# THE SHIFTER REJECTED SERIES

## BOOKS 1-3

AMELIA SHAW

USA TODAY BESTSELLING AUTHOR
# AMELIA SHAW

# CHAPTER 1

# TALIA

In six days, I was marrying the next Alpha of the Northwood pack. Maddox Brady. My fated mate.

Lights flashed around me and the room spun with the beat of the heavy techno music the DJ was playing. I didn't dare get up from the stool where I teetered, lest I fall flat on my face. Yet, despite my intoxication, the simple fact was, I'd never been happier. I loved Maddox and couldn't wait to marry him.

"Another round of tequila shots!" I called to the bartender, though I wasn't sure he'd bring them. He'd said something about cutting us off earlier, but surely, he'd been joking?

"You can't handle another round, Talia," said Nyssa, my best friend.

I leaned forward on my stool and straightened my pink and white sash. We all had them. Mine read, 'Bride-to-be'.

"This is my last night as a single lady!" I sang the words, amazed at how loud I could be when the music thumped around me like a drum in my ear. "Gotta make every minute count."

Nyssa laughed. "The mating ceremony's not for another week, Talia. You've still got time."

"Here, I got you another one," Celia whispered, handing me a small glass of clear liquor. My other best friend had come through for me.

I took the drink, my hand wobbling as I brought it to my lips. I snorted, then tipped my head back, throwing the shot down my throat.

"Wow." I grimaced at the burn and handed Celia back the glass. Then I took a deep breath and focused on the warm feeling of the alcohol spreading through my veins.

Oh, yeah. That has to be the last one. Or I'll never make it home.

Thank goodness the wedding was next week and not tomorrow.

Then again, if it was tomorrow, I would never have gotten this smashed.

"Are you excited for the wedding night?" Nyssa asked me, wiggling her eyebrows up and down.

Celia snickered, while I rolled my eyes. They all knew I couldn't wait to finally consummate my relationship with Maddox.

My fated mate.

My true love.

The future Alpha of our pack.

"Of course, she is!" Celia answered for me.

Celia was my oldest friend. We'd known each other practically from the day we'd been born. Her mom and mine were friends from way back, and we'd been raised together as more sisters, than anything else.

Celia turned to me with an eyebrow raised. She was by far the most sober of us. "You never told us what the real reason was."

I leaned forward on the bar stool, careful not to crush the peanuts lying on the surface of the bar top, then squinted at my friend. "For what?"

Celia glared at me. "For waiting this long to have sex with him!"

I gasped at her forwardness, then put a hand over my mouth and giggled.

I shook my head, not wanting to answer.

She jabbed me in the arm with her finger and I swayed on my seat. "Whoa…"

"Come on, Talia! You can tell us!"

Nyssa nodded. "Yeah. I want to know why, too."

I hefted my top for the tenth time, trying to cover up the ridiculous amount of cleavage this outfit showed off to the room, and shrugged.

"We just… decided to wait."

I didn't want to admit it hadn't been my decision. Maddox had been adamant though. We needed to get married first.

Celia pulled another stool over to the bar and huddled closer so she could hear me better. The music was loud, and the people dancing and drinking on this warm summer night were even louder.

I closed my eyes, enjoying the heat of the room and the warmth in my blood. As the next Alpha's mate, I was watched constantly when we were at home. In the pack. In town. At formal gatherings.

I tried to be as perfect as possible. For Maddox. For the current Alpha of the Northwood pack. And also, for my dad.

But tonight was my bachelorette party. I could finally let down my hair and not worry about anyone else and what they might think of me.

The steady beat and thump of one of my favorite songs came through the speakers. I jumped to my unsteady feet, wobbling on the tiny heels Nyssa had made me wear.

"Let's dance!"

I pulled my two best friends to the dance floor. They were my entire bridal party and all I needed. I began to sway and twerk and giggle away.

This wasn't my last night of freedom, of course. But it was one of my last nights as a single woman. Soon I would be a mate, a wife, and the future Alpha's mate, with all the responsibilities that came with that position.

And I couldn't wait.

"Is Maddox doing his bachelor party tonight too?" Celia asked, dancing forward to whisper the question into my ear.

I twirled toward her. "Doesn't matter, 'cos I'm here with you!"

I grabbed her hands and spun around, almost falling on my ass, but managing to stay on my feet.

Just.

We laughed and danced, and drank more, thanks to Celia.

Close to dawn, we all caught a cab back to the pack, then staggered into the house I shared with my father.

"Your dad doesn't mind if we stay over?" Celia asked, throwing her dress to the floor and crawling into my bed with her underwear still in place.

I dragged the curtains shut, blocking out the rising sun. "'Course not. You guys are family."

The girls smiled as they settled on either side of the bed.

I took a drunken moment to appreciate how lucky I was to have these two in my life. As an only child, these girls were the closest thing I had to sisters.

I stripped off my own clothes, relieved when my short skirt and too-obvious top were in a pile on the floor. I enjoyed being pretty like every other girl, but boobs and legs on show everywhere was not usually my style.

"The house is really quiet. So is the rest of the town," Celia whispered, her eyes closing as she nestled into the pillow she'd landed on.

I crawled onto the king-sized bed and slid under the covers between my friends.

"Dad's out. He said there was some pack business thing they had to do today."

Nyssa huffed out a laugh as she rolled over. "You're the future Alpha's mate and you still don't get told anything, huh?"

"Yeah..." I lied and closed my eyes.

I knew where they'd all gone, which was probably half the reason I'd drunk so much tonight. But we'd gotten on the water around two a.m., and now that I was well on the way to sober thanks to my wolf metabolism, the anxiety had set back in.

Maddox, my dad, and the rest of the men in our pack had planned an attack today. On a neighboring pack they considered a major threat.

The Long Claw Pack. Their Alpha was legendary for his strength, as was his son, Galen. Though I hadn't met either of them.

Personally, I hated the wars the wolves fought amongst themselves. It didn't make sense to me when we had so many other natural enemies. We all had our own territories, so why wolves constantly fought for more power, was beyond me.

And I hated the fact that the men I loved put themselves in danger like this.

I rolled onto my side and let exhaustion sweep me away. I tried not to dream about the dangers my family were in. After all, my dad and Maddox were my whole world.

Galen

My eyes sprung open at the sound of running footsteps thumping through my dad's house.

The door to my bedroom flung open and I sat bolt upright in bed.

"We're being raided." One of my betas, Tommy, pushed the door wide. "It's those fuckers from the Northwood Pack. They're here."

I jumped out of bed and rapidly pulled on some old jeans. One of the fifty pairs I kept for moments like this: when I knew I was going to shift, and probably destroy the clothing in a split second.

"Go," I told Tommy. "I'll be there straight away."

Tommy ran out the door again.

I didn't bother with a sweatshirt. This was going to be a fight, not a conversation. I didn't need to dress properly.

I chased after Tommy, ducking into my dad's room on the way, where he lay in his bed, fast asleep and as pale as the sheets he lay on. He had a light sheen of sweat decorating his brow.

Dad hadn't been well for months, so there was no way I was waking him now. If he knew they'd come, he'd want to join the fight, and in his current state, it was highly unlikely he'd survive. He could barely stand, let alone shift and defend our territory against a bunch of strong wolves.

I wasn't ready to be Alpha of my dad's Long Claw Pack. Not yet.

And I wasn't ready to live in a world without my dad in it.

"Galen!" Tommy hissed from the front door. "Come on!"

I hightailed it out of my dad's room and reached the front door. "What do we know?"

"The Northwood Pack is about to attack. Our scouts have seen them coming through the woods."

"How many are there?" I asked, already mentally preparing for the fight we were about to have.

The neighboring pack had always hated our borders, though I wasn't sure why. There was bad blood from way back before I was born, and no one had ever mentioned what happened back then.

But why attack? And why now?

Had they heard my father was dying and our pack would need to fight without our Alpha? That was the most likely explanation for this timing.

Assholes.

They thought we were weak without my dad. We'd just have to prove them wrong.

"At least thirty strong," Tommy said. "Maybe more."

I nodded once. They'd brought most of their pack. The men anyway.

I hope their Alpha is with them. I'd love to take him out. Or his pussy of a son. Maddox.

"Let's go."

I was next in line to my father, born from a long line of Alphas. I could lead our men in this fight. And, victorious, or not, I would never abandon them.

Tommy and I ran through the town, waking up our fellow pack mates and shouting out orders. "Lock the doors. Make sure your families remain safe."

All our women were strong fighters, if need be, but it was their job to protect our children if something happened to the men.

It was our role to protect them, so that hopefully they'd never have to fight to save their babies.

I called out to my Betas. "Let's get to the forest edge."

Our town was built well and was only vulnerable from two sides.

I had at least forty men, so I could afford to divide our forces.

"Split up! You five go to the east." It was unlikely the neighboring pack would attack that way. Their lands lay to the south. But I didn't want to leave any of our borders unmanned, just in case. "The rest of you follow me."

We ran to the south side, where the forest butted up against the town. My heart pounded like a war drum in my chest. Adrenaline zinged along my veins.

The only question in my mind was whether I needed to shift straight away, or later. We didn't carry weapons, but my claws were razor sharp, as were my teeth.

"There!" someone cried, and I squinted into the darkness of the forest.

The sun was only beginning to lift its head. Whisps of red and orange hues rose about the horizon, lighting up the blackened sky.

Deep in the forest, wolves stalked toward us. They'd already shifted, their beady yellow eyes standing out against the darkness around them.

Well, I'm not getting caught out with my fragile human body. They're clearly not here to talk. That's for damn certain.

I let go of my humanity. My wolf rose inside me, growling loudly as it took over.

I dropped to the ground onto all fours. My whole body vibrated as my skin sprouted fur, and I transformed into the huge beast of my forefathers.

My black wolf form.

And then it was on.

They charged, and every man around me shifted. The dawn filled with the snarls of the wolves from two packs—mine, and theirs.

There was no warm-up, no formalities, as the neighboring pack ran out of the woods toward us. This was going to be a fight to the death, and I damn sure wasn't going down today. Not on my land. Not on my father's death watch.

I flew at the nearest wolf rushing forward, my mouth open, teeth ready.

He snapped in my face, missing his mark as I twisted. I tore around the side of him, ripping my teeth through his fur and tasting blood on my tongue.

The wolf yelped and skittered sideways, before teaming up with another gray wolf near him and coming back for a second try.

They both faced me, their lips raised in matching snarls. I charged, aiming for the new wolf, and head butted him, then bared my teeth to the one I'd already injured.

He should have run when he had the chance.

This time I grabbed him around the throat, my ears burning with his whimper a moment before I tore out his throat. Blood gushed into my mouth.

His neck snapped as he fell to the ground, his head tilted at an odd angle, and I turned to growl at the other wolf.

They'd come onto my land, into our town, to what? Kill us all? Even the women and children?

Not today.

The other wolf started to back away, before lifting his head and howling. It was a high-pitched sound that set my fur on edge. He was calling for help.

I charged, my mouth open, and sunk my teeth around the wolf's neck and shook him. Hard.

Enough to warn, not kill. If he came at me again, I wouldn't give him a second chance.

He scrabbled into the dirt to get away from me, and I let him.

He whined as he backed away, toward the forest.

I backed up a few steps also, watching as their pack rejoined forces and grouped together near the forest's edge once more.

Where was their leader?

There. A large black wolf who met my eyes. He was still in challenge mode, but he was wavering. I could read the uncertainty in his expression.

I stepped over body after body of dead wolves to get back to the rest of my pack. The guys, my betas, were blood-smeared and panting, but looked mostly okay.

I stood at the head of the Long Claw Pack and growled at the intruders that had come from the Northwood. It was their call. Would they regroup and try again, or would they turn tail and retreat? We wouldn't chase them if they chose the latter.

The large black wolf howled once, and as one, the whole pack turned away. Their Alpha, the one in charge, had called an end to the fight.

Good decision.

I let myself begin to relax. They were leaving.

Then suddenly, a large gray wolf growled and broke away from the retreating group, running around their pack to head straight at me.

This lone wolf was trying to take me out? Seriously?

But he wasn't alone for long. As he ran, others followed, until he'd managed to pull several wolves away from the main pack. They were all coming toward me now.

I shook my head as I faced them.

Idiots.

They'd just lessened the numbers of their main group by ten, all the while bringing the party to me. Perfect.

I dug my feet into the dirt and launched at them.

Then the whole pack came at us. They'd obviously decided to join the second wave.

We fought hard, and I killed two more of their wolves before the other side called another retreat.

I stared after them as the remaining wolves ran for their lives through the woods, back the way they had come. In that second attack, they'd lost at least five more pack members, and I almost growled at the stupidity of it all.

I let go of my shifter, rising from my animal posture to stand on two feet again.

My naked skin was covered in sweat and my heart thumped loudly in my chest as the adrenaline took time to dissipate.

"Should we go after them?" Markus asked, having transformed back to human beside me. He was huffing and puffing from exertion.

Blood poured down his chest from a wound in his shoulder.

I shook my head. "We will avenge this attack, but not today. Right now, we patch up our injured, and burn the bodies of their fallen."

They'd gotten what they deserved, coming onto our land to try and kill us while we slept. They had twelve dead, if I counted correctly, and many others of them had been injured. A huge hit to any pack. They were weaker now. There would be no coming back until they regrouped, which gave me time to plan our attack.

I glanced around at my own pack members. Several injured, and two dead.

There would be justice. Our pack would have its vengeance.

# CHAPTER 2

# TALIA

My father limped into the house after I'd said goodbye to a still hungover Nyssa and Celia.

I'd barely slept all morning, worried about my father and Maddox and how they were doing during their attack on the neighboring pack. But even so, I'd not expected them to be back so soon.

"Dad!" I ran out to greet him as he practically fell through the front door. "Let me help you."

I put my arm around his waist and partly carried him to the couch, where he dropped onto the cushions. He was bleeding from wounds in his leg and chest.

Not life-threatening, by the looks of them, but not pleasant. "I'll get the first aid kit."

"Thanks." He groaned as he hoisted his leg up onto the couch.

I grabbed a bottle of water and the box of supplies I kept on hand in the kitchen, then rushed back to my dad.

"What happened?" I asked, wincing at the blood gushing onto our couch. "That's gonna need stiches."

"Thanks, Talia," he said, lying back and getting comfortable on the cushions behind him.

I sighed and pulled up a stool. That meant I needed to do the stitches for him. Dad didn't really like going to the doctor in town. I'd done this before, but I still didn't like it.

I threaded the needle and flicked the lighter so I could burn the end to sterilize the metal. With a shifter's metabolism, infections were rare, but for the few seconds it took to do the extra step, I figured it couldn't hurt. I liked to be thorough.

"Can you tell me what happened, Dad?"

He sighed, a heavy, world-weary sigh. "I did something stupid."

My head flew up and I stared at him. "What do you mean?"

"I tried to go for the young Alpha."

I bent my head to the task, carefully, but firmly holding the torn flesh of my dad's leg together so I could slide the needle through.

"What was the mission, exactly?"

"To take out the old Alpha, and his son Galen, if we could."

"But why?"

Dad shrugged. "Pack politics aren't my thing, Taley, you know that. Let's talk about something else for a minute. You're about to get married. That's the most important think that can happen in your life."

I glanced up. "You really think so? The most important?"

Dad nodded solemnly, then winced as I continued to sew up his leg wound. The chest laceration would be next, but it wasn't bleeding as much. "Yes," he said. "Everything else is easy to fix if you make a mistake. Wrong house, wrong job. But choosing a mate... or having Fate choose one for you... that is the biggest decision of your life. It shapes who you are, who your children will be, and how you live your life."

That was the most I'd heard my dad say in one go in a very long time.

"Is that how you felt about Mom?" I asked gently, concentrating on my stitching and not looking up at my dad.

He usually didn't like to talk about her, no matter how much I asked.

"Yes," he said simply.

I risked a glance at his face to see a soft smile playing at the edges of his lips.

"She was... incredible," he said with a sigh. "The most amazing woman I've ever known."

Hot tears gathered in my eyes, and I blinked them away, trying to concentrate on my sewing task. "Why don't you ever talk about her?"

He groaned, shifting slightly in obvious discomfort. "I don't know... too painful, I guess."

I sniffed, trying my best to hide the emotions I was feeling and the tears that were still gathering, ready to flow.

I coughed to clear my throat and tied off the thread. I was done with my sewing.

"Because she died?"

I faced him squarely this time, and my dad stared straight at me. "Yeah."

"I know you never wanted to talk about it before, but how did she die, Dad?" Every time I'd brought up the topic, he changed the conversation, or flat out refused to talk about it.

"You almost done?" Dad asked, indicating his leg.

A punch of disappointment hit me in the chest. I was going to be left wondering again, it seemed.

"Ah, yeah. I might just wrap it up lightly. And the chest, too. Hang on."

I pressed gauze to the fresh stitches and wrapped tape around the leg wound, then spent a few minutes cleaning and taping the gash on his chest. It was shallow and didn't require stitches the way his leg had. For a human, this quick patch-up job wouldn't be adequate; nowhere near it. Neither would my stitching have been.

But my father wasn't human. He was a strong, huge, wolf shifter. And as far as I knew, my mother had been the same.

Not that I remembered her particularly well.

Once I was done, he lifted his leg and swung it off the side of the couch. He panted and cursed a little, but then smiled at me. "Thanks."

I nodded and made to get up from my stool.

Dad reached out for me and grabbed my arm. "Can you stay a bit? Sit with me."

He had never asked me to do such a thing before.

"Yeah, of course. Is there something you need to tell me?" My heart sickened. "Is Maddox okay? He came back from the fight, didn't he?"

I jumped to my feet and stared out the window, my stomach suddenly churning.

Several pack members stood around talking, but no one was coming this way. No one even seemed to be looking at our house.

That was a good sign.

"Maddox is fine." I relaxed slightly at his words. Then he added, "He didn't get too close to the front of the action." I couldn't help but notice the disgust in his voice when he said it.

Conflicting emotions rose in me. The instant desire to defend my mate, and the knowledge that dodging action in a fight was a cowardly act, in shifter terms.

It was a cowardly act, in any language.

"You know his dad doesn't let him do anything dangerous, when he can help it," I said, and swallowed hard against the acid that rose in my throat.

Our Alpha only had one son, like most shifters in our pack. One child. One son. And the Alpha made sure to keep his heir safe.

Other pack members thought that was the wrong thing to do. They believed that the only way to harden up a wolf shifter— especially a fighter and someone who would one day be a leader —was to throw him into the fray. Experience bred the best generals. But that wasn't my decision to make.

On a personal level, I was glad that Maddox was home, and he was safe. I'd never really had to worry about him in the past, which was probably why he hadn't been the first thing on my mind when Dad had come back injured.

"Anyway." Dad coughed hard. "About your question."

I moved closer. He had my full attention now. "You mean about Mom?"

He nodded. "There isn't a lot to tell, Taley. I wish I had some grand, amazing story to tell you, but she just... died. It was an accident."

I swallowed hard. I'd been eight years old when my mom died. Which meant I had some beautiful memories of her kindness, her hugs, and her voice, but not a lot of concrete things that would help me interpret what my dad was trying to say.

"What do you mean exactly by... it was an accident?"

My heart was pumping a little too fast in my chest. Did he mean that she'd fallen off a cliff while on a hike, or had he accidentally killed her while in a wolf-shifter rage or something? What?

"It was a car accident," Dad said quietly. "She was driving home from work in the city. She was a nurse. She'd picked up some late shifts to help pay the bills. I was.... out of work again. I just..."

He stopped to run a shaking hand through his hair. "She should never have been driving home that late. It was past midnight. Raining..."

My heart broke to hear the lump in his throat, the regret and pain he was pushing past to speak about what had happened.

He blamed himself? I reached over and grabbed his hand. "Things like that happen, Dad. It sucks, and I hate it. But it wasn't your fault."

It couldn't have been. He wasn't the rain. He wasn't the car. He wasn't even the one driving.

I shuddered at the thought of the guilt someone would feel to be driving a car, only to crash and kill their passengers. That load would be something that would truly break your heart. But Dad hadn't been there. He shouldn't blame himself.

When he raised his gaze to meet mine, there was so much love burning behind his eyes, it took my breath away.

He squeezed my hand tight. "You're the only reason I'm still here, my beautiful daughter."

I frowned and held tight to his hand, relishing in the rare show of affection from my father. "What do you mean, Dad?"

"I mean that I don't think I would have lived the past fifteen years without you." He smiled and reached over to cup my cheek with his other hand.

I covered his hand with mine. "You've been my whole world, Dad. Thank you... for everything."

I swallowed hard, forcing the emotional lump down.

We hadn't always gotten along, of course. Like most girls with their dads, especially during my teenage years when puberty kicked in, I tried testing boundaries as all teens do. But he'd supported me, loved me, given me a home, and kept me safe.

In this world, I couldn't ask for more.

There was a long, drawn-out moment, where I felt entirely happy. Filled to the brim with love, and the knowledge that I had everything I could ever need.

Family. Love. And a bright future with Maddox by my side.

Then there was a knock at the door, and the spell was broken.

"Hello?" I called out, getting to my feet.

The door swung open and one of the pack members, Maverick, stepped into the room. He had a gash above his eye and a bandage wrapped around his shoulder. "Alpha called a meeting. One hour."

His tone was harsh.

I stared after him as he turned and left without another word.

What was that about?

I glanced at my dad who made grumbling noises and shifted on the couch, hoisting himself to the edge. He looked like he was about to stand up.

I put out my hand and pushed against him. "No. You can't get up. You need to give your leg time to heal."

Dad shook his head and pushed himself to his feet. "I'm going to have a quick shower. Then it's time to face the music."

He took a step to test his leg's strength. Then slowly, but with an obvious level of pride in his own resilience, he limped down the hallway.

A shiver of unease wriggled down my spine and I hurried after him.

"What do you mean, face the music?" I grabbed his arm and gently spun him around. "What did you do?"

My dad's mouth twisted. "I told you. I tried to take out their Alpha, and it didn't work."

Tears burned in my eyes, hearing the finality in my dad's words. "So? You made a mistake. It's not like there haven't been raids on other packs before; raids that weren't always successful."

"Ah. But this time I made a mistake that cost a lot of other pack members their lives," he said slowly, removing my fingers from his arm.

"But... everyone makes mistakes, Dad. I'm sure they'll forgive you... They always do."

He smiled but didn't say anything else in reply. Instead, he stepped into our small bathroom and shut the door in my face.

I stood in the hallway, my heart filled with worry and my gut tight with dread. What were they going to do to him? Punish him in some way? Toss him out of the pack? Surely, they wouldn't do such a thing to my father.

He was going to be the next Alpha's father-in-law.

Of course. Excitement grew inside of me at the thought, and I rapped on the bathroom door. "I'm going to get changed and find Maddox. I'm sure he'll help. See you at the meeting."

"Okay, sweetie. I love you."

"Love you too!" I yelled, then bolted into my room for a quick change of clothes. Earlier, I'd just thrown a cotton dress over what I'd slept in last night, but I needed to try a bit harder if I was going to convince Maddox to help me.

I had some nearby baby wipes that I used for emergencies, or when the water wasn't running. I did a quick wash of my body, having not showered since last night, and pulled on my black jeans—Maddox's favorite on me—and a tight pink sweater. I took a moment to brush my long hair, because my soon-to-be-husband liked it out and flowing down my back.

Soft and feminine, he said.

I grabbed my house keys and my cell phone, though the coverage out here was terrible, and ran out the door. I had to find Maddox and ask him for support. I had a horrible feeling about what might be about to happen to my dad, and I needed to stop it.

My stomach swirled and my heart hammered in my chest the faster I moved my legs. People were everywhere in the streets, walking toward the center of town where the meeting was being held.

The townspeople often told me that my father was well liked by the Alpha. He'd been excused in the past for mistakes that no one else would have gotten away with. I wasn't sure of the details of those mistakes, but whatever had happened in the past, that didn't seem to be the case this time.

I started running toward the Alpha's house. Surely Maddox would be there? I had to find him and beg his help.

And fast.

**CHAPTER 3**
# TALIA

The Alpha's house was locked, and no one was home. I went to Antony's house, Maddox's beta, but still couldn't find anyone.

So, I ran about like a mad woman, searching every house I had access to.

Were they all already at the meeting?

Fuck!

Then the Alpha's booming voice echoed through town. He was projecting his words through the loudspeaker.

"Damn it." I was late to the meeting now, and I hadn't accomplished what I'd set out to do.

I ran toward the center of town. I hadn't kept an eye on the time, and I was sweating from the stress.

My only hope was that my worries were unfounded. Surely the Alpha would pardon my father? He always did. He was a hard Alpha, but not unkind.

Normally.

I reached the edge of the gathering and stopped, taking deep breaths to try and calm myself down. I placed a hand on my heart, feeling the hammering beneath my palm, and took some time to slow my breath.

It's okay. It's going to be okay.

"The attack this morning was... a disaster," the Alpha was saying.

I peered through the crowd, between the heads of the people in front of me. There was a small stage the council had set up for such meetings. It was only two feet off the ground, but it meant that most of us could see whoever was speaking.

My gaze slid from the Alpha, to Maddox, who stood at his father's right, tall and proud, and gorgeous.

My heart leapt in my chest at the sight of my mate. Electricity sizzled in my veins and happiness bubbled through me. There was the person I was meant to spend the rest of my life with.

My love.

My fated mate.

I frowned as I stared at him. Something was different. He wouldn't meet my gaze, even though in the past he would have found me in a crowd this size within moments.

He swayed from foot to foot, and rubbed his hands together as though he was cold.

I was sweating from all the running around. I should have worn a skirt.

I wiped my brow with my forearm and let myself start to relax. It was going to be okay. This was just procedure.

"We lost many souls today. Andrew Murphy, Blaze McGuphry..." The Alpha went on to list more and more men.

So many? There were tears all around, and a loud sob echoed to my left.

My throat closed up, and I swallowed down hard, forcing the tears back. It was such a loss to our pack. So many men. Fathers. Sons. Husbands.

Had my father's mistake caused that? Horror filled me with

the realization this might not be something easily forgiven, like in the past.

"We would never have lost so many if it wasn't for the irresponsible actions of a single pack member, Trevor Linetti." The Alpha held out his arm and gestured toward the edge of the stage.

My father stepped up; his face set as he walked resolutely forward.

I put a hand over my mouth to stifle a gasp. What were they going to do to him?

"This is not the first time that Trevor has done something to endanger the pack. Many have wondered why I've spared his life in the past."

There was a murmur of agreement from the pack.

Oh, my God.

I had to get to my dad.

"Excuse me." I pushed through the people in front of me and began to work my way through the crowd. I had to beg them to spare him. I wasn't sure what I'd say, but I had to convince the Alpha not to hurt him.

I shoved through more people, but I was still twenty feet away. The whole pack had turned out for this.

"His wife Margaret was an exceptional woman, and many of you would know that she brought special gifts to the pack. But she is no longer around, and after Trevor's selfish, despicable actions from this morning, I can no longer shield him from the pack's anger."

There was a loud growl and a surge of energy.

"No!" I yelled, and that was when I finally caught my mate's eye. Our gazes connected and I felt the same pull, the same tug of desire and heat that I always did.

"Maddox!"

He looked down and away, breaking our eye contact and ignoring my plea.

No!

"Trevor Linetti," the Alpha continued, "you are sentenced to death for your crimes against this pack. And your remaining family will be cast out, forbidden from returning, on pain of death."

Sentenced to death. Oh, my God.

I desperately looked for Maddox again, but he'd moved out of my sight. I didn't care at this moment. I had to get to my father.

I pushed and shoved and ran, stumbling over a woman.

"I'm sorry. Get out of the way. Please!" I screamed out toward the stage. "Dad!"

He didn't turn. Instead, he dropped to his knees in front of the Alpha.

My dad said something I couldn't hear. The Alpha shifted into his massive wolf form in a ripple of light and magic.

"No! Please... No!" I shrieked, throwing myself at the small stage.

The people around me jumped back as if not wanting to touch me. I ploughed forward, falling to my knees just as there was a collective gasp from the crowd and a muffled scream from a woman behind me. A sickening crunch filled my ears and blood spattered everywhere.

Too late.

I reached out for the edge of the stage, gripping the wood with my claws as my wolf shifter rose inside of me, struggling to get out.

I couldn't see, couldn't hear anything but that crunching sound on repeat. Over and over.

My fingers slid in the blood and the tang of it rose to fill my nostrils.

I tried not to vomit as I stared at the mangled body on the stage.

The Alpha had just killed my father.

Right in front of my eyes.

~

I RAN through the woods in my shifter form. How I got here, I had no idea. Trees flew past as images of my father's headless, lifeless body dropping to the stage floor echoed in my mind.

It had to be a dream.

No. A nightmare.

A nightmare to end all nightmares.

I couldn't have designed a worse fate for myself. My only living family... gone. The man I loved—the man I was mated to—standing by, watching and doing nothing, as his father killed mine.

Romeo and Juliet had nothing on me.

I ran and ran, until my legs gave out and I collapsed onto the grass. The sunshine danced in my fur, making a mockery of my sorrow.

I was going to be sick. How dare the sun even show its face on a day like today?

It was the end of my life as I knew it.

Dad was gone. Dead. And I was to be banished from the pack. My own pack. Casting me out at the moment I was most in need.

And Maddox... My thoughts skittered away. I couldn't bear to think of his betrayal at this moment.

I closed my eyes, waves of grief washing over me. The devastation was so complete, my anger couldn't even try to rear its head.

My father had done what his Alpha had asked of him, and that same Alpha had thought it his duty, his right, to end my father's life.

What was I going to do now?

My ears pricked up at the sound of running. Two sets of paws hitting the earth, if my ears were correct.

Was the pack coming for me already? Was I to be put to death as well? The week before my wedding?

I didn't even care right now. They could take me, and I would join my parents. At least then I wouldn't be alone.

I didn't even lift my head, just rolled onto my side and stayed there, waiting for fate to deliver the death blow.

The running grew closer, followed by the panting breath of two wolves.

I refused to open my eyes, the pain in my heart making me wish I could crawl into a dark hole and die.

Literally.

There was a ripple of magic, and a shift in the air. Then two sets of human hands were on me.

"Talia! Are you okay?" Nyssa asked, pressing a kiss onto the top of my head.

"Of course, she's not okay, you idiot!" Celia practically yelled at her. "Did you see what the Alpha did! Did you hear what he said?"

I hadn't realized how much I wanted to cry, until this moment. As my sadness became overwhelming, my wolf shifter let go, and my human body returned.

The forest was cold, and my friends' hands were warm on my skin.

"Oh, my God." I began to sob, letting the tears finally fall.

I curled up into a ball and rocked as I vocalized all my pain, while my two friends wrapped their arms around me. I screamed and cried, and howled, and still they held me.

Eventually, the tears dried up, and I was left feeling like a husk of a person, unwilling and unable to form a single coherent thought. Or feel anything other than darkness.

"The pack's isolation cabin is not far from here. Let's go there and get warm," Nyssa said softly.

I shook my head, not able to answer.

"Come on, Talia. Up you get," Celia coaxed, putting one arm around my back and somehow managing to get me onto my feet.

My knees gave way.

"Grab the other side," Celia called, and Nyssa pressed in close.

If it had been any other time, I would have remarked on the strangeness of their naked bodies pressed against mine. But this was not the time for lighthearted jests.

Instead, their closeness kept my heart from breaking completely.

They half-carried me through the woods, my feet dragging in the dirt and forest floor debris.

"Put me down. Please. I just can't..."

My voice was hoarse, and my stomach was empty. Had I vomited at some stage? I couldn't remember. Everything back at the pack grounds was dark after that moment...

"No," Celia hissed. "We are not staying out here, naked and alone. We are getting to the cabin so we can get some clothes and talk about what we're going to do next."

The vehemence behind her words bolstered my strength and I somehow managed to get my feet under me and join them in the awkward stagger to our new destination.

Finally... finally, I saw the wooden cabin through the trees.

"We're almost there, Talia," Nyssa said, breathing hard. "Almost there."

Together, all three of us, like some naked, four-legged race, clung to each other as we aimed for the cabin.

When we finally staggered up the front steps and stood on the stoop, Nyssa pushed open the door and we fell in.

Celia groaned as she staggered to a nearby couch and I hit the deck, crawling over to the bear skin rug in front of the cold fireplace.

"Give me a minute. I'll light a fire," Nyssa said, her teeth chattering.

I lifted my head and stared out the window. The sun was beginning to fall out of the sky, and shadows crossed the window.

Just how long had I been out in the forest alone?

Celia grunted as she heaved herself up off the couch. "I'm gonna lock the door, then find us some clothes."

She slid the large bolt into the deadlock, then started going through the cupboards lining the walls.

"Got it!" Nyssa said, and I managed to pull myself up into a sitting position as the first flickers of flame in the cold grate began to burn.

I swallowed against the dryness in my throat. "I haven't been here in... forever." I couldn't even remember the last time I had run as far as this. Several years, at least.

The cabin was a large box with no internal walls. There were beds against one wall, kitchen stuff on the opposite side, and all the living area in the middle where we currently sat.

There was a toilet outside, but I wasn't venturing out there right this minute.

"Yeah, I haven't been here in a while, either," Nyssa said, settling cross-legged beside me and staring into the flames.

The fire was growing by the minute and my once goose-bumped skin was beginning to warm.

"Here," Celia said, throwing some clothes in our direction. "There's sweaters and jeans, and a few tops. Not exactly our sizes, but at least we'll be warm."

The clothes she'd thrown at me were for a man, four times as big as I needed. But I slipped on the huge sweater with relief and tucked my bare legs up inside and laid my head on my knees.

There was a long silence before Nyssa finally put her hand on my back. "What are you going to do, Talia?"

I sighed; all my tears dried up. "I don't know. I really don't know."

"You're the next Alpha's fated mate. Surely, they'll take you back," Celia said, coming to sit down next to me on the bear skin rug and stretching out in front of the fire.

I squeezed my knees even harder. "I hope so. We're fated mates... right? No one rejects their mate."

My question was answered by silence, so I finally lifted my head and repeated my question. "Right?"

# TALIA

I stared at Celia, the stronger of my two friends. The harsher one. The physically bigger one. She'd never shied away from telling it to me straight.

"Celia?"

She pressed her lips into a firm line, then nodded. "You're right. No one has ever walked away from their mate. You guys are fated! Nothing would mess that up."

Nyssa shuffled forward so we were sitting in a sort of triangle, and I could see both of them. "How are you feeling about it all though? Like, Maddox's dad killed your dad. How are you going to... get past that?"

I didn't have an answer to that one.

"I just want Maddox," I said. "I want him to come here, and wrap me up in his arms, and tell me everything's going to be okay."

Celia and Nyssa glanced at each other, then converged on me like they had out in the forest, holding me close.

I didn't fight them. I allowed them to press even harder into me, closed my eyes, and inhaled their mingled earthy scent.

"We'll never leave you," Nyssa said. "You're our best friend, no matter what."

"Always," Celia added. "You can count on us."

We climbed into the bed without dinner and somehow, exhaustion took me. We slept through the night.

When I woke up in the morning, the birds were singing in the trees surrounding the cabin, and faint rays of sunlight filtered into the room.

I pushed the scratchy blanket off me and stretched, my stomach rumbling for food.

"Morning," Celia said, though she was a grouch in the morning.

"How are you feeling?" Nyssa asked, sitting up and staring at me like I would do something stupid if she dared take her eyes off me for a single minute.

"Um… hungry," I said. "And… ready to go back."

I still felt strangely numb in my mind. Like someone had slammed down a huge wall between my memories and me. I couldn't feel much except for an aching in my chest, like I had a hole in my ribcage.

I lifted my hand and rubbed at the spot over my heart where my father's love used to sit. "I need to go back and see what they've done with my dad, and I really need to see Maddox and find out what we're going to do."

"Let's get going ASAP, then," Celia said.

Nyssa nodded. "We need food too."

We all took off the clothes we'd borrowed, folded them up, and shut the door to keep the wild animals out of the cabin.

"Let's do it," Celia said.

It was time to go home, so we shifted back into our wolf forms for traveling.

Nyssa and Celia were both a nice gray, but I'd always been black. Just like my mother.

Together, as a small pack of three wolves, we ran home. When we hit the main road in our town, we all went our separate ways to find our houses and get clothes.

When I reached my home, I shifted as soon as I stepped onto the porch.

My heart was in my throat as I opened the door, the words stuck in my head as I fought the desire to call out to my dad. To ask how his night was and tell him about mine.

I glanced around the room. It was like nothing had changed. Like he wasn't dead.

I rushed to my bedroom, running from the memory of what had happened yesterday, a whirlwind of emotions set to chase after me if I dared to think about it too long. They would drag me into the pit of despair if I gave them half a chance.

I had the fastest shower on record, but one was needed, none-theless. I was covered in sweat and tears and dirt; I was pretty sure neither Maddox nor the Alpha would be happy about that if I were to turn up on their doorstep, unwashed.

Then I dressed, not sure if I needed to be getting ready for a funeral, or not. So, I reached for my most comfortable pair of black leggings, a long dress, and a heavy silver belt.

I walked out of the house without a backward glance, tears in my eyes and emotion clogging my throat. Yesterday had been the worst day of my life, bar none. Surely, today couldn't be any worse?

People stared at me as I walked down the main street in our small village.

We were about a fifteen-minute drive away from the main town we all frequented. Our closed shifter community made it safe for us to live the way we needed to, but also kept us close enough to civilization for access to school and shops.

The closer I walked to the Alpha's house, the more people

stared at me. Members of a community I'd known my whole life were pointing at me. A few people shot glares my way.

What had I done wrong? I was the one whose only family had been brutally killed by our Alpha.

That thought made me resolutely stomp forward.

The Alpha's house was the biggest in town. Double story, with huge windows, a large wooden door, and an imposing brick façade.

I lifted my chin and marched up the steps. I didn't know what I was going to say, but I could already sense that begging was on the cards.

The biggest question in my mind though was, what was Maddox going to do? Surely, he'd be on my side in this. He didn't like to go up against his father. But that was because he was a good son, and a loyal pack member. Not because he didn't love me.

I lifted my hand to knock on the door. It flew open before I had the chance to touch it. I stared at the man standing in the doorway.

"Hello, Talia."

I swallowed hard. "Maddox. I've come to talk to your dad. Is he home?"

My mate nodded. "Yeah. He is. Come in. I wasn't sure if you'd left already."

"Left?" I repeated as I walked inside.

Maddox shut the door behind me.

He didn't answer, but simply ushered me into the large living room where his father sat on the couch. Three of his council members stood behind him.

My stomach dropped, and I reached for Maddox for comfort.

He shook my grasping hand off his arm and marched away.

I couldn't help the soft cry that ripped from my throat. "Maddox... don't walk away. Please... I..."

Maddox kept walking, until he was around the couch and standing on his father's right side.

When he turned to stare at me, his face was stone cold.

I gasped and pressed my hand to my mouth. I was supposed to get married this week. To the man standing right in front of me, staring at me as if I was a stranger. I was going to spend my life devoted to him, loving him, raising his children.

I didn't understand why he was acting like this.

"I don't..." I shook my head, and then dragged my gaze down to his father when he made an annoyed noise in his throat.

The Alpha might have been the only one seated on the couch, but his presence dominated the room. "Talia Linetti, I told you yesterday. You are no longer a member of this pack. You are banished. I will allow you seventy-two hours to leave town and get across state lines, or the pack will hunt you down and deliver to you the same fate that befell your father."

My mouth gaped open, unwanted tears filling my eyes and spilling down my cheeks despite my best efforts to hold them in. "But... I'm supposed to get married next week. To... Maddox. How... why...?"

The words tumbled from my lips, yet I had no real idea what I was saying. My world had tipped on its axis, and I had nothing concrete to hold onto.

The Alpha stood and I craned my neck to look up at his six-foot-six frame, fear shivering through me. Even at his advanced age, he was the most dangerous man I'd ever seen.

"I will leave you and my son to speak, but my word is law. You will never return here, Talia. Your father was a disgrace, and you will take his shame to your grave."

The Alpha turned to leave.

I forced my voice to work, though it sounded rusty and weak. "Where is my father, Alpha? His body? I would like to see him one more time. Say... goodbye."

My lip trembled as I spoke, and I bit it hard. I felt like a pathetic child acting so terrified in this moment. But he was the most powerful man in my pack, and he had just murdered my father.

"He's been taken to the pack's burial site," the Alpha said, and walked out without another look.

His betas, the other three men in the room, all left with him.

As soon as the door shut, I staggered toward my mate. I landed on my knees on the couch, staring directly at Maddox standing behind the furniture.

A pained sob wrenched itself from my chest as I stared at my husband-to-be. "Tell me I'm dreaming. That I'm in a nightmare and one day I'm going to wake up from this. Maddox. Please..."

I reached out for him once more, for his gorgeous, perfect hands, desperate for comfort from my mate, but he pulled away, out of my reach.

No! Please.

"Talia. Stop. You heard the Alpha." Maddox turned his back on me, his ass making his jeans look way sexier than he had any right to at this point in time.

"But we're fated!" I pushed myself to my feet. "You and I are meant to be! You've said it a thousand times. It's why we're getting married. It's why we waited so long..."

I gulped down the words, bitterness lacing my tongue.

What was the reason we'd waited so long? If we were mates...

Some mates couldn't wait even a minute to start fucking. They saw each other, and that was it. Boom. They were together from that moment on. But Maddox and I had dated for years. He said he'd wanted to wait until our wedding night to finally take me.

I'd always thought it was the most romantic thing I'd ever known. A shifter who would fight his most basic instincts to show respect for his partner. To wait until our official mating to impregnate me.

But maybe it had been more than that?

Maddox shook his head. "It doesn't matter."

"Of course, it matters!"

He stared at the wall opposite him, as if he couldn't bear to look at me anymore.

I stumbled around the couch and stood in front of him, forcing his gaze onto me. "Maddox! I love you. We have to find a way to change your father's mind."

His jaw tightened and his teeth set in that obstinate way he'd had since we were young.

"No, Talia." His eyes were cold. Empty. "I reject our bond, and I reject you. We will never be mated."

# CHAPTER 5

# TALIA

I stared up at Maddox, dumbstruck. "No. You can't. A wolf only has one mate. You'll never have another... I'll never have another. It's not how it works."

He started to crack, a small hint of the man I had known beginning to shine through in his sad smile and the pain in his beautiful blue eyes.

Finally, he took my hands in his and gripped them tight. "We don't have a choice, Talia. The Alpha's word is law. You know that."

"But..."

"No buts," Maddox said, then pulled me into a tight hug.

I breathed in his scent, inhaling deeply. And it was all there. The familiar woodsy smell. The sweetness of his cologne.

I began to cry. "This is so unfair."

And it was. All of it.

I couldn't possibly lose my father and my mate in the same twenty-four-hour period. Could I? Fate would never be that cruel.

He pulled back from the hug and shoved me away.

I stumbled then pushed forward, seeking the reassurance of

the man who'd been my boyfriend, my mate, for three years now. "Please, Maddox... please..."

He strode to the door and opened it.

When he glanced back, there was pain and regret written all over his face. "I'm so sorry about your dad. I tried to help, but..."

He shrugged.

I nodded. I knew. He was helpless to change his father's mind while his dad was still the Alpha.

"Go and see your dad," Maddox said quietly, "Goodbye, Talia."

I raised a hand to beckon him. "Madd—"

The door closed and I was alone in the room.

Rejected.

It was unheard of. Impossible. I shook my head, and a wave of unexpected pain coursed through me. My head felt like it was about to explode from the stress and grief. I staggered a little from the impact of the sudden headache, clinging to the couch so that I didn't pass out. That was the last thing I needed, to give the Alpha another reason to hate me.

Adrenaline rippled down my legs and I found myself propelled forward by a will that didn't even feel like my own.

I needed to see my dad. And then I had to get the hell out of here.

My trembling legs moved me forward, through the town and toward the cemetery. Where would they have put him?

I glanced around, terrified of what I was about to see. How would my father's body look after a night out in the elements?

Then I saw it. The newly dug grave, in a familiar spot. I stumbled over to the headstone I had knelt at for over ten years, my mother's final resting place.

There, now beside her, was a new burial. The dirt was freshly turned over and instead of a tombstone, there was a simple wooden cross planted in the ground.

No words. No name.

He had been buried as a traitor.

An angry sob rose in my throat, so I tried to concentrate on the one thing they had managed to get right. He'd been buried beside my mom. His mate. The love of his life.

The tears flowed freely again, down my face in hot, wet torrents. I wiped them away with the back of my hand, numb to most of the feelings now. But my tears wouldn't stop.

They didn't even let me say a proper goodbye to him.

I stayed there, on my knees, in the dirt, until my legs ached from the position and my face was finally dry.

When I could stand, I pushed myself up and began the slow, painful walk of shame back home. Through the streets of our town, past the homes and judgmental glances of the pack that now shunned me. Away from the mate that rejected me. I walked until I fell in my father's front door and then I simply laid on the floorboards until morning.

Galen

I stepped into my father's bedroom and hurried to his bedside.

"Son. You have news?" he asked, pushing himself up and leaning back against the pillows.

"You don't look well, Father." I couldn't help the words. His cheeks were ashen and sunken. His eyes, dark holes in his head.

He was no longer the strong Alpha I had grown up with, and I had no idea how to stop the decline.

"Don't worry about me, Galen," he said, swatting his hand through the air in a dismissive gesture. "I'm stronger than I look. Always have been. Now, tell me what happened this morning."

He didn't reprimand me for not waking him, and for that I was grateful. I didn't want to admit to the truth—that I hadn't dared wake him because he was so unwell and weak that I didn't want him in the fight.

"The Northwood pack attacked at sunrise."

My father's dark brows lowered. "Bastards. What happened?"

I inhaled sharply. I'd spent hours with my men after the fight, assessing their injuries, sitting with them as they were stitched and bandaged. Pouring alcohol over wounds, and down throats for pain management.

Wolf shifters were strong, deadly creatures, but we were still mortal.

"Three dead, ten badly wounded. But we won the fight."

My dad's eyes glittered with anger. "You need to make them pay, Galen. This cannot stand."

I nodded. I knew that revenge would be on the cards, but how strong a force my father wanted, I didn't know.

"We killed at least ten of their men. Their pack won't be nearly as strong as it once was."

My father sat up in his bed. "Serves them bloody right! Coming here to fight us on our own lands, totally unprovoked." He shook his head and tsked loudly. "Their Alpha must have rocks in his head."

"The men want to retaliate," I said, about to speak further until I saw my father's tiredness sweep over him. I stopped talking.

He leaned back once again, exhausted from this mysterious sickness that no one could name.

"You should do that, Galen. You are our Alpha in my stead."

I stood up, staring down at the strongest man I'd ever known. "I'll speak to them, Father. We need to formulate a plan. I'll see you later."

I headed for the door.

My father chuckled. "You don't have to sleep here at the house, son. I might be unwell, but I don't need a babysitter."

I grunted. "The bar doesn't need a babysitter, either. My apartment can wait."

My father closed his eyes, and I slid out, shutting the door quietly behind me.

Until my father relinquished his role, or passed on from this life, he was our Alpha. He lived in the Alpha's house, where I had grown up.

I owned a bar in town, about twenty minutes away, and I lived in the apartment above. It was a hectic life, but I loved it, and running the bar passed the time between pack obligations.

I walked down the hall and out the front door, where I was met by three of my Beta wolves.

David, Markus, and Theo.

"Hey, guys."

"We need to plan how we're going to get them back," Theo said, puffing up his chest.

I waved my hand. "Follow me. We'll go to the meeting hall and talk there."

The guys fell into line behind me, and we walked down the main street of our pack's town until we reached the small hall where we held weddings, funerals, and birthdays.

I opened the front door and entered the currently empty space. "Pull up a chair and let's get this party going."

I grabbed one of the chairs stacked against the wall, dragged it into the center of the room, and sat down.

The other three guys did the same. The Betas were my oldest friends. We'd gone to school together, hunted together, chased girls together, and now we sat and planned a war together.

It was strange the way some things changed, and others stayed the same.

When everyone was settled, I took the opportunity to study them. Most of them were uninjured from this morning's fight, except for Markus, whose eyebrow was covered in dried blood, and his neck had a neat row of stitches showing above his collar bone.

I swallowed hard, an ache forming in my gut. These men would put their lives on the line in a heartbeat, to keep our pack safe.

I was grateful more of the pack weren't injured, but I dreaded the fights to come.

"So," I said, "tell me what you're thinking."

The guys glanced at each other, then Theo moved forward, pinning me with an intense stare. "We need to pay them back. Like... now."

I held a hand up to calm him. "We do, and we will. Going right now, without a solid plan, would not be smart. We killed a lot of their pack..."

"Which leaves them vulnerable!" David hissed. "We should strike now."

I shook my head, my gaze sliding over to Markus, and the way he shifted uncomfortably in his seat. Did he agree with the others?

I focused back on David. "Our pack has been hurt too. We don't want to go off half-cocked and get more of our friends killed because we didn't wait for them to heal."

David lifted his chin in a show of defiance. "Wolves heal fast."

I sighed. "I know. So, you don't need to be patient long. A few days, a week maybe, and we'll be back to full force."

"Except for Damian, and Toby," Markus said quietly.

"And Rocko," Theo added.

Our fallen comrades. We'd been lucky to only lose three men, but it was still three too many, for a fight we had neither expected, nor started.

Anger pooled in my gut. We would get vengeance for our men.

I leaned back in my chair. "God rest their souls. Have their burials been arranged?"

Markus nodded. "The pack has decided to do one funeral a day for the next three days, so their families have time to prepare, and mourn."

That was a good idea, rather than forcing the pack to attend all three funerals in one day.

I clapped my hands together. "So, we allow ourselves a week to heal, and prepare for war."

The three Betas nodded, in agreement with my timeline at last. "We should increase our security," Theo said, "in case they try something again."

I shot him an approving look. "You're right. We'll double it. Four men on watch every shift from tonight."

That would stretch our numbers a little, but it would just mean covering people in their day jobs when those on watch duty needed to sleep.

"So, when do we attack?" David asked, the bloodthirsty question making me want to roll my eyes.

That sort of dumb thinking had gotten the other pack's members killed.

"We don't, necessarily. We need to be smarter than them."

"What do you mean?" Theo asked.

"I think we need to do more than just walk onto their land and start another fight," I began. "I don't know what, exactly. But there has to be a better way to seek vengeance than just copying their own stupid move. If we just do the same as they did, the outcome will be similar, until finally there'll be no men left in either pack."

"Then what do you suggest?" Markus asked.

I spread my hands wide. "I don't know yet, but there's gotta be a better way. Throw any ideas at me that you have."

There was a long moment of silence, and I could almost hear the cogs in their brains turning.

"What about kidnapping the son of the Alpha?" Theo said.

"He's a wanker. I've seen him in town. Big guy, but weak. He's a coward."

"Really? Tell me more…"

We spent the rest of the afternoon throwing ideas around.

By the time the sun was setting over the forest, we were finally done and had a few ideas on how we might be able to cripple the pack nearest us.

I'd always hoped the war we'd fought on this soil for generations would end with me, but here I was, not even in the shoes of the Alpha yet, and I was planning my first attack.

I didn't like the idea of it. But this pack meant everything to me. And I would defend all our pack members with my life, even if it meant going on the offensive.

I lumbered back to the Alpha's house, unwilling to leave my dad and go home to my apartment just yet. He seemed weaker every time I saw him, which was so frustrating. It was unusual—almost unheard of—for a wolf to die of sickness.

Especially an Alpha.

We died of heartbreak, or injuries sustained while fighting, or an accident like my mother. Simple old age was the most common, when our hearts gave out, but wolf shifters lived far longer than humans. We did not die from some strange unidentifiable disease in our fifties.

My father hadn't seen me mated, hadn't met his grandchildren. It was unfathomable to me that, at thirty years old, I may lose my remaining parent.

Our Alpha. Who was supposed to be the strongest of us all.

I crept into the house and checked out the fridge. It was stocked full of ready-made meals, and I smiled. Our pack looked after one another. The wives of Father's council would have made these meals.

Lasagna, stew, pasta, and rice dishes.

They'd been cooking for him since my mother had passed, and I had to assume the care had only increased since he'd been ill.

"Galen? That you?"

I turned toward my father's voice. "Yeah, Dad. Thought I'd stay here tonight."

"You raiding the fridge?" he called out.

I laughed. There was nothing wrong with his hearing.

"Yeah. There's some lasagna here that looks good. You want some?"

"Sure. Bring me a plate."

I smiled as I heated the food in the microwave. A healthy appetite was a good sign he was feeling better.

On the days when he didn't eat, it wasn't good. I could see the pain in his face on those days. They were the worst.

I took the food and went to sit with Dad in his room.

I inhaled my dinner, not even realizing how hungry I was until I glanced up and found he'd barely taken more than a few bites.

"Good?" Dad asked, a smile in his tone despite the still-full plate.

I grinned, trying to keep things as normal as possible. "Yeah. Very good." The cheese sauce was creamy, the meat rich, and the pasta cooked to perfection. "Nancy's recipe?"

My dad chuckled. "Yeah. Good guess."

Nancy lived next door and was married to my dad's oldest friend.

I set down my plate and he handed me his. "Finish mine off too. I don't need to eat anymore. I'm full."

My stomach dropped and I set his plate aside. I couldn't do that. Not now. "Dad..."

"I need you to promise me something, Galen."

I leaned forward. "Anything."

Whatever my dad wanted, I would do.

"You have to promise me that you'll avenge the pack. This

morning's attack was a sign that news of my sickness has gotten out. The other packs think we're weak. Vulnerable. You can't let them get away with it. It will..." My father stopped to cough. "It will..." He coughed again.

"It's okay, Dad."

He shook his head. "It's not okay, Galen. When an Alpha dies, and his son resumes the new role, it's the most common time to attack another pack. It is considered the easiest time to take over. But you must show them all that we are still strong. I know you can do this. You are strong. A born leader."

My breath caught in my throat, and I forced a laugh. "You're not dying yet, old man."

He smiled at me, and behind his eyes there was an ocean of pain. "Not today. But it won't be long, Galen. You have to promise me that you won't let them take over our pack—your pack. Your legacy. You need to strike back while you can."

"Dad, I..."

"Promise me." My father growled.

The hairs on the back of my neck stood on end as I offered up the only words my father wanted to hear.

"I promise, Dad. I'll avenge our fallen men. They won't take this pack from me. No one will."

Then I closed my eyes and hung my head, the weight of the world on my shoulders.

### CHAPTER 6

# TALIA

I had three days to leave town, forever. Three days to leave behind everything I had ever known and loved.

Today was officially the worst day of my life. And I had horrendously bad days to compare it to.

The day my mother had died.

The day my father had been killed.

And now, the day I'd been ousted from the pack I'd grown up with and the day I'd been rejected by my fated mate.

I slept on the floor of the lounge room at my dad's house the night before, unable to get up. I could barely move. I hadn't eaten in so long that my stomach felt like it was consuming itself.

I still didn't want to eat. I wanted to cry. And curl into a ball and stay there.

So, I did.

I went to bed, pulled the covers over my head, and woke up to the sound of a rooster crowing, and a loud knock at the front door.

I sat up, bleary eyed and confused.

What day was it? What was I meant to be doing... Oh.

Reality hit me with the force of a two-by-four piece of wood.

Thump. Right across the chest, making my ribs squeeze tight and my heart drop to the base of my stomach with a sickening lurch.

I now had two days to get out, to leave my pack... forever. It was an unfathomable reality. I put my hand to my head. The headache had come back in force.

The knock on the door came again.

"Talia! Open up."

I scrambled out of bed to the sound of Celia's no-nonsense voice. I raced to the front door, tripping over my own feet, and wrenched the door open.

"Celia."

She looked me up and down, then charged inside past me. "We need to find you somewhere to stay, some clean clothes, and some money. Have you got access to anything of your dad's?"

Nyssa was standing behind Celia, her eyes full of tears. "I'm so sorry, Talia."

Then she put her arms around me and hugged me tight.

I couldn't stop my own tears as they welled up and coursed down my cheeks. Damn it. I'd thought I'd run out of those.

I pulled out of my friend's comforting arms and reached for the front door, shutting it behind Nyssa and then locking it for good measure.

"What were you saying, Celia?" I asked, wiping the tears from my face. I loved Nyssa, and a large part of me wanted to wallow in her care and affection, but I was more in need of Celia's no-nonsense guidance and help.

She was level-headed and I needed that right now.

"You need a shower, and you need to pack. Essentials, mostly. Your favorite clothes. Photos. Jewelry. Things that you can't replace."

I nodded. She was right. I had my dad's old car to travel in, so I could fill that up with stuff. But there wasn't a lot of room in the little hatchback. Especially since I had no idea where I was supposed to go.

"Okay." I blinked. My brain was foggy. "So, my first step is to pack?"

Celia and Nyssa exchanged a worried look.

Then Celia took a deep breath. "No. You shower. Nyssa, make Talia something to eat while she's showering, and pack whatever food is portable. We need a plan. I'll start packing clothes. I pretty much know everything you own."

I couldn't help smiling a little. She probably did. We spent so much time together, Celia would have seen everything I'd ever owned.

"Thanks, guys."

Celia flapped her hands at me. "Go. Shower. And wash your hair. You're a mess. I'll meet you in your bedroom after you're done."

A sense of calm settled over me. I could deal with my pain and my grief later. For now, I was following Lieutenant Celia's instructions. "Yes, ma'am."

I went straight to the bathroom, stripped off the clothes I'd slept in, and climbed into the hot shower. Celia was right. I was a mess. Covered in dirt, grime, snot and tears, and with my brain only on half-power. Hopefully the hot water would help kick start the latter, at least.

Turns out I was numb to the normal pleasure of a hot shower. Instead, I mechanically moved, doing what Celia wanted, but no more.

I scrubbed myself clean, washed my hair, and climbed out. I managed to wrap a towel around my head and body, before Celia stuck her head in the door.

"I'm packing your clothes. You grab some toiletries. Toothpaste and toothbrush. Toilet paper too."

Then she was gone again.

"Toilet paper?" I repeated, then shrugged and grabbed a few rolls and packed my small toiletry bag.

I'd bought all new stuff for my honeymoon next week, suitcases and everything, but they were locked away in my father's bedroom, and I wasn't going anywhere near that space.

I wasn't sure I could handle the reminder of where my life should have been headed, but instead had taken an abrupt turn toward Hell.

"Keep it together," I whispered to myself as I picked up what I needed from the bathroom and headed to my bedroom.

Celia had turned the place upside down. There were clothes everywhere as she went through every item, packing what she thought I might need neatly into a black suitcase on the floor.

"Have you got more bags? Another suitcase maybe?" she asked.

"Um. I have a backpack or two, I think."

"Get them."

I grabbed what she wanted from the cupboard, then moved over to my clothes and stared at the pile.

What to wear on the day I escaped my pack?

"Wear something comfortable to drive in, and warm," Celia said. "You have to be over state lines by tomorrow night, so you'll be driving most of the day, I'd say."

I nodded, turning away to hide the tears that welled in my eyes.

I grabbed an old comfortable pair of blue denim jeans, a black tank, and a gray sweater.

"Boots?" I asked her.

Celia wrinkled her nose. "I'll pack those. You wear sneakers."

She went back to dissecting my wardrobe.

I dressed and tried not to think.

"Talia!" Nyssa called from the kitchen. "Come eat!"

I glanced at Celia who waved me away. "Go. Go. We're on the clock, here."

I groaned and trudged to the kitchen.

My heart was beginning to pump a little harder, a little faster now. It hadn't given up on me, which was a good thing.

I think.

"There wasn't a lot in here," Nyssa said, placing a plate down in front of me loaded with toast, scrambled eggs, bacon, and tomatoes. Despite her apology, the plate looked like more than enough to me. I was still struggling to get my stomach working again. It was full of anxiety and grief and there wasn't much room for food.

"I did the best I could," she added, and I sent her a grateful smile.

"Thank you, Nyssa."

She nodded at me, her eyes filling with tears, before she turned away to the pantry. "I found a box in the recycling and I'm going to fill it with food you can eat while driving, and some canned goods and stuff. And I'll make you some sandwiches as well, 'cause I know you forget to feed yourself when there's no one else to cook for."

I shrugged. "It's better when there are others to feed. Makes it worthwhile."

She glanced over her shoulder and grinned at me. "I agree! So, eat!"

I picked up my fork and knife and slowly began to consume what she'd put on my plate. On a normal day, I would have devoured the whole lot, but my stomach ached after the first few bites. I forced myself to keep going. I hadn't eaten at all yesterday, and I needed my strength if I was to get out of here alive.

I shoved more food down my throat, until I was almost gagging on the bacon.

"Thank you," I said, pushing the half empty plate toward Nyssa.

She popped her head up from where she was kneeling on the floor, going through the cupboards. "That's more than I expected. I'm going to pack you a little bit of cutlery, and plates, and glasses, and stuff." She glanced at her watch. "We've only got half an hour or so left before you should be on the road. Is there anything personal you want to take with you?"

I opened my mouth to ask her why they both seemed to think I had to get out of the house this morning. Didn't I have another forty-eight hours?

"Um, yeah."

"Then go grab it," Nyssa said with a weak smile.

I took a steadying breath and headed to my father's bedroom, where my mother's jewelry was stored along with the photo albums my father had kept close to him.

I ran my hand over my parents' wedding bed. I'd always thought I'd live in this town, with my pack, until the day I died. I couldn't believe I was being forced out, through no fault of my own. And that my father was no longer with me in this life.

A pang shot through my heart, and I bowed my head to hide the rush of emotion.

"Do you need a bag to put those things in?" Nyssa called.

I snapped out of my fog and turned toward the door. "No, I'll take Dad's suitcase with me. It's all good."

It wasn't, but I was trying to keep my head above water, lest the depression drown me.

I grabbed my dad's travel bag and packed everything I could see that was literally irreplaceable. Photos. Jewelry. Then I remembered where all the certificates were. The deed to the house. My birth certificate. Surely that stuff was important, too?

I ran down the hallway and into the small study that was once my nursery. There, in a small set of drawers, was everything my father deemed important.

I grabbed the various papers and stored them in my dad's black bag. Maybe one day I'd be able to come back here.

When I walked back into the kitchen, the front door was open and Celia was taking boxes of clothes to the car, packing them in the back seat and the trunk.

"Grab your quilt, too," she called from the car. "You know, the one your mom made."

"Oh, yeah." I couldn't believe I'd forgotten it.

I ran back to my room and opened my blanket box, pulling out the hand sewn quilt my mom had made me for my eighth birthday not long before she died.

I wrapped it up and headed outside. Nyssa packed a box of food and several plastic bags into my car.

"You guys are really wanting me to leave, huh?" I asked, trying to make it sound like a joke.

But then Nyssa released a sob, and guilt washed over me.

I rushed toward her. "I didn't mean it like that!"

She wrapped her arms around me, and I squeezed her tight, feeling like, for the first time, I was having to comfort her instead of the other way around.

"I'm going to miss you so much," she said.

"Aren't you guys going to come with me to town, at least?" I asked. "We could have a farewell lunch... or..."

Nyssa pulled out of my arms and took a step back toward Celia. They looked at each other, and Nyssa said, "We can't."

Celia handed me the car keys, then took out her wallet. "I've scrounged up everything I could find for you."

She pulled out a wad of cash.

I put my hands up and refused to take it. "I don't need that. I can get a job. Work my way across the state."

She moved closer, folded the cash over and pushed it into my jeans pocket. "You're gonna need gas, and food, and a place to stay. The money was meant to be a wedding present so... yeah."

Celia stepped back, thrust her hands into her jean pockets, and pressed her lips into a thin line.

Tears welled in her eyes, and I bit down on the inside of my cheek to stop from crying. "Why can't you come with me?"

I wasn't sure I wanted the answer, but I also needed to know for sure.

"The Alpha," Nyssa said quietly. "We've been banned from helping you, and we're under orders to hunt you down if you're not gone by sunrise on Thursday."

I shivered at the threat behind the words. The Alpha's, not Nyssa's.

"But you already did help me." I gestured to the house. "You packed me up and..."

I trailed off. They were helping to get rid of me.

"Oh. You were just making sure I away on time."

Nyssa shook her head. "It's not like that. We convinced the Alpha to let us help you pack up. We told him we could make you leave faster, but that's not why we did it. We don't want you hurt, Talia. You're our best friend. We wanted to help you, and... send you on your way with the knowledge that we love and care for you."

Nyssa's voice broke on the last word, and Celia wrapped an arm around her.

I nodded once, appreciating their motives. But it was time to go.

"Okay. I'll call you when I arrive... wherever I'm going."

Celia opened the car door for me.

"There's more money in the glove compartment," she whispered.

I actually managed to laugh, the sound rusty and painful in my throat as I slid into the driver's seat. Laughing was far better than crying, and I had already done so much of that in the past couple of days. "I'll see you guys later, I guess."

The girls smiled as they shut the car door. I started the engine.

I had no idea where I was going, but I put the car into gear and drove away.

Away from the only family, and the only home, I'd ever known.

# CHAPTER 7
## TALIA

I only had one human friend in town, Kylie. We worked together at the restaurant I waitressed at for extra money on the weekends.

Part of me considered just filling up the tank with gas and driving until I ran out of fuel. I could head for the state line right now and not look back. After all, I had cash, and food, and a blanket if I decided to sleep in the car.

But every instinct told me to take a little more time and not just run off with no plan in my head. I needed to work out a plan of action. I decided to stop in town and speak to Kylie and get organized. I needed to pull money out of the bank and do a little shopping for supplies. I had two days after all, before the Alpha's deadline.

And what was my rush to get somewhere else? It wasn't like I had anywhere else to go. I was completely alone and helpless in this shit storm.

I drove the fifteen minutes to town, gripping the steering wheel of my dad's old car and glancing down at the yellow light on the gas gauge every minute or so.

I'd definitely need gas before I went anywhere else, that was certain.

When I hit the edge of town, I slowed as I drove down the main road. I had to find Kylie, and the best place to start was the restaurant we worked at. I'd go from there.

She'd given me her cell number ages ago, but my phone was AWOL as of yesterday, and I had no idea where it was, or if I'd ever get it back.

Better to start fresh. I'd buy a new one, get a new number, then contact Celia and Nyssa when I'd crossed the state line and was safe.

I shook my head.

Safe from the clutches of my own pack, who'd been told to hunt me down and kill me if I didn't get away. How ludicrous. How terrifying. That people who I had considered family, would kill me just because of a mistake my father had made...

I shook my head, trying not to follow that thought any further, and pulled into an empty spot outside the restaurant. There were a few people inside, early lunchers probably.

I got out, locked the car, and walked in.

"Hey Talia! I didn't know you were working today," One of the waiters, Stevie, called out. He had always been lovely to me.

"I'm not. I was just looking for Kylie. Do you know if she's around?"

Stevie frowned. "Not sure. Do you have her number?"

"I did, but I lost my cell, and I have to buy a new one."

Stevie pulled his phone out of his pocket, hit a few buttons, then handed me the phone.

I put it to my ear.

"Hello?" Kylie said in her sing-song voice.

"Kylie! It's Talia. I came to the restaurant looking for you, but Stevie decided calling you would be best." I grinned at the waiter as he went back to the register.

Kylie laughed. "Yeah, he's practical like that. What's up, hon?"

"I, ah, need a place to stay tonight. I'm leaving tomorrow and was hoping I could stay with you for just one night."

I needed to organize some bank stuff, and mentally, I wasn't quite ready to haul ass across the state. I was shaky on my legs and still feeling stunned.

I wasn't sure I'd make it in my current state. I needed rest, and food.

"Of course, but what do you mean you're leaving? Aren't you getting married, like... next weekend?"

I rubbed the ring finger on my left hand, where my engagement ring used to rest. I'd put it into the jeweler a few days ago to have it cleaned, to make sure it sparkled for my big day.

I hadn't picked it up again, though I probably should. I could pawn it... maybe.

I put a hand to my head. "I'll explain later. Can I have your address again? I lost my cell, so I'm kinda a mess without it."

She laughed, told me the address, and we hung up.

"You okay getting there?" Stevie asked.

"Yeah, I've got a pretty good sense of direction."

Like most shifters, I had a good memory, and could find my way pretty much anywhere.

It also helped that Kylie only lived a couple of blocks from the restaurant.

I waved at him. "Thanks, Stevie."

"Anytime."

I got back into Dad's car, and before I knew it, I was sitting on Kylie's couch with a mug of hot chocolate and a warm blanket over my lap.

"Tell me everything," Kylie said, leaning forward in her chair, clearly wanting all the gossip.

I gave her a wan smile, and then concocted a humanized version of everything that had happened—which pretty much meant I had to lie about a lot. Kylie didn't know I was a wolf-shifter. Like most humans, she lived in blissful ignorance of the paranormal world around her.

At the end of my story, Kylie's mouth had dropped into a comical 'O', but her eyes were sympathetic.

"I'm so sorry to hear your dad passed, Talia. You must be devastated. Did you know he had heart issues?"

I shook my head, feeling slightly guilty about the lie. "It was sudden and unexpected."

"And then Maddox dropping you like a hot potato at the same time? Oh, honey, I can't even imagine what you've been through. I'm so sorry."

Her supportive words almost started another flood of tears, but I swallowed down the grief and concentrated hard to avoid crying. If I began again, I likely wouldn't be able to stop.

"You said that Maddox and you were, like, meant to be. Arranged since birth, yeah?"

I nodded. There was no such thing as fated mates in the human world, so I'd explained to Kylie that Maddox and I were in an arranged marriage.

My town was closed to outsiders, like most wolf-shifter towns. Kylie had never been there, and she had often expressed the thought—in an almost-joking sort of way—that we were some sort of cult, or something.

I shrugged. "It's all forfeited now. His family told me to get out of the state, or else."

Kylie frowned at me. "What do you mean, or else? They wouldn't hurt you or anything, would they?"

Of course, they would.

"No, I don't think so," I lied. "But rules are rules. And I have to go."

Kylie bit her lip. "Where to?"

I took a sip of the hot chocolate, grateful for the sweetness that washed away the bitter taste in my mouth.

"I don't actually know."

"Do you have any family, any friends? Anyone you could turn to?"

I thought about it for a minute, then realized there was one family member still living, and I hadn't even thought of her.

"There is, actually. A distant aunt. My mom's auntie, I think. She lives in Kansas. Wichita, I think."

Kylie whistled. "That's about a ten-hour drive from here."

I nodded. "I can do that in a day."

If I left by lunchtime tomorrow and didn't stop much, I'd be over the border in five hours or so, and another five hours to Wichita. That left me about twelve hours of wiggle room, or more.

"Do you have her number?" Kylie asked, grabbing her cell phone and sliding it over to me.

"I don't have it on me... But give me a sec. It could be in the car. I grabbed an address book before I left."

I ran outside, grabbed the box of things I'd gotten from Dad's room, and walked back inside. As suspected, there was his old-fashioned address book among the other documents and personal effects.

I flicked through the black leather book and found Aunt Sylvia's details.

"Thank God for my parents being the type of people who wrote everything down," I joked.

Kylie handed me her phone. "Yeah, I'd be screwed without my cell."

I moved into another room and called Sylvia. I hadn't seen her since I was very young, and in fact, could barely remember her to be honest. Our chat was brief, but it gave me hope. She was happy to help and said I could live with her for as long as I wanted.

Relief swept through me. I had a place to run to, where before I had nothing. And now I could begin to make plans for the future.

When I walked back into the room, Kylie was pouring chips into a bowl, and had candies and chocolates in another.

When I raised a questioning eyebrow at her, she shrugged. "Hey, you've just been through hell losing your dad, you've broken up with your guy—who should have hung around to support you, the asshole—and I probably won't see you for ages, from the sound of it. Unless I want to visit you in Wichita. I don't see why we can't pig out and have a major calorie fest before you leave."

I grinned at her. As a wolf shifter, calories weren't something I worried about. We burnt off so much energy, our metabolism just wasn't comparable to humankind. "Sounds perfect, Kylie. I really appreciate your support."

"That's what friends are for."

I sat down on the couch and reached for a handful of M&M's. I would miss Kylie when I left.

"Is there anything you need to do before you leave tomorrow?" Kylie asked as she walked into the kitchen, then came back with bottles of wine, one white and one red. "Which do you prefer?"

I groaned. After my hen's night, I didn't think I could stomach another drink. Not this year. "Neither, but I would love a soda."

"I've got heaps."

Kylie disappeared again, and came back with an assortment, and loaf of cheesy bread. "Wanna watch a movie?"

I nodded. "Sure." Anything that would take my mind off what had happened would be a blessing.

She found a chick flick that I knew would make me cry, and I shook my head. "Actually, can we do something with action? Not sure I can cope with a romantic comedy."

Kylie grinned, turned on Kill Bill, and we settled into the couch.

I stared at the screen. Perfect. Blood, and guts, and revenge. At least I wouldn't cry.

"Oh, you didn't answer me before. Is there anything you need to do before you leave?"

I shrugged, picking up the bowl of chips and plonking it in my lap. I was going to eat until I was sick. "I don't know. Maybe organize some money; bank stuff."

I had savings, and Dad did, too. He'd linked our accounts years ago.

He had said it was to help me with money management, but looking back, he'd obviously thought ahead, especially since he'd given me access to his accounts. Had he known something like this might happen one day? Had he suspected that I would be kicked out of the pack altogether for his transgression?

"Do you need clothes? Food? Anything like that?"

I shook my head. "Nope. All good in that regard."

I think...

She nodded. "Then we relax here for the rest of the day, get an early night, and head to the shops in the morning."

I sighed. "That sounds like a great plan."

"I've got a huge bathtub here too, if you wanna soak? That always makes me feel better after a bad day."

I glanced over at my only human friend and sent up prayers of thanks for her. "That's exactly what I need. Thank you."

I spent the rest of the day eating myself into a food coma and fighting off the ebbs and flows of depression that ate at my resolve. I had a long hot bubble bath, then crawled into the bed in Kylie's guest bedroom.

Part of me knew that I should have already been in the car and driving across state lines to get away from Maddox and his dad while I still had time. But I needed this night more than anything. It was a great reprieve from the stress of the last few days. I needed the moment to recoup my strength and prepare for the next few days of travel.

I sighed and stared up at the ceiling. Travel? Who was I kidding? I was running away. Escaping the pack I had called family only days before.

Everything was turning out completely different to what I'd planned for my future.

My life wasn't meant to be headed this way. Since I'd turned eighteen and the Alpha's son had felt a mating bond with me, my life had been blessed.

Now, I was in the seventh ring of Hell.

Alone.

Orphaned.

Abandoned.

Rejected.

And soon to be hunted.

At least I had a place to run tomorrow. Family to call on, even if it was a distant relative I barely remembered.

But it was a start. The beginning to a new life I'd never asked for, wanted, or expected.

What would Maddox do now? Forge another mating bond? Was that possible? Our mating bond hadn't been consummated, after all. Did that change things? Or would we both be destined to mourn each other forever? Would Maddox mourn me until the day he died?

I snorted at the thought. Not likely. Maddox was the Alpha's son. He was a soldier, doing whatever his father wanted. And he had made it clear through his rejection of me, that he was not there for me. He had shown the world—at least, the shifter world —that I was not his number one priority, mate bond or not.

I'd always thought of him as being loyal to his father, and the pack. But he'd abandoned me in my moment of need, so what did that make him? Certainly not loyal to me, the woman meant to be his wife.

The word coward circled in my mind, but I couldn't say it aloud. My love for Maddox still ran deep, as deep as my current feelings of betrayal.

I rolled over, nestled under the warmth of Kylie's blankets, and quietly cried myself to sleep.

THE NEXT DAY, I dragged my depressed butt out of bed, then managed to drink a strong coffee before Kylie got me to drive her to the shops.

If I was honest with myself, I probably wouldn't have gotten out of bed if it wasn't for her. I would have stayed there and counted the minutes until the Alpha, or his minions came for me. Would they really kill me?

"Thanks for the lift," Kylie said as we got out of my dad's car outside the restaurant where we worked. "I suppose I'll tell the boss you won't be doing any more shifts?"

I rounded the car. "Yeah… unfortunately." I rocked on the balls of my feet. "Thank you for yesterday, Kylie. I needed that day so badly. Things have just been so crazy."

I ran both hands through my bedraggled hair and Kylie pulled me in for a tight hug. "I'm gonna miss you."

I closed my eyes and hugged her back, enjoying her warmth and taking comfort from the friendship she was offering. "I'm gonna miss you too."

When I pulled back, I had tears in my eyes. I wasn't just moving away from the pack, but from my job, my friends, and everything I had ever known. Everything familiar.

Kylie glanced at her cell phone. "I better get inside. I'm gonna be late."

I gave her one more quick hug. "You go, I'll get all my errands done, then head for the border."

"Drive safe."

I nodded. "I will. Thanks, hon."

Then I headed toward the bank, hurrying past two people I didn't know to stand on the edge of the street. I waited for the lights to change so I could walk across and go to the bank.

I was knocked sideways, almost into the road, and staggered before righting myself. I whirled to see who had bumped into me.

Two guys from my pack—well, my former pack—turned and glared at me before continuing on.

I rubbed my arm, which ached from the hit, and stood in my spot, staring at the bank across the street.

My pack had turned on me. It was clear that I was no longer welcome in this town. I needed to get out as soon as possible.

I raced across the road as soon as the light turned green.

Out of the corner of my eye I spotted Shelly, a friend of my dad's.

I raised my hand to wave and opened my mouth to call out to her.

Shelly lifted her hand to wave back, but her husband grabbed her arm and tugged her around to face away from me. They both walked away.

Shelly cast an apologetic look over her shoulder as they left but didn't fight her mate when he dragged her away.

I pulled my shoulder bag closer to my body and hurried to the bank. I'd thought town was a neutral zone, where all shifters and humans could cohabitate without fear of a fight breaking out.

Obviously not.

I pushed open the door to the bank and went straight up to the teller. I pulled out all my IDs and said, "I'm moving interstate and need help transferring money around, please. And I need to pull out some cash, too."

I didn't take out as much money as I'd originally planned. Celia, God love her, had filled my glove box with cash, so I'd be right for a while, as long as I didn't need to purchase an apartment, or something big, straight away.

When I walked out of the bank, I took a deep breath of fresh air in through my nose and soaked in the warm sunshine on my face.

Life may have thrown me lemons—hell, it had cut my throat and shoved lemons into the wound—but I was alive. I had a chance of surviving all of this.

I would grab some brunch from the café and be on my way. It was only a five-hour drive to the border, then five to my aunt's house.

Then, and only then, would I be safe from the pack I had formerly called family.

~

Galen

I stared at the superb-looking woman standing on the footpath outside the bank. She had her eyes closed, her head tilted up, and the wind was in her hair. She looked like some beautiful goddess, pausing in our town to drink in the humanity around her.

"Is that who I think it is?" I asked Tommy, staring at the woman across the street.

When she opened her eyes and a small, almost wistful smile lifted her lips, I almost sucked in a breath. That smile only made her more beautiful.

Lust kicked me in the groin, and I clenched my teeth in annoyance at my lack of self-control.

Get it together.

Tommy sidled up next to me. "Who? That chick over there? The blonde one?"

I nodded, following her with my eyes as she walked down the street and opened the door to one of the only good cafes in this town.

"Yeah, isn't she Maddox's girl?" Tommy asked. "Weren't they getting married or something?"

I nodded. "Yeah. That's her, all right."

I'd only seen her from a distance in the past, holding Maddox's arm and laughing up at him. The same kick in the gut had happened then, too, but I had successfully ignored it. Mostly.

A plan was forming in my mind. I had to think about the best possible way to avenge my fallen pack members, following the latest attack. And taking the next Alpha's mate, a key piece in the structure and hierarchy of their pack, was a perfect way to do it without further bloodshed.

I clapped my hands together. "I think I have an idea. But we need to follow her."

Tommy didn't question me as I jumped in my car, turned the key, and stared out the windshield at the woman.

How old could she be? Twenty? Twenty-one? Maybe a little older.

Something twanged in my chest as I watched her look left and right, then run across the road to jump into an old car.

I rubbed the spot on my ribs that ached in a foreign way, then pulled my car out of its park and followed her at a distance.

What was that strange feeling in my chest? Jealousy? It couldn't be.

There's no way I would ever be jealous of that coward, Maddox.

I glanced across the car at Tommy, who always kept his ear to the ground and knew more about the packs around us than anyone. "How much do you know about this chick and the next Alpha? Is it a love match? Or a power match?"

Sometimes, wolf packs did their version of an arranged marriage, putting the Alpha with the strongest or most powerful of the women. The girl I was following looked quiet and not at all tough but looks were often deceiving.

"They say it's a love match," Noah said from the backseat, and my stomach dipped again. "Fated mates, actually, if what I heard in the pub last week was right."

She was fated to that loser? This time, the burning in my chest was unmistakable. Yep. Jealous as a wolf watching the full moon rise through the thick glass of a cage.

I wanted a mate. A wife. A woman who I could come home to, love, and protect. Who'd have my babies, and guard them with the fierceness of a wolf-shifting mother.

Sure, I'd been in no rush to find her in recent years, and no one was pushing me into mating someone I didn't want, which I was grateful for.

But a fated mate connection? A true love match? Just like my parents before me. I secretly wished for that. I wanted an equal partnership. One built on love, trust, and preferably the perfection of being touched by Fate.

The girl was likely heading back toward her pack grounds, based on the direction she was driving, and I shuddered. "She's driving home."

"What do you want to do?" Tommy asked me.

Whatever we did, the decision had to be made quickly. We couldn't just drive onto her lands. That would be suicide for all of us. The packs in this area had rules about boundary lines. Town was a neutral zone, and a peaceful area. Even if we were at war, the fight wasn't allowed to spill into the town where the humans were.

And if we ventured onto each other's territory without a direct invitation, it was war.

"I'm going to follow her," I said. "On foot. I'll try to intercept her before she reaches their land, or at least, not too far in from the boundary. You drive my car home and I'll meet you back there in a few hours."

I pulled over the car and opened the door.

Tommy grabbed my arm. "If they find you, you know you're as good as dead."

I rolled my eyes at him. I was one of the fastest in our pack when in shifter form. "They'll have to catch me first."

I jumped out of the car, ripped off my shirt and jeans, and threw them in the back seat so I didn't ruin them.

Maddox's mate was getting further and further away. "Go, Tommy. Before they sense you. I won't be long."

If I all went according to the quickly formulated plan in my head, and with a bit of luck thrown in too, I'd be bringing home the girl with me.

"Galen..."

I ignored Tommy's protest and let my shifter take over my body. I would need to run fast to catch her now.

As soon as my wolf paws hit the ground, I was moving. I darted off the road and wove my way through the trees, following the soft puff of smoke that trailed behind the old car but cutting through woodland area in a shortcut that would bring me close to the road further ahead.

My heart was pounding. Being so close to an enemy pack's territory, and contemplating snatching the mate of the Alpha's son—especially when we were currently at war with said pack— was dangerous.

Very. My father would have my head, if he ever found out.

But this was a gift horse we couldn't afford to ignore.

The girl was leverage and payback all rolled up into one.

I kept following her. As we hit the edge of her pack's town, the girl didn't turn in to drive down the main strip of road like I'd expected her to. Instead, she veered around the town's outskirts and kept driving.

Where was she going?

My heart hammered hard as fear prickled along my veins. I needed to turn back. If they caught even a whiff of my scent this close, it would turn them rabid. This was dangerous, but God, I wanted to take them all down so badly. How stupid had they been to think they could just stroll onto our land and kill enough of us to take over the whole pack?

My father might be ill, but the rest of the pack remained strong and steadfast.

I kept running, veering around the pack grounds, keeping to the trees and trying not to be caught by anyone who might pose a threat to me.

I didn't think anyone in this pack had the balls to kill me, nor the strength now that we'd killed a dozen of their men. But without another heir, and with my father so sick, I was the only Alpha my pack had. They'd be lost without a leader.

And I might be skating on thin ice chasing after Maddox's mate, but I was damn sure I wasn't going to let them catch me.

I would survive this, and more than that, I would make sure no one took my pack from me. No matter what I had to do.

# CHAPTER 8

# TALIA

I pulled up my car next to the burial ground on my pack's land and turned off the engine. The smell of the chicken sandwiches beside me was making my mouth water, but I was saving them for the trip.

Back in town I'd gotten in the car with my fresh food, my new bank account details, and some cash, and then it hit me. Once I left, I'd never be able to visit my mother's gravesite again. Nor would I get to say a proper goodbye to my father.

Damn that idea to hell.

Tears threatened again, but instead, I'd pulled up my big girl panties, ignored all my instincts that told me returning to the pack was too dangerous, and drove straight here to the burial ground and my mother's grave.

I still had twenty-four hours. They could shun me, bump into me, and ignore me all they liked. But they couldn't stop me from seeing my parents one more time. I had as much right to be here as any of them.

I stepped out of the car, shut the door, and pocketed the keys.

"Okay. I can do this," I said to myself, then I took a big deep breath and walked over to where the pack had buried my parents.

My father's plot was still covered in freshly turned soil. But there were still no flowers to decorate the site, and no gravestone to mark the final resting place of the man I'd loved. And unfortunately, I didn't expect there ever would be.

I knelt in front of my parents and tried to smile. "I'm going to miss you both so much."

I didn't want to be all choked up and unable to speak. I needed to get this out. To be able to say my final goodbyes properly. I swallowed hard and took a fortifying breath.

"I contacted Aunt Sylvia, and she seemed excited to have me stay with her. It'll be a whole new start. A new life, in a new town, a new state, maybe a new pack... I'm not sure what sort of life Aunt Sylvia lives. Human or shifter. I don't really care. I just..."

I wiped my nose with my sleeve.

Kneeling here, I could almost feel my dad's grief, his regret at how everything had turned out. I turned my gaze to stare at where my father's body lay buried beneath the earth. "I'm so sorry I couldn't do more to help you, Dad. I should have known... Maddox should have told me... I'm so..."

I couldn't get the final sorry out. My throat closed up and there was no talking.

I love you, Dad.

I turned to my mother and tried to speak, but there was nothing I could say or do to get the words out.

I gave up and spoke to her inside my head, where the prayers went.

Mom. I love you. And I am so, so sorry I didn't take better care of Dad for you. I tried... I promise, I tried. But I wasn't good enough to keep him... from this.

I began to sob as the thoughts poured through me, and even though part of me wanted to stay there forever, I knew I couldn't.

I pushed my hands into the cold earth and staggered to my unsteady feet. I glanced up at the clear blue sky and blinked rapidly.

"I need to go. The pack have orders to hunt me down if I'm still here come morning, so I'd better…" I motioned to the old car that stood behind me. "I hope I get to come back one day. But I… who knows?"

I clenched my hands into tight fists and willed the despair away.

This was my last chance to say what I needed to. I just had to concentrate hard enough to stop sobbing.

I took several breaths, in and out, forcing the tears back, and the bile down.

Finally, I opened my eyes and stared at the place where my parents both rested.

"I love you both. So much. Thank you for being my parents. I promise to try and make you proud. Bye for now…"

And with my head held high, I managed to walk away without shedding another tear.

I wasn't staying here to be killed like my father had been. I'd lost my parents, my husband and the man who had been my mate, but I hadn't lost my life. Not yet anyway.

I got back in the car and wiped my hands off on a wipe, then reached for my chicken sandwich. The first bite was pure bliss and the second was better. By the third I was feeling a little more normal. My stomach was growling, but there was now a sense of peace in my body.

My shoulders relaxed, crawling down from the place up near my ears.

I glanced out my windshield at the clear sky and open landscape. I was about to drive across the state line for the first time ever.

The unknown awaited.

I quickly ate the rest of my sandwich and turned the key. Shit. I needed gas, and then I could leave. There was a gas station on the highway, between the two pack's lands.

As far as I knew, it was a neutral zone.

Maddox had never let me visit there, but he wasn't running my life anymore.

I could do anything I wanted. It was such a strange feeling.

I drove to the small station, filled up my dad's car, and set off. It was two hundred miles to the border. I should make it on this tank, but if I didn't, surely there'd be another place to get gas somewhere on the highway.

The fact that I didn't know that kind of thing freaked me out. I hadn't realized how sheltered a life I had led, being looked after by Dad and "managed" by Maddox. But I was too far gone now to turn around.

I took a back track and turned onto a dirt road, looking for signs to the highway, slowing down to peer out the window.

I slammed on the brakes as a huge black wolf jumped onto the road in front of me. My car fishtailed and swerved.

Panic wove through me as the car stalled.

"Come on. Come on." I twisted the key over and over, but the car wouldn't turn over.

Then the black wolf transformed into a huge man with long hair down to his shoulders, and the largest body I'd ever seen.

Huge, hulking shoulders, massive thighs...

He skulked toward me, ripped open my car door, and reached over me to unfasten my seat belt. All before I had moved a muscle.

I was frozen in place, shocked into silence by his sudden appearance, and by the sheer enormity of his superbly proportioned body.

He grabbed me by the wrists and wrenched me out of the car.

"What are you doing?" I choked out the words as I stared up into his dark eyes.

He still looked feral, which some men did after shifting back from their wolf forms. The animal was still inside him, larger than life and pushing hard to get out.

"You're Maddox's mate." The words were hard to make out around the sharp teeth still present in his mouth.

How did he know who I was? As far as I knew, I had never seen this man before.

He shook me, and my teeth practically rattled in my head.

"Yes! Yes. I'm Talia," I squeaked out. I was still processing that I wasn't Maddox's mate anymore. And in this moment, when the enormous man had pulled me out of the car, I wasn't thinking straight.

Was he looking specifically for me? Was he going to hurt me? He wasn't a shifter from our pack, but what if he'd been hired by the Alpha to track me down, and kill me?

Fear rushed through my veins. I could feel my shifter rising inside me. I wasn't a good fighter, but I was fast. Could I get away from this guy? I wasn't sure. But if it came down to my life, then I'd fight with everything I had.

"You're coming with me," he said, grabbing tighter to one wrist and pulling me off the highway and into the forest.

He almost yanked me off my feet, he was so strong.

I glanced back at my dad's old car and tried to plant my feet, tugging in the opposite direction to where he was dragging me. I couldn't stop him, but I did manage to slow him down a touch.

"My car! Everything I own is in that car. Please."

He grunted like he hadn't heard me, and I yanked my arm back, fighting hard to turn around. When I managed to pull my arm out of his grip, I pivoted on one foot and tried to make a run for it.

I made it one step before he grabbed me around the waist and threw me over his shoulder like I weighed less than a bag of flour.

I cried out, pounding my fists against his back. "Please! I can't leave the car there! Please!"

My money! My clothes! Everything that was important to me was in that car. It was all I had left of my life. All I had left of the connection with my dad.

He stopped walking as though he was considering my plea. There wasn't a sound around us. Not even a bird chirping.

All I could hear was the pounding of my heart in my ears.

"You got the keys?" he demanded.

I shook my head. "No. They're in the ignition."

I hadn't even had time to pull them out.

He grunted dismissively. "No problem. I'll send someone back for it. Only my pack uses these back roads. They're on our land."

My pack. Our land. Who was this guy? Was he an Alpha, too, like Maddox's dad?

"Fuck it." I let go of the fight, relaxing against his back to conserve my energy. It was no wonder why Maddox had always told me not to go to the gas station in town.

It was theirs? A neighboring pack?

He could have explained that, and I've have given it a wide berth.

The big and very naked shifter walked for so long I began to get numb and tingly in my hands. I was just about to say something to the guy, when there were shouts and men came running toward us.

Had we reached their pack town? I tried to lift myself up and turn around so I could see who was there, but my captor just used his other hand to push me down. "Stay there."

I groaned but didn't fight him. What was I going to do if he put me down anyway? Run away from a rival pack group of super fit men?

I was dead. Clearly, it was only a matter of time as to when.

"Markus. Go get her car and bring it here. Don't touch any of her stuff. It's on Dawsons Road, a mile out from the gas station."

"Will do."

Relief flooded through me. He'd asked them not to touch my stuff.

I was being kidnapped, probably to use against my old pack and Maddox. But that small amount of understanding and thoughtfulness about my belongings made tears prickle at the backs of my eyes. He listened. He cared.

I hung my head in shame.

God, you really have stooped to a new level of low if you're happy at the tiniest bit of kindness thrown your way by a kidnapper.

"I'm gonna throw her in the shed. Make sure everyone knows to stay away," the kidnapper said, and my ears pricked up.

He was gonna do... what?

Then my big naked abductor sauntered away from the others and back into the forest, with me still draped over his shoulder.

I glanced up as we walked away. The pack guys he'd been talking to still stood around in a small group, watching us. I gave up caring what anyone thought. This was pretty much as undignified a position as one could get, but at least no one was laughing at me, or pushing and shoving me into the road.

Like my own packmates. Former, I reminded myself.

The concerned looks on these men's faces as the big guy carried me off were obvious.

They were about my age, probably a bit older.

What was this guy's plan?

We continued on in silence until the pack was long out of sight. I zoned out, trying not to think too much. There wasn't much I could do like this.

Eventually, my captor lowered his shoulder, and I fell onto my ass on a hard wood patio.

"Ow," I said, rubbing my tingling hands and staring up at the still naked man before me.

Holy shit, he was big. Everywhere. I averted my gaze from the part that was just about eye height right now.

"Get inside," he demanded, and I shivered at the sound of his voice.

Damn, if he's not an Alpha, I'll bite my own ass.

He must be the Alpha of this pack, whatever it was.

But what the hell was an Alpha doing kidnapping me?

I pushed myself to my feet, my legs trembling. "What are you going to do with me?"

He grinned as though he had all the time in the world and crossed his beefy arms over his even beefier chest. "I don't know yet. But I can tell you that you better get that ass inside, or..."

I was running for the log cabin before he even finished the sentence.

As a virgin, I had an insane amount of fear wrapped around the first time I would have sex. I'd always assumed it would be with Maddox, on our wedding night. That dream was now in tatters, but that didn't mean I had to submit to the nightmare of being taken by force by a stranger who would never understand how terrified I was.

I pulled open the door and raced over the threshold, a tingle of awareness shooting up my spine as I stumbled into the house.

"Oh, no." I knew that feeling.

Magic.

The place must be warded.

I stumbled around, crashing into a bookcase, then a couch, before finally falling to my knees on a worn rug.

The magic was knocking me out.

I lifted my head and stared at the naked Alpha looming over me. Dark spots danced at the edge of my sight, and my brain was beginning to shut down.

"Please don't hurt me," I whispered, fighting against the magic of whatever sort of spell had been woven into the door of this place.

He frowned as though he didn't understand why I was struggling. Could he not feel it? The magic was strong, so strong. But I needed to be clear with my words, so there would be no mistake.

"I'm a virgin... please... don't..."

I couldn't fight the effect of the magic anymore.

I fell toward the floor and everything went black.

# CHAPTER 9

# TALIA

Galen

She was a virgin?

God, no...

I dove forward to catch her before her head smashed against the ground, tangling my fingers in the long red and gold strands of her hair just in time.

"Fucking hell," I muttered as I lowered her unconscious form to the rug, then gathered her up again in my arms.

What sort of Alpha would leave a woman like this... his mate... untouched?

"A fucking idiot, that's who," I answered my own question.

I walked the rival Alpha's soon-to-be-wife into the bedroom and placed her gently on the bed.

Untouched... fuck. It was unheard of in this part of the woods. We took what was ours, and it was given willingly.

I shook my head and walked away, wishing I'd been able to tell the girl before she fainted that no one in this pack was going to rape her. Not unless they wanted their head placed on a fucking pike out the front.

This woman, who was barely more than a girl, had nothing to do with the fight I was having with her pack. I would keep her as a bargaining tool, sure. But I wouldn't hurt her, and neither would any of my men.

"Hey! Galen!" someone called from outside, but I found myself unwilling to leave her, which was insane. She wasn't mine to protect. She was my prisoner, the mate of the rival pack's next Alpha, and nothing to me. Then why was it so hard to walk out the front door and greet my Betas as if nothing was amiss?

I stared at the excited faces of David, Markus, and Theo.

"Did you do it? Did you really do it?" Theo asked, jumping up and down like a puppy.

I growled at him to calm down as I prowled off the step. I needed some clothes, but I didn't want to leave this place to go get them. "You guys brought spare jeans with you?"

They shook their heads.

Then Markus said, "I'll go get you some."

He trotted off.

"Be quick," I called, and watched him speed up.

He'd read me well, and that was something I needed in my lead beta. I hadn't formally chosen my men yet, or the council members I wanted to add from my generation when my father's time came to an end.

But I was always on the lookout for people who were loyal, clever, and good fighters.

All of which Markus was.

"So?" Theo asked again. "Is she here? Did you really kidnap their next Alpha's mate?"

I nodded. "I did. Her name is Talia, and none of you are to touch her. Do you understand?"

Theo frowned. "Why would we?"

David crossed his arms over his chest like he was offended. "As if."

I shook myself, trying to drag myself back to a base level of calm. She'd thrown me off, that girl. Maybe I shouldn't hang around until she woke up. I needed to get away from her, run off this tension.

I looked at David. "Because she's young, and scared, and she's not to be hurt. Can I leave you in charge of her while I go check on my dad?"

David walked up the steps that led into the cabin. "Yeah. You can trust us."

I nodded, fighting the need to growl at them the closer they got to her.

"Let me know when she's awake."

Theo frowned at me. "She's asleep? Seriously? Wow. She must have been pretty tired."

"Yeah. Magical sleep. I had one of the local witches put up wards around the cabin. If anyone that isn't from our pack steps over the threshold, they pass out. I hadn't expected it to work quite so well, or so quickly."

I frowned at the window that was off the bedroom I'd left Talia in. Hopefully she'd be okay.

"Clever," Theo said. "Great place to keep prisoners, and ensure they remain under control."

I didn't really want to think about how many people we may need to hole up there in the next few weeks, months, or years. Nor the fact that it would likely be me making those decisions in future, rather than my dad. So, I ignored his comment and turned to take the jeans from Markus, who had returned quickly as I requested.

"Thanks," I said, pulling them on, then took the gray tank from him with a grateful smile. "That's great."

I tugged on the shirt and clapped Markus on the back. "I'm going over to speak to Dad, then to the bar afterward if anyone needs me."

That should help me lose this strange feeling about the girl.

The virgin.

No. Maddox's girl, I reminded myself. Off-limits, for about a thousand different reasons.

I trotted down the hill and jogged through our town, my heart rate higher than it should be. I moved faster, wanting to burn off whatever excess energy this was. I ran the length of the pack grounds, then circled back, watching as Tommy drove Talia's old car through town, then parked it outside my dad's place.

I jogged up to him, a nice sweat covering my skin and cooling me down. "Thanks for doing that, Tommy."

He nodded at me. "Anytime."

He threw the keys at me and frowned.

"What's up?" I asked.

He shook his head. "I don't know. Something's weird about this. It looks like she's packed up to move away or something. There're pillows, clothes, blankets, photos, even cash in there. You sure she's the Alpha's mate you think she is?"

She had confirmed it, and I was sure I'd seen her that one time hanging off Maddox's arm. But why she'd packed up her car for that sort of trip, I didn't know.

I shrugged. "No idea. I'll ask her when she wakes up."

I headed inside my dad's house. "Hey, Dad! You home?" I picked up a note left by a neighbor that said there was dinner in the fridge.

A chuckle came from the nearest bedroom. "No. I'm out running through the forest."

I smiled at the jest, but there was little humor in my heart. My father hadn't shifted in months, let alone gone for a run through the woods.

I pushed open the door to his room and walked inside. The smell struck me, hard. It smelled of decay, and a little of death.

"We need some fresh air in here, Dad," I said, trying to keep the tone light.

"I like it dark in here," Dad grumbled.

I ignored him, going over to the windows and pushing two of them open, while keeping the curtains drawn so it was still semi-dark.

"There. You'll breathe easier now," I said, before plopping down on the chair next to his bed. "How's your day been?"

He shrugged. "Same as most days, no worse. What's happened?" Dad narrowed his eagle eyes at me. "You look … concerned."

I struggled not to laugh. That was my dad's word for worried and excited at the same time.

"I am concerned," I said. "I've taken a step to fulfil my promise to you. To stand up for our pack and avenge our fallen."

Dad pushed himself up in bed until he was sitting up and leaning against the headboard. "What have you done?"

I leaned back and grinned. "I spotted a girl in town."

"A girl? What sort of girl?"

"Maddox's girl," I said with a grin. "Their next Alpha's soon-to-be-mate."

My dad swallowed, his eyes gleaming with interest, but his tone was cautionary when he said, "The town's a neutral zone."

I nodded. "I know. So, I followed her, and when she drove back to her pack, I shifted into my wolf form and ran after her."

"Galen! You could have been killed."

I swiped my hand through the air, dismissing his worry. "She visited a graveyard. There was a freshly dug grave there, but no marker. Then afterward, she headed to the gas station to refuel."

My dad's eyes brows flew higher on his forehead. "Our gas station? That's not neutral ground."

I grinned. "I know. So, I grabbed her, carried her back here, and threw her into the cabin, where the magic I had arranged to have instilled in the boundaries knocked her out."

My dad's mouth opened, but nothing came out.

I wanted to laugh, but instead, a shot of self-pride raced through me at his pleased expression. He was also shocked. That was a first.

"What are you going to do with her?" he finally asked.

I shrugged. "Not a hundred per cent sure, but we can definitely use her as leverage against the Northwood pack. I'm certain of it."

He nodded, glancing away. "Yes. It's a bold move, son."

I sighed. "I know, but I don't want any more blood spilt if we can stop the war now. I figured that if we were smart, showed a united front and strength, her capture would get the others to back down. We can release her once they agree to that, and our show of goodwill in letting her go without harm should mean they can't easily attack again. Unless they want to lose face across all the packs in North America."

My father nodded slowly. "Yes. Though your plan hinges on the girl being valuable."

I grinned. "Why wouldn't she be? She's the fated mate of the Alpha's only son."

"Fated? Shit!" My dad's laugh was strong and made the hairs on my arms stand on end.

That was the sound of my father from when I was younger, when he was fit and strong and able. I loved the sound of that laugh.

"You are one lucky man, Galen. But smart, too. That was a good call, son," he said with a grin, then began to cough.

And cough. And he didn't stop.

I jumped up to help but he waved me back. He coughed until blood stained his fist, and then he tried to wipe it away on his blankets.

"Dad! Your hand! It's…"

"I know," he said, the annoyance shining through even though he sounded hoarse.

He cleared his throat, threw back his head so that his hair cleared his eyes, and stared at me.

"Why do I feel like I'm in trouble?" I asked.

Dad shook his head. "You're not. I am."

I narrowed my eyes. "You're in trouble? What for?"

What could he have possibly done from his bed?

Dad sighed. "I think you need to publicly take over the role of Alpha."

My mouth gaped open. "That's just not done, Dad. Not…" I broke off, unable to finish. Not yet. Not till you're dead.

The role of Alpha passed from father to son upon their father's death. Not before. Unless a challenger came in to battle for the role, but that rarely happened. An Alpha was born the largest and strongest of our kind. Not many Beta wolves were strong enough to survive a battle against an Alpha. Not even if they teamed up.

Dad reached over and grabbed my hand, squeezing it tight. "You have to, Galen. Otherwise, if someone outside of the pack chooses to challenge me, I'll have to fight."

To the death.

"I would avenge you," I said, my wolf teeth cutting into my lower lip as I began a partial shift in anger.

My dad pressed his lips together and nodded once. "You must take the role now. To show strength in our pack."

I shook my head. "It isn't done, Dad."

"That's because Alpha's are never sick. We are strong, until we die in battle. Or of old age. This sickness—whatever it is—is going to kill me, Galen. And I would rather my last memories be of my son rising to the role he was born for."

Tears and emotion clogged my throat as I stared down at my father. What was it, this illness that was killing him? If we could work out what it was, maybe he had a chance. But no one knew, not the shifters, nor the witches, nor anyone, it seemed.

Finally, I nodded. "Okay, Dad."

What else could I do? Deny the final wishes of a dying man?

Besides, like always, his request made sense. My father was the most sensible person I knew.

Dad lay back against his pillows, exhausted. "You will be a great Alpha, Galen. You love our people. You're strong and loyal. And you have a good moral compass."

I chuckled, brushing off the compliments. "Be careful, Dad. You'll blow my ego up too big and I won't fit through the door."

My dad shook his head. "Nothing wrong with being honest."

"True."

We sat that way for a while, in the quiet. In peace.

I'd originally had plans to head back into town and check on the bar, but instead I stayed with my dad and talked more about how I would take over officially, and how to plan a ceremony that in the history of our people, had never happened.

By the time we were done, the sun had dropped out of the sky and it was time for dinner. I heated something up for Dad from one of the dinners that had been dropped off by pack females, then glanced outside, where Markus was resting by the car Talia had been driving when I found her.

I handed Dad his lamb stew and cocked my head. "Markus is outside. I'm gonna go speak to him, then I'll be back."

Dad waved his hand. "Don't hurry back. You do have a life outside this sick old man."

I clenched my jaw in denial of his words, but without anything to say back, I just stomped over to the front door and opened it up.

"Hey Markus. Come in for a beer," I said.

God knew I needed one.

What a day.

I'd done my first kidnapping, and unfortunately it was the beautiful soon-to-be wife of my enemy. And I didn't even hate her enough to be mad at her. She'd looked so terrified when she'd seen me on the road.

A virgin? I shook my head. Was that idiot Maddox insane as well as stupid?

I groaned as I threw open the fridge and pulled out some drinks.

Now my father wanted me to take over as Alpha, years before I should.

"Here," I said, handing Markus the beer.

"Thanks." He gave a nod before he tipped the drink back.

"Any news?" I asked. "About the she-wolf in the cabin?"

Markus shrugged and leant against the counter. "Not really. She hasn't moved since last night."

I frowned. "She's not even awake yet?"

"Nope." Markus finished off his beer and sighed. "I'm gonna head home for some dinner. Theo said he'd do the night shift."

"I'll go talk to him."

I tossed my empty beer bottle in the recycling and headed up to the cabin. The night was quiet and cool, just as I liked it. I kept my ears open and my eyes wide, checking to see if our enemy was coming once again for us in the night.

I still couldn't believe the Northwood Alpha and his pack had thought to take me out. Or my father.

What the hell had they been thinking?

I trudged up the hill and waved to Theo, who was standing guard on the patio.

"You okay to stay here over night?" I asked him.

He nodded. "Yeah, no problem. I'll call you if she wakes up."

I wanted to stay here as well but that was stupid. Theo could watch her. She was just a prisoner after all.

There was only one thing. "Remember that there's safety on

the other side of that door for you. If some of her pack come looking for her, just go inside and they'll pass out the moment they try to cross the threshold."

Theo saluted. "That's great. Thank you."

Despite the strange tug to stay, I turned and walked away. My dad needed me, and I would stay with him again tonight. I didn't know how much time I had left with him, which would kick me in the guts enough when he died, but the idea that I'd have to be Alpha soon was even harder.

How was I going to look after all my people without my father at my side?

# TALIA

When I opened my eyes, I was staring up at a ceiling I'd never seen before. It had white plaster, but low hanging rafters that reminded me of a log cabin.

But not mine.

I sat up and gasped, furtively looking around. This wasn't my pack's cabin. All the memories of being kidnapped came rushing back in. And then the rush of magic as I stepped through the door. It must have been warded, and knocked me out.

How long had I been unconscious? Had anyone...

Fear flooded me and I quickly checked my body for injuries, running my hands over my neck, my breasts, and legs. Nothing seemed sore, or ill-used. My clothing was all still in place.

Relief flooded me. I hadn't been touched. I'd know if I'd been hurt, or abused in some way.

A memory hit me, of a large black wolf shifter stopping me from driving out of town.

Shit! What time was it? My seventy-two hours might be almost up, or worse. I may have already run out of time altogether.

I jumped off the comfortable bed and raced to the window. I threw back the gray curtains and was blasted with sunshine. Judging by the position of the sun, it was at least the next day.

I raised my hand to shield my eyes. "Crap!" I said out loud. "I'll never make it over the state line now."

I had to try, though. What else could I do?

I raced to the bedroom door and pulled it open. The front door wasn't far. I stumbled over my feet trying to get there, another memory rising and confronting me. The shifter... the man... had carried me here. He'd promised he wouldn't hurt me.

Despite his size, and intimidating aura, he'd been... kind. For a kidnapper.

He'd obviously been true to his word, and not hurt me. So far.

But if I didn't get out of here soon, the kidnapper and his pack would be the least of worries. My own pack were going to hunt me down and kill me the way they'd killed my father.

I pulled open the front door, but the moment I tried to step over the threshold, an invisible force threw me back. I landed heavily on my ass.

Damn it. The ward was still in place. And it worked both ways, in and out of this cabin.

I rolled to the side to rub the offended spot on my rear.

A huge man with blond scruffy hair blocked the doorway. "You're finally awake."

He growled at me as though I'd done something wrong, like I was lying about sleeping in and being lazy, even though I was the one being held prisoner; and had no choice about whether or not I was awake.

I jumped to my feet, my wolf shifter rising within me. "Why can't I get out of this cabin?"

The guy, who seemed younger than I first thought now that I was looking at him properly, quirked a smile at me. "It's warded. You can't get through."

"Well, obviously its warded. But I have to leave! You don't understand."

He frowned at me. "Why? Worried your boyfriend will miss you?"

I opened my mouth to tell him the truth, and then realized the only reason they'd captured and not killed me, was probably because they thought I was still Maddox's bride-to-be.

Tears clouded my vision and I blinked them away.

I opened my mouth to respond, and the guy, who couldn't be much older than me, backed away. "You just stay there. I'll go get Galen."

Before I could reply, he hurried away.

I clenched my hands into fists and strode forward, bouncing back off the invisible shield again, like I'd smacked into something solid.

"Fuck!"

I ran my hands through my hair, frazzled at the entrapment. What the hell was I going to do now?

How would I ever manage to get away from this pack? Or my pack? It felt like the whole world was about to be on my tail even if I did manage to run.

On the other side of the living room, a huge window let in the morning sun. I bolted over to the window, threw open the pane, and felt a moment's excitement before I was forcefully pushed back against my will once more.

The windows, too?

"Shit!"

There was a knock at the open door, and a blond guy slid two plates along the floor toward me.

Food.

I walked back over to where the same young guy, with tousled hair and the beginnings of a beard, was staring at me like he'd never seen a girl before.

"What's your name?" I asked him as I picked up the plate with my sandwich on it. The same one I'd bought yesterday and taken a few bites out of.

I was so hungry I didn't care. The sandwich was stone-cold now, but it was still delicious.

"Galen's on his way," he said, not answering my question. He disappeared from view by walking along the patio so I could no longer see him.

Galen... was that the name of the Alpha who grabbed me yesterday?

I took another bite, chewing and swallowing despite the goosebumps of fear that covered my skin, and the tumultuous feelings rolling around in my belly. I was starving. How long had I been out for? Was it more than a day?

"Who's Galen?" I called out in between bites.

The guy stepped back into my line of view. "He's our Alpha's son."

I rolled my eyes. Of course, he was. I seemed to attract those assholes.

"Great."

The kid disappeared again, and I took my plate of sandwiches, and the extra plate of cookies he'd pushed into the room, over to the couch and sat down.

It was obvious I was in enemy pack land, being held captive. Although I could easily have let fear consume me, at this point, I didn't have a whole lot to lose.

They were feeding me and keeping me safe, overall, which was more than I could say for my own pack. But if I could convince the Alpha's son to let me go, I would jump in my car and hightail it straight over the border.

I finished my sandwich but couldn't bring myself to eat one of their cookies, even though they looked homemade, and delicious, with little chocolate chips throughout

I swallowed hard, my throat beginning to ache. I needed a drink.

I wandered over to the small kitchen, found a glass in one of the cupboards, and turned on the faucet.

Clean water flowed out, and I smiled as I filled my glass. So, they weren't complete barbarians after all.

"Making yourself at home?" a deep voice asked from behind me.

I sprayed a mouthful of the water I'd been drinking all over the cupboards in front of me, then slapped a hand over my mouth, trying to stop the rest coming out.

I swallowed hard and spun around to confront my kidnapper. "Don't sneak up on me like that."

His eyebrows flicked up, and I got my first good look at his face. I was sure I'd seen him in town at least once. Who could miss a guy towering over six foot six, and as big as a fridge? He had an air about him, too, that drew the eye and held it. He looked like he came from Alpha blood. There was something robust about him —beyond his size—that gave the distinct impression he was a leader of men.

But despite that air, and the hard set of his jaw, his eyes seemed kind.

I set down my glass and walked back over to the couch, sinking onto the cushions to assume a submissive position.

I didn't feel submissive right in this moment. Part of me wanted to punch him in those hard abs for daring to kidnap me. But I didn't want him thinking I was challenging him in any way. The best way to get out of here was to make him think I wasn't a threat. To him, or to anyone else in his pack.

He crossed his arms over his big meaty chest, his biceps bulging.

I swallowed. This was one Alpha who looked like he was strong enough to lead a whole pack of shifters. I couldn't help the quick thought that flickered into my head, comparing him to my now-ex-fiancé. Maddox didn't really like to exercise, or work out, and his father never made him do any physical labor because he knew his son didn't like it.

Maddox was lean and long, not heavily muscled. I'd always liked Maddox's slim body, but this guy was all male.

"What were you doing on our lands yesterday?"

"Your lands?" I squeaked as I repeated part of the question. "I was just filling up my car with gas, and driving home."

"You weren't driving home. Don't lie to me." He growled. "You were headed in the complete opposite direction to your pack, and town. So where were you going? With enough cash to buy a new car, and enough clothes and possessions to move house."

I blinked rapidly as tears pooled in my eyes. I had to come up with a good lie, and quickly.

Focusing on being kidnapped had actually helped me contain my grief, but this guy's questions brought it all rushing back. "My father died." I covered my mouth to stifle the sob that rose. It was still ridiculously hard to say out loud. "I decided to go visit my aunt. She lives in Wichita. She said I could stay with her for a while."

He narrowed his eyes. "What about your future husband? What did he have to say about that?"

"Maddox?" I repeated. I must have sounded stupid, to him, but my brain was slow in concocting a story.

He nodded. "Yes. Why would he let his future wife leave the state? Especially if you've just lost a parent. I wouldn't let you leave my side, if you were mine."

I blinked at him.

If you were mine.

Well, I'm not yours, I thought. I'm not anybody's, anymore.

His words made me realize that no one outside our pack knew what had happened to my father and myself.

I frowned at him. "Is this about Maddox? Did you kidnap me to get to him?"

He didn't answer, but I saw the truth in his eyes.

Now I really couldn't tell him Maddox had rejected our bond. I'd have nothing to bargain with if they planned to use me against him. Hopefully, when they did inevitably find out, they wouldn't kill me and toss my body over the pack lines just to prove a point.

"Answer my question," he said.

I stood up, not because I really wanted to, but something told me to get on my feet. I wouldn't die on the ground, like a dog.

"Maddox told me to take some time to mourn my father. He loves me." I stuck my nose in the air, though it took everything in me to lie like that.

Galen, if that was his name, glared at me. "Were you part of the hunting party that killed two of my men?"

My mouth dropped open. "Your men... Oh, my God, you're the pack they attacked..."

That's what this is all about!

When the big Alpha took an aggressive step forward, I held up both of my hands and took retreating steps back. "No! Of course not! Women in my pack aren't allowed to fight. That's men's business."

"Where were you when it was all happening then?" he countered.

I narrowed my gaze at him. "If you really must know, I was in bed with a hangover from my bachelorette party the night before."

His mouth practically fell open, before he turned and marched away.

He obviously hadn't been expecting that response.

When he reached the door, he turned around and glared at me. "Your pack will pay for what they did to my men."

"What's that got to do with me?" I demanded. "I wasn't even there."

"Your Alpha ordered the attack, and your 'fated mate'," he said, as though the term disgusted him, "will pay for his part in it as well."

I was in the middle of something bigger than I had realized. I began to sob as I ran to the door after him. "Please. Just let me go. I won't tell Maddox you grabbed me. I'll just drive to Wichita to be with my aunt. She's expecting me."

He turned to look at me from the fresh air outside the cabin. "You'll stay my prisoner until I've come up with a plan to use you against your pack."

"But..."

He waited, but I didn't have anything else to say. How could I tell him that it wouldn't work? That my pack didn't want me anymore? In fact, if he killed me, he'd be doing them a favor. They had orders to kill me on sight.

"Please..."

Another guy came running up, bounced up the stairs, and whispered in the Alpha's ear, before bounding off again.

Galen speared me with a wordless look, one I couldn't read, and then without saying another thing, the huge shifter man turned and ran after the other man, disappearing from sight.

# CHAPTER 11

# GALEN

Fucking hell. Dad had been taken to hospital in town, which could only mean one thing. He'd gotten so bad one of his neighbors must have called the paramedics. That wasn't a good sign.

I ran until I reached my truck which was parked outside Dad's place, jumped in, and took off. "Damn it," I fumed out loud, even though there was no one to hear me. "He was okay last night."

I'd been working out when they came to tell me Talia was awake this morning. I'd been out for over an hour, and I hadn't thought to check on Dad before I went to the cabin to see Talia. He'd still been asleep when I got up.

I drove way over the speed limit and didn't care, reaching the small hospital in less than ten minutes.

I swung my vehicle into the closest parking spot and ran inside. When I found my dad, he was in an ICU room, hooked up to a myriad of beeping machines and an oxygen mask covering his face.

"Are you family?" a nearby nurse asked.

I nodded, swallowing the lump in my throat. "I'm his son."

She directed me to a chair next to his bed and said, "A doctor should be along soon." The sympathy in her words only added to my anxiety.

I waited, nervous energy engulfing me.

The staff were jittery, as humans always were around wolf shifters, and they were confused by the lack of records in relation to my dad.

"He's never really been sick before," I said.

The next few hours were terrible. I sat in the room that smelled of detergent and dying people and watched my father's chest rise and fall. At least the machines were keeping his breathing relatively even.

He didn't wake up and no doctors came to check on him in the time I sat there.

Eventually, I had to leave.

I got up and turned to go, only to run into a gray-haired doctor, with glasses sliding off his nose.

"Finally," I said, and he stared at me with wide eyes. There may have been a touch too much growl in my tone. I took a deep breath and released it slowly.

He extended his hand. "Doctor Michaels."

"Galen," I said, pulling my frustration in by the reins. "This is my father."

"Incredible case," the doctor said. "He has no medical history in this hospital whatsoever."

I wanted to roll my eyes. Of course, he didn't. Wolf shifters didn't get sick. Not that the doctor knew he was a shifter, of course.

"I explained to the other staff that he's always been well. He's never been here before, because he has never needed to be here."

"When did this start?" the doctor asked, and we got into a history of my father's mystery illness.

In the end, the doctor offered to run what sounded like a

hundred tests, and promised he'd contact me as soon as he knew more.

Despite the tardiness of his arrival, he seemed to be competent, and I relaxed a touch, leaving my dad in this human doctor's relatively capable hands.

"Where can I leave my number?" I asked him. The doctor directed me back to the nurse's station.

I wrote down my details on the papers they shoved at me. "I'm only ten minutes away, so please call me when he wakes up."

"Of course," the nurse replied, though I got the feeling she wasn't certain he would wake up at all.

When I headed out of the hospital's parking lot, the sun had passed the highest point in the sky, and was well on its way down.

I ran a hand through my hair.

How many hours have I been sitting in that chair?

I pulled my cell phone out of my pocket and checked the time.

"Jeez. Three o'clock already."

I swung past the bakery for a couple of hot pies and headed back out of town again.

I didn't see any of the enemy pack members in town, but the situation with Dad occupied my mind, so I wasn't really looking. It was the one great thing about the treaty we all held tight to, safety within town. Our own pack borders couldn't be crossed without outright war, but the main town was a green zone.

Had we gotten into fights over the years? Hell yes.

At my bar? Often.

But no one had been killed in town in my lifetime, and I hoped it never got to that. There were laws that all shifters abided by when it came to humans and leaving them to their ignorance was one of them. If we turned our quiet little town into an all-out turf war, there would be hell to pay.

I drove straight back to the cabin where Talia was being kept. I wanted to make sure the wards still held, and that she wasn't making a nuisance of herself.

I pulled up in front of the cabin and got out of the truck. I had competent staff looking after the bar for me at the moment, so I planned to drive back into town after this and sleep in my own bed rather than head back to work. I was closer to the hospital that way.

Markus was sitting on the porch, his eyes closed, his arms crossed over his chest.

I stomped up the steps.

He came awake on a start, jumping to his feet, then swaying with fatigue.

"You okay?" I asked him, grabbing for his arm to steady him.

He nodded. "Yeah, I'm just tired. Did the night guard last night."

Which meant the poor guy had been awake all night running the perimeter and had probably only got a few hours of sleep before he was needed for something else.

"I'll take over. You go home to bed."

"I've got night run on again tonight," he said.

I checked my cell phone for the time. "You can go home and get a few hours' sleep before then."

Markus sighed. "Thanks, Galen."

"Anytime," I said, patting him on the back.

I watched him walk away, then turned to stare through the door of the cabin.

Talia was sitting on the couch, cross legged, not doing anything. Just staring at me.

"Can I get you anything?" I called out to her.

"Yeah, a way out. Then my car keys."

I laughed. I couldn't help it. "Anything else?"

She pouted and I wanted to go up there and wipe that look right off her face. Preferably with a kiss.

I shook myself, growling in self-annoyance.

She's the asshole Maddox's mate. Pull yourself together.

"You okay?" she asked, standing up and walking toward the door opening.

I ran a frazzled hand through my hair. "Yeah. Just had a bad day. Do you need anything from the car? Clothes, perhaps?"

She inhaled deeply, her nostrils flaring as though she was controlling her temper. "Yes. I'd like my clothes."

Did I trust her not to make a break for it? No, I didn't.

"Tell me what you want and I'll get it for you."

She crossed her arms over her chest, which was more ample than I'd originally thought. I tried not to stare. "It would be easier if I just came out and grabbed the things I needed," she said.

I raised one eyebrow in her direction. "Can you guarantee me that once you get to your car, you'll just grab all your stuff and walk calmly and quietly back to the cabin?"

She lifted her chin, only a fraction of an inch, but part of me kind of loved the defiant streak. "Yes," she said.

I burst out laughing. "Sure you will. I'll just grab some shit and be back in a second."

I jogged back to my dad's place where we'd parked the car she'd been driving when I'd stopped her and grabbed a blanket and a suitcase. Then I trotted back to the front door of the cabin.

I didn't hesitate as I walked over the threshold and deposited her things at her feet. "Here you go."

Her pupils dilated as she stared at me, and I found myself wanting to grab hold of her. Which was insane. She wasn't mine to grab.

I backed away.

"Do you have witch in your blood?" I asked.

It wasn't unheard of for the witches to mix with the wolf shifters, though it was rare.

She frowned, before shaking her head and kneeling on the floor to open the huge suitcase I'd brought inside.

She started to take out clothes, choosing some new jeans to change into. "No. Both my parents were wolf shifters."

She glanced up at me as she got back to her feet holding a new top and some underwear.

I tried really hard not to stare at the bra she held. I was a grown man, after all. The sight of some basic, white, cotton underwear should not get my motor running like it suddenly was.

I took another step back.

Definitely a witch.

She tilted her head to the side and looked at me in an assessing way. "I wish I was a witch, then I'd be able to work out how to break that damn ward and get out of here."

I chuckled as I backed up over the threshold. "I think I'll stay here overnight. I'll sleep on the porch. Just in case your fiancé comes looking for you."

There was a flash of something that looked like hurt in her dark eyes, before she glanced down at her feet. I wasn't sure what it was, but it certainly looked like she was upset at the mention of her fated mate.

Maybe she was disappointed he hadn't started looking for her yet?

In fact, why hadn't he? If she was my mate, I'd have razed half the county to find her and get her back.

"Where's your cell phone?" I asked, realizing we hadn't checked her for one.

She picked up her jeans, clinging to the fresh clothes. "In the car, I think. I lost my old one and picked up a new one in town yesterday, but didn't have time to charge it or anything."

I frowned at her. Since when would someone travel as far as she had said she was going, without charging her phone? That made no sense at all.

"I'm going to go have a shower and get changed?" She phrased it as though it was a question.

I nodded, as if she were my guest. "Go for it. But the hot water will only last about three minutes. Fair warning."

That wasn't true, but I didn't want her disappearing for hours and using up my town's water supply.

"No problem," she said and bolted toward the bedroom.

I sat down on a chair on the porch, and the idea of a hidden cell phone began to play over and over in my head.

I got up off the chair and jogged down to her car. I checked the front seat, the back, and the trunk. No obvious sign of a new cell phone anywhere. Or an old one for that matter.

I looked back at the cabin. How could I have fallen for such an obvious trick? She could be on the phone to him right now telling him where she was, and how alone I was.

I ran back to the cabin, barged through the open front door, into the bedroom, and opened the closed bathroom door.

"What are you..." My accusation froze in my throat as her scream ricocheted around the bathroom walls.

She was completely naked beneath the spray of water, and she certainly wasn't holding a cell phone.

"Get out!"

I backed away, scanning the room for signs of a charger, or anything that would indicate she had a phone in here with her.

"I'm sorry," I managed to mumble. "I thought... never mind."

I bolted out of the room and slammed shut the door. Now that was an image that was seared onto my brain. How would I put that aside?

I huffed out a breath and began to look around the bedroom for anywhere she might have plugged in a phone: on the dresser, under the bed, and beneath the pillows. But there wasn't a cell, or device to be seen.

I grabbed my head with both hands and squeezed, trying to

get the sight of Talia's gorgeous ass... perky breasts... perfect nipples... virgin body... out of my head.

"Damn it..."

I shook my head and bolted out of the cabin. Did I trust myself to sleep here with her within arm's reach all night?

I growled at myself. Of course, I did! I'd never taken a woman against her will in my life. Never would.

But damn, she was hot! Curved thighs. Tiny waist. Dark pink nipples... I'd only gotten a flash of the front of her, before she turned her back and curled up against the tiles, showing me her perfectly rounded ass.

My God, she was beautiful.

Maddox was an idiot, for not turning up the second she went missing.

"Damn it all to hell."

She was an Alpha's mate, and I could see why. Just not this Alpha's mate. And that fact was going to drive me insane until I had her... or she escaped.

Whichever came first.

# CHAPTER 12

# TALIA

'd never been so mortified in my life, or embarrassed, than when the Alpha Galen walked in on me. Naked. No man had ever seen me like that. Not even Maddox.

I felt violated. But in the strangest way, I also felt safe.

The embarrassment in his eyes as his gaze raked my body had matched mine, I suspected.

Whatever he had rushed into the bathroom to do, it hadn't been to ravish me, either with my permission or against my will.

Galen's men so far had been respectful, but I'd been terrified to go to sleep. I'd imagined waking up to one of them in my bed, on top of me, hurting me in the most basic, horrible way.

But after seeing the way Galen had responded to finding me in the shower, I knew I was going to sleep okay tonight. He'd been so embarrassed his cheeks had flushed red and he'd bolted out of the bathroom so fast there had been a trail of smoke behind him.

Sure, he'd looked at me, all of me, but truth be told, I would have been hard pressed not to stare at him if I'd found him completely naked too.

I finished my shower, staying longer than three minutes just to test out what he'd said, despite the way my heart raced in my chest, and my shifter shimmered just beneath the surface, ready to jump into wolf form if the need arose.

When I crept into my room, I was wrapped in two towels, just to make sure Galen wouldn't see anything more than my ankles if he was sitting on my bed.

But he wasn't there. The room was eerily empty.

I dried myself and changed into a casual top and a pair of jeans from my suitcase, wishing I'd brought my slippers with me. And my dressing gown. But I hadn't exactly known what to pack for this trip, not to mention the fact that I'd been so out of it after Dad's death, my best friends had packed for me.

Once covered, I snuck out into the lounge to find it also empty. Disappointment hit me, hard. I was as shocked by the feeling as I was by the fact that he wasn't inside anymore.

Where did the disappointment stem from?

"Hello?" I called out.

Galen stuck his head in the front door, his eyes doing a cursory glance of my now dressed body, as if checking before he entered. Then he stepped into the room.

"My... about apologies before," he began, tucking his hands behind his back. "I... I want you to know that despite the fact you're our prisoner, and your pack tried to kill me and my father and all of our male pack members, I would never harm you in... that way."

I liked the fact that he felt like he needed to say it. I couldn't really say why. Maybe because I understood what sort of life we led. That things got dangerous, and people got killed, and yet watching this huge man apologize for walking in on me naked was humbling.

He could have taken me if he'd wanted to. He still could. He was far stronger than me, and there was no one here to stop him.

I had the distinct impression he was pretty much the boss

around here, even if there was an Alpha father somewhere in the background of the pack.

"I—"

He cut me off by lifting his hand and taking another step forward. "I swore to you yesterday that no one would hurt you, and I mean it. I..."

He shook his head, a frustrated growl coming from him.

It was a beautiful thing to see, watching his tough side war so fervently with his good side. He was an Alpha who would protect his women and children. I liked that in a man.

Unlike Maddox, a traitorous voice said in my head. He didn't even try to protect his woman from the sentence of death.

I bit the inside of my lip to punish myself for even thinking such nice things about my captor and such bad things about my ex-mate. What was wrong with me?

"All good. No harm done," I said. "Is there any food? I'm kinda starving."

He nodded, nipped out of the cabin, then a little while later, brought back into the room a huge plate covered with meat, bread, and potatoes.

My stomach growled at the smell of garlic and butter.

"Here you go."

I rushed toward him, taking the plate gratefully, though there wasn't a utensil to be seen. I didn't care.

"Thank you."

I hurried back to the couch and began making myself a lamb, or beef sandwich. I wasn't sure which one it was and I didn't care. It smelled delicious.

"I'll stay tonight," Galen said, although he'd already told me that.

I nodded and mumbled, "Okay."

He made it sound like he was protecting me, instead of what he was really doing, which was making sure I didn't escape.

The potatoes were warm and crisp, and even as I picked one up and bit into it, I moaned. Wow, that was awesome. Salty. Just how I liked them.

Galen didn't leave. Instead, he wandered to the end of the couch and sat down, and watched me eat. Strangely, I didn't get self-conscious. I figured he had to deal with the sight of my hunger since he was the reason I was so starving.

I ate all the meat, half the potatoes, and most of the bread too.

"Is this bread homemade?" I asked, staring down at a crust dripping with butter. It didn't look like something bought from a shop.

"Yes," he said, smiling softly. "My dad's next-door neighbor is a great cook. She brings food over all the time."

I chewed on the end of the bread. "Where's your mom?"

I was pretty sure I knew the answer, but part of me wanted the personal conversation. Wanted the connection in this lonely, devastating time.

I shouldn't feel that way about Galen, of course. He was the enemy. But since Maddox had thrown me out so spectacularly, I found myself yearning for any type of contact. Even with a kidnapper.

Galen sighed. "She died about ten years ago."

I bit my lip and mimicked his sigh, leaning back against the couch. "Mine too. And now that Dad's gone, I suppose I'm an orphan."

Galen didn't respond, so I took the platter to the sink and did a quick wash. Then I lay it on the couch cushion next to him. When he didn't move, I sat back down in my original spot.

The room was still warm, despite the fact it was dark outside now.

"Where's your dad?" I asked, wondering where the true Alpha was in all of this.

Most wolf packs, like the one I'd grown up in, only had one

leader. And he stayed the Alpha until the day he died, or someone came in and took the title from him.

Maddox had said something about Galen's dad being sick. Maybe? I couldn't really remember now. The last week had turned into an absolute blur of a mess in my head. I still couldn't remember why my pack had attacked Galen's in the first place, let alone everything that had followed.

"He's, um..." Galen faltered, sliding a hand over his neck and tugging at his hair as though frustrated.

"Is he okay?" I asked, pulling my legs up and wrapping my arms around them.

I was feeling sleepy now. My belly was full, and after the rush of adrenaline from the shower mishap, I was coming down and wanting to rest.

I laid my head on the tops of my knees and stared at the big shifter, who was so much more attractive that I'd first thought. He had hair that curled down to his jaw line. And his eyes were so intense.

When he finally turned to look at me, his jaw was tight, his teeth clenched. He looked angry, but I could already tell it wasn't at me.

"My dad's... sick. He got taken to hospital this morning. That's why I've been gone all day. I was with him."

I sat up, slipping my legs down. "Oh, I'm so sorry. That must be... strange. I mean, for an Alpha to get sick. It's unusual. Isn't it?"

Galen nodded, swallowing so hard his Adam's apple bobbed up and down.

"Yeah, it is. And no one can work out what's wrong with him. It's just..." He tapped his heels on the ground a few times. "It's not good."

Then his gaze slid to me, and this time I could see the anger banked inside his dark eyes. "I believe that's why your pack attacked us. They think, with my dad sick, that we're weak. That we don't have an Alpha at the helm any longer, but they're wrong. We do."

He stood up, and sudden fear quickened my blood stream.

His hands were clenched, and the set of his jaw told me how upset he was about everything that had happened.

"I'm sorry," I said, though I wasn't sure how I could have changed either scenario.

Galen walked toward the door, then doubled back and paced along the wall, behind the couch. "I know it's not your fault. It's obvious your pack keeps you in the dark about these things. But you need to know, we're not weak! We killed at least ten of your men, and you only got three of ours, and we weren't expecting it."

Pain and tears clogged my throat. "I'm sorry for your loss. I promise, I didn't know anything about the attack. And I lost my father that day too."

Galen stopped pacing. "My pack killed your father?"

"No. He made it back to the pack..." How did I say this without outright lying? "But he died shortly after. I know it's not your fault. So please don't blame me for what happened either."

I wrapped my arms around myself and squeezed tight. "I lost so much that day, and because I'm just a girl, they didn't tell me anything! I couldn't prepare myself... I didn't know..."

The sobs began to rise in my throat and I couldn't stop them this time.

Galen strode across the room, yanked me to my feet, and held me in his arms.

I pressed myself into him, crying against his huge chest. And this time I didn't fight the grief, nor stop myself from mourning my father the way I needed to. They'd taken him from me. I wasn't ready. It hadn't been his time.

It wasn't fair.

I'd lost everything, and I'd done nothing wrong. I'd loved my father. I'd loved Maddox. I'd been kind, and loyal, the best person

I knew how to be, and everything I'd been taught made up a good female pack member.

And this was how they repaid me? Killing my only remaining parent, and taking away my future, and my past, in one fell swoop.

Galen held my head to his chest and murmured, "Shh..." as I cried until I was exhausted and could barely stand from the pain in my heart.

He picked me up and carried me to the bed. I lay limp in his arms, too devastated to consider what I was doing. He lay me down and pulled up the blankets like I was a child, and he was caring for me.

I felt numb. Dead inside. I could barely see through my aching, tear-filled eyes.

"I'll go sleep on the couch," Galen murmured as he backed toward the door. "But if they need me at the hospital, I'll have to leave."

I nodded and turned onto my side, nestling into the pillows.

I wasn't sure why he was being so nice to me, but I wasn't looking a gift horse in the mouth after all the bad luck I'd had lately.

"Thank you," I managed to choke out. "You've been very kind, Galen."

I would figure all this out in the morning and decide what to do. For now, I closed my eyes and fell asleep, dreaming of big black wolves... and death.

# CHAPTER 13

# GALEN

When I woke up around sunrise, my neck ached, and I couldn't feel my left arm.

I rolled off the uncomfortable couch and landed as quietly as I could so I didn't wake the girl sleeping in the room next door.

"Ouch." I stretched out my neck and hung my arm down straight to let the blood flow connect back to my brain.

Then I shook the dead arm because I hated how it felt.

Feeling came back in electrical pulsing bursts. I got to my feet and groaned. Last night was not the best night's sleep I'd ever had, but strangely, it wasn't the worst either.

"You've been so kind, Galen." Her voice kept replaying, over and over in my head. She had sounded so forlorn; so broken.

Where was that fucking mate of hers? Why hadn't he come to rescue her?

Comforting Talia had been weirdly soothing to me. I was surrounded by stress and pain with my dad and everything else that was happening at the moment, and feeling helpless about so many things.

But with her last night, I'd been able to help her, comfort her, and that had made the big wolf inside me happy.

Which confused me even more. She wasn't my woman; she wasn't even of my pack. It shouldn't have felt so good to be with her.

I walked to the bedroom door, which was still wide open, and stared into the room. Talia was lying on the bed, the blankets flung back and her face resting in sleep. Her lips were slightly open and her gorgeous blonde and red hair was spread across the pillows.

I turned away before I could admit that what I was feeling was close to passion, or lust, or desire.

I refused to covet another man's wife. Even if they weren't yet married. It just wasn't acceptable. I wasn't religious by any stretch, but the original commandments were a pretty solid way to live your life, in my view.

There was a knock on the front door, then David stepped into the room.

I pulled shut the bedroom door. "Hey man. You here to take over?"

David nodded. "Yeah, if you want me to."

"Please do. I need to go into town, check on my dad and the bar." I needed to work tonight. There were only so many nights I could let the bar staff run things without me.

"Cool. Anything you want me to do? Specifically?"

"Yeah, make sure she's fed. And don't touch her."

David's eyebrows shot up. "Touch her? Why would I touch her?"

I huffed out a laugh. David was into guys; always had been. "Sorry, man, I just mean... you know. Leave her alone."

"Easy," he said, and walked back into the sunshine. "I'll just sit on the porch until you get back."

Concern coursed through me which I tried to squash. No point worrying over a woman who was our prisoner. She couldn't escape. And with David outside, no one would get in.

"I might send one of the witches here to check on the wards, just to make sure they'll hold up against an attack if Talia's pack come to get her."

"Talia?"

Oh, crap.

I tried for a casual shrug. "Yeah. That's her name. I won't be long man, thanks."

I waved goodbye and jogged down the steps.

I needed to be rid of the strange level of protectiveness I felt around Talia. She was the enemy, but my wolf didn't seem to care. I liked her. She seemed... sweet. And bright. And loyal to a fault.

Great qualities in a mate.

"Oh, shut up." I growled at myself. "She's already somebody else's!"

And the last time I'd had the chance at a great mate, I'd failed to protect her.

I didn't deserve another.

In my truck, I sped off toward town, not bothering to look at the speed limit. I could tell by the way the trees were flying by that I wasn't doing anywhere near as low as sixty.

I went into the hospital, where I was advised that Dad's condition hadn't changed. He was still on oxygen, and although the nurses said he'd woken up once or twice, he was sound asleep now, and I wasn't going to wake him again.

I checked on the bar, and everything was as it was when I left it a few days ago. I made a few phone calls and got my manager and best barman in for the night. I'd open, but I wouldn't necessarily be there for the whole time.

I'd trained some good staff, mostly humans from town, and some shifters from my pack. The bar ran like a well-oiled machine, with or without me at the helm.

I had just gotten the bar in order, when someone knocked on the locked front door. I yanked open the door and startled.

"Maybelle," I said, greeting the witch who had always been a friend of our pack. "I was thinking of calling you this morning."

I held open the door, and she drifted in. "I know. I could sense your need of me." She glanced around the room, narrowing her eyes as though looking for a problem. "How can I help you?"

I grinned at the powerful mage. We paid her well, in money, liquor, whatever she wanted. And she had helped us out with her magic skills a number of times over the years.

"I have a prisoner, from a neighboring pack, that I'm keeping in the cabin. I wanted to make sure the wards you set up last year are still holding strong."

Maybelle sniffed the air, then slid toward me. "You smell... different."

I crossed my arms over my chest. "Yeah, sorry. I'll have a shower as soon as I can."

"No, it's not that. I can smell another shifter on you, and she's... odd."

I frowned at the witch. "What do you mean?"

Maybelle took another sniff. "I mean, she's not a normal shifter."

"I don't understand." I frowned. As far as I could tell, Talia was perfect.

Maybelle stepped away, her eyes swirling with the purple of her magic. "I don't understand, either. I would like to meet her."

"Yes. Please. I need you to check the cabin also. I want to know that if her pack tries to rescue her, they won't be able to pass the threshold."

Maybelle nodded. "I can do that, but perhaps, tomorrow?"

I didn't question her. She was an odd creature, and did things at her own pace. If she didn't think there was any urgency to the situation with Talia, I trusted her judgment.

"Thank you, Maybelle."

She stepped toward the door, then glanced back at me. "Has your father told you of the demons that roam in our world?"

I froze and stared at her, the hairs on the back of my neck standing on end. Was this one of her weird premonition things? Another spanner in the works was the last thing we needed right now. "Ah... yes. He has. Though I've never seen one."

Demons were evil. Everyone agreed on that, at least. They were part of the paranormal world, of course, but unlike the rest of us, demons worshipped only darkness.

Maybelle stared into my eyes. "You will. I've sensed them moving around, testing people."

"What should I do when I see one?" I asked her, not having any idea what the answer would be. Were they deadly to us? Should I be concerned for my pack? Could I even kill one if I wanted to?

"Do not be afraid of it," she said. "They are here only as scouts; messengers for their evil masters. They won't hurt one such as you."

Then she swept out of the room without another backwards glance. I sighed. Witches were strange, and I could never quite work out how their minds worked. Though they often came in handy when it came to magic needs relating to the pack. I filed away all the information Maybelle had just given me, and got back to what I was meant to be doing.

Sorting out the bar.

After more phone calls, I ran up the stairs behind the bar that led to my small apartment on the top floor and had a quick shower. I scrubbed my skin, wondering what Maybelle had meant about Talia smelling strange.

Was it possible that Maybelle had sensed the girl wasn't mine? Or from my pack's blood lines? Or was it something else? I didn't try to guess further, and pushed the questions to the back of my mind.

Too many other things to question, and the way of the witches wasn't mine to question.

I put on a fresh change of clothes, packed up some boxes of whiskey and bourbon, and got in the car. I was strangely excited to be going back to the pack, though it annoyed me that part of the reason was because I wanted to see Talia so much.

It was wrong.

She was taken. Mated. And not to me. When I arrived home, a guy was sitting on the steps of my father's house. I'd never seen him before. He wore a black leather jacket and had a buzz cut, which made his dark eyes stand out even more.

I smelt the shifter on him, but like Talia, he wasn't one of mine.

A lone wolf. A shifter and—I had the feeling—a dangerous being.

I parked the truck and got out. "Hey."

No one usually visited our pack unless they were family members. And if they were family, they wouldn't be sitting on the Alpha's front step, waiting for who knows what.

The guy got to his feet. He was a good six feet tall and built well, like many of my betas.

He didn't seem to be an Alpha, but he wasn't necessarily a follower, either.

"Can I help you?" I asked, walking right up to him and looking down from my six-foot-six height in obvious challenge.

He grinned up at me, as if aware of my ploy and not fazed. "I'm Darius. I came to speak to the Alpha about joining your pack."

"Well, my father's not here at the moment, so you've got me in his stead." I narrowed my eyes at him. "Any reason you want to join our pack?"

Darius nodded. "I've been traveling across the state, but I'm sick and tired of the constant moving. Always looking out, with no one to watch my back. I need to set down some roots. And I heard good things about your pack."

My brows rose. I didn't necessarily believe or disbelieve him. It could be the truth. But a grain of skepticism was always healthy. "And the reason you can't go home?" I drilled.

His smile faltered. "Well, I... My mate died last year. In childbirth. I... can't go back. Too many bad memories."

His words sliced across my heart with the keen sharpness of a knife.

I dropped my arms down and cleared my throat with a rough cough. "Sorry to hear about that."

He shrugged. "Thanks."

I glanced around, still suspicious about his timing. "Any reason you chose our pack over the other three in the area?"

Darius didn't seem to miss a beat. "I did speak to one other pack before coming here, but they're in a bit of a messy state, and I don't want to join anyone else's drama. Plus, I'd rather be on the winning side."

I raised an eyebrow. "Because you need protecting?"

Darius laughed. "Nah, I like a good fight."

He looked like he could handle himself too. Despite the baggy leather jacket, I could see the strength in his legs and in his core. This guy knew his way around a gym, or he'd done some serious outdoor work, over a long period of time.

"Okay. I'll give you a week to prove you're not going to be a nuisance, and you can bunk in with some of the other bachelors in town. My Beta Markus has a spare room at his place."

Darius grinned. "I appreciate the opportunity."

"Is there any other reason you chose our pack?" I asked, still worried about this stranger's reason for coming here right now.

"Well, two actually. I heard you run a bar in town, and I know my way around a drink pourer. And a hot grill."

That was good to know. "And the second reason?"

"Well, I had some news I wanted to share with you, though I didn't want to just come out with it at the start. You'd think I was some sort of snitch."

I crossed my arms over my chest and narrowed my eyes. I wanted to convey my thoughts about snitches, though at the same time I wasn't going to ignore Darius if he knew something I needed to know too. The pack came before my pride.

"I've already said you can stay, so if you wanna tell me something extra, now's the time."

He shrugged off his jacket and pulled out a packet of cigarettes. "You mind?"

I shook my head. "It's your life."

He huffed out a laugh, then lit his cigarette. "You're right."

He inhaled deeply, then blew out the smoke in the opposite direction to where I was standing.

He was definitely fit and strong, but it would take me at least a week to determine his character. For all I knew, he was a pack member of our nearby enemies. I didn't know all of them by sight.

Though, I was pretty sure I'd have recognized him if I'd ever seen him in town, or in my bar, before now. And I hadn't.

"So?" I prompted.

He stared at me. "The other pack I tried to join, they're in a mess, right?"

"Yeah," I said, assuming he meant our lovely neighbors. Talia's pack. "They attacked us, and we fought back. They lost a lot of men."

He nodded. "Yeah, but it's not just that."

"What, then?"

"They're hunting someone."

Hunting someone? Didn't he mean, hunting for someone? I narrowed my eyes. "Who?"

I assumed it must be Talia. I mean, why wouldn't they be hunting for her? I was astounded they hadn't come for her yet. Not that she would have been easy to follow, the way she'd been driving.

"The Alpha's son's former fated mate. They threw her out of the pack, and gave her three days to leave town. But they can feel her, and they know she's still around. They have orders to kill her on sight."

Former fated mate? Maddox had rejected her? My mouth dropped open. It must have been the other way round. Surely, it must have been Talia who rejected that loser, Maddox. "They're looking for Talia... to kill her?"

How was that possible? What on earth could that girl have done to receive that sort of wrath?

"You know who they're looking for?"

I nodded. "Yeah." I rubbed the space between my brows, trying to will away a sudden headache. "I grabbed her the other night. One of my Betas knew who she was, but she seemed to be headed out of the state and I thought... Fuck."

I'd stopped her from leaving town. She'd been running away from her pack. If they'd given her three days to get away...

She'd hit the deadline and it'd passed her by some time ago.

I grabbed my head on both sides of my skull and squeezed hard. "Shit."

What the hell was she playing at? Pretending she was still important to her pack? Though she had offered to leave, and not look back, hadn't she? Had that been the truth? Was she really heading to an aunt in Wichita?

What had she lied about?

"Thanks for letting me know, man. I'll introduce you to some of the guys, then I better go deal with Talia."

I found Darius somewhere to sleep, and introduced him around. Then I headed back to the cabin, fire in my belly and anger clenching my fists. What the hell was this shit?

She must've been lying from the moment I got her. So, what was the truth? And could I trust her to tell me anyway?

I stormed up the steps and into the cabin.

Talia was lying on her belly on the rug, reading a book. Her feet were crossed, and her gorgeous thick hair was out and flowing down her back.

My heart hurt just to look at her.

She looked up at me, startled.

"You need to tell me what's going on," I said, putting a growl into the words.

She jumped to her feet, her eyes huge and suddenly fearful.

"What do you mean?" she whispered.

"I just found out that your pack is hunting you and you're to be killed on sight. And... ex fated mate? What the fuck is that about, Talia? I thought you were set to marry the next Alpha of your pack."

She chewed on her bottom lip, a tremble going through her body. I could practically smell the fear on her.

"I was."

"What? Speak up."

"I was!" she said, more forcefully, before wrapping her arms around her middle.

"Well, what the hell happened?"

This was a fucking mess. Here I was trying to avenge my pack and fulfil a promise to my father without killing more people, and the plan had gone up in smoke.

Worse than that. I'd stopped her from escaping their clutches, and most likely signed her death warrant, so I'd truly screwed up on that front, too.

"I... He..."

"Spit it out!"

She jumped. "I... I..."

She stopped, swallowing, and I couldn't take any more.

"Argh! I'm going for a run," I said, unable to get a hold of my temper. It was all too much. Too many mistakes. Some of them fair and square in my court.

I ripped off my shirt, noting the way her pupils dilated when she saw me half naked. Another thing to be pissed about. All this time, she was available, and I hadn't even known it. Fated mate be damned.

She was a rejected mate.

And now she was in danger. This was a lethal combination for the protector in me.

"I'll be back later."

I ran out the door and leapt off the patio, shifting halfway through the air, and landed with my paws on the dirt.

I took off.

What a fucking mess this was.

# CHAPTER 14
# TALIA

Oh, my God. He looked so furious. He's going to kill me when he gets back.

The only thing that had been keeping me alive was the fact that I was Maddox's mate, and therefore useful to Galen.

And now, he had somehow found out the truth.

I paced up and down the room, my book and my relaxed mood now totally forgotten. I wasn't safe anymore and thanks to the witch's wards, I was still trapped.

My wolf rose up within me, and for the first time, I didn't try and stop my shifter from bursting through. My jeans and tank top shredded as my black wolf emerged.

My heart was pounding so fast I was shaking.

"What the..." One of Galen's Betas stepped over the threshold, and I saw my opportunity to escape.

I hadn't been able to get past the threshold last time, but with one of their pack short circuiting the magic, and with me in wolf form, I had a chance.

I ran for the door. The guy tried to stop me, putting his arms out, holding tight to the door frame.

Perfect. Thank you.

I leapt through the air, pushing my two front paws into the guy's chest, and both of us sailed through the door and onto the ground.

I shook myself, looking around the area for a way out.

I'd made it out of the cabin, but I had to go. I had to leave everything behind. My life was at stake now. Not just from my pack, but from Galen's as well.

Two wolf shifter packs would be after me.

What chance did I have, to survive even a few hours, let alone through the night?

I turned toward town and started running. My old pack would get me if I went anywhere near the forest. But the town provided a neutral zone for all the packs. My only chance at this point was to reach neutral ground. Maybe Kylie would hide me again, until things died down a little?

At this point I didn't know. And I didn't care.

All I knew was, I had to get away from Galen and his pack, right now.

I ran down the road, dodging people and traffic, my heart pounding like a steam engine.

I ended up at a fork in the road that I didn't recognize. Both road signs said they led to town, but which way would keep me safe from Maddox's pack?

A commotion came from behind me, from the direction of the cabin I'd been staying in. I could hear fighting and yelling. Then the howl of a wolf sounded, long and mournful.

The sound called to my essence; my blood. I almost turned and ran back to greet the caller, having to use all my willpower to stop.

Fuck.

I shivered. Galen knew I was gone. I had to keep running, and not into town. I needed to put distance between me and the Alpha's son.

Both of the Alpha heirs.

I ran through the forest and away from the town, in the opposite direction of Galen's pack.

Oh, shit.

They caught up to me before I had gone anywhere near far enough. I didn't know whose land I was on—Galen's, Maddox's, or the neutral zone—but it didn't matter. I was surrounded.

I was going to die.

Three white wolves came at me from all sides. I panted, backing up. From their scent, I could tell without even looking at their familiar wolf forms that two of them were Maddox's Betas, young guys I'd known my whole life. How did they justify chasing me, let alone getting ready to kill me? We had been friends in the past. I couldn't fathom trying to kill a friend.

I whined, to show them I was scared. That I was defenseless. We'd never been taught to fight in my pack. The women didn't do that.

Instead of showing any care or compassion, they snarled back at me and I yelped. Panic set in. They were serious. They were really going to follow the Alpha's decree.

Where could I go?

The largest wolf showed me his teeth. I turned tail and ran. They caught me easily and knocked me down into the dirt.

I growled and turned, but one of them grabbed my back leg, biting into the flesh and hauling me along the ground. I cried out at the pain, kicking my other leg in an attempt to be free.

A third wolf stalked over to me. He was older and huge. One of the Alpha's council members, by the looks of him.

I stared up at him and whined. He growled, his lip quivering as he showed me his white sharp teeth.

There would be no mercy. I was going to die today, at the hands—or teeth and claws—of my own pack. And I had no one to blame except myself. They had given me time to escape, and I'd squandered much of it, before being stupid enough to be captured by Galen and his men.

A loud, threatening growl rolled over me like thunder in the distance. The white wolves looked up.

The large Beta was hit in the chest by a huge black wolf, and rolled backwards, knocked off his feet.

The possible reprieve gave me added strength, and I fought with the wolf holding my leg, snapping my jaws at him until he let go. I jumped to my feet and growled, watching in awe as the black wolf took on all three of the smaller white wolves at once.

He headbutted them and snapped his jaws, biting at their necks with his razor-sharp teeth.

The two smaller wolves were bleeding and limping, but the larger one recovered more quickly, and stalked toward the black wolf that I had to assume was Galen.

He was magnificent—and terrifying.

Galen charged and grabbed the largest Beta around the throat, lifting him high. He shook him like a rag doll and dropped him. With a snarl, he tore the Beta's throat out with a vicious tug and snap of his neck.

It was over, just like that.

He threw back his head and howled, his jaws soaked with blood, and I gaped at the scene before me.

Blood and guts everywhere, and the triumphant black wolf in the middle of it all, breathing hard.

The large Beta was obviously dead, his chest no longer rising and falling. Only then did Galen shift back.

I couldn't help but stare at him.

He was dripping with sweat, naked, and shaking with adrenaline. He was a warrior standing over the fallen body of his enemy on a battlefield.

I let go of my wolf even though all my instincts told me not to, and shifted back to human. Naked, and vulnerable, and crouched on the ground at Galen's feet, but no longer afraid. Not when Galen had just charged in to save me.

I stared at him, wanting to say thanks but unable to formulate words. No one had ever stood up for me the way he had just done. Not even Maddox. Especially not Maddox.

He was panting, and blood dripped from wounds in his flank and his side.

When he turned to face me properly, his eyes were still shifted. "I fucking hate killing those bastards."

He spat on the ground, more blood painting the earth.

I was shaking as well as naked, but Galen didn't have desire in his eyes as he stared at me.

"Thank you, for saving me," I said through my chattering teeth, finally managing to get the words out.

What else could I say? He really had saved my life. I owed him, big time.

I swallowed hard and forced myself to calm down. Talk rationally. We're naked, surrounded by blood and guts, but we need to remain calm.

"How can I repay you?" I asked as I sat up slowly. "I can go, if you want me to. Now. If you'll let me grab my dad's car, I can leave right away. Go to my aunt in Wichita like I'd planned."

Galen shook his head and bent down toward me, fierce and strong. "No, you'll never make it. Your old pack will hunt you down well before you hit state lines."

"I have to try." I began to sob, biting my lip. "I don't have anywhere else to go. My mom's gone... my dad too. There's no one else. The only family I have left is in Wichita. Galen, please. Let me go. I have nothing... and no one..." My voice cracked, and I stopped. I couldn't be any more pathetic, begging at his feet like this.

Quickly I got to my feet.

He ran a hand through his hair, pushing the thick curls off his forehead. "I'm offering you a place in my pack, Talia. Come back with me. I'll protect you."

Shock pulsed through me. "You'd really do that?"

Tears of gratitude burned in my eyes. How was it possible that after the ugly twist of human nature I'd seen in my own pack over the past few days, Galen—the enemy—could be so different?

He nodded. "I would do that, and I am. Come home with me. Be a part of my pack."

I wrapped my arms around my shivering body. "But... why?"

He shrugged, his eyes finally shifting back to completely human. "Because you need us. And I like you. I think you would fit in well with us. Do I have to give you another reason? Do you really want to travel all the way to Wichita, and live outside a pack, in a mostly human environment?"

I shook my head and held in the sob that rose. He liked me? I liked him too. He was a good man—he had shown that in many ways even in the short time I'd known him—and he would be a fantastic Alpha when the time came to inherit the throne from his father.

"I... accept. Thank you."

My heart, which had been so broken a few days ago, filled up to the point that I could barely speak.

He nodded once. "Let's shift, and get back to the pack. It's safer that way, assuming you can travel in wolf form?"

I nodded. "Of course I can. And I'd be honored to run beside you."

He grinned, then chuckled. "I feel a strange amount of protectiveness over you. And I'd prefer if the rest of the pack didn't see you like this."

He indicated my nakedness and I laughed, an unfamiliar weightlessness filling my chest. I couldn't remember the last time I had felt so cared for.

I should never have survived these few days, not with so many things against me. My dad's mistakes. My pack's blood lust. Galen's need for revenge.

Somehow, I'd made it through everything. So far.

I had the feeling I was still on borrowed time, though.

I smiled at the man who had officially just become my hero. "I have to tell you something, Galen. Even if I feel that it is inappropriate to say, I believe I owe you the truth."

"Tell me."

His jaw became tight, as if I was about to deliver news that was hard to take, or bad.

I laughed to try and break some of the tension. "You're the only man who has ever seen me naked. So yeah, I'd appreciate it if you don't show me off to the rest of the pack like this."

I held my arms out and shrugged, with the intention to show off my lackluster breasts and wobbling stomach.

Galen's gaze, now that it was human, flared suddenly. There was more lust in his eyes than I was comfortable with. But I stood, proudly, a new member of his pack.

Galen dragged his fingers down his face. "For fuck's sake, Talia. Don't say things like that."

I didn't respond. I just let go of my human body and dropped down into my wolf.

Then Galen transformed before me.

His huge black wolf stood beside me, towering above in a much larger form than mine, then he threw back his head and howled.

I shivered.

All that power. He was incredible.

I looked once at the dead white wolf lying on the ground, then shook my head and turned away.

I followed Galen back to his pack, my new home.

# GALEN

I took Talia back to the cabin to gather her clothes from her suitcase, and to my father's house to gather mine. Being naked in front of that girl was far too dangerous. She was too beautiful, and now that I knew she was available, my wolf howled for her.

And that comment about being the only man who'd ever seen her naked? For fuck's sake, the girl would drive me insane with comments like that! My wolf practically leapt with joy inside my chest.

I commanded my Betas to meet me at the bar, got Talia to drive her car behind me, and we all met at my place. I figured we could both stay there for a while. I would be close to the hospital, and with the weekend coming, I had to work.

"So, you said you work here?" Talia asked, glancing up at the sign outside my bar that read, 'Howling Wolf'.

"Yeah... kind of," I said, unlocking the front door so that everyone else could join us for a meeting. "I own the bar, and the apartment above it. I live up there."

She stared at me, surprise in her wide eyes.

Before I could answer the unspoken questions in the air, the front door opened, and Markus, David, and the new recruit Darius, wandered in.

"Hey guys. Come grab a seat. I want you to officially meet Talia, and work out our next move."

The three Betas came over to where we hung out around the bar and grabbed bar stools.

"Hey," David said, lifting his chin in greeting to Talia.

She jumped up and sat on the bar top, her legs dangling like a kid sitting on a ledge.

"Hi."

I shook my head. She seemed to effortlessly manage a fantastic combination of naivety and sensual allure.

I turned away from her so that I could focus on what I needed to say. "Guys, this is Talia. I've offered her sanctuary within our pack."

"Sanctuary?" Markus repeated. "Why does she need—"

"Talia is going to stay here, with me," I said, interrupting Markus. I didn't need to explain myself to him. Then I heard my words as though from another place.

I tightened my jaw. I hadn't expected to say it just like that, but now that I had, I wasn't taking it back. "She needs our help and we're going to give it. Her pack is after her. They plan to kill her if they catch her, and since we now share a common enemy, that makes us allies."

The guys, to their credit, took my news in their stride. Mostly. The only show of surprise was a couple of raised eyebrows, and surreptitious glances at Talia.

"So, what do you need from us?" David asked.

"Help," I said simply. "I want Talia kept safe. She knows her pack well, and will be key in our revenge, and in staying one step ahead of them."

I glanced up at Talia, who nodded once. We hadn't actually

discussed her helping me get revenge on them for attacking our pack, but she seemed solid in relation to the idea, and I appreciated her not contradicting me in front of my Betas.

The guys and I talked about how we were going to obtain the revenge we sought, and threw around a whole lot of suggestions. We went back and forth, and in the end, came up with a few ideas, but no actual solution. Not yet.

Talia got up about halfway through the discussion and wandered around the bar, trailing her fingers over the furniture. Concern was etched on her face. I wondered if she was concerned about her old pack, or something else.

I would ask her as soon as we finished here.

"Galen, I'm going for a quick walk," she whispered, once she had circled back to me. Then she spoke more loudly, for everyone to hear. "Do you guys want anything from the bakery?"

I shook my head, as did the others. "No," I confirmed. "Do you need any money or anything?"

"No. I've got my own. I won't be long." She smiled at the guys, then slipped out the front door.

The bakery was nearby, and this was neutral ground, in town. She'd be safe enough for now.

As soon as the door closed, Markus turned to me. "What's with you and her?"

I took a sip of my beer, then shrugged. "Nothing. What do you mean?"

Markus and David glanced at each other. "You're acting kinda... possessive toward her. I mean, she's cute and all, but she's the other Alpha's mate."

I clamped my jaw down. "Not anymore."

I leaned back in my chair and crossed my arms over my chest. They needed to shut up about her being another Alpha's mate. It was in the past.

Markus's jaw dropped. "What do you mean?"

I groaned, not sure I should be the one to tell them Talia's news, but what choice did I have? They'd find out soon enough.

"The Alpha of their pack rejected her. They've kicked her out."

"What?" Markus said, then grunted. "Those bastards."

"It's true," Darius said, finally speaking up. "I heard it straight from some of their Betas when I met them the other day. It was a love match. Fated mates. So, she must be pretty devastated if her mate has rejected her."

There was silence around us as everyone in the room digested the new information. I hadn't really thought about what Talia must feel about her breakup.

"We better head back," Markus said, jumping to his feet.

"Darius," I said, "you interested in working a shift tonight in the bar? If I'm going to watch Talia, then I need an extra hand here."

I'd still need to work, but an extra set of eyes on the drinks, and the guys starting brawls, was always handy. Especially if I was running upstairs regularly to check on my new pack member.

"Yeah. Of course," he said. "Can you show me where things are now?"

I nodded. "Sure."

Markus and David headed home, and Darius came around behind the bar and started going through the stock with me.

Then it occurred to me that Talia wasn't back yet.

"Hey, how long's Talia been gone?" I asked, walking back around to the front of the bar.

"Don't know." Darius tucked a cigarette behind his ear. "Do you think she might be in trouble?"

"No, the wolf packs around here have laws about fights in town. It's a neutral zone," I explained. "There'd be hell to pay if they broke that law. We all have to abide by it."

Darius shrugged. "Yeah, but she's a single female, on her own.

And her whole pack is out to get her. Can you guarantee they'll all toe the line?"

My gut clenched tight, and my heart sank.

No. I couldn't guarantee anything, when it came to another wolf pack.

Why had I let her stroll out the door like that? If anything had happened to her, it would be on me.

My wolf surged to the surface, and I forced it back down. Here in town, I needed to stay human.

"I've gotta go." I raced for the door and pulled it open. "Where the hell did she say she was going?"

Darius came up behind me, even though I hadn't asked him to back me up. "The bakery, or something like that."

"Yes, that's right." I raced off.

The bakery was on the next block. With Darius hot on my heels, I ran down the street in search of our lost wolf.

Talia

I didn't know how to repay Galen and his pack for their kindness. Until I remembered how much the male shifters in my old pack liked their food. These guys would surely be the same. A trip to the bakery was the least I could do to say thanks.

I didn't just go to the bakery. Considering Galen had saved my life, I thought he deserved a bit more food in his belly than a few pies. And his pack members as well.

I didn't have a kitchen, but I could get them some treats. I had money, thanks to Dad. So I went to the bakery, the fruit and vegetable market, and then the candy shop.

My arms loaded with food; I began the trek back to Galen's bar.

I headed down an alleyway that would save me time in my trip back. I knew this town; it was neutral, and therefore safe.

Dark silhouettes in the distance emerged from the shadows and out walked three large men I recognized. All in their thirties. All from my old pack. Noah had a shaved head and an orange-tinged beard. Justin was blond and quiet; while Reed had dark eyes and dark hair.

They were all deadly.

I froze.

Their faces lit up when they saw me, like it was the fourth of July.

They shared a look and the way they licked their lips in preparation of the kill made my stomach lurch and my heart begin to pound. I dropped the bags I was carrying.

There were too many of them to take on alone, and yet I didn't want to simply run away. They would only chase me down and getting them excited by the hunt wasn't a good idea.

I could do this. I just had to stay calm. Breathe. Maybe I could talk my way out of this. After all, we were in town.

I picked up the bags and with careful, deliberate steps and began to back out of the alley.

"Hey! Traitor! Where are you going?" Reed called out.

I kept walking, faster. My heart pounded in my chest, but I didn't dare shift. We had rules, after all.

Running footsteps thudded behind me. A large hand grabbed my shoulder and pulled me back.

The food went flying, the paper bags breaking open and pastries spilling over the cobblestone path.

I spun to face them, my hands tightening into fists. They hadn't shifted yet, and I assumed that was because of the rules about town. None of the humans were allowed to see us in wolf form.

But I was one girl up against three guys. It didn't matter

whether we were in wolf or human form. They outnumbered me, and would outperform in strength, ten times over.

Galen, where are you?

"What's up?" I managed, though my stomach was tight, and fear made my pulse quicken.

"What's up?" Noah asked, sauntering closer. "Why are you still here? You're meant to be long gone. You were given fair warning."

Reed was on my right, and he advanced on me. I took a step back, feeling a stone wall at my spine.

Damn, I was trapped.

"I was meant to be over the border by now," I whispered, trying to keep them talking while I worked out a plan. "But I had car troubles and had to come back to sort it out."

'Car troubles' was one way of explaining what had happened, I supposed.

"You should have gone while you had the chance," Noah said. "Now we're gonna have to kill you, because the Alpha wishes it."

I swallowed hard, standing as tall as I could, even as they pressed in from all sides. My hands clutched at the wall, seeking to draw on its strength. "But the town is a neutral zone," I said. "Like Switzerland."

Or that was how it had always been explained to us.

Justin took a couple of steps back. "She's right, guys."

"Yeah, but who's gonna know?" Reed said, his nasty face twisting up into a scowl. "The Alpha wants her dead, and his word is law."

"But—" I began.

Noah whacked me across the face.

I staggered sideways, my eye exploding with pain.

I stumbled away, trying to keep my balance and stay on my feet, but also trying to break up the little pack hunt they had going on.

"You need to stop," I said, squinting at them with my bad eye. "You aren't allowed to attack me here in town."

Justin hung back, a worried frown on his face, but Noah and Reed advanced on me. Their sneers were matching. "The rules are there to protect our packs. But if no one shifts, you're just a girl who got mugged in an alleyway," Noah said.

Reed swung his fist at me. I only just managed to duck out of the way.

They were serious. They were going to beat me to death right here and now and blame it on a robbery gone wrong.

"What? So, you're just gonna leave my dead body in the alley?" I asked, hating the croaky sound of my voice. I had to stay on my toes and keep moving around so it was harder for them to hit me.

Noah and Reed looked at each other and laughed.

"Hell yes. Good idea."

Reed swung again, and this time he clipped my ear. Hard.

I went down, the cold cobblestones pressing into my hands.

Shit. Get up.

I jumped straight back up to my feet, ignoring the pain in my head.

I tightened my hands into fists and punched Reed in the gut as hard as I possibly could.

He grunted and fell back a few paces but laughed at the same time.

"Really? Didn't think you had it in you."

Noah stepped up instead of Reed and punched me across the face, making me lose sight for a moment, then I fell onto my back on the cold stones.

Get up. I couldn't fight these guys. I had to run.

I groaned and rolled around on the stones, willing myself to get to my feet. My movements were slower this time. I was having difficulty keeping my vision in focus. But then I saw them laughing and clapping each other on the back.

They thought they had already won.

I groaned again, and staggered a bit more, putting my hand up to my head and acting more disoriented than I really was, so they would think I was really gone.

It worked. They gloated as I wiped at my mouth and moaned.

They turned to give each other a high-five, and I lunged forward and kicked Noah in the nuts. In the same move, I rounded and punched Reed again in the belly. Reed swiped at me as I pivoted and ran past them up the alley, back toward the street. I tripped over the smashed groceries but managed to remain upright, and simply kept on going.

Don't stop. Don't stop.

My breathing was ragged as their footsteps charged behind me.

"Help me!" I began to scream as I approached the alley entrance, appealing to anyone who might hear, or care.

Too late.

One of the men grabbed my hair and pulled me back, hard.

Tears sprung to my eyes as I stared up into the ugly face of my attacker. Reed. His teeth had partially shifted, and he glared down at me with death in his eyes.

I wouldn't beg or plead for my life. Not with him. Not with any of them.

I bared my teeth and growled up at him, even as he yanked again on my hair, tilting my head further back.

Nearby, someone yelled. Galen? I hoped it was Galen, and I hoped he would rip these guys apart.

Reed twisted to face whoever was coming.

The movement gave me a slight reprieve and I got my footing, then kicked him hard in the knee. He grunted and pulled my head down. I went with his pull, then twisted out of his grip.

It was Galen. He and the guy he had introduced as Darius raced toward us.

Galen reached us first, and punched Reed in the head over and over, until the latter fell to the ground, his nose broken and bleeding all over the place.

Then he came at Noah, who pulled a knife from his belt and held it out in front of himself in a defensive posture. He swiped at Galen, who jumped back and knocked Noah's arm out of the way. Galen brought his arm down on Noah like he was bowling a ball.

Crack. Noah went down and didn't get back up.

Reed went for Galen while his back was turned, but the new guy jumped in and turned to fight at Galen's back, lunging at Reed.

He threw a punch at Reed's face. Reed staggered back.

Justin looked between his buddies and Galen, then turned and ran away, down the alley.

I stumbled sideways; one eye already closed. Pain pushed me to pass out.

I stood my ground as Darius threw another punch at Reed, knocking him out cold. Noah was still on the ground, his face covered in blood. He was either unconscious or dead. I didn't know. And I didn't care at this moment in time.

Now who looks like they got mugged in an alleyway?

I staggered over to my heroes. "Thank you, for saving my life. Again."

Galen twisted to stare at me, his eyes shifted into his wolf.

He took another step closer and pulled me up into his arms, holding me tightly against his body.

"My hero," I whispered, patting his chest.

Galen growled something totally unintelligible, and I began to laugh. Until the darkness took me.

# CHAPTER 16

# GALEN

I carried Talia back to the bar and considered calling an ambulance. Her face was a mess.

"What do you think?" I asked Darius, as I laid her down on my bed at my apartment above the bar. "Should I take her to the hospital?"

"She's a full wolf shifter, yeah?"

I nodded. "Yeah. As far as I know."

"Then she should heal quickly. You got some ice for her face?"

"Yeah. Down in the bar. Can you get it?" I wasn't leaving her anytime soon. In fact, she was banned from leaving my side ever again.

Darius headed off and I knelt down beside her, brushing her hair off her face. "Every time I leave you alone for ten minutes, something like this happens to you."

Darius came back with multiple small plastic bags of ice and several dry dish cloths. "Great idea," I said, taking the little bags and placing them on her swollen lip and cheek.

"What sort of men do this to a girl?" I said out loud, to no one in particular.

"Cowards," Darius answered, walking over to the corner and sitting on the chair there. "Three against one isn't a fair fight even if you're talking about men, let alone someone as young and small as Talia."

I nodded, because I couldn't say anything else. My wolf had risen up inside me, and it was hard to quiet. I clamped down hard to stop him from ripping through my body and causing a shift here and now.

"They deserve to be hunted down. Those... savages."

Talia groaned, and her eyelids fluttered open. "Who are?"

"You're awake," I said, holding the ice to her jaw. "And I'm talking about those monsters who attacked you. Are you okay? Do you want me to take you to the hospital?"

My father was there, so it would probably save me time, having the two people I was looking after stay in one place.

"No, I'm fine," Talia said, closing her eyes. "I heal fast."

"I'll head back to the pack for a shower," Darius said. "What time do you want me here for work?"

"Shift starts at eight. People start coming in around nine, and it gets busiest around eleven."

"Be back at eight," Darius said, and then left.

I withdrew my hand from Talia's face so I could stand up and pace. "I can't believe those guys had the nerve to attack you in broad daylight. On neutral territory, too. They could have killed you."

This girl was trouble with a capital T. Her pack wouldn't stop until they had her.

"They intended to," she said softly.

I glanced down at her, and she smiled up at me, one eye swollen shut. "You saving me is beginning to become a habit."

I sighed. "Yeah, well, maybe I'm trying to make up for the mistakes of my past."

"What do you mean?"

I groaned and grabbed the chair from the corner of the room, then dragged it over so I could sit by the side of her bed. "I don't really talk about this..."

She smiled, but didn't say anything, which was exactly what I needed, a moment to think.

I bent forward, resting my elbows on my knees. I couldn't believe I was even contemplating sharing this information, but somehow, the words tumbled out of my mouth. "Her name was Jessie. She was my girlfriend at the time, and we'd been together for a year or so."

"She was a pack member?" Talia asked.

I nodded. "She was. We went to school together. We'd been friends a long time. Then we fell in love..."

I shrugged, the pain of speaking about Jessie getting to me. My heart still hurt.

"What happened?" Talia asked, her voice gentle, soothing.

"She died," I said, though it burnt my throat to admit it.

Talia gasped. "How? What happened?"

"We were attacked." I gulped loudly. "In the woods. I don't remember it very well. Maybe ten people jumped us. All men. I fought them off as best I could. I told her to run."

I shook my head, staring at the wooden floor beneath my feet.

"I was beaten unconscious and when I woke up, she was dead, lying a few feet away from me. A head wound so bad she wasn't able to heal."

I swallowed hard, the pain of Jessie's death still haunting me. The failure.

"It wasn't your fault," Talia said, hefting herself up to stare at me.

I lifted my gaze to look at her. "I know that..."

"I don't think you do. You're blaming yourself, when you didn't hurt her. I bet you got really hurt too. How bad were your wounds?"

"Ah..."

It was easier to show her.

I stood up and reached over my head, drawing the shirt off my body.

I pointed at my shoulder. "Knife wound here. Slashed my belly." I indicated the thick white scar dissecting my abs. "Plus twenty stitches in my head."

I put my hand up to the raised flesh cutting across my skull behind my ear. "Broken ribs, nose, eye socket."

I swallowed hard. I shouldn't have survived, and the doctors at the hospital couldn't believe I had.

Talia swung her legs over the side of the bed and stood up, the swelling on her face already noticeably improved.

I raised my hands to cup her cheeks, staring at her injuries. "You're healing already."

She smiled. "Good genes."

She put her hands on my chest, and my heart stopped and then restarted double-time.

"You shouldn't have survived wounds like this, Galen," she whispered, running her fingers along the ugly, white flesh of my belly wound. "Wolf shifters are hard to kill, but we are not immortal, nor death-proof."

"Yeah, ah..." Think, idiot. "The doctors didn't believe I'd make it. Especially after I carried Jessie all that way."

Her gaze flicked up to mine. "You what?"

I shrugged. "We were in the middle of nowhere, and I had to get back to the pack. I couldn't carry her body in wolf form, so I just... carried her."

And God, that had hurt. I'd passed out once on the way home, woken up, and kept going. The blood loss had been the hardest to deal with. Though the shoulder wound especially had been deep.

Talia trailed her fingers up my chest, bypassing my sensitive nipples and going to my shoulder.

"I can't believe you lived through that. You're... incredible. So strong."

I held her fingers against my shoulder, enjoying the warmth of her. Then I took a step away, breaking contact.

"I'm not incredible. I failed the woman who could have been my mate, my wife. It was my weakness that cost her, her life."

"No," Talia said, strong and sure. "It was the evil of those other men, whoever they were."

I nodded once, reaching for a clean black tank from a drawer next to my bed. "It certainly was."

She wrapped her arms around herself. "I am so grateful for everything you've done for me. But what am I going to do now? I don't want to endanger you, or your pack."

I pulled on the shirt, stretching it over my body and covering myself up once more.

"I want you to stay," I said. "If I thought I could get you out of the state without them catching you, I would. But I don't think it's safe to attempt it yet."

Talia nodded, then sighed. "Yeah, you're probably right."

I glanced toward the door to the bedroom. "Look. I need to get the bar ready for the night. I won't leave, don't worry. I'll get some food delivered, and it's gonna be loud, but hopefully you can get some rest."

She bit her lip and climbed back onto the bed. "Thanks."

I went out of the bedroom and shut the door that connected the stairs from the apartment down to the bar. I'd get her some food, work all night, and make sure no one came near her.

Then I'd sleep on the couch and hopefully get a good night's sleep myself.

It was beginning to niggle at me that I'd shared so much of myself with a girl I'd only known a few days. And for most of those days, I'd considered her a bargaining tool.

I had to reconsider my whole position on Talia, and how I was going to use the information she gave me to do as my father had asked and avenge our pack.

~

Talia

I closed my eyes and listened to the intense beat of the music rising up from below. My belly was full, thanks to Galen, and I was warm and dry.

Also, thanks to him, I was lying in a comfortable, clean bed, safe from the pack that hunted me.

I still couldn't believe I'd almost died today. Twice.

Galen had been my knight in shining armor. Or fur, in our case.

He was so much stronger, and more truly Alpha, than any man I'd ever known. I couldn't even begin to compare him with Maddox. There was no Alpha in Maddox—I could see that now. When it came to Galen, not only was he huge, and strong, and powerful, he was thoughtful. Understanding. Empathetic.

When he told me about his girlfriend dying in a brutal attack that almost killed them both, my heart had broken for him. He must have blamed himself for such a long time after; and it seemed to me like he still did.

Survivor's guilt must have been the absolute worst. It was similar in some ways to my father.

I turned onto my side. The sounds of the music in the club beneath me should have kept me awake. Instead, I found the constant noise soothing. I knew Galen was down there, watching out for me.

I trusted him. He wanted me to be a part of his pack, and he'd proven twice now that he was willing to kill to save me.

Maddox had never done such a thing. If anything, in truth,

he'd thrown me out. His father had wanted me gone, and despite him being my fated mate, he hadn't stood up for me.

What did that say about our relationship? About Maddox himself?

I moaned softly, burying my head in the pillow. My head ached, but thanks to the medication Galen had given me after dinner, I was beginning to drift off.

Sleep tugged at me, pulling me down into the darkness.

My body was sore, and my heart had been broken. But I was still here, and I was still fighting for my life. And now I had a tiny bit of hope for the future, where earlier, I had none.

Yesterday, I hadn't been so sure I would fight if it came down to it, but today proved to me that I would and could.

Despite losing everything, I desperately wanted to live. To see where the rest of my life's journey would take me.

And at the moment, my journey had led to Galen.

To his pack, with his scars, and his strength.

There were a lot worse places to be, and that included my old pack grounds.

# CHAPTER 17

# GALEN

Sleeping on my couch in the apartment was almost worse than sleeping on the old sofa in the cabin. When the sun rose, I woke up and rolled off the couch, falling to the ground with a thud.

From the bed, Talia moaned softly, but didn't wake. She was probably still a little doped up on pain medication.

I got to my feet and walked over to her, staring down at her glorious red and gold hair, and her beautiful face, as she rested peacefully on one of my pillows.

She was looking so much healthier this morning. Most of the bruising and swelling was gone, leaving only remnants of the blood-smeared battle she'd waged yesterday.

She couldn't fight, that was obvious. But she'd tried, and that said something for a female up against three males.

I was proud of her. Even though she wasn't mine to be proud of.

Well, she was officially a member of my pack now, so I supposed that I was allowed to be, at least a little. She could use some fighting lessons, though.

I crept into the small kitchen and made eggs for breakfast, checking my cell phone for any messages from my Betas.

I'd told them I would bring Talia back to the pack this morning for her own safety and introduce her to some of the women. Then, while she was occupied, and safe, I'd hunt with some of the men.

I needed it. My nerves were stretched tight, and I had to get out for a run.

I still couldn't believe that I'd told Talia about Jessie. I didn't talk to anyone about her, not even my dad. It was a gruesome and dark part of my past that I never liked to look back on, let alone speak about.

But Talia's very presence made me want to open up and talk to her. I didn't know how she did it, or what had possessed me to show her all my scars. But I had. Literally and figuratively.

"Good morning," came her small voice from behind me.

I turned around, frying pan in hand. "Hey. You want some breakfast?"

She nodded and rubbed her eyes like a sleepy kid.

But there was nothing childish about the miles of leg that showed beneath the oversized sweater she'd worn to bed last night.

Her thighs were creamy and smooth, and made me want to toss breakfast in the sink, throw her over my shoulder, and take her back to bed.

I coughed to clear my throat. "Come sit down."

I shoved off the papers and crap that had accumulated on my dining room table and put a couple of plates down.

Talia sat, and I served her, the softness of the aura that surrounded her making me sigh.

"Eat up. I've got juice, and coffee if you want?"

"Thanks. This is great," she said, grabbing a fork and beginning to eat the scramble I'd made for her.

It had been so long since I'd had a woman stay in my bed. Too long to count, actually. I was a little rough on the whole breakfast-with-another-person thing.

"We'll go back to the pack this morning. It's safer there for you," I said, picking up my plate and sitting down next to her to eat.

"That sounds great." She ate a few more forkfuls, then asked, "Where will I stay? At the log cabin again?"

I laughed. "No, you're not my prisoner, and I don't like the idea of you being trapped in a house."

She grinned at me. "You didn't seem to mind a couple of days ago."

I shrugged. "A lot has changed in two days."

"Yes, it has." She stared at me, her eyes wide and vulnerable pools that I wanted to dive right into.

I broke eye contact, scooped up the last of my eggs, and went to the sink to wash up.

This girl wasn't good for me. I felt as young and vulnerable as an eighteen-year-old with his first crush. It was unsettling.

"You wanna get changed, and we'll go right away?"

She stood up and brought her plate over to me. "Yeah. Of course. Thank you so much."

I grimaced out a smile and started the dishes, so she'd walk away. I was going to put her in Dad's house, but maybe I should shove her down the back of the pack with some of the other women her age.

But what if her pack came to grab her? And hurt some of our females?

Nope. That wasn't happening. There was only one place where she would be safe, and that was right beside me.

Talia walked back out of the bedroom a few minutes later in a pair of black leggings and a gray t-shirt. "All ready."

"Great," I said, though my mouth was dry. "Give me five minutes and we'll go."

I went and changed quickly, my hands shaking while I did. I was filled with nervous adrenaline. Damn, I really needed that run.

I grabbed the keys, locked up, and escorted my new pack member to my truck.

"Jump in and buckle your seat belt," I told her, hopping in my side. "I still can't believe the nerve of your old pack. They attack us out of nowhere. Then they try to take you down in the middle of town, even though town is considered neutral."

I turned the key in the engine, and we started driving along the road.

"Yeah, I reminded them of the neutrality when they attacked. But they just said that as long as they didn't shift, they could attack me, and everyone would think I'd been mugged and murdered. Just another dead girl in an alleyway."

She shivered, and then stared out the window, and although I couldn't see her face, I could hear the pain in her voice.

"I'm sorry this happened to you."

She nodded but didn't look at me. I hadn't asked why she'd been kicked out of her pack, and I wasn't sure she'd tell me if I asked.

It seemed deeply personal.

For a fated mate to reject her, something terrible must have happened. Had Talia been caught with another guy? Or had Maddox himself fallen for another?

Or was it something completely unrelated to their relationship? The timing seemed too coincidental, that she'd been thrown out of the pack the day after the fight.

But I didn't ask.

She'd tell me in her own time, or it would all come out soon enough. Secrets and lies tended to be unearthed, even when people wanted them buried.

"We're almost there," I said as we passed the large iron gates that led onto my pack grounds. "I'll set you up in a bedroom at my dad's house, then you can rest and relax. How are you feeling today?"

She sighed and glanced over at me. "A bit heart broken, but hey… I'll live. Hopefully."

I pulled over in front of my dad's place and looked straight at her. "You're safe here. I promise. As long as I've got breath in my body, I'll fight for you."

She trembled as though my vow had physically affected her.

I reached out and squeezed her hand, wanting the connection, for some unfathomable reason.

She glanced down at my hand and smiled. "Thank you, Galen."

I nodded, then pulled my hand away, my palm tingling from the contact. "Great. Let's go."

I settled Talia into my dad's place.

Then I called Darius, who'd been a real asset in the bar last night and in the alleyway fight yesterday. I was beginning to trust him, even after this short time, and at least I knew he could hold his ground. "Come over to my dad's place and stay outside until I get back. Have a smoke, whatever. Just keep an eye on her and don't leave her alone."

"Yeah, not a problem."

Within five minutes, he was on my doorstep.

"I won't be long," I told him. "I'll be back as soon as I can."

Markus waved at me from the front step of his place, and I jogged after him. My shifter was aching for a run.

"Let's go, man. What are we looking for today? Rabbits? Foxes?"

Markus shrugged. "Whatever. Food is food, right?"

I nodded. I wasn't hungry, and I never ate a live animal while in wolf form. But it was good for the pack to bring home game, and good for the local pest problem, too.

Not to mention the fact that us guys got to run and fight and kill stuff.

It was basic, but our wolves needed it.

I was gone long enough to fulfil that need in me, but as soon as I started to feel anxious about being away from Talia, I turned tail and raced home.

When I got there, Darius was nowhere to be seen.

"Hello?" I called out, and Mary-Anne, one of my dad's neighbors, popped her head over the fence.

"Galen!" she said, smiling at me.

"Have you seen Darius or Talia?" I asked her, worry making my skin itch.

"The new Beta and the girl?" she asked. "Yeah. They said Talia needed to get something from her car, and you'd left it in town."

"Shit. I did."

We'd driven it in yesterday, and she'd been too unwell to drive it back.

I hated having to change the plan all the time, but the goal posts kept shifting and the end game was still unknown.

"Thanks, Mary-Anne."

"They said they wouldn't be long."

I grimaced out a smile and headed into the house for clothes. I'd begun to trust Darius, but not one hundred percent yet. I didn't know him well enough to believe that Talia would be fine with him outside of these pack grounds.

And I certainly didn't trust Talia's pack not to attack her again if they had the chance. I'd been there to save her the past two times, and I needed to make sure I was there again.

I threw on some clothes, grabbed the keys, and jumped in my dad's truck, since they'd taken mine to the bar.

My teeth were clenched tight as I pulled onto the main road and headed back into town.

They were probably fine. I would see them driving on the other side of the street and they'd call me a fool for worrying.

But I didn't turn back.

I was a fool. This girl wasn't mine. I barely knew her. And yet, I was determined to keep her safe.

My truck was still parked out in front of the bar. The hairs on the back of my neck stood on end.

Where the hell were they?

I barged into the bar. "Talia? Darius?"

"Just out the back!" Talia called.

My heart leapt in my chest and tension eased from my body.

I unclenched my fists and strode through the bar, grabbing a beer from the fridge on my way through. My nerves were shot.

"You should have waited for me..." I started to say as I walked out the back door, then caught sight of Talia.

She was standing by her dad's old car, staring off into the distance.

"Talia!"

She didn't respond.

"Hey! Talia!" I called again, walking toward her. I waved my hand in front of her face.

She looked frozen in place, and her eyes were glazed over. What the hell was this? It looked like someone had cast a spell over her. So, where was the witch who was working the magic?

And where the hell was Darius?

I caught something in the reflection of Talia's eyes and twisted, fast. Fucking hell. It was a demon. They were so rare I'd never actually seen one, only heard of them, but there was no mistaking what it was.

It stood like a man, but it had no face. No features, no clothes. It was a blackened shadow with flames for eyes.

"Get out of here!" I growled at it, stepping in front of Talia to block the demon's view.

It lifted its hand, as though anxious for the woman behind me. That's weird. My father had told me of demons' alluring qualities, and I could see from the way Talia continued to stare in its direction that it was calling her. Just like a siren's call.

Town rules be damned. I let the shift rip through me, and my black wolf leapt forth. I planted my feet on the concrete in front of Talia and bared my teeth at the demon.

It flared, the brightness of its flames burning hotter. Dark magic. These things were fucking evil. And it had to be stopped from getting whatever it wanted to acquire from Talia.

I growled, but the demon didn't move. These things were deadly.

I launched forward, running straight at it.

Its arms dropped, and then it disappeared from view as it ran down the street. I stopped short at the corner of the building and shifted back to human before anyone in town saw me.

I was naked now and panting hard.

I stuck my head around the corner, but the demon was gone.

I shook myself. "What the hell was that?"

I turned and jogged back to Talia, my heart thumping in my chest.

She shivered, then dragged her gaze up to my eyes. "You're naked. What happened?"

"A fucking demon just turned up and attempted to lure you away. Don't you remember anything?"

Her mouth dropped open. "A demon? Are you insane?"

I growled in frustration.

Darius called through from the bar. "Hey, Talia. You still here? We've gotta get going. Galen—" He stepped through the back door and stopped dead. "Is already here."

"Hell yeah, I'm here. I told you to watch her. Keep her safe. Do you think that meant bringing her here, where she almost died, and then leaving her alone?"

Talia put her hand on my arm, drawing my attention. "It's my fault, Galen. I'm sorry. I didn't know how long you'd be, and I thought getting my dad's car and parking it where I'm going to be living was smarter."

I scratched my head and took a long deep breath. "Let's just get going. You both get back in your prospective cars and head off. I'll be two minutes behind you. I've gotta go grab some more clothes."

I stormed into the bar and ran up the stairs. The jeans I'd just ripped to shreds in the unexpected shift had been my favorite pair.

I tugged on sweatpants and a t-shirt, irritated and angry. What the hell was a demon doing in town? And what did it want from Talia?

Maybe time would tell, but one thing was for sure. Once we got back to the pack, I wasn't letting the woman out of my sight again, even if it meant sleeping in the same room as her and making her come on runs and patrols with me.

I couldn't trust anyone else to look after her, and after failing to protect Jessie, I wasn't losing Talia, too.

The human part of me knew that she wasn't mine to protect. But the wolf part wanted her claimed, and whilst I couldn't do that, I would do the next best thing. I would protect her as if she was mine.

# WOLF OF BLOOD

USA TODAY BESTSELLING AUTHOR

## AMELIA SHAW

# CHAPTER 1

# TALIA

After the incident with the flaming hot hypnotist in the alleyway, aka the demon, Galen banned me from going into town. Especially alone.

I'd been ordered to stay on pack grounds, with the proviso that I could help the pack if I wanted to. Which, of course, I did. Considering how many people were trying to kill me, Galen's over-protectiveness was fine by me.

The pack Alpha, Galen's father, had woken up in hospital after he'd collapsed and refused to stay there once he realized where he was. So, he was home resting once more.

Galen wanted me close at hand, so he moved me into the Alpha's house and into a spare bedroom. That made my task of finding a job to keep myself occupied a lot easier. I made the Alpha's meals and cleaned the house for him, much like I would have done for my own dad—before he was killed.

I found it a surprisingly satisfying job to make sure the older Alpha was comfortable. He was nothing like the Alpha from my old pack. Galen's dad was a nice man, and so much gentler than anyone I'd been used to from my old life. He spoke to me, and others, with respect. In my experience, that was rare in a man of his bloodline.

After a slightly stilted start, we'd fallen into a comfortable daily rhythm.

"Talia?" the Alpha called out from his bedroom.

I raced over to his room and hung in the doorway. "Yes, Alpha?"

"Could you go up to the Grayson's house and get our weekly quota of eggs? They're the farm on the corner with the white picket fence."

I smiled at him, admiring the way he always made my job that little bit easier with extra details about the people and properties that were still unfamiliar to me.

"Of course!" I replied, pulling off my rubber gloves. He'd caught me in the middle of doing the dishes. I was always especially happy to do anything that got me out of the house when I could.

I was grateful for the protection of Galen's pack, and the freedom Galen himself, afforded me. But my wolf was dying for a run and itching to get out in the fresh air.

I grabbed a sweater because the skies were darkening, and it looked like rain.

"Be back soon," I called toward the Alpha's bedroom, before opening the front door.

I inhaled deeply, smelling the moisture in the air. It was going to pour down. And soon.

I headed toward the edge of town, looking for the house with the white picket fence.

A few of the pack members that I passed gave me hesitant smiles, and I waved in response. They weren't sure about me, that was clear, and I understood why. I wasn't just unfamiliar, or a stranger like Darius. I'd been a member of an enemy pack that had recently attacked and killed some of their men.

I was grateful they were being as nice as they were. After all, if it had been the reverse and they were the strangers in my old pack... well, let's just say I was relieved not to be stoned in the street.

I wrapped my cardigan around my body tighter as a cool breeze whipped around me. The storm was truly on its way. I hurried a little faster along the road.

When I spotted the white picket fence in front of the house on the corner, I jogged up and knocked on the door, then retraced my steps back to stand by the front gate. The people in this town were suspicious of strangers and I didn't want to upset anyone by being on their property without permission.

There was the distinctive scent of chickens, and they were clucking, though I couldn't see them anywhere. They must be out back in the yard, or down the side of the house.

An older woman with a suspicious look on her face opened the front door and walked out onto the porch, holding a carton of eggs. "Are you here on behalf of the Alpha?"

"Yes," I said. Everyone knew I was staying with Galen's father. "He sent me down to fetch some eggs. Looks like you already knew that."

I softened my words with a small smile.

She strolled toward the gate, her long gray hair blowing around her face. "The whole town's talking about you. You're the girl Galen stole, then saved from the Northwood pack."

I wrapped my arms around myself. "Yeah. They forced me out of my pack and told me to I had to leave the state." I shrugged. "But Galen stopped me, and now I'm here."

The woman stood on the other side of the fence. Her keen gaze roamed over me, and I remained still, allowing her to look. I had nothing to hide. Quite the opposite. I wanted these people to know me and learn to trust me. I wasn't here to hurt them, and eventually they'd work that out.

She finally handed me the eggs, and when I checked inside the carton, several of them still had little chook feathers attached.

"You look like a good girl. If you need anything else, especially for the Alpha, come ask for Joan. Okay?"

"Thank you, Joan." I clutched the eggs to my belly. "I appreciate it."

"You better go." She nodded behind me. "The storm's almost on us, and it looks like a big one."

I gave her one last grateful smile, then turned tail and headed back in the direction of the Alpha's house.

I was about fifty feet away from my destination when someone yelled out. "Talia! Talia!"

I stopped dead in my tracks. I knew that voice. Female. Familiar. *No way. It couldn't be.*

I whirled around, looking for the face that went with that voice.

"Talia!"

*Oh, my God.*

"Celia!" I gasped when my best friend's face popped out of the shadows near the tree she was hiding behind in a neighboring yard.

I looked around, checking that no one was watching me as I slowly made my way into the yard and over to Celia.

I leaned against the tree, with my back to the trunk, so that it would look like I was simply taking a break on my walk.

"Celia? What are you doing here?" I hissed.

Galen's Betas ran security around the pack all day and all night. How had she gotten through undetected?

"I had to. I needed to speak to you." She kept her voice to a whisper. "I'm so glad you're okay. The Alpha's increased the directive. He told everyone in the pack to kill you on sight. He said that some of his Betas were killed in a fight outside of town and it had something to do with you. I got so worried that you'd be next."

I closed my eyes and leaned my head back against the tree trunk. "Yeah, they came for me and tried to kill me. We had to deal with them."

There was a beat of silence, then Celia asked, "What do you mean, we? Who killed the Betas?"

"Galen," I whispered, glancing around once more to make sure no one was looking our way. "The Alpha's son."

"Are you okay? I mean, have they hurt you?"

I shook my head. "No, not at all. He hasn't hurt me. None of them have. They've been... well, he's... protected me."

"Listen, Talia." Celia forged on as if I hadn't just told her that an enemy Alpha and his pack were protecting me. "You need to get away from all of this. Get in your dad's car at night fall and drive across the state borders. Get as far away from here as you can."

I frowned at her insistent words, and her tone was even more frantic.

"Why, Celia? What's going on?"

"Maddox is planning something terrible for you, Talia. He... he... You need to leave. He's going to kill you. And you don't deserve it. You've done nothing wrong."

That wasn't news to me. My own pack had tried to kill me a couple of times now. The shock factor was still high, but the facts were clear. My old pack wanted me dead, and Galen's pack offered a safe haven. For now.

"I know I haven't," I said. "They killed my dad, Celia. Right in front of me. Then Maddox rejected our mating bond and threw me out of the pack. Do they really have to kill me as well? They already destroyed my life."

My throat tightened with hot tears, and I stopped talking. Everything was such a mess and every time I thought about what had happened in the past few weeks, it just seemed like a terrible nightmare.

"I'm so sorry, Talia." Celia's voice was so low I almost didn't hear it.

I turned to answer her, but she was gone. I blinked a couple of times at her quick disappearance.

A man I didn't recognize, with long dark hair, stepped around the side of the house. "Can I help you?"

"No. I'm sorry," I said, still clutching the eggs. "I just had to stop and catch my breath. I was on my way back to the Alpha's house, from Joan's."

He nodded but didn't introduce himself. "You better get back then. The heavens are about to open."

"Yes, sir." I put my head down and hurried back into the road just as the first drops of cold rain hit my face.

Hopefully, Celia had gotten away without being discovered.

I rushed up the porch steps and opened the front door of the Alpha's home, then turned and looked back down the road. Celia had been dressed, so that meant she hadn't gotten here in wolf form. She must have driven and parked nearby, then walked over to find me.

The girl was crazy. What she'd done was such a dangerous move. Galen's pack were on high alert, and they wouldn't have thought twice about taking Celia down if they thought she posed a threat.

Would she be able to get away safely?

What if they caught her?

Lightning cracked in the sky above, and I shut the front door against the gust of chilly wind that blew against the house.

"Brrr... It's cold out there," I said to the empty kitchen, trying to put my worry about Celia aside as I placed the eggs on the countertop.

The Alpha called out, "Talia. Is that you?"

"It's me, Alpha. I've got the eggs. Would you like some lunch?"

"No, thank you. But you make some for yourself."

I smiled at the generosity of the man. He wasn't hungry, and yet he was offering me his food.

"Thank you, Alpha."

My stomach was in knots. Celia had risked her life to come here and track me down. Against her Alpha's wishes.

Against *Maddox*.

She was a friend, in the truest sense of the word.

But the message she'd come to deliver was one I already knew, so I wasn't sure why she'd risked her life to tell me that. My old Alpha had ordered our people to kill me on sight and confirmed that I was being punished for my father's mistakes. So, was there a more urgent message I needed to hear?

Had something made Celia more panicked? Was Maddox himself now coming for me? What had changed to ramp up the danger?

I didn't know, and I needed to talk to Galen to hash things out with him. But he was working with the pack today.

I spent the afternoon on autopilot, cleaning the Alpha's kitchen and making a dinner that I hoped everyone would enjoy.

When Galen finally arrived home at the end of the day, I practically sagged with relief. I could talk to him. Try and make sense of everything whirling around in my head.

"Hey," he called out, nodding at me as he pulled off his gray sweater. He shook the rain from his hair before he tucked the longer strands behind his ear. "Food smells good. How was your day?"

"Can I talk to you?" I asked without preamble, shivering unexpectedly in his company.

He stared at me as though assessing my query for hidden meaning, and then nodded. "Give me a minute to check on my dad, then we'll talk."

"Okay."

Galen disappeared and I poured myself a glass of water to

make the time go faster, then turned on the oven and put in the garlic bread I'd prepared earlier.

When Galen got back, his lips curved into a soft smile. "He's in much better shape with you around."

I tried to smile but shivered instead. "I like being here, Galen. Your dad's nice."

And it made me feel useful being here. The Alpha couldn't walk anywhere except to the bathroom, so making sure he had water, food and blankets, and anything else he needed, felt like a valuable contribution to the household.

I wasn't sure how they'd handled things before I got here but leaving him home alone all day didn't seem like a good thing to do to him.

"Now, what's wrong?" Galen asked, pulling up a stool and sitting at the kitchen counter.

He stared at me, waiting, and my bravery shrunk. So, I diverted, fast.

"Are you hungry?" I asked. "I made dinner."

"I am, but I want you to tell me what's got you shivering so much. I've seen you face death a couple of times now, and you weren't this shaken up."

I took a sip of water, then laughed a little at his expression. It was nice to know that he didn't think I was weak, even though that was how I saw myself. "You're right. I think it was just seeing Celia that got to me."

"Celia?" Galen repeated, his eyebrows drawing together.

"Yeah. Celia." A wave of sadness passed over me, threatening to suck me down into the depths of darkness.

I shook myself and straightened my spine. My pack had come to kill me not once, but twice now. I'd survived, and I would continue to survive whatever else was coming my way. Now was not the time to break down.

"Celia is one of my best friends. She has been since childhood. She snuck over here, and hid, so she could talk to me."

Galen stood quickly, the stool legs scraping on the kitchen tiles as he did.

"One of your old pack was here?" His tone was shocked. "She got through our security without detection?"

I nodded. "Yeah, I suppose."

Galen crossed his arms over his chest. His expression darkened. "Well, that's not good. I'll talk to my guys. But what did she want?"

I swallowed hard, readying myself to tell him the truth. "She came to warn me. She said that my ex-fiancé, Maddox, is planning to come and kill me."

And although that wasn't a new piece of information, it was what Galen would do with such news that worried me.

CHAPTER 2

# GALEN

"Your fated mate is planning to kill you?" I asked, not sure I'd heard correctly.

Did she mean Maddox, himself, or did their pack have a new plan I needed to know about?

Her face hardened, her eyes flashing. "He's not my mate."

"I meant—"

"No. I know what you meant," Talia snapped. "But Maddox and I aren't mated. We never even had sex. And even though we were fated..."

She stopped talking and swallowed hard, her throat working.

I nodded in acceptance of what she said. Acceptance... and sympathy. I couldn't imagine being rejected by a fated mate. Not only that but being betrayed by the one person who was supposed to be your soul mate. The ultimate betrayal.

"I misspoke," I admitted, watching her carefully to see if she was about to break.

Not Talia. She was strong. She raised her chin and faced me squarely.

"Okay," I said. "So let me get this straight. One of your friends from your old pack risked her life by sneaking through our perimeter to warn you that Maddox is out to kill you."

We already knew that the pack had orders to kill Talia on sight, of course. But this felt different. There was something more personal and determined in this latest development.

Talia nodded, then leaned heavily on the counter like she couldn't stand upright without support any longer. "It's never going to end, Galen. Is it? They're always going to hunt me. Come for me. And they're not going to stop until I'm dead."

Tears tracked down her cheeks and she lifted her hand to wipe them away. "Celia told me that I needed to just get in my dad's car and leave. Do you think I should?"

I gaped at her. "You want to leave?"

I was shocked she'd even suggested it, but why was I? I shouldn't be. When I found her, she'd been running away, so why wouldn't she want to continue that path now?

Anger and frustration burned in my chest and my breathing hitched in my throat. I really didn't want her to go. The very idea turned me cold as ice, and angry at the Fates that were forcing her to choose a path I didn't agree with.

"No! I don't *want* to leave." She shook her head. "This town is my home, now, but Celia could be right. Maybe it's better to run away to fight another day. I don't know. What if my being here endangers your pack?"

"My pack is strong, Talia," I said, infusing confidence into my tone. She was right to be concerned on that front, but I was right, too. We *were* strong. "And you live here, now. If you don't want to leave, then stay."

I could protect her. My pack would too, under my instructions. Even though some of my Betas thought I was nuts for offering to help Talia, they'd do as I instructed.

"I'll never be safe. Here or anywhere," she whispered. "Would you help me if I decided to leave, Galen? Run with me to the border? Do you think we'd make it?"

"In wolf form?"

She was talking about five hundred miles.

"No," I said, honestly.

I could run for days in wolf form and Talia was a fast shifter, but even so it was too far, with too strong an enemy. If they snuck up on us at night and killed her, I would never forgive myself.

She released a tiny sob. "Then I'll drive, like Celia suggested. Take my dad's car. I'll go tonight."

"No, you won't," I told her firmly. "You'll stay here tonight. Safe. Under the Alpha's roof. Then tomorrow, I'll fix this."

I could feel a plan forming in the back of my mind, but it wasn't one I was ready to share yet.

"How?" Her eyes were huge and wide as she stared at me. "How are you going to fix it?"

There was only one way. "Do you trust me, Talia?"

She nodded. "I do."

My ribs squeezed tightly as pride blossomed somewhere deep inside, dark and hidden.

"Then let me organize what I need to do with my Betas, and tomorrow, I'll deal with it."

Talia nodded, wiping away a few more tears that had strayed onto her beautiful cheeks.

She didn't ask any more questions, which was likely an advantage of her being raised to be an Alpha's mate. Talia's instincts led her to follow directions and inherently trust a man that had my bloodlines.

But there was a flip side to that trust and submission. It meant that the Alpha in me wanted to protect her even more.

"You want some dinner now? I'll take some into your dad in a moment." Her shoulders slumped as though we'd had a fight and she'd lost, which was quite the opposite of what had happened.

"Yes, please. Tell me how Dad's been today for you."

After she delivered dinner to Dad, Talia chatted with me easily about my father while we ate. The food was tasty and showcased her talents in the kitchen. Eventually, I excused myself to talk to my Betas and prepare for the next day.

I ripped into them about our security lines, not caring when they all showed shock and dismay. After all, a female wolf from a neighboring enemy pack should never have been able to get onto our territory without detection. And especially not to be able to reach Talia so easily. The very idea of it galled me. Thank God she'd been a friendly, and not one sent to kill Talia.

I informed my Betas of my plan and what I was willing to do to save our pack from future fights, and hopefully prevent Talia from losing her life. The guys were ready to string me up when I voiced my thoughts, and they called me every crazy name under the sun, but I wouldn't be moved.

There was only one way of saving Talia, and I was going to do it. Whatever it took.

THE NEXT MORNING, I didn't tell my dad where I was going or what I was planning. There was no need to worry him until I got back. Then, once he heard what I'd done, he could tear me a new one.

Assuming I survived, of course.

I woke up early, dressed into some old, shifting clothes, and left the house.

I'd only taken a few steps from the front porch when I heard her voice.

"Galen! Wait!"

Talia came running out of the front door in nothing more than her black panties and a tank top that showed her sexy midriff. No bra.

Her breasts bounced as she ran down the stairs and her nipples peaked against the material of her top in the cold morning air.

"Where are you going?" she asked as she crossed her arms over her chest, shielding her nipples from the cold. And my view.

I straightened my spine and hardened myself against the desire sweeping my body. "I'm going to have a little talk with Maddox."

"You're..." Her mouth dropped open. "You're going to... *talk* to Maddox?"

I nodded. "There's only one way to save you, Talia."

My Betas knew what to do if I didn't come back. They had a strategy now, and I'd named Markus as my successor. I'd made note of it on the papers in my room in case anyone had questions.

I wasn't ready to die, but I wasn't going to stand by and let Talia die either.

Her eyes filled with tears and her bottom lip quivered. She knew me better than I'd thought. "You're going to challenge him."

"Yes, I am."

He was an Alpha's son. So was I. He had fury driving him, but I had more. I had Talia.

"Galen. No... please..."

The time for talking was done. I stripped off my t-shirt and pushed my jeans down my thighs, letting my wolf rise up inside my soul and tear through my human body.

Part of me wished I could grab and kiss her, take her taste with me into battle. But if I stopped to touch her now, I wasn't sure I'd be able to fight afterwards. I needed every bit of unsatisfied lust to fuel my rage.

Instead, I stood before her as my large black wolf, set on protecting the woman before me, then turned tail and ran—across my own pack lines and into enemy territory.

I kept running as the sun rose over the horizon, lighting the way. There were buildings up ahead, and houses. I made my way through the streets, the bubbling of my anger boiling through me.

Then I stopped, right in the middle of their town. I shifted back to human, my body hot and slick with sweat. My chest heaved with each breath I took, and my wolf howled inside my mind, craving violence.

Women stopped to stare at my nakedness, then rushed past me. An old guy gaped at me from the side of the road.

"I want your Alpha!" I bellowed into the street. "Now!"

A group of men marched down the street toward me.

I stood firm and faced them, clenching my hands into fists. "I am Galen… future Alpha of the Long Claw Pack."

I scanned the group as they surged forward and locked eyes with a guy about my age, perhaps a little younger. He had a soft, pretty-boy type of face and it turned my stomach to look at him. I knew who he was by my reaction. I didn't need it confirmed.

"Maddox. I challenge you."

The group of six men stopped before me and an older man, with graying hair and a huge build, stalked forward. "I'm the Alpha of this pack, not Maddox. You want a challenge? Challenge me, pup."

I lifted my chin. "If I win, you leave Talia and my pack alone."

He dismissed my words with a flick of his hand. "You gotta win first."

He began tugging at his clothes as though I would be fighting him.

I shook my head. "I'm not fighting a man older than my father. I want Maddox. Is he too cowardly to step up?"

The pretty-faced man I'd spotted earlier rushed forward. He was taller than the Alpha and stood at the right hand of his father. "No one calls me a coward. You want me? Then you get me."

My gaze locked on him, and a growl rolled through my chest. This was the fuckwit who'd left Talia untouched. The man who'd rejected her and tossed her aside when all she'd wanted was to serve him.

*Asshole. You never deserved someone like her.*

The Alpha thrust out his arm, stopping his son and never taking his eyes off me. "No. I'm the Alpha of this pack. I'm the one who gave the order. Talia had her chance to get out of the state. She didn't take it. That decision and the consequence falls on her, not us."

I clenched my teeth. "I want the threat taken off her."

The Alpha began to strip. "Boy, if you win, only then will we talk terms. But you won't win."

The growl that ripped through the old Alpha as he shifted was one of feral, nasty strength.

I responded in kind. Maddox would not step up now that his father had called it. I was already naked, so I quickly shifted to my wolf form, shook out my fur, and planted my paws firmly in the road.

We were evenly matched in size and weight. This fight would not be easy to win.

It might possibly be a fight to the death.

He launched at me, his snapping teeth, aiming for my throat.

I sprung back, out of his reach, and then twisted on my paws to face him again. This time, when he launched, I was ready.

His huge maw with vicious teeth snapped together an inch from my neck as I jerked away. I lunged in to score a bite on his shoulder. I ripped through his thick fur to expose the flesh beneath, and held on, tasting blood. It fired my senses, that taste, and I shook him, *hard*, before letting go.

He yelped and limped backward. Then we were on each other again, biting and growling and swiping at each other.

The sounds we made must have been horrendous for those watching, and vaguely I wondered where Talia was right now.

Then I put her out of my head, because I had to concentrate on staying alive.

I had never fought someone so evenly matched. My usual size and weight advantage was nullified against this enormous Alpha.

He caught me on the back leg and held on. It took all my strength to throw him off. I backed away, shaking my head to re-orient myself.

That one hurt. A lot.

I spared a glance downward to see blood gushing from a huge wound on my leg and another gash on my hip.

When had he got me there?

Blood was everywhere. His *and* mine.

I couldn't worry about injuries now. I glared at my enemy, noting the red fire of blood lust in his eyes. My lip curled up, and I snarled, battle-lust raging through my body and infusing me with power and energy, despite the blood loss.

His shoulders bunched as he readied to leap at me again. I held my ground, lowered my head, and charged him first.

I caught him round the neck, and I dropped my weight to the ground, pulling him down with me. I locked my jaw, refusing to give up, even under a torrent of scratches and scrabbling all over my body as he fought to release from my grip.

If I let go now, I would be a dead wolf.

From this position, I could only see one of his eyes, and it was full of rage and a hint of fear.

Then he stopped scrabbling as the rage dissipated and the fear in his expression grew. He arched his neck further, which would allow me to finish him off if I so desired. It was a classic sign of defeat. He was signaling to me, and to anyone watching, that I had won this battle.

The Alpha was conceding the fight.

I detached my locked jaw from around his throat, tasting his blood as it ran down my gullet and fighting the urge to give him one last shake and finish him off. This bastard had tried to kill Talia. He deserved death in return. But I needed to back off and let the negotiations begin. That wouldn't happen if I killed him.

It was done. I won. And Talia would finally be safe.

I let go of my wolf, needing to withdraw from the red haze of anger and adrenaline. I slid back into my human body with exhaustion, feeling barely alive as I climbed to my feet and stared around.

My gaze locked onto Maddox, who stood as still as a statue, as if he was shocked at the outcome.

Blood poured from my wounds, but I ignored it.

"Let's talk terms," I said.

# CHAPTER 3
# TALIA

I couldn't believe Galen had left to fight my old Alpha. What if he was killed? My chest filled with dread at the thought.

I ran back inside and dressed. The sun was barely up and much of the town was likely still asleep.

Not me. Instead, I paced and worried, until I couldn't bear my whirling thoughts any longer. But what could I do? I couldn't stop the fight, and if it didn't go Galen's way, where could I go?

Tears fell down my cheeks until I became so angry at my own frustration, I scrubbed at my face under the kitchen sink tap. Then I took a few deep breaths to calm myself, before I went to ask Galen's dad if he needed anything.

Luckily for me, the Alpha gave me a list of errands, which was a useful distraction. I ran from one house to another, collecting food and dropping things off as he'd requested.

I didn't tell the Alpha where Galen was, feigning complete ignorance when he asked if I knew where his son had run off to so early. I didn't see any of the Betas along the route. They were likely already working or on patrol. They were probably avoiding me too, because after all, I was the reason their Alpha-to-be was putting his life at risk.

My stomach was completely tight with tension. I couldn't eat. I could hardly breathe. Galen, my protector, my captor, the man who had become my friend... he was, quite possibly, in the fight of his life right now. *For me.*

Was he hurt? Had he been killed?

What would happen to me, and to this pack, if something happened to him? It wasn't like Galen's dad could miraculously make himself well and jump out of bed to take over leadership once again.

The not knowing was the worst possible thing, and by the time my errands were done, all I could imagine was the worst outcome.

What if Galen never came back?

I rushed back to the house, put away the food I'd collected for the Alpha, then went to the bathroom to have a quick shower. I felt somehow unclean and even though I knew water couldn't wash away my worry, I couldn't resist cleaning myself from top to toe under the hot spray.

If Galen died, then I would surrender to my old pack. I didn't want anyone else getting hurt on my account and with Galen gone, who would keep this pack safe?

I wanted to live—of course, I did—but not at the cost of anyone else's life. Especially those who had tried so hard to help me.

I scrubbed my flesh hard, from the soles of my feet to the scalp on the top of my head. But everywhere on my body was itchy and aching in a strange way.

*Oh, please let this not be a premonition of any sort. Or if it is, please be a good one.*

I wanted Galen home, now. I wasn't sure how it had happened

so quickly, but Galen had become someone I trusted. Someone I cared about.

Once I was raw and clean, I dried myself and dressed, then walked outside and sat on the front step of the porch.

And I waited.

All day, I waited, moving off the porch only to make the Alpha some lunch and clean up after, before returning to my watching post on the porch.

If Galen had won the challenge, wouldn't he have returned straight away? It was close to dinner time now and the streets were empty of people.

If he'd lost, would Maddox's pack have taken immediate vengeance? Was that why there was no one around? Should I be readying myself to head back to my old home and hand myself in to whatever dreadful fate awaited me there?

"Oh God, what should I do?"

I jumped to my feet, biting my lip so hard I tasted blood. I considered my options. Should I try to find one of his Betas? Markus, maybe? He'd help me, surely? Would he run with me to the pack lines and see if we could find out what had happened to Galen?

Just when I was about to throw all caution to the wind and try to track him down myself, a large black wolf appeared in my vision, trotting down the street toward me. No, trotting wasn't accurate. He was limping down the street.

Limping quite badly, in fact.

It was Galen. No one else was that big or strong. Besides, I would know him anywhere, whether in wolf or human form.

He came straight toward me, and I rushed to meet him.

"Galen."

He was alive. My eyes filled with tears of relief.

Blood matted his fur, and I rushed back to the house to open the door and let him in.

"Come. Quickly," I said, gesturing to him.

Galen hurried towards the door, but he grimaced with every step.

"Everything okay?" the Alpha called out from the bedroom. "Do I smell blood?"

"All good. No problem," I called back, then motioned for Galen to follow me. "It's...uh... my monthly... you know."

My cheeks heated. I couldn't believe I'd just said that, but nothing else came to mind to explain the scent of Galen's injuries.

"All right. Sorry, didn't mean to pry," came the Alpha's muffled reply.

"Come to my bedroom," I whispered to Galen. "I'll get the first aid kit."

Galen limped down the hallway, bloody footprints trailing behind him. I grabbed everything I could find to help him: bandages, water bottles, disinfectant, needle and thread, and clean cloths.

Then I raced down the hallway to my room, where Galen, completely naked in his human form, sat on my bed, swaying with exhaustion and blood loss.

"Hey..." He groaned as he pressed a hand to his head.

"You okay?" I asked, shutting the door behind me.

He was covered in so much blood, it looked painted on. Red was splashed over his face and down his chest.

"Yeah, I'm okay. A few injuries, but mostly I just need a shower."

I held up my supplies, trying hard not to look too long at the incredible body before me.

The one sitting on my bed.

Every time I saw Galen naked, he took my breath away with the strength and beauty of him. Even now, dirty and streaked with blood, he was damn beautiful.

"Do you need any stitches? Can I help you with any of your

injuries?" I'd patched up my dad enough times after fights to know how to do most first aid. Especially on a wolf with a high pain tolerance and fast healing power.

"Ah, yeah." He turned to the side. "I think my back needs a little attention, and my leg. Near my ankle."

I dropped to my knees on the ground before him, keeping my head bent to stare at his ankle and foot.

The flesh had been mauled and blood still gushed out of the wound onto the floor beneath him. The pool of red was beginning to grow. I needed to stop that bleeding, fast. God knew how much he'd already lost, getting back here.

"This is gonna need stitches."

"Can you do it?"

I didn't raise my head, knowing what I would come eye to eye with if I tried to look up at him. I wasn't mature enough for that today. Nope. No way.

"I can."

"Then please do."

He extended his leg to give me full access and I got to it, washing away any grime with water, then applying the disinfectant before using the needle and thread to sew the flesh back together. It was a rough but passable job. Galen inhaled sharply above me while I sewed, but he didn't make any other sound.

When I was done, I added a waterproof covering, then bandaged up the wound and put some clips on to hold it all together.

I hopped to my feet without staring at his groin, an almost impossible feat. The heat of my desire for him settled deep in my belly, and my breath kept hitching in my throat.

"Your ankle's done. Can I look at your back now?"

He nodded, not speaking, but twisted away so I could check out the scratches and teeth marks on his back. The skin was a mess, but it would heal. There was one gash over his hip deep enough to show flesh and bone, but I wasn't sure if stitches were needed or not. It wasn't bleeding anymore. I cleaned that wound out and added a few butterfly sutures and a waterproof dressing to hold it together. It didn't seem to need more than that, and with Galen's healing, it would hopefully not take too long to mend.

I studied his back some more. "Gee whiz. Did Maddox do all this to you?"

He huffed out a laugh. "Wimp wouldn't fight me. This was his father."

A chill coursed down my spine. "You fought the Alpha?"

How had he survived that encounter?

Galen turned back to face me and this time, I couldn't help but notice the way his cock lay thick and heavy against his thigh. My stomach clenched and I lifted my gaze up to his with effort.

"Yeah. Why?" he asked.

"Oh, because he's... very tough." I swallowed hard and walked away from him. "I don't think you need stitches for anything on your back, but I could look again after a shower. I can disinfect it then, too. Do you need help getting in and out?"

Galen got to his feet and his cock wasn't flaccid anymore.

*Wow. Even with all that pain...*

"No. I'm fine. But if you could look over my back again afterward, that would be great."

"Use my shower," I said, indicating to the ensuite I had, thanks to Galen giving me his room. He was sleeping in a spare room. "I'll clean up and be here when you get out."

There were several pools of blood on the floor and the blankets on the bed would need a wash now.

"Thanks." He limped to the bathroom.

I hurried to the kitchen to gather paper towels and more water; my face aflame. The water was running in the bathroom, and I tried to slow down my heart rate.

He'd fought my old Alpha and survived.

No one I knew, or had even heard of for that matter, had fought our Alpha and lived to tell the tale. He was a monster of a man, and his wolf was equally vicious.

So, what had happened to him?

Had Galen killed him?

Maybe I didn't want to know the answer to that one.

I hurried to clean up, stripping my bed and putting the blankets and sheets straight into the washing machine. I mopped up the blood on the floor and put the water down an outside drain, then went back in and remade my bed with sheets and blankets I found in a cabinet.

When the shower finally turned off and the door to the ensuite opened to reveal a still very naked but much less bloody Galen, my heart soared.

"How are you feeling?" I asked, then swallowed the excited squeal rising in my throat.

He pushed wet hair off his face, his naked torso rippling with muscle. "A lot better, actually."

He slung the towel around his waist, low on his hips, and limped forward. "Can you check my back again? It's still sore."

"Yeah, of course." I rushed forward, stepping behind him while he was still standing. I set my hands to his flesh, pressing my palms flat and spreading my fingers wide.

The strength of his body radiated out in a wave. I quivered, then clenched my teeth, hard, forcing whatever that feeling was to retreat. Now was not the time for anything other than caregiving. Galen had been hurt, because of my presence here in his pack, and I needed to focus.

After taking a long, slow breath, I moved my hands down his spine to the indent of his lower back, checking marks and wounds as I went.

He was hot to the touch, his skin smooth beneath my fingertips.

"They look okay," I whispered, pressing against the claw marks on his shoulder, then checking the one at the base of his spine near his hip where the wound was a lot deeper. The butterfly sutures seemed to have survived the shower and were holding well. "Can I put some antiseptic cream on these ones on your back?"

As long as the gashes didn't become infected, Galen's wolf genetics would step in and heal him quickly.

"Yeah." His voice was deep and gravelly. "That'd be great."

I rushed over to my pile of supplies and grabbed the white tube. Then, with shaking hands, I squirted some of the cream onto my fingertips and applied it to the remaining wounds.

"Is that okay?" I asked as he stiffened beneath my touch.

"Yeah. Just cold." His voice was still croaky.

I covered all the claw marks with the antiseptic.

"I think I'm done," I whispered.

"Thanks." He swayed a little on his feet. "I think I need to sit down again."

*Crap! I knew he'd lost too much blood.*

"Of course!" I said, grabbing his arm and tugging him across to the bed.

When he sat, I climbed onto the bed as well, sitting behind him cross-legged and facing his shoulder, so that if he fell, I could make sure he landed on the mattress and not the floor.

"Are you okay?" I asked, placing my hand on his arm.

He nodded but didn't turn toward me.

I coughed to clear my throat, my gaze sweeping over his incredible muscles. I wanted to touch him more, caress him. Learn each groove and curve of him.

But I had a burning question I needed an answer to. "Did you, uh... kill the Alpha?"

Galen turned his head, his eyes blazing with his wolf as he stared at me.

I gasped, unable to look away.

"No. I didn't."

"Then what happened?" I whispered.

He'd come home after being at the other pack all day and considering that an Alpha's challenge usually meant a fight to the death, Galen's injuries were quite mild, really.

"I fought him and won. But I refused to kill him. Instead, I made him concede. Then Maddox and I talked terms while some of their other pack members carried their injured leader away somewhere."

"Terms?" My gaze dropped to his mouth as he spoke, and it took a moment to process what he'd said. "You talked terms with Maddox?"

"Yes. You're free." He said it like a simple statement of fact. "You're safe. They won't come for you, Talia, nor for my pack. Not anymore."

Tears welled up in my eyes and fell, but I continued to stare at him. He'd done it. My savior. He'd freed me from the tyranny of an unfair pack Alpha and a death decree hanging over my head.

I covered my mouth with my hand so that I didn't sob out loud. Instead, I swallowed hard. "Galen, I...."

He looked away. "It's okay."

"Thank you," I rushed to add, "I owe you my life."

He shook his head. "You don't owe me anything."

I put my hand on his arm, and he groaned as though my touch hurt him. "Why won't you look at me?"

His jaw tightened, a muscle ticking just beneath his ear. Then he said through his teeth, "Because if I look at you, I might do something we'll both regret, and I don't want to do that. Not after everything you've been through."

A feeling flashed through me that I couldn't even begin to describe.

Hope? Fear? Or was this pure need?

I didn't know what it was, but I knew I needed to move closer. I pressed my hand against his back, then leaned forward so that I could touch my lips to his flesh, too. I kissed his skin, tasting the natural saltiness there.

He groaned and twisted around, sliding on top of me in one move and pushing me back into the mattress.

I welcomed the feel of his body heavy atop mine. Then I wrapped my legs around his waist, carefully trying to avoid his injuries, and pulled his face down to me for a kiss.

When our lips met, I gasped at the pleasure that shot through me. I wanted more. I arched up into his naked body, needing to get closer.

He moaned as I moved my fingers into his hair, holding him tight against me, his tongue sliding into my mouth.

I groaned at the pleasure arrowing deep into my core.

God, I wanted him. More than I'd ever wanted anyone.

With that thought, the pain of the past came crashing down into me like an avalanche. My father's death. Maddox's rejection.

I couldn't do this. Not yet.

I stilled, and Galen clearly felt the change in me.

He pushed himself up on his hands and stared down at me. "Are you okay?"

I nodded, pressing my fingers to my mouth. I could still feel the imprint of his lips on mine, the scratch of his unshaven face on my cheek. I reached up and stroked the hair back from his forehead, but I didn't try to kiss him again.

He must have read something in my expression, because he gave a quirky little grin and shook his head slightly.

He was still on top of me, with barely a towel covering his body, and yet I could sense no aggression in him. No need to take or force me, even after the day he'd had. His natural state seemed to be more protector than aggressor, and I relaxed beneath him when I realized he had accepted my need to go slow.

He dropped his head and pressed his lips against mine, just holding there, like he was saying goodbye. Then he rolled to his side and stood up beside the bed, wincing.

"Sorry. I can't lie down on my side too long," he said. "My back's too sore."

I sat up and tucked my knees into my chest, embarrassed I'd pulled away from him barely one kiss into... whatever that might have developed into. "I'm sorry. I just..."

"It's totally fine." His tone was clipped. "I forgot that you're... untouched. I didn't mean to scare you."

I shook my head. "You didn't! You're... amazing. And I'm so grateful for what you did for me this morning."

His eyebrows drew together as he re-tied the towel around his waist to cover himself. "I hope that's not why you let me kiss you. I don't need that sort of gratitude."

I hopped off the bed. "No, it wasn't like that. You're..."

I swallowed hard.

How did I say this without sounding ridiculous? "You're beautiful. Especially when you're... not dressed."

My face flamed, but it was worth the hideous feeling of embarrassment that shot through my whole body when he answered my stumbling explanation with a sudden grin.

"Yeah, well—" he began, but we were interrupted before he could go further.

"Galen!" a male voice called out from inside the house somewhere, sounding like one of his anxious Betas.

Galen's head whipped around. "That'll be Markus," he said, walking toward the door to my bedroom. "Thanks for patching me up, Talia."

"Of course," I whispered, as he walked out the door. Then I

added, to myself, because he'd already left. "Thank you for saving my life, Galen. Again."

I sat down on the bed, wishing I could melt into a puddle and disappear. The truth was staring me in the face, and it was impossible to deny. I wanted Galen, the next Alpha to this pack.

# CHAPTER 4

# GALEN

I headed toward the front door, where Markus stood.

"Hey!" I called out to my Beta as I walked down the hall from the bedroom, my ankle feeling better with each passing minute. Talia must have done a good job of matching up the flesh with her stitching because the wound was already healing.

"You're back," he said, relief in his tone. "Thank God."

I grinned at him. "You didn't doubt me?"

His eyebrows drew together. "Of course not, but it still felt like an unnecessary move."

I shrugged. "I won, and demanded they leave Talia and our pack alone. They agreed. So hopefully the attacks will stop. For now, anyway."

I wasn't under any illusion that the peace I'd brokered with my blood this morning would last forever. Grudges this old and that ran so deep rarely disappeared overnight.

"Just give me a minute to get dressed and we can talk more then," I told him, pointing at the door of the spare room I'd been using.

"Oh, that's what I came to tell you!" Markus said, slapping the side of his head like he'd forgotten something important. "There's absolute fucking chaos going on in town. I think we should get in there."

*In town? What now?*

"Okay, come with me and give me the run down," I said, indicating he should follow. I hurried into my room, threw my wet towel over a chair, and started grabbing my clothes. "What's going on?"

"I just got a call from Mikey, the guy who runs the liquor store. He said the witches are going insane. Blowing stuff up. Something's wrong, and I think the humans are gonna need our help."

"Shit..." I groaned, tugging on my boots, then cursed when the shoe hit my healing ankle. "What do you think it is?"

There was only one thing I knew that drove witches, as a group, insane like that. But I could be wrong. Hopefully I was.

Markus shook his head. "Not sure. I don't think I've ever seen anything like Mike was talking about."

I hadn't seen the madness in person, but my dad had told me the stories.

"I think I might know," I said grimly. "Let's go. I'm gonna grab Talia."

Markus frowned at me. "You're bringing her with you?"

"Of course." She was safest with me. "Let's go. Talia!"

She came running down the hall, her red and gold hair flying around her face. "Yeah?"

"We need to go into town, now. I'll explain on the way."

She nodded and followed us down the hall and out the front door.

I jumped in my truck. Markus sat in the passenger side and Talia hopped in the back, hovering in the gap between us.

When we were on the road, heading into town, Talia piped up. "So, what's happened? Why the rush?"

I glanced in the rear-view mirror, meeting her gaze. "I think the demons are infecting the witches."

"Demons? What do you mean?" she asked, a note of fear in her voice.

She was right to be concerned. Demons brought a whole other level of batshit crazy to the situation.

"Seriously?" Markus said. "How do you know that?"

"I've heard about it before," I told him, putting my foot down harder on the accelerator. "Demons affect all of us differently, but when a demon touches a witch, they go insane. They'll fight and scream and throw magic around the place. They're aggressive, too, according to the stories. I can't imagine what they'll be doing to the townsfolk."

I planted my foot even harder against the accelerator and the truck raced toward town. I wanted to be wrong, but since I'd seen that demon trying to seduce Talia out of the alleyway, I'd known they'd surface again.

That sighting hadn't been a chance encounter. It was the beginning of something big.

"Is it permanent?" Talia asked. "The changes to the witches?"

Good question.

"No, it's not. It only lasts a day or so. It's like an infection. It works through their system after a while, but they can do a lot of damage in that time."

More than I wanted to think about.

The town came up on the horizon and, even from this distance, smoke billowed up from the buildings.

"Oh, Jeezus. I hope we're not too late," I muttered.

I hit the outer edges of town and drove down the main street. Chaos and mess were everywhere. When a witch blasted a human man with magic, knocking him through a glass shop front, I slammed on the brakes. The truck fishtailed down the road and narrowly avoided a rabid group of howling witches that appeared seemingly out of nowhere.

"Holy shit," Markus said, while Talia's expression in the rear-view mirror was round-eyed with shock.

The car slid sideways and somehow landed right outside my bar and apartment with a loud screech.

I glanced at the building where everything seemed quiet and normal. *Thank fuck.*

"Talia, you get in there and stay safe. Markus and I need to help the humans."

Markus jumped out of the truck and we followed suit, Talia slamming the car door shut. It was an insane scene with black-robed women walking the streets flinging magic this way and that as if uncaring of any consequences.

People screamed, fires burst out of shops, and a huge crash sounded in the distance. That one sounded bad, like a big car crash.

"Fuck. I've gotta go check that out." Markus ground out between his teeth.

I grabbed hold of Markus's arm. He was already chomping at the bit to run after the berserker witches. "Be careful, and if you can help any humans without shifting, please do. They don't need to see wolf shifters on the same day they realize witches and magic are real."

Markus nodded and took off running down the road.

Talia looked at me, her jaw set. "I'm going to help."

"No. I want you safe."

"Then why did you bring me?"

I opened my mouth to respond then realized that she had a point. If I had really wanted her safe, then I should have left her at home with my dad. "You're right, but can you try and stay out of the witches' way? Try and help any humans get in their cars and leave rather than engaging with anyone non-human."

She nodded. "No problem."

We took off in opposite directions, and even though a part of me wanted to keep Talia by my side, we now had bigger issues to worry about than her stupid old pack.

As I rounded a corner, I came face to face with a witch whose hair frizzled out in every direction. She had a look of madness in her eyes.

She shot spears of magic straight at a hairdressing salon. I launched myself at her to push her off-balance. I didn't want to shift unless I had to, but when she lurched straight back onto her feet and swiveled to face me, a light of rage had joined the madness in her expression.

She threw back her head and cackled, and there was nothing human or rational about that sound whatsoever.

*Uh oh.*

There was no time to strip off and shift nicely. Instead, I leapt into my wolf form and stood on all paws before her, growling a warning.

She ignored me, throwing her arm forward and sending a blast of flame straight at my already-injured hip.

I ducked away with only a tiny puff of air between me and incineration.

I didn't want to hurt her, but she was leaving me no choice. I readied myself to launch. A small wolf landed on all four paws between us, growling and snarling at the witch.

*Talia?* Little Talia wanted to defend *me?*

A mixture of respect and fear rippled through me. If the witch got to her with one of those flames, she would be nothing but ash. A howl tore out of my throat... but then I quieted, shocked at what was happening.

The witch was staring at Talia and slowly backing away. Talia advanced, step by growling step.

It almost looked as if the witch was afraid of my little wolf defender, and that the fear had cut through some of the madness at last.

The witch released a strange shriek, and then turned and ran off down the street. I let her go. She no longer seemed inclined to shoot magic flame.

The small wolf in front of me stared after the witch. I came up beside her and nuzzled her shoulder in thanks. She cocked her head to the side, looking in the direction the witch had run, then shook her body in a violent manner, as if she'd experienced something distasteful.

Then she seemed to come back into herself. She touched her nose to mine, just for a moment, but the ripple that ran through me had nothing to do with fear, and everything to do with lust.

I needed to shift back to human, and fast, and finish the task at hand, before I lost concentration.

AFTER THAT CRAZY-HAIRED WITCH DISAPPEARED, something seemed to change in relation to the insanity going on around us. The tension lowered a notch, and at last, within only a few hours, all the witches responsible for the damage came to my bar to find me.

They were mostly back in their right minds, remorseful and worried about what this meant for their future in the town.

"Firstly, you need to go home. Heal yourselves," I told them. "But it may be best that you don't come into town for a while."

"Some of us weren't affected," a young blonde in the back of the group piped up. "Not many, but a few of us. What should *we* do?"

"You could focus on fixing the damage done in town, then, by those of you who were hurt by this event. Fix the broken windows and the shops. Do everything you can while the humans are hunkered down in their homes tonight, then you'll probably need to talk about getting some memory spells cast."

An older witch with bite marks on her face nodded. "I can start that process."

"Leave," I told them. "Those of you that are capable, fix the town. The rest of you, go home and rebuild your health and your strength."

The witches left en masse, most of them beaten and bruised, and all of them regretful. Many had been hurt by the wolves and others had injured themselves in their frenzy. Paramedic and police sirens sounded in the distance, likely coming to help the humans even though the danger seemed to have passed.

It was a mess. All of it.

I wanted them out of my bar and gone.

THE NEXT AFTERNOON, I went back to town to check things out in the light of a fresh day. I stood outside the bakery and studied my surroundings. The witches had done a great job of putting the town to rights. Most of the shops looked the same as they always had, and the streets were clear of debris.

From the smiles on the faces of most humans walking past the bakery, the witches had thrown some memory spells around as well, because there wasn't a frown—or a police car, for that matter—anywhere to be seen.

I jumped out of the truck and walked over to my bar. I had to unpack a shipment of alcohol that had arrived that morning.

"Come on in," I called to Talia, who I'd brought with me. I still didn't want her out of my sight. I didn't trust anyone to be as vigilant as me, and after she'd saved my life yesterday, I owed her.

She sat at the bar while she waited for me to finish the work that needed to get done, drinking water and being altogether too patient. Anyone else would have been bored, or complaining, but not her.

It took me an hour to put everything where I wanted it. Talia offered to help, of course, but I figured it would take longer to explain where everything went than to do it myself, so I just got the task done.

I released a sigh and wiped the sweat off my brow as I finished the final box and returned to Talia. "Give me five minutes to call the bar manager, then we can go."

It was close to dinner and my stomach was grumbling.

Of course, that was when my front door opened.

"Galen?" The voice was female and one I didn't recognize.

I twisted around as a group of women walked into the bar. Four of them, with uncannily bright blue eyes harboring the light of magic that gave them away as witches.

Their spines were straight, their clothes dark, and there wasn't an injury among them. These four clearly weren't part of the coven that had created havoc yesterday.

"Yeah, that's me," I said, walking forward to confront them.

I wasn't worried about their intent because I had protective wards on the doors of this place. There was no way they would have gotten through those, if they'd meant me or my people any harm.

The group stopped in the middle of the bar.

One of the women stepped forward and lifted her chin. "We've come to ask for sanctuary."

I crossed my arms over my chest and stared down at her. "Come again?"

"We live a few towns over and heard about what happened here yesterday."

I nodded. "Yeah, it was a damn shame. The witches from our local coven have never caused the town any problems before."

In fact, I'd considered some of them friends, until yesterday. Today, I was a little more wary.

"We heard you were a kind man, with an even temper," the woman said. She had obviously been deemed spokesperson for the others.

I let my amusement show on my face. "You don't need to blow smoke up my ass. What do you want?"

The woman blinked like she didn't understand what I meant.

Then she inclined her head with a regal tilt. "We want sanctuary."

I let my arms fall to my sides with a casual air, but inside, I said to myself, *oh crap*. I plonked down on a bar stool next to Talia, giving myself a moment to process her request.

The head witch's gaze roamed over Talia as if she'd only just noticed her. She frowned a little before turning back to me. "Will you help us?"

"You're gonna have to be clear about what you actually need. I'm not a church." And I'd never offered sanctuary to anyone before, except Talia, and I'd kidnapped her first.

"No, but you're a strong Alpha with pack lands where we can hide."

My mouth dropped open. So, she wasn't kidding about the sanctuary.

"Why do you need to hide?"

All four of the witches rolled their eyes in unison. The one at the front took another small step forward. "You know there are demons around. We can't protect ourselves."

"And you think I can?"

What was I going to do that their magic couldn't?

The witch to the leader's left, sporting a head of curly red hair, stepped forward, her voice urgent. "Please. We can help your pack with whatever you need. Food growth, potions, healing. We just need somewhere safe to stay for a while. Please."

It was the second please that got me.

I rubbed my face, and then hauled myself to my feet. "Let me talk to my father, the real Alpha of our pack, and I'll let you know. Okay?"

The redhead looked like she was going to protest but the one at the front put a hand on her arm and shook her head.

Then she turned to me. "We'll come by tomorrow for your answer. Thank you for your time, Galen."

They left, just as mysteriously as they'd arrived.

I turned to Talia, who hadn't spoken a single word while they were here. "Any comments? You've been pretty quiet today."

She shrugged. "I have lots of comments, but it's your choice, Galen. You're the Alpha."

I ran a hand through my hair and collapsed back onto the stool beside her. The funny thing was, I wasn't. My dad was still with us, so technically *he* was the Alpha of the pack, not me. I felt like a kid dressing up and pretending to be the leader. Nothing about this responsibility felt real, or normal.

"There is something I'd like to tell you," Talia whispered.

I narrowed my eyes at the paleness of her face. "Of course. Anything."

She glanced down at the floorboards and my heart sped up. Was it something to do with those witches that had just left? Or something new?

What was wrong now?

# CHAPTER 5

# TALIA

I blew out my breath. I didn't really want to have this conversation, but I needed to tell someone what had been eating at me since the witch attack yesterday. Galen seemed to be the most knowledgeable and trustworthy person around me.

"How much do you know about the demons?" I asked him.

Galen frowned. "I thought you wanted to tell me something? That's a question."

"It's sort of related," I admitted. "I want to talk about the demons, but I was wondering how much you know about them. You knew straight away that they were the reason the witches were going berserk yesterday, so... can you tell me what else you know about them?"

He sighed and leaned back against the bar, looking way too strong and sexy for my liking. Being around Galen made it hard to concentrate on anything else, sometimes.

"Well," he said slowly, "I only know what my father's told me."

"Which is...?"

He scratched his chest through his t-shirt with one hand and a strange quiver of heat rippled through my belly.

"That the presence of demons affects us all differently," he said.

"Us?" I asked, not understanding.

"Yeah, the paranormals. Apparently, wolves get more aggressive, more agitated. The witches become insane, like you saw last night. They don't seem to affect humans as much, but that's just a guess."

I nodded. "So, if they come near you or me, you think it'll make us more aggressive?"

He shrugged. "That's what Dad always said. But I don't think we start acting ferocious after just one encounter. I think they need to be around for a long time, or maybe they need to touch us. I'm not really sure."

Our gazes clashed.

"Why?" he asked.

I couldn't put it off any longer; I had to tell him. "Um... because I saw one yesterday."

Galen jerked, sitting up straight on his bar stool. "You did? Another one? When?"

"After you were attacked, and I saved you from that witch. As she ran off, I saw something move out of the corner of my eye. It was a demon. Another one." I dug my fingernails into my palms, enjoying the sting of the little bit of pain.

There was something about the demons that fascinated me. I knew I should fear them because they were bad. And on one level, I was scared. But I was also strangely intrigued by them.

When I saw one, I always felt the need to move closer, to see if the fire they were made from burnt me, or whether it would totally consume me, if I touched one.

"Okay. What happened? Did it call to you again?" Galen's tone was demanding, suspicion etched into every line on his face. Was he suspicious of the demonic presence? Or of me?

I nodded, unable to explain the pull properly. It hadn't been like last time, when I'd felt like I was in a trance and unable to control myself. This time, I'd been fully conscious, and yet I still wanted to move forward and be with the demon. See where it took me.

Galen groaned and shook his head, looking away.

I understood he was frustrated with me, and this whole situation. The demons were a new force and seemed to be wreaking havoc everywhere. The last thing he needed was some sort of beacon for the things, especially considering I currently lived in his unwell dad's house.

The silence dragged on, so finally I said, "Ah, is it okay if we run an errand on the way back to the pack?"

I wanted a few things and since Galen didn't really like me being in town by myself, I should take advantage of this time to do a bit of shopping.

Galen glanced up. "What sort of errand?"

"I have to go to the drug store, and then a friend's house. I left my address book at her place, and I ought to call my aunt. She'll probably be frantic by now."

I'd realized yesterday that I still hadn't called my mother's sister to tell her I was staying in town. I'd accidentally left my address book at Kylie's place.

Galen dragged himself to his feet. "I suppose. But I've gotta get back to Dad. Will it take long?"

I was about to tell him I'd be quick when the front door opened and two guys from the pack walked in.

"Hey Markus. Darius," Galen said, nodding toward the men.

"Hey." Markus nodded back. "You weren't answering your phone. Your dad wants you."

Galen groaned and walked around the bar, picking up his cell from where he'd stashed it.

"Shit. I think it's on silent." He grabbed his keys. "Come on. We've gotta go."

I jumped to my feet and pressed my hands together, palm to palm. "I really must go to Kylie's, and the drug store. I'm sorry I didn't think to go earlier by myself."

Not that he would have let me go anywhere alone.

Galen ran a hand through his hair, a frown tugging at his brows. "My dad needs me."

"I can take her," Darius said. "Happy to help."

Galen stared at the new wolf. I glanced between all three of the guys in front of me. I wasn't totally comfortable with Darius, but I wasn't worried about him either.

He never looked at me inappropriately, but he was definitely interested in me for some reason. I wasn't sure if it was because of my relationship with Galen, or if there was something else.

"I'm okay with that, if you are," I said, addressing Galen.

He glanced at his cell, probably balancing out the time it would take to do what I needed to do, versus getting back to the pack.

"That would be great, actually," he said, then turned to Markus. "You coming with me?"

Markus watched me, before his gaze moved to Darius. "Nah, I'll ride with them. All my shit's in my car anyway. You go. Your dad needs you."

Galen raised his eyebrows at me as he asked, "You sure?"

I nodded, my heart tugging in my chest at his show of concern. "Yeah. Absolutely. I'll only be an hour or so. See you back at the pack then."

Galen nodded and left, and I was alone with the two other wolf shifters.

Darius, who'd been smiling a minute ago, was now frowning heavily, lines creasing in his brow.

"You didn't need to stay with me," he said to Markus. "I can drive your truck fine."

"I don't think so," Markus said with a grin.

I grabbed my bag and headed out the door. The sun was slowly dropping out of the sky, but it was still light enough for the shops to be open a little longer.

"Thanks for doing this," I told Darius as we waited for Markus, who took a little longer to head out the door.

"No problem," Darius said, looking annoyed, his lips pulled tight and down.

It seemed like Darius was pretty pissed off that Markus was coming with us. I had no idea why. I was only doing a shopping errand and I thought it was pretty clear to the whole pack that I was Galen's to protect.

I wasn't available to any other wolf.

We jumped in the truck and drove straight over to Kylie's house. She was home, luckily, and gave me my book that I'd left there.

I didn't stop to explain what was going on, just thanked her, reassured her I was okay, and ran back to the car.

"Where to next?" Markus asked from the front seat.

"Ah, the drug store please," I said.

Markus drove me to the only drug store in town, humming away while Darius glared out the window the whole time.

He was definitely annoyed. Had he wanted me to himself? Why would he? Didn't he know that Galen would hurt him if he did something to me, or tried anything romantically?

When Markus pulled up outside the shop, I jumped out. "Thanks. I'll only be a minute."

I walked inside, glancing around. I needed the women's

section, for my monthly which was due. Which aisle were the tampons in? I turned to the left, set on quickly hunting down what I needed, and almost ran into Samantha, a friend from my old pack.

Happiness flooded me. We'd grown up together and her family had lived only a few houses down from mine. "Sam! I..."

Sam's eyes widened when she saw me, then a dirty look crossed her face like she'd sucked on a lemon. She lifted her pointed chin in the air and turned her head away. "Don't talk to me."

I stared at her, shocked to my core.

"Oh, ah..."

What could I say? That, in that moment when I'd seen my friend, I'd forgotten my old pack hated my guts? That they'd been told to kill me on sight?

"Sorry."

As I turned away, Sam grabbed her cell phone out of her bag and began to text frantically.

Panic hit me in the chest with the weight of a fist. She could be calling for help, or she could be just bitching to someone back at the pack. Either way, I needed to hurry.

I raced away from her, looking for the aisle I needed. *There.* I snatched up the few products I needed for the week ahead and ran to the counter to pay.

Three people stood in line in front of me, and I clung to the small boxes in my hand. I couldn't afford to stand here forever. Should I just drop them and leave?

One person finished their purchase and walked away, then there were only two people in front of me.

I tapped my foot, a shriek rising in my throat. Sam seemed to have disappeared, but the panic in my heart hadn't. Should I cut and run?

I glanced out the window beside the counter. Darius and

Markus were out the front, sitting in the car and both looking bored. There wasn't any danger. It was all in my head.

There wasn't anyone coming for me. I had to calm down.

Only one person in front of me now.

*Breathe. Just breathe.*

Galen had brokered a deal for my freedom, hadn't he? He'd told me I was safe. I had to remember that.

Memories of last night came flooding back, including the kiss we'd shared. It had been, by far, the hottest kiss I'd ever had.

In the past, I'd often wondered about sex, and how on earth it could feel natural to have a man put his dick inside my body. The very act sounded freaky and weird, and although I'd had confidence that with Maddox it would be okay, the idea of it had never seemed natural to me. Not at all.

But being with Galen yesterday had been totally different. I'd finally understood how sex could be simple and, dare I even think it, natural.

It would have been too easy to open my legs for him. Way too easy. In fact, every part of me had wanted my clothes to melt away so I could feel his hot, naked body against mine.

He would have whipped his towel away and kissed me, surged into me...

I shook my head, heat flooding my cheeks at the thoughts crowding my mind. Galen was dangerous for me. He made me feel different. Unlike me. He made me want to do things I've never done before.

The next person ahead of me was done, and it was my turn.

The salesgirl called me forward and I paid for my things, then headed outside. The sun was going down, and I was heading back to the pack for dinner. Everything was going to be okay.

I stopped dead in my tracks. Four men ran toward me down the street, all of them ex-pack members.

"Shit!" I raced for the car, yanked open the door, and jumped into the back seat. "Go! Those guys are coming for me."

Markus switched on the engine and threw the car into gear just as a fist bashed against my window.

"Get out of the car! Traitor!" Anthony yelled at me through the window.

I screamed, terrified he would break the glass with his next punch. "I thought Galen made a deal with you!"

"Fuck Galen!" Anthony yelled, his eyes showing a devilish hint of red.

*Oh, no. Not the demons again.*

What had Galen said? Demons made wolves extra-aggressive.

"Hold on!" Markus called as he hit the gas and we jumped into traffic, swerving to miss a car, then we zoomed out of town.

I put on my seat belt with trembling hands, then twisted around in my seat to see the four guys still running after our car.

"Whoa, that's insane," I whispered at the sight of them pumping their arms and legs and trying to catch us.

"They better not shift," Markus said, changing gears and pushing the car even faster. "First the witches, now that bloody pack. Did you see his eyes?"

I settled into my seat, relaxing now that we were further away from town. "I thought I was seeing things."

Markus shook his head. "Not if you saw that red glimmer. Bloody demons."

He growled.

My gaze strayed to Darius who stayed remarkably silent. Didn't he have an opinion on the presence of demons? Or the fact that my old pack had just tried to grab me again, despite the deal Galen had supposedly struck with them?

But he didn't say a thing.

We were only a couple of minutes from the edge of pack territory when a woman darted out on to the road in front of the truck, waving her arms.

Markus yelled out, "Holy shit! Hold on."

He slammed on the brakes, the car fishtailing and skidding on the road.

I grabbed for the safety handle and clung tight, thankful I'd put on my seat belt when we left town.

I jerked forward, then slammed back as the car came to a stop.

"Stupid bitch. What is she doing?" Markus huffed as he opened the door and jumped out.

I followed, scrabbling to grab the handle and get out without my legs collapsing under me from nerves. I wanted to know what on earth this was about.

The woman knelt on the road, her knees in the dirt. She wore patched, colorful clothing which only the witches around us wore, but from which coven she belonged, I didn't know.

"Please," she begged. "You need to help me. Take me with you."

Her face was tear-streaked, and blackened ash was evident on her clothes, like she'd been burned. Or gotten too close to a fire.

"Are you okay?" I asked, unable to stay quiet while the Betas simply stood there, gaping at her.

"No. I'm not. Please. We need help. The demons are every-where. My coven members are... hurt. They need help."

"No way." Markus shook his head. "We need to look after our own pack. And you need to go home."

"No, please..." She sobbed again, and my heart wrenched in my chest. We should help her. She didn't appear to be a threat to us.

Markus took my arm and pulled me back toward the car. "Come on, Talia. We need to get back. It's not safe here."

"But..." I stopped. I knew he was referring to my old pack members, who even now might have shifted and be racing after us. It was unfortunate for this poor woman, because if it wasn't for the fact that my pack were still hunting me, I would have stayed and fought for her right to be heard.

But Markus was correct: we needed to leave, and fast.

"Okay."

*I'm sorry*, I mouthed at the woman. She bowed her head and sobbed some more.

We climbed back into the truck and drove around the witch who was still kneeling on the ground.

I stared out the back window and watched her figure get smaller and smaller in the distance. My head spun with questions.

Was she part of the coven that had attacked the town yesterday? Maybe... but that didn't feel right.

Or was she part of the coven who'd come to ask Galen for sanctuary today?

I glanced at the front seat where Darius and Markus were sitting in silence. *Shit.* Should I say something to them about the witches who'd come to speak to Galen? Was it my place?

Probably not.

When we got back to the pack, Markus dropped me off at the Alpha's house and I bolted inside. Galen was nowhere to be seen.

"Talia, is that you?" the Alpha called out from his bed.

"It's me!" I stashed my products in my room then ran to him. "Hello, Alpha. Are you okay?"

He was sitting up in bed, but his skin was pale, and he had dark smudges under his eyes. "Yes, I'm all right. Is Galen back yet?"

My heart thumped. Galen wasn't back? I walked up to his bedside. "Didn't he come and see you earlier?"

"Yes, but only for a moment. Then he sensed something outside, shifted, and took off. I'm not sure what he sensed, but he hasn't returned."

Fear tugged at my heart. Had it been another of my ex-pack members come to get me? Or something more dangerous?

I picked up the empty jug of water next to his bed and said, "I'll let you know when he gets back. I'll get you some fresh water now, then go wait for Galen. Is there anything else you need?"

He stared at me with his assessing gaze, then shook his head. "No. I'm fine. Thank you."

I hurried to the kitchen, filled up the jug for him, then returned it to the spot next to his bed. Job done, I then ran to the front door, where I sat down on the stoop and waited for Galen to return.

I had a lot to tell him. And a lot of questions to ask.

# CHAPTER 6

# GALEN

I was talking to Dad when I sensed the demon. Even though I shifted and took off, chasing down the scent, I never found the creature that had dared to come onto my pack lands. I followed the trail all the way to our border to the east, but I didn't go any further.

With everything that had been happening lately, with the witches and also with Talia, it wasn't worth being away too long. So, I turned around and headed home again.

I wanted to check on Dad and see if Talia was back yet. Stupid demons were making everything worse. We already had the issue of the pack wars but add in crazy witches and demons trying to attract Talia for reasons I couldn't fathom, and my temper was bubbling through the roof.

I wanted to rip those demons apart.

I slowed my gallop once I neared home. Some of my people turned to me, smiling and waving as I trotted past. They probably assumed I'd just wanted to let off some steam with a run.

I needed a shower and something to eat.

I needed a woman too, but that wasn't happening anytime soon.

In fact, I didn't remember the last time I'd sated those urges within myself. Too long.

Talia was sitting on the front doorstep as she often did, waiting for me.

I shifted back to my human state as I reached the foot of the stairs. My heart pounded in my chest, not from the run or from the remnants of anger still pulsing through me, but from the desire I felt for her, and the lust mirrored in her eyes when she stared with a hungry look back at my naked body.

I lifted my chin, daring her without words to look her fill. As a wolf shifter, I was comfortable with my body and used to being naked around my pack. Talia should have been too, being a shifter herself. But there was a naïveté to her manner that was unusual in our pack.

Talia didn't look at me like she'd seen a hundred men naked before. With her, it was totally different. She made me feel something I'd never felt. Not even with Jessie.

I clenched my jaw at the single thought about my old girl-friend and forced my body not to react to Talia the way it wanted to.

Too late.

Heat and blood pulsed through me. There was no stopping the way my cock swelled in reaction to her.

I pretended to ignore my hard-on and jogged up the steps to push past her. "I need a shower. Give me five minutes and I'll be out to talk."

I rushed down the hall and shut the bathroom door behind me. I glared down at my swollen cock and growled. "You need to get your mind out of the gutter and on to the problem."

Cold water blasted out of the shower head and doused my overheated body.

I scrubbed my skin with the washcloth and soap. When I couldn't take the needling coldness any longer, I got out of the shower, dried myself, and put on a clean pair of jeans, sneakers, and a t-shirt.

When I finally felt a little more in control, of both my wolf and my human side, I walked into the kitchen where Talia was waiting with a plate of toasted sandwiches.

"I thought you might be hungry." She pushed the plate forward.

My stomach growled. Hell yes, I was hungry. I'd totally forgotten about dinner after the incident with the demon.

"Thanks." I sat down on the kitchen stool with relief, loving the way the yellow cheese oozed out onto the plate between the nicely toasted pieces of buttered bread.

I picked up the sandwich from the top of the pile and bit into it. I moaned as the greasy meal satisfied at least one kind of hunger that had been building inside of me.

I ate one, then the next, then set about devouring a third. When I finally finished, and licked my fingers clean, Talia came around and sat on the stool next to me.

"Your dad said you sensed something and went out to look for it?"

Her tone was questioning, politely asking for an answer.

"It was a demon," I said. "I scented it hanging around here. Which I don't really understand as we've never had a demon on our pack land before. At least, not to my knowledge."

I reached for the glass of water Talia put in front of me. "But with all the trouble they're causing at the moment, I guess I shouldn't be surprised. I mean, why stop with the witches?"

"I agree. I don't think they've stopped with just tormenting the witches."

My brows rose and I turned on the stool so I could face her properly. "What do you mean?"

"Well, some of my old pack members tried to attack me at the drug store earlier."

A growl rolled through my chest. After everything I had done to ensure at least a few years of peace? *Those assholes.*

"They fucking *what*? Are you okay?"

She nodded. "Yeah, I'm fine. Markus did a good job of driving the getaway car."

My gaze flew over her pale face, her thin neck, all the way to her hands. She seemed untouched but even so, anger swelled inside of me.

"Those bastards. We made a deal. I beat their Alpha. I let him live. They never should have been anywhere near you."

What was I going to do about this now? I'd tried everything I knew to keep Talia safe, and now the packs were going to be at war. Again.

I should have killed that bastard Alpha of theirs.

I looked at Talia and reached for her, unable to keep my hands to myself. I cupped her cheek and stared at her beautiful face, those dark eyes staring up at me with all the trust I could ever hope for in a woman.

"I'm so sorry," I said. "I never should have left you alone."

"I wasn't alone. I was with Markus and Darius. And it wasn't your fault." She narrowed her eyes at me. "You've done more for me than anyone has ever done, and I don't think it's entirely Maddox's pack's fault either."

I dropped my hand away from her face. "What do you mean?"

"They had a red glow in their eyes..."

I cursed again. "That does sound like a demon's touch."

"Exactly. But why? What do they want?" Talia asked. "And why now?"

I shook my head, unable to answer. I crossed my arms over my chest and grunted. I had no idea what the demons wanted, but I didn't want to stick around and just wait to find out.

"There's one other thing you should know." Talia bit her lip.

I narrowed my eyes at her. "Yeah? Tell me."

"We met a witch on the road. Actually, we almost ran her over."

"You what?"

Since when did witches lie down in the middle of our roads? They knew where all the pack borders were and mostly stayed clear of us.

"She begged us for help. Wanted us to take her home with us." Talia swallowed hard, her throat working with emotion. "I wanted to help her, but... I'm really worried about the witches, Galen. They're not safe. We need to help."

I groaned and thrust my fingers through my hair, pushing the wetness left over from the shower out of my eyes. "Talia, you know that's not a good idea."

"Then why didn't you tell those witches today that you couldn't take them in?"

I looked away, slightly annoyed at the reminder, and the knowledge that she could read me so well. "Because you never say no to a witch, not directly, and not without thinking about it first."

"That's not the reason," she said quietly.

I sighed. "You're right. I don't want to say no to them. I want to help. Just like you do. But my pack is not going to like it. Especially not after what happened in town yesterday."

The fight with the witches had left several of our pack wolves hurt, and most of them angry and wanting revenge.

"The witch today was from a different coven. I'm sure of it," she insisted. "And you're the Alpha while your father is unwell, Galen. You get to decide. Make the others understand."

I stared at her, loving the sudden fierceness in her face. "Why do you want to help the witches so much, Talia? You don't owe them anything. In fact, you took part in the fight yesterday to protect the humans. And me."

I still couldn't believe she'd stepped in to save me from that crazy witch. Sweet Talia. She looked so soft and fragile, beautiful like a rose. But she had a keen mind, and from what I'd now seen, the inner strength to step in and fight when she was needed. A courageous heart was a great asset in a pack member—and mate.

"We're all in the same boat," she said. "All fighting against the demons, and those witches need our help. I can't imagine turning away someone who truly needed help when I might be in a position to offer it."

I groaned as I stood up off my seat, then stretched my back. "I need to call a pack meeting. See what everyone has to say, because despite the pack hierarchy, and my ability to make decisions on behalf of them all, I still want to hear what everyone thinks."

Talia grinned as she got to her feet and stood before me. "Sounds like a great plan. Should we go now?"

I nodded. "Why not?"

A lot of the women would be putting their kids to bed, but I could rally up my Betas and get at least some others from the pack to attend.

I stuck my head in to check on my dad, who was sleeping soundly, then rallied the troops. Within five minutes, I was standing on the small stage at one end of the town hall, surrounded by five of my men, and looking out on the rest of our pack as members trailed in. It wasn't everyone, but there were enough here that I could get a sense of where people's heads were at.

When everyone was seated, I held up my hand to quiet the buzz, then began to speak.

My first announcement was met with surprise, and then anger. "A coven of witches approached me in the bar today, and I'm considering offering them the refuge they asked for.

"You wanna do… *what*?" Markus asked, his mouth tight and anger flaring in his eyes.

I crossed my arms over my chest, looking down at the other pack members. The same disbelief and anger filled their gazes.

Talia sat in the front row of seats and the heat of her gaze warmed my face.

"You heard me."

"But… why would we do that?" David asked.

I sighed. Why did I need to explain this to them? Couldn't they see that we were in a war?

"Because we need allies in this. There's a war on, whether you want to admit it or not. The demons are here for a reason, and I don't think it's just to cause havoc. They want something. So, until we work out what they're here for, we need to be in as strong a position as possible."

"Aligning with the witches won't make you stronger," Darius said, crossing his arms across his chest. "Look what happened yesterday."

I frowned at the man who'd been an outsider only a week ago. "The witches have powers we don't have. And they've always been good to have on side. I use them to keep my bar safe, and they put up wards around the cabin that kept Talia locked up as well."

All eyes slid to Talia sitting in the front row of seats.

I didn't look at her to see how she was handling their stares. Her face was probably as red as her hair.

Instead, I drew everyone's attention back to me. "Listen, guys. We need to work together on this."

"We?" Darius demanded. "Who's we?"

"My pack," I said, glaring at him, before looking at all the pack members who'd assembled in the hall.

They were observing my discussion with my Betas with interest, and from the collective look of trust in their eyes, would abide by any decision I deemed the right one.

"We need to consider this option, then *I* need to decide what's best for the group as a whole."

"No disrespect, Galen, but you know this is all Talia's fault," Tommy said, gesturing to her.

My eyebrows flew up. "Excuse me?"

"He's right," Theo said. "None of this would have happened if you'd let Talia go. Instead, you grabbed her, and kept her, even when it was obvious that she was going to be more trouble than she was worth."

*Never. I'd never say that.*

"None of this is her fault." I growled at my guys. "Not the fact that her old pack kicked her out, or the demons causing havoc in town. These are separate issues."

"Galen, he has a point," Markus said quietly.

"You're wrong," Theo said, glaring at me.

They weren't going to stop and the anger in me was building. They were wrong about Talia and pointing their fingers at the victim in all this was making me even madder.

"No!" I all but roared at them. "Talia is not up for discussion here. She is my responsibility and all of you will keep your goddamn mouths shut."

The guys took a step back. Talia's hand crept up to her throat as she stared at me.

I panted hard, my breath heaving in and out of my chest.

"Enough." I growled again. "Now, I don't know how many families, children, or women are in this witch coven, but if I offer them sanctuary, and I said *if*, they will need housing, land, and food."

Theo groaned. "Fuck. We don't exactly have a lot of extra anything, Galen."

"I know. But we have land, and they have magic. So, let's see what they offer when I speak to them again, okay?"

The guys grumbled around me, and I tried to calm my wolf down. I didn't mind the fact that my guys didn't agree with me. In fact, I welcomed the challenge. But throwing their hatred at Talia while we were discussing the witches wasn't fair.

"Talia and I will go back to the bar tomorrow, and I'll talk to the coven some more. But just in case I decide to offer them sanctuary, and that's a big *if*, I know how you all feel and will take it on board."

They all nodded, seemingly okay with my response.

I continued. "But I need more information from our pack too. So can you guys, Markus and David, go and speak with any of the other bachelors, see if they have spare rooms, see if you can shuffle some of the people around to make some space?"

Markus groaned. "Okay. Will do."

I glanced at my watch. It was dark now. Time for bed.

"Everyone." I addressed the group as a whole. "Head home. I'll run the perimeter tonight. You all get some sleep."

As the crowd filed out, Talia's voice piped up.

"You can't do that all night," she said, her first words since stepping into the meeting hall. "You're still injured."

I wanted to roll my eyes. "I'm fine."

I hadn't had a woman looking over me for years, and it felt... strange. But not unwelcome.

"She's right," David said. "I saw you limping home after your fight with the Northwood pack. You all right?"

All eyes turned to me with a more critical air.

I put up my hands. "I'm fine. A few scratches, but Talia sewed up my leg and my back will heal. No problem."

"I'll do the first half of the night, if someone can cover me after three a.m.," David said, ignoring me and glancing around the remaining group.

Theo put up his hand. "Me and Billy will take over at three. Have you got someone to double up with you?"

David nodded. "My brother will run with me."

I risked a glance at Talia, pride blossoming in my chest at the way my Betas rallied to support not only me, but each other.

"Thanks, guys."

I took Talia's elbow, and we walked home. Together.

# TALIA

I was shivering, and I couldn't stop. Galen and I had walked back to the Alpha's house, and he was setting up to sleep on the couch while I was sitting on my bed shaking like a leaf.

I glanced toward the ensuite bathroom. Maybe a hot shower would help?

I pushed myself to my feet and moved into the tiled room. I flicked on the water, my teeth chattering so hard they were clacking in my mouth.

Steam began to rise, fogging up the mirror. I was freezing, damn it. What was wrong with me? I pulled off my clothes and dropped them to the floor, and hopped under the water.

"Ahh..."

Heat enfolded me, beating down on my shoulders and back. I shivered again, but when I turned and let the hot water flow over my face and down my chest, the shaking finally began to subside.

Why had the Betas all blamed me for the recent stuff that had happened to them? I hadn't caused the initial attack to the pack, or my father's death, or Galen kidnapping me, either.

I'd been playing with the cards I'd been dealt the best I could but feeling their anger toward me was... hard.

I hadn't wanted any of this to happen and if my world hadn't been horrifically turned upside down, I would be married to Maddox now, living in the small house he'd built for us and dreaming of a future filled with children.

I would never have met Galen.

Sadness tugged at me at the thought, the feeling dragging me down, closer to the darkness of despair. I'd done a good job recently of pushing away the emotions that surrounded me about my father's murder, and my mate's rejection.

But now, I couldn't seem to stop the sudden need to lie down and not get up again.

I turned off the water, dried myself quickly, then staggered back to the bed. I managed to pull on some panties and a tank top to sleep in before there was a knock at my door.

"Talia?" Galen called through the closed door.

"Yeah?" My pillows were so close. I needed to just climb in between the covers, and then I could finally sleep.

*What a day.*

"Can I come in?"

I sighed. It was his room, and his house. What was I going to say? No?

"Okay."

The door opened and Galen snuck in quietly, then shut the door behind him.

He was wearing a loose pair of running pants and a cut away black tank that showed every inch of his muscled arms. "I wanted to check on you and see if you were okay."

I nodded at him from where I sat on the bed. "I'm fine."

"You don't look fine. You look upset, actually."

I shrugged and stared at the carpet before me, feeling numb. "I just wanna go to sleep."

Galen walked closer, then sat on the bed next to me. "I'm here if you wanna talk."

I closed my eyes, afraid I'd cry again. The man next to me had seen enough of my tears for a lifetime. "I don't. I just need sleep."

Galen stood and moved to the top of the bed. "Okay, then. Climb in."

He held back the blankets for me. I didn't stop to think about how sweet and caring the gesture was; I simply crawled up the mattress and slid between the covers.

When I lay my head on the pillow and closed my eyes, I could still feel his presence in the room.

I glanced up and saw him staring down at me. "Are you going to stay?"

He shook his head, but then knelt down beside the bed and used a gentle touch to push the hair off my forehead and stroke my head. "None of this is your fault, Talia."

I sniffed, still intent on never crying in front of Galen again. "I know."

"No matter what anyone says. My pack, yours. Maddox, or the Alpha. None of them are right. You're a victim in all of this."

My heart ached to hear him say everything I needed to hear. To know that he understood how I felt made all the difference.

"Thank you," I managed to whisper, before I shut my eyes again.

I couldn't do any more tonight. It had been such an intense day. Between Galen's fight this morning, to the meeting tonight, I felt stretched too thin. Hollow in places I'd once been full.

Galen pressed his lips to my temple and said, "If you need me, I'm only a room away. Okay?"

I nodded, and he quietly left.

That night I dreamt about being pregnant, though I never saw the baby, nor the man who'd given it to me.

I knew it wasn't Maddox's. Somehow, I knew it was Galen's.

*Galen*

The next morning, I got up early, grabbed a banana, and went out to meet my guys who'd been on guard duty all night. I needed a distraction, and preferably some good news.

I still didn't know what I was going to do about the witches who'd asked to move onto pack land. My job as acting Alpha in my father's stead was to keep my pack safe, but if I chose to take in the witches, I could be putting everyone in danger—witches and shifters alike.

Darius was against it; that was obvious. And so were most of my Betas and other pack members. Not Talia. She thought as I did —that the witches needed our help, and we should give it if we could.

For me, witches had always been great allies in a fight. They could be valuable when it came to the final fight, which there always was in wars like this.

The witches had already shown their weakness to the demons' influence, but that didn't mean they couldn't help to strengthen our numbers.

I still needed to think about it.

Once I'd checked in with my guys and learned nothing had come up overnight that worried me, I went home.

Talia seemed to still be asleep, her door shut, which was unusual for her. She was generally up at the crack of dawn, but yesterday seemed to have broken her somewhat. We all had our limits and she'd gone through a lot lately.

So, instead of checking on her, I snuck into my dad's room, where he was already sitting up and drinking water.

"Morning, Dad."

"Hey, son. How are you this morning?"

He was pale, and looked thinner than he had yesterday, but his mood was happy.

I smiled as I sat down on the chair next to his bed. "Needing some of your advice, if that's okay?"

"Always," Dad said, shifting on the bed so that he could sit higher. "What's wrong?"

I leaned back in the chair and sighed. "It's the witches."

"What about them?"

"Did Talia, or anyone else, tell you about what happened in town the other day?"

Dad nodded. "Tony came by and gave me a run down."

Tony was Markus's father, and one of my dad's oldest friends.

"Well, yesterday, another coven came by the bar and asked me if I'd let them move on to our pack grounds."

My dad's eyebrows rose high on his forehead, but he didn't say anything, so I continued.

"Sanctuary, they called it." I huffed out a laugh. "I don't know what to do. The demons are a real threat to the witches, and our pack. So, would I be endangering our people if I moved them in, or would their magic give us protection? I'm not sure which way to go."

Or what was going to be needed in what I felt was an inevitable fight.

Dad leaned back against his pillows. "What do you want to do?"

That was an easy answer. "Me? I want to help them."

They needed my help, and I'd always struggled to turn anyone away who was actually in need.

The strong were there to help the weak; that was the purpose of men like me.

"Then perhaps that is the answer," my father said.

I groaned. "That's not giving me advice, Dad. The pack doesn't want the witches here. In fact, some of my Betas are blaming Talia for everything bad that's happened. It's a mess."

My dad grinned, his bright white teeth flashing in the dim light of the room. "You're a good man, Galen. You're a great leader for our people."

My heart squeezed hard in my chest. I wasn't ready to lose my dad, not yet. "Tell me what to do, Dad. You're still our Alpha."

"Do what your gut tells you to do," he said. "Even if it means going against your pack, or your Betas. You're the Alpha for a reason, and your instincts won't let you down."

I clenched my jaw a little too tight, then asked, "What about Talia?"

"What about her?"

"Should I let her go? Drive her to the border and let her get to safety?"

The very idea of never seeing her again hurt on a level I didn't want to admit.

Dad shook his head. "No. It's way past that point now. You need to keep her safe, and safe for Talia at the moment is with you."

Relief winged through my chest at his words. I'd hoped that was the case, but even I knew I was blinded by my feelings for her. "You think so?"

My dad nodded. "I do. I know you've been alone since Jessie passed..."

"Dad..."

"We never really talked about it, Galen, but..."

I got to my feet. I didn't want to discuss what had happened to the woman I'd loved. "It's okay, Dad. It was a long time ago."

"Galen."

I walked to the door and opened it. "Thanks for the chat, Dad."

An awkward silence stretched between us.

Talia's bedroom door opened, and she walked out into the hallway, fully dressed in jeans and a yellow t-shirt the color of sunshine. "Morning."

My heart did a little dance at the sight of her face. "Good morning. How'd you sleep?"

"Like the dead," she said with a smile, slipping past me and walking into Dad's room. "Good morning, Alpha. Can I make you some eggs for breakfast?"

Dad perked up, the light of happiness flickering in his eyes. "Yes, please."

"Scrambled?" She walked over to his windows and opened the curtains.

"Yes. Just two."

"I know, Alpha." Talia smiled, then walked over to me. "Would you like some breakfast, as well?"

I nodded, enjoying the fact that she was looking after my father so well, even though my wolf was a touch jealous at being second priority in her mind. "Please."

Talia headed to the kitchen, and I watched her leave.

I was already protecting Talia from the very real threat of her old pack, and the demons that seemed more than a little interested in her. Could I afford to split our defences and take in the witches as well? My heart said yes, though the worry that came with it was a heavy burden.

I nodded at my dad as a way of saying thanks and goodbye, then followed Talia into the kitchen. "After breakfast, we'll head into town and speak to the witches, okay?"

Talia lifted her gaze from the egg cracking she'd been doing and met my gaze. "Okay."

She stared at me, as though she was considering her next words, but then she bent her head to the task and continued making breakfast.

I took five minutes to have a quick shower, check on my

injuries that were healing nicely, and dress into a shirt and a pair of jeans.

I had a meeting with a coven, after all.

Thanks to Talia, we ate a hearty breakfast before driving into town.

"Do you know what you're going to tell them?" she asked, when we were about halfway to the bar.

"Yeah, I do."

"Good," Talia said with a nod and a smile, and I couldn't help but laugh.

Did she read minds, too?

# CHAPTER 8
# TALIA

I'd just gotten around to pouring some waters for Galen and myself when the witches burst in the front door of the bar as if they couldn't contain their eagerness.

There were more of them today—by my count about nine of them—but the same woman with long dark hair was at their lead.

"Good day." She bowed her head at Galen, her expression grave.

The redhead from yesterday stared at me, and I wasn't sure why. She was assessing me intently, that was for sure. And she didn't seem happy with what she found in her assessment, either, though I couldn't pinpoint how I knew that. Maybe a slight tightening of the skin around her eyes and the way her lips pursed as she finally turned away.

Did she want Galen for herself or one of her friends? Was she thinking I was a threat to him partnering up with one of the witches? Because I wasn't. Sure, we'd kissed a little, but nothing was certain between us.

"Hello. I didn't get your names yesterday." Galen stepped close to the leader, gesturing for the group to come further in and take a seat wherever they could.

The dark-haired leader pointed to her chest. "I'm Marguerite, and this is Telly." She indicated the redhead, standing to her left. "And Sarah." She pointed to her right.

My gaze was drawn to Sarah. She had long blonde hair and bright blue eyes. She looked about my age, and seemed as terrified as I'd likely feel, walking into an Alpha's place of business and demanding refuge.

"You all know me. I'm Galen. This is Talia." He indicated me, but the witches barely spared me a glance. Except the redhead, who looked in an uncomfortably intense way.

"Have you decided on our fate?" Marguerite asked.

I wanted to roll my eyes at the dramatic words, but declined the childish move. Giving him the weight of their coven's 'fate' seemed a little heavy to me. It wasn't up to Galen to save them, or protect them if he didn't want to, for that matter.

"Yes," Galen answered calmly. He was more mature than me, clearly. "You are all free to come and stay on my pack lands. I will grant you sanctuary while the demons are still a threat to us all."

Relief rippled through the room.

"Thank you," Marguerite said, holding her hands together in a prayer-type of position and bowing her head over her fingers.

"We do have to discuss the particulars, of course. Timing, and how many of you there are. What we do about housing, food, that kind of thing," Galen added.

Marguerite exchanged glances with Telly, to her left, before answering. "There are only the nine of us. We are a small coven. All unmarried. No children. The witches you see here are our whole group."

Galen glanced back at me, and I nodded, but didn't speak.

That certainly made it easier on the pack, assuming these women would all pitch in and help.

He crossed his arms over his chest. "When do you want to move in?"

Marguerite smiled, the first time I'd seen that look on her face, and it transformed her from serious to attractive. She looked much younger when she smiled. "Would now be too soon?"

Galen laughed and the sound ricocheted around the room. The tension in the air began to dissipate as the witches responded to his friendly signals.

"Well, yes. Give my pack and me a few hours to get the place ready for your arrival. But if you'd like to meet at the territory border around seven this evening, we'll escort you in and arrange everything then."

Marguerite inclined her head, serious once again and as regal as a queen. "Thank you, Alpha. We will all see you at seven."

The nine of them swept out of the room in a flurry of black clothes and flowing hair.

I exhaled the breath I hadn't realized I'd been holding. "Why do I feel like they're gonna be trouble?"

Galen twirled to look at me, his eyebrows shooting sky high. "Don't say that. You were totally *for* the plan to move them in. I can't have you changing your mind now."

The vehemence in his tone surprised me. Why would my single opinion sway a man like him?

I slid off the bar stool where I had been perched with my glass of water. "Oh, I haven't changed my mind. It's just that nine women who don't usually share their space with men, or children, or... anyone non-magical, are about to move in with the pack. They might cause a little more trouble than I first thought."

I chewed on my lip, worrying the flesh. "But I still think you're doing the right thing bringing them in."

Galen nodded, though his brow was furrowed.

"What's wrong?" I asked, though I was pretty sure I knew what was worrying him. "It's a lot, isn't it? You're protecting me, your pack, and now a whole coven of witches. Female witches who you didn't even know at all before yesterday."

He stared at me, his eyes wide and his wolf burning deep within.

I took a couple of steps closer to him. "You're not even Alpha yet, and you're doing fantastic things, Galen. For your own people, for others, and for me."

I was within touching distance of him now and couldn't stop the desire to reach out and close the gap.

So I did. I took his fingers in mine, tangling them together so that it felt as if our pulses beat as one. I stood like that for a long moment, staring at the ground and loving the feel of his skin against mine. His pulse raced in tandem with mine. Then he tugged me closer still, and I pressed my hands against his chest, his heart thudding beneath my palms.

"Talia," Galen whispered.

I shivered. He had the sexiest voice. I dragged my gaze up and my eyes clashed with his. He wasn't moving, wasn't trying to kiss me, and yet the pull toward him was intense. I was dying to kiss him.

I went up on my toes and closed the distance between our lips, pressing my mouth against his and moaning at the perfection of how it felt when he kissed me back.

Galen's hands slid around my waist, holding me against him.

I parted my lips and welcomed the feel and the taste of his tongue into my mouth.

He kissed me deeply and for so long, I began to get dizzy from a lack of air. But he didn't try and move anything further, and eventually he released my mouth. Both of us panted.

When I finally lifted my head, my eyelids were heavy and I felt partially drugged. "Do we need to leave soon?"

He groaned.

"Unfortunately." He pressed his forehead against mine and sighed. "I'd love to take you upstairs and explore that beautiful body of yours, but we need to get back and warn the pack that nine witches are incoming."

I giggled at the picture he created with his description. "Yeah, I don't think Markus, or Darius, are going to be too pleased to hear that."

Galen chuckled and pulled back from me, as if he didn't want to let go. "You're right. But it's not up to them."

The Alpha was back. I wrapped my arms around my body to stave off the sense of cold left by his withdrawal. I'd been through so much the last few weeks. It had been so nice to be warm and safe and wrapped in Galen's arms. I had forgotten for a few minutes that we had a lot of responsibilities to face. "Anything you need me to get before we go?" I asked him. He shook his head. "Not at all."

He held out his arm and we headed out the door and into the truck. We drove home in relative silence, both of us absorbed in our own thoughts.

When we got back to the pack, I went to help Galen's father at his home while Galen headed off to prepare the rest of the pack for the imminent arrival of the witches.

Eight hours later, they arrived. All nine of them carried several bags each, and were laden with boxes of potions and crystals. They looked like some sort of strange, walking apothecary.

Galen strode up the main road to greet them, but I hung back. I wasn't sure what my role should be, here, and whether I should try to help, or not. This wasn't my pack, after all.

"Talia."

The summons came from above. I turned and craned my neck. The voice had come from the open bedroom window of Galen's father.

"Would you come here, please?"

I ran to the house and entered the Alpha's bedroom.

"Is everything all right, Alpha? What can I get you?"

It turned out he was simply a little hungry, so I made him a light dinner and then, after he'd eaten, I turned on the shower for him. The Alpha hadn't gotten out of bed in a week so, although I was surprised he had the strength to wash, I understood the need.

I put one of the kitchen stools in the shower for him and changed the dirty sheets and bedding while the water ran. Then I rushed back and hung around outside the door in case he needed me. But he managed a rather long shower, dressed himself inside the bathroom, then staggered out again.

I slid under his arm and used my body to help him back to his bed.

He'd even had a shave and looked twenty years younger.

"Oof..." I hefted him onto the bed just as the door opened.

I glanced over my shoulder and couldn't help but giggle at the shocked look on Galen's face. You'd think he'd caught me in bed with his father, naked.

"Everything okay?" I asked him as I pulled back the fresh blankets and lifted his father's legs up and onto the bed.

The Alpha groaned as though in pain, and Galen seemed to snap out of his trance and rush forward. "Do you need help?"

"I think we're okay," I said, then glanced up at the Alpha's pale face. "You pushed yourself a bit much just then."

The Alpha relaxed back against the pillows. "Ah... yeah."

The pain in his expression was intense and I frowned. "Galen, can you stay with your dad? I'm going to get something."

I raced out to the kitchen, and grabbed a glass of milk and

some pain killers. I knew he didn't like to take them, but some-times a reprieve from the body was a good thing.

When I rushed back into the room, I handed him the tablets and the glass of milk, and he swallowed them down without complaint. That alone was testament to the amount of pain he was really in, and a wave of worry washed over me.

"I'll let you sleep," I said, grabbing up the dirty sheets and blankets and balling them in my arms.

I glanced at Galen, silently letting him know his dad really needed rest, then walked out the door.

Galen didn't follow me, and I heard him and his father talking quietly. So, I put on the load of washing, adding extra detergent as the sheets didn't look like they'd been washed in weeks. Longer, even.

By the time I came back to the kitchen, Galen was walking out of his father's room, shutting the door behind him.

"He needs sleep," Galen said, and I nodded. Then he followed me into the kitchen and sat down on the stool.

He blew out a long breath and ran his hand through his hair.

"You okay?" I asked gently.

He met my gaze. "Yeah, I'm okay."

"Then what's troubling you?"

He huffed out a laugh. "The witches. They're already turning things upside down and they've only been here an hour."

"In what way?"

"They don't like the houses we've made available to them. They don't want to share rooms. They wanted dinner, but didn't bring anything with them to cook."

I shook my head. "Sounds like they need a bit of a wake-up call."

They were refugees of a sort. They should be grateful for whatever they were being offered by the pack. I knew I was.

"Maybe some of them could be put in the little cabin where I was, initially?" I suggested. "At least they'd be further away from the main pack."

Galen grinned at me. "I did think of that, and sent four of them out there. There's two bedrooms. They can share."

They certainly could. Or they could magic up some more space.

Come to think of it, they could probably magic up their own dinner if they were that hungry.

"So, what are you going to do?"

Galen got to his feet, pushing up on his arms from the counter. "Tonight? I'm going to bed. It's too late to worry about what I've done now. I've put myself on night shift, so if you hear me sneak out about three a.m., I'm just running with my pack members. Thanks to the witches being here too, I've increased our night-time guard to three men per shift."

I crossed my arms over my chest. "That's gonna stretch you a bit thin. I'd be happy to do some of the running. Are there any other females like me that would help too?"

"Like you?" Galen asked, tilting his head to the side.

"Yeah. Unmated, or at least, no kids. Happy to help."

Galen nodded slowly. "There are, actually. That would help us. Thanks for the advice."

He headed off for a shower and I decided to make a quick batch of raspberry drop cookies, nervous energy still buzzing through my system.

While he was settling into his bed on the couch, I placed a couple of cookies on a plate next to him, with the rest cooling in the kitchen. "See you in the morning."

He stared at me, our gazes locked together. So many unsaid things burned in his eyes and sat heavily between us. Yet, I knew it wasn't the right time to explore any of it. Not yet.

"Good night." I went to my room, showered, and crawled into bed, my body tired but my mind still alive and racing.

Maybe I'd get up with Galen when he left at three a.m. and learn the route they ran around the property. That could be fun.

I closed my eyes and resolved to listen for the moment he left, but the next time I opened my eyes, sunshine streamed in the windows. I'd slept right through to morning.

"Damn. Gonna have to set an alarm for that, in future."

# CHAPTER 9

# GALEN

"No, Telly, you may not ask a family with three small children to leave the house they built with their own bare hands." I glared down at the redheaded witch who'd had the audacity to ask me to move another family out of their house, because she and her coven sisters 'needed more space'.

Telly glared right back, a strange silver mist floating in her eyes. "Galen, how do you expect us to live like this?"

She gestured around the house to which she'd been assigned. It had been a beautiful home, and yet in the space of a single day, the witches had turned it into what my mother would term, 'a brothel'.

There were clothes and bras and things I couldn't even identify, thrown everywhere. Herbs hung in bunches from the windows, while crystals littered every spare surface.

I crossed my arms over my chest. "I expect you to be grateful for the roof over your head. And if you're not, then I can recommend approaching the Northwood pack next door."

I tilted my head in the direction of Talia's old pack. The

witches would be killed on sight if they entered Northwood pack territory, and Telly and I both knew it.

She slammed her lips shut, but there was an angry fire burning in her gaze that made me think this conversation was by no means finished.

Just as I opened my mouth to suggest they clean up the place, the front door to the house swung open and the coven leader, Marguerite, sauntered in.

"Galen, I've set new wards in place for the perimeter of your pack grounds, and had Markus show me where your father's house is."

I turned toward her, my anger at Telly's attitude dissipating at the mention of my dad. "You met the Alpha?"

She shook her head. "Not yet. I simply lay down my strongest ward over and around his house, so that Talia and the Alpha will be the safest if a fight eventuates. Of course, those wards will fall if I'm ever killed, but I believe they will hold firm until that day."

I shivered at her words as a premonition fluttered across my mind. Then it was gone, and I realized it was simply concern for Talia and my father that had sent such an image into my head.

I smiled at the witch. "Thank you for that."

"Your father is sick," Marguerite said, her words not a question. "I sensed it."

I answered her honestly, even though my inclination was to protect my father. "Yes, he is. We haven't been able to identify what's wrong with him."

She nodded, her brow furrowing deeply. "Sarah is the best of us at healing potions. Perhaps I could send her over to see if she can help?"

I inclined my head. "Any help with him would be appreciated."

Marguerite smiled at me and walked me to the door. I ignored Telly, who was still standing across the room, scowling at me.

Once outside, Marguerite took a deep breath and wrapped her shawl tighter around her body. "It's lovely out here, Galen. The ground is sacred, and your people have trust, and love for you. That is a rare thing in this world, but I know with the wolves that love runs deep and true."

Her words bolstered me in a way I couldn't describe, helping to chase away the ghosts of self-doubt that had haunted me through the days since Dad became ill and I'd had to step up.

"My father is a great Alpha."

She nodded and smiled at me. "And you will be, too. You already are."

I snorted. "You're only saying that because I let you into my pack."

The witch's eyes sparkled with a mischievous silver. "That's part of it... definitely. But there's a lot more to this battle than even I know."

I turned to face her properly. "Battle? What do you mean?"

Her smile disappeared. "My instincts are telling me that my witches and I need to put up some better protections on your pack grounds. And on your people. Something's brewing, Galen. Something unsavory, but I can't pinpoint exactly what. You've done a huge favor for us, letting us move in like this, and I feel like we should repay you in some way."

I inclined my head. "Any help you can give us would be appreciated."

This was what I'd hoped for. Support from the witches was one of the main reasons I'd agreed to their request.

I pointed toward the house behind us. "Can you make sure your women stay in line? Harassing my shifter families because your witches want a house to themselves is not... productive. Not for any of us."

It was damn selfish, and ungrateful, but I was trying to be nice so I didn't use those words.

Marguerite inclined her head. "Of course. I will have a word to my sisters."

"Thank you."

A shriek sounded from a house next door to the one we were standing in front of. I shook my head, frustration clawing through me.

Right now, I felt as if this had been a bad idea, but there was no going back now.

And if the witches could help us with strengthening wards, or perhaps even assisting Dad to beat whatever illness ailed him, then a bit of fighting over housing arrangements might be worth the angst.

Another high-pitched shriek sounded, and I rolled my eyes.

Maybe.

Darius was walking down the street toward us, so I lifted my chin and nodded. He didn't respond to my greeting. Instead, the moment he saw I was with Marguerite, he did an abrupt about-face and strode off in the opposite direction. I frowned after him but didn't follow.

Darius didn't like the witches; that had been clear from the moment I'd seen him fighting them in town. His aggression toward them was out of place, and his fear of getting physically close to any one of them was strange.

But the why was unclear. Had he had a run-in with witches in his past that he hadn't told us about? Had he been burned somehow? Or was this hatred of the coven sisters something more?

I took a step in his direction, considering whether to chase him down and ask him directly, but changed my mind as he disappeared around a bend in the road. I wanted to get back to Talia and check on Dad.

I turned away from Marguerite and the various arguments coming from the houses, and headed down the road, back toward my own house. I stopped along the way to talk to a couple of young pack members about some chores I had for them to do later in the week. When I arrived home, the blonde witch Sarah was already standing by the front door.

"Marguerite sent you?" I called out to her as I approached.

Wow. That was quick. We'd only just mentioned it, and here she was, having beaten me back here.

She bobbed her head, seeming shy. "Yes. I was hoping to speak to your father."

I jogged up the steps. "That would be great. Come in."

I opened the door and the witch walked inside my home.

Talia raced out to meet me, as she often did, and stopped abruptly. Her gaze narrowed on the young blonde.

"Talia, this is Sarah. She's good with healing, and she's here to check on Dad and see if there's anything she can suggest."

"Well, he's sleeping," Talia said with a suspicious frown.

"Could I just see him?" Sarah asked, glancing between Talia and myself.

Talia looked up at me, then nodded once when she realized I was okay with it. "I'll show you where he is. Galen, your lunch is on the counter."

The two of them headed upstairs as I sat down and ate. It was strangely comfortable handing over to Talia, and admittedly nice to relax for a few minutes while someone else did my job.

The thought of how much I already trusted Talia shocked me more than I wanted to admit. It was as if she had been in my life —in our pack—for a long time. And it felt good. Right, somehow.

Just as I was finishing up my third turkey roll, Talia and Sarah walked back into the kitchen. They both looked a lot calmer than I expected.

"You two bonded?" I asked with a grin.

Talia rolled her eyes and moved around to the other side of the counter. "Sarah was respectful of the Alpha."

I almost laughed at how protective Talia was over my dad, but then again, she'd just lost her own father and had become my dad's primary carer. It made sense. And I appreciated it, far more than I'd said.

I transferred my attention to the witch. "What can you tell me, Sarah?"

Sarah placed her purple and black tote bag down on the counter and began rummaging through it. "I have some cleansing powder in here. I doubt it will be strong enough to fix whatever's wrong with him, but it might help lessen its hold a little. It will definitely help with some of his pain."

She pulled out a little bottle with a blue liquid in it. "Give him five drops in a jug of water every day, until I can find a way to diagnose him properly. I'll come back tomorrow with more equipment, if that's all right with you?"

I nodded slowly. A correct diagnosis was vital in figuring out how to heal my dad.

"I'll take that," Talia said, holding out her hand for the bottle.

Without question, Sarah handed over the medicine. "It might taste a little tart to him, and that's okay. It's very mild, so won't do him any harm."

Talia wrapped her fingers around the bottle and held it tightly.

"Thank you," I said. "You are welcome to come back tomorrow."

Sarah smiled. "Yeah, I'd like that. Thank you."

She bobbed her head and left, leaving Talia and I alone in the room.

Talia exhaled loudly, like she was exhausted.

"You okay?" I asked her.

"Yeah. I'm just worried about everything and everyone. The pack, the witches, your dad, you. It's all just a mess at the moment, isn't it?"

I pressed my hands into the cool countertop. "Yeah, it is."

Sure felt like a mess to me.

"Tell me more about the witches," Talia said. "Are they being really painful?"

I couldn't stop the sudden laugh that bubbled up. "Oh, yeah. A right pain in the ass."

I spent the next hour telling Talia little stories about what had happened when the witches arrived last night, and what they'd gotten up to already this morning. Almost everyone the witches had come into contact with so far had had their noses put out of joint, it seemed.

By the end of the debrief, I felt the heavy weight of the world lifting off my shoulders. "Thanks for the chat," I said as I stood up, "but I need to get back to it."

Talia smiled at me and picked up the plate I'd left in front of me. "I'll be here. You can vent to me anytime. See you at dinner."

I thanked her again and left, feeling unusually happy. Despite the situation we were in, Talia made me feel content on a bone-deep level.

Markus came running up to me as soon as I exited my front door. I sighed, expecting another petty witch complaint.

"More demon attacks in town."

The shock hit me like a punch to my guts. "What the hell?" I pulled my truck keys out of my pocket. "Who did they attack?"

"I heard it was some of the humans this time. Scaring them, setting houses on fire."

"Oh, for fuck's sake." I stalked over to my truck.

Markus ran up to me and grabbed me by the arm. "They're gone now, by all accounts. There's no reason to go in."

I slid my keys back into my jean pocket. "That's good, I suppose. But what does this even mean? I don't understand what they want. Other than causing chaos and mayhem. There doesn't seem any rhyme or reason to it."

At least none of the guys could say it had anything to do with

Talia. She was safely inside my father's house, and the demons had come nowhere near us.

"I don't either, Galen. But I think you should close the bar for a couple of weeks. The guys are getting tired. Between shifts at the bar, running extra security around here at night…"

He trailed off, and I groaned.

"You're right. I'll drive in tonight and put up the signs myself."

"Thanks." Markus clapped me on the shoulder and walked away.

I hadn't closed my bar for more than a long weekend, for… well, ever. I didn't take holidays and I had a loyal team on board. This was totally unforeseen. But Markus was correct. I didn't need to be at my apartment at the moment, nor did I need the stress of work. Right now, I needed to focus on my pack, my people, the witches, my dad, and Talia, and ensure everyone under my protection remained safe.

Because only God knew what was coming for us next.

# CHAPTER 10

# TALIA

Sarah returned as promised the next day and performed some spells on the Alpha. She placed pink crystals in his room and invoked an incantation, while I watched carefully to ensure he remained safe. I had made sure he drank all his detox water the night before, and readied another jug for today.

By the time Sarah finished her spellcasting, the crystals had turned from pink to a smoky black color. She studied them closely, a worried look bringing her brows together.

"What's wrong?" I asked, the moment we stepped out of the Alpha's bedroom.

"He's sick," she said.

I stared at her. Was she crazy? "Ah, yeah. Stating the obvious, much?"

She shook her head, seeming distracted, so I directed her into the kitchen and pulled out the leftover roast chicken I'd made for dinner last night. "Are you hungry?"

"Yes, that would be great, thanks." Sarah slid onto a stool and picked up another pink crystal from her bag. "These are healing crystals. They aren't very strong, but you saw what happened to them after only an hour in the Alpha's room."

"He did that to them?" I asked, pulling out plates and grabbing some tomatoes and spinach from the fridge.

"If you mean turning the crystals black, then yeah. He's… sick," she repeated, and this time I noted her extreme concern.

I pushed a plate of chicken salad at her and picked up my fork. "You keep saying that. We know he's sick. What aren't you saying?"

Sarah bit her lip. She looked about twenty years old, which made me think it would be nice to have someone around who was my age and wasn't terrified of me.

"Come on, Sarah. Just say it."

"He's dying." She burst out with the revelation and my heart skipped a beat. "He's not just sick, he's dying, and I'm not sure why. None of the spells I cast told me anything, other than the fact that he doesn't have a lot of time left."

I sucked in a deep breath and let it out slowly. "I know. I've been feeling it, too. But I don't know what to do for him, other than try to keep his pain under control and give him as much support and care as he wants."

"I can give him more potions, pain killers, and detoxes. It might help to slow the process. But until we know what's causing him to spiral downwards, I can't do anything else."

I sighed. "Thank you for everything you've tried so far, Sarah. It is much appreciated."

We ate our chicken in silence after that, and once we were done, I quickly washed up and then went to check on the Alpha. He was fast asleep and seemed to be breathing easier than he had been earlier. Maybe the detox was helping. At least a little.

"I've gotta run a few errands," I said to Sarah. "Pick up some food for the Alpha. That kind of thing. Wanna come along for the walk?"

Her face lit up. "Sure! I'd love to get out and explore a bit more of the town."

I liked Sarah. She was good company, and as we walked around town, collecting fresh eggs, bread, and muffins, we chatted about life, and magic, and working at the restaurant in town.

I missed Kylie and the others who worked there, but it was just too dangerous to go in and see them now. I hoped they were all still okay.

"I better head back, but thanks for the chat." I clung tight to my basket of goodies with one hand, and waved goodbye to Sarah with the other. "I enjoyed your company."

She smiled shyly. "Me too." She turned away, then back again. "Would you mind if I came back tomorrow? I've had an idea and I want to try something else."

"Sure." I watched her leave, and then returned to the Alpha's house.

The Alpha called out for me the moment I stepped inside.

"Hey Talia! Could I get something to eat?"

I glanced at the clock. It was too late for lunch but too early for dinner. His sleep had thrown things out a little, but I was glad he'd felt able to rest for so long. That was surely a good sign. I hoped.

"Of course, Alpha! I'll be right in."

He rarely asked for food. I was usually the one forcing him to eat. I put together a plate of cheese, ham, tomatoes, and fresh slices of bread slathered with butter.

When I took it in to him and placed it on his lap, he was looking brighter than he ever had, to my eyes.

"You're looking well." I stared at his warmer-than-usual complexion in surprise.

"I feel well," he said, picking up a piece of ham and eating it with gusto. "Not sure what that blonde witch did, but it definitely helped."

Shock held me rigid, but I forced a smile to my face. The spells and crystals—or maybe it was the detox drops—were really working!

"Sarah wasn't sure she did anything right, but obviously she did. Alpha, I'm..." I swallowed hard. "I'm really glad to see you looking like this."

He grinned at me and proceeded to eat everything on his plate with an appetite I'd never seen on him.

I turned away to get him another glass of detox water and tried hard not to cry. I would have loved to meet Galen's father a few years ago, when he was a normal Alpha: strong and fit, running about town. For the first time, I could see traces of that man, and it brought home to me how unwell he had been, up to now.

The man I had known so far was frail and bedbound. It wasn't right.

When Galen arrived home that night, he seemed more stressed than normal.

"Hey, are you okay?" I asked, once he'd finished the pie one of the neighbors had brought by for him.

He shrugged. "Yeah. Closed down the bar indefinitely, today. First time ever. It was a bit... strange."

I felt his sadness so strongly, it was as though the emotions coursed over me in waves. "I'm so sorry. I hope it won't be for long."

He sighed and took the plate around to the sink to wash up. "Yeah, hopefully not."

"Your dad ate a large meal this afternoon. He looked much better after Sarah's visit and a long nap," I said, hoping to cheer him up.

He shot me a quick, surprised grin, and then hurried upstairs.

He returned a few minutes later. "I looked in on him, but he was sleeping. He did seem to have a bit of color in his cheeks, though, which is good."

Galen sat on the couch, seeming less stressed than when he'd first arrived home. I busied myself finishing the clearing up, and once everything was done, I sat at the opposite end of the couch to him, with the TV playing some drama. I wasn't giving any attention to it. I was too aware of Galen. Where he was, how he moved, even how he smelt. Everything about him both excited me and made me a little afraid. Of myself more than anything else. He was too much of everything. Too brave, too courageous, too hot, too sweet.

Far too Alpha for the likes of me.

I wanted to reach across the expanse of space that separated us and touch him, to feel the warmth of him against me once again. But I didn't know if I had earned that right. In the end, I kept my hands to myself.

"How was your day?" He turned toward me.

"Good. Actually, as I mentioned, Sarah was here for a while, and then she walked with me while I picked up the food orders for your dad. I like her, Galen." It was surprisingly nice to have made a new friend in this strange world in which I'd found myself.

Galen smiled at me. "That's great. I'm glad you've made friends with one of the witches. Having powerful allies is always a good idea."

I hadn't really thought about it like that. "Yeah, I guess. For me, it's just nice having someone my own age to talk to."

During the day, I rarely saw anyone but the Alpha, and he slept a lot.

"Do you wanna come closer?" Galen asked, lifting his arm and indicating I could cuddle into him, if I wanted.

Did I want? Of course, I did! I pressed my lips tight so that I didn't give myself away by squealing with excitement and scooted across the couch cushions so that I was sitting next to him.

He placed his arm around me and tucked me into his side.

I put my head down onto his shoulder and sighed as his body heat and a sense of protection enfolded me.

"You know…" he began, and I closed my eyes against the wave of pleasure that passed over me when he spoke. His voice had such a melodic effect on me.

"Yeah?" I prompted when he stopped.

"I know everything that's happened to you recently has been horrible, so I don't want this to come out the wrong way."

I tried not to laugh at the awkwardness in his tone. He was clearly trying to tell me something positive, but possibly going about it in a backwards way. Galen was thirty-ish and an Alpha wolf, yet he could be so bashful sometimes. I loved it.

"Okay. I'll try not to take it that way," I said with a grin.

"I'm glad you're here," he said in a low growl. "With me."

I sat up so I could look straight at him. I wanted him to see my sincerity. "Me too."

He cupped my face and kissed me. Softly at first, then harder, deeper, until I was pressed into his chest and gasping, needing to get closer. Desperate for more.

He pulled back and tugged on my waist. "Jump up. Straddle me."

I didn't wait to allow any embarrassment to rise. I just jumped up onto my knees and swung a leg over his hips, wanting to kiss him for as long as he'd let me.

I slid my arms around his neck and met his lips with mine, moaning at the pleasure, the rightness of this connection.

He slipped one hand beneath my t-shirt, sliding around my waist and up my back.

When he flicked open my bra, I gasped against his mouth, then pressed in deeper as his fingers fluttered across my skin.

My eyes closed again as I sunk into the pleasure his touch evoked.

His hands came around the front of me, cupping my freed breasts almost reverently, softly, his thumbs flicking over my taut nipples until heat poured through me.

I grabbed tight to his hair, wanting more.

"Galen!" the Alpha called out, and I jumped.

Galen's hands stilled, and I slid off his lap and stood in one fast move.

Galen stayed seated, his eyes smoldering with the heat of unmistakable passion. His lips were still parted and red from my kisses.

I giggled at the sight of him so obviously aroused, then covered my mouth with my hand. I probably looked exactly the same.

But at least the Alpha hadn't called for me.

Galen's lips tweaked up into a rueful grin. "Yeah, Dad. Coming!"

He got to his feet and adjusted his jeans, the bulge beneath the zipper more obvious than either of us would like his father to be aware of.

"Great timing, huh?"

I smiled softly. I was kind of enjoying all these great kissing sessions we were having. Made me want him even more.

"Should I wait up for you, or...?"

Galen glanced in the direction of his dad's room, then back at me. "I've actually got a few pack business things to discuss with him, so maybe you should head to bed."

Then his eyes lit up with a teasing light I knew well. "Do you want me to join you in there?"

I reached out and grabbed for his hand. "Think you can keep your hands to yourself?"

He chuckled. "Nope."

I didn't want to reject him, but with the advantage of a few minutes off his lap, my brain had switched back on again and I realized I wasn't ready for more yet. So I lifted his hand and kissed his fingers. "Maybe another night?"

His eyes sobered, but I could tell he understood. There was no malice or anger in his gaze.

"Definitely," he said, and I shivered at the promise in the word.

I pressed a chaste kiss to his lips, then stepped back, parts of me aching that had never ached so badly before. "Goodnight, Galen."

He growled a little, shook his head, then walked off.

I ran to my room, a hysterical laugh hovering on my lips. At least I knew for sure he wanted me, and that was an amazing thing in this new, unknown world.

Everything else was as solid as water, impossible to hold, and could just as easily slip through my fingers.

# GALEN

I tossed and turned through the night, dozing in between fits of being wide awake. *God, I wanted Talia.* But the ramifications of what that would mean, for her and for me, were too much to comprehend at this moment.

It was both a help and a hindrance that my dad liked and trusted her so much. It softened me too much knowing he thoroughly approved of the woman who'd once been destined to be a rival Alpha's mate.

I rolled over yet again, trying to resist the urge to punch my pillow in frustration. A warning howl came through my window. The sound hit me like a shot. I jumped up off the couch and ran for the front door, yanking it open. The protection wards rippled around me.

Someone gasped behind me. Talia had woken up, alerted, as my whole pack would be, to whatever danger was coming for us.

The wards rippled again. It felt like they'd been punched.

Whatever was coming was big and no doubt deadly.

"Talia! Stay here with Dad!" I yelled over my shoulder, praying she'd do as she was told, then jumped off the porch, shifting mid-air and landing with my paws on the grass.

Down the street, men ran out of their homes, and even the women were shifting too, ready to protect their children if it came to it.

Black and gray wolves fell in behind me as I raced the length of our main street. I met up with Markus, who was bleeding, his right eye damaged and his ear ripped off.

I didn't bother shifting back so we could speak properly. I had a small amount of telepathy with my wolves, especially my Betas.

More feelings than true words.

But Markus was communicating, and I tuned in hard to listen.

*Talia's old pack. We're under attack.*

I stared hard at Markus. That sounded bad, but why was there a note of fear in the air around his non-verbal communication? We had taken on the Northwood pack before and won.

I cocked my head, asking the silent question of Markus.

*It's not just them. They have vampires with them.*

Vampires? It was rare for vamps and wolves to fight together. Someone must have worked a deal, or perhaps even magic of some kind, to get the vampires on their side.

Fuck.

I growled low, then turned and vocalized my orders to my men via barking, growling, and projecting instructions into their minds. Thank God for telepathy.

*Be careful. Surround and protect the town. And know this is possibly a fight to the death. Chase off anyone who doesn't belong. Watch out for the vampires. Rip off their heads if you want them to stay down.*

We took off, circling the town and putting ourselves between the coming enemy and our home.

Maddox's pack had breached our perimeter and were already

in our forest, rows of beady yellow eyes glaring at us as they stalked forward through the brush.

I halted, waiting for them to emerge into the open space between our town and the forest edge. This was our home turf, and we had the advantage. Let them come to us.

My pack stopped too, taking the lead from me.

The enemy wolves emerged, spread out and snarled. Behind them stood several vampires—master level by the look of at least one of them. My hackles rose. I lowered my head, readying, and watched as a red haze misted over the lead vampire's eyes.

So much for the peace treaty I'd made with the Northwood pack.

There was a moment of hesitation, each side weighing up the other, and then the wolves charged. I launched myself at the nearest black wolf and landed on top of his back. I tore at his fur and flesh, ripping a hole in his shoulder, before he managed to shake me off.

Howls and grunts rose as the sounds of battle intensified around me. I had no time to consider anything, except launch, attack, evade.

My mouth filled with hot wolf blood as I bit and ripped into them. I came face to face with a huge wolf—it wasn't Maddox, but it must have been one of his Betas—and our lips lifted in a snarl before we were on each other.

He managed to claw my hind leg before I got him by the throat. I sank my teeth deep, holding on and shaking him, until the growling snarls turned to a whimper. I dropped him to the ground, hardly even noticing when he slunk away almost on his stomach.

Another one down. How many to go?

I risked a glance around. In every direction, wolves engaged in deadly combat.

Some of the younger women in my pack had shifted and were

rushing in to help. Equal parts pride and worry filled my chest. I scanned their ranks, praying Talia had obeyed my command to stay with my dad and that she hadn't shifted and decided to join the fight.

I couldn't see her among the smaller female wolves, thank God, and my heart thudded in relief. At least I knew she was still likely behind the protective wards in my dad's house. One less person to worry about.

My Betas, meanwhile, were right in the thick of it.

On my right, Tommy was engaged with one of the vampires. His lip was raised, and his vicious snarls rose above the sounds of battle as he stared down the vampire with the red gaze. I trusted Tommy in that match-up. If anyone could take out a vamp and survive, it would be Tommy.

Beyond him, David was facing off with a Northwood shifter. They were evenly matched in size and weight, but David was a master at fighting, and I sensed he would be okay.

On my left, several feet away, Markus fought two shifters at once. I started over to help him but an attack on my flank diverted my attention. I was pulled back into my own skirmish until I managed to fight yet another shifter off.

There seemed to be too many of them. Where had they all come from?

My men—and my women—were strong, but we were outnumbered in this, and many of the vampires still stood waiting, as if they intended to swoop in at the end.

My gaze clashed with the master vampire, and a haze of red filled his vision.

He wanted to kill me, badly. And with the adrenaline of battle rushing through my veins, who was I to deny him?

I leaped over the head of a snapping wolf and landed directly in front of the lead vamp. He took a tiny step back, as if he hadn't expected that from me, and then grinned.

"Ready to die, wolf?"

I didn't bother with an answer, but simply lifted my lip and showed him my teeth, before launching straight up at his scrawny pale neck.

He was lightning fast, though, dodging away from my snapping jaw, before jumping onto my back. I twirled and shook, trying to dislodge him, but he had engaged his taloned nails and hung on for grim death, no matter how hard I tried.

I dropped to the ground and rolled. That got him off me, but then he was back in my face, hissing, his fangs fully extended and red blood lust in his eyes.

"You need to die, but not before I suck you dry, wolf."

He sprang at me again, so fast he was a blur even with my shifter vision. I felt the pain of a bite on my neck. I tipped back my head and howled.

It was a howl of rage more than anything else, but not one I expected to be answered.

A blast of silver light almost blinded me, and the pain in my neck disappeared.

I turned my head to see Marguerite and Telly, with several other witches, running toward the battle ground.

Marguerite shot me a glance and nodded. It had been her stream of blast magic that had dislodged the vamp off my back.

She and Telly turned and stood, back-to-back, and began blasting streams of silver out into the battle. Other witch pairs did the same.

I had to trust that they knew what they were doing and would only harm the Northwood invaders or the vamps, and not members of my own pack.

I would thank the witches later, if we all survived. For now, the battle was still raging.

There were rogue vamps, and enemy wolves, to destroy.

## CHAPTER 12
# TALIA

The sounds of a huge battle raged outside, and my wolf clamored inside my chest to burst free. But I'd promised Galen I would stay with the Alpha.

"Talia! What's happening?" the Alpha's voice rang out.

I ran to his bedroom and sat down on the chair next to him, even though I could barely stay still. I was jumping out of my skin, but he needed me.

"We're being attacked. Galen and his Betas have gone to defend the town." I shivered as I spoke.

"Who is it?" the Alpha asked, narrowing his eyes at me.

"I don't know." I said, shaking my head. "It could be my old pack, but... I honestly don't know."

It was the truth. Strange sensations rippled over my skin, as if there was some kind of magic in the air. It may have been my old pack, but if so, they had brought more than their wolf shifters to this fight.

The Alpha threw back the covers. "I need to get out there."

"No way!" I pushed on his chest, pressing him back into the bed. He was weak enough that it was easy for me to hold him in place. "You can't do that. If something happened to you, Galen would kill me."

The Alpha glared at me. "Well, I can't just sit here and do nothing."

I pressed a hand into my temple. *Think. Think. How could I stay here and protect the Alpha, but help at the same time?*

Then I had it. "Your house has the best wards in the whole town. We should get as many people in here as we can. The older women. The children. The vulnerable ones who can't fight. You and your house can protect them, Alpha, if Galen and his men fail."

As long as the witches weren't killed, they would be safe in this house, too.

The Alpha's eyes lit up. "Go. Get them. Now."

I rushed out of his room and into the street. I looked left and right, but where did I even start? Next door!

I ran to their front door. "Norah! It's Talia. Come out. Quick."

The Alpha's neighbor opened the door, her eyes wide with fear. I could tell she already knew we were under attack. "What is it, Talia?"

"The Alpha's home has the best warded protection. The witches have surrounded his house with shields. Come. He wants everyone inside his house, now."

Norah nodded, grim determination taking over her expression. "I'll take this side of the town, you go down that way, toward the south. Knock on every door."

I nodded, and then bolted to the next house, glad to have someone else to help with the task.

Between us, Norah and I called every woman, child, and elderly or frail pack member, and soon there was a stream of people rushing toward the Alpha's house. It wasn't a huge space, but they'd fit.

When I reached the final house, where a woman named

Abigail lived with her four children, I gathered up her baby in my arms. "Go, Abigail! Go! I'm following you!"

The snarls and howls rising everywhere around us were terrifying. Some of the women had shifted into protector mode as I knocked at their doors but had shifted back when I told them the plan.

I ran for the Alpha's house with Abigail's baby in my arms. The heat of danger prickled along my spine. The tingle of menace erupted in my brain.

This wasn't just an attack by wolf shifters.

There were demons around. I could sense them.

This was very bad.

The front door was open, and I hurried up the porch, yelling at everyone gathering inside. "There's the back bedroom, too. Spread out. Get comfortable."

"You can come up here too, children." the Alpha called out down the stairs, and I exchanged a smile with a nearby woman I hadn't met. Relief filled her gaze.

"Yes," I told the little ones, all clinging to their mother's legs. "Go up and see your Alpha. He'll tell you a story. I'm going to go check on your dads."

Norah grabbed my arm. "No, Talia. Stay."

I shook my head. "I need to check on the witches, and get them here too, if I can. You all stay here. The wards are strong. Be safe. I won't be long."

I took off down the street in the direction of the witches' houses.

Someone behind me called out my name, loud and long, in a sing-song voice.

My heart sank.

I swiveled around and saw him. Maddox. He was naked, obviously having shifted back from being in his wolf form. Blood ran down his neck from some kind of small wound, but otherwise, he looked healthy and strong.

Surprisingly so. Had he not participated in the battle?

Then I did a double take. The red glimmer of a demon's influence shimmered in Maddox's eyes.

Oh, God. Maddox was mean enough, but with a demon riding him as well?

He rushed closer and I held my breath, trying to control the fear.

"You disloyal little slut." He spat at me.

My mouth dropped open. A slut? Seriously? I'd been kissed three times by Galen, after Maddox had rejected me and thrown me out of my own home.

Who was the disloyal one in *that* scenario?

"Have you opened your legs for that feral new Alpha?" He sneered. "I bet you have. Has he got between those thighs that refused to open for me?"

"Refused... You're insane." And he was. Delusional at best. He'd twisted everything good and made it into something crazy. "You're the one who wanted to wait!"

I couldn't believe I was trying to reason with him at this moment. I mentally shook my head at my own actions. Leave him, and run, I told myself. But something stayed my legs.

I'd been desperate to know what physical love felt like with Maddox. He was the one who'd never wanted to enjoy me in that way.

"Bitch." He began to growl. I could feel the ripple in the air that meant he was about to shift. He would attack me, then, for sure. Which meant I only had one option.

Despite my promise to Galen, I had to shift myself.

"You're going to die." He spoke through sharpened teeth that had already begun the shift. The red of his eyes intensified. "There's no-one around to save you now."

I pulled forth my own shifter as fast I could, my clothes tearing into shreds as my wolf leapt forward into freedom.

He leapt for me, his huge jaw crashing together in a bite that just missed my head.

He was so much bigger than me, and stronger, but I was faster. *Thank God.*

I weaved and ducked around him as he launched and bit and swiped at me with his clawed paws.

I couldn't keep this up forever, but I had no choice. It was fight or die.

I darted in, scoring a quick bite on his right hind leg. He swirled and landed a bite of his own on my front leg before I managed to dance out of reach. The snarling that erupted from his throat had an added sinister quality that I suspected came from whatever demon was influencing him.

It was terrifying, knowing I was facing down not only a crazed ex, but one who was most likely being controlled by a demon.

He lunged at me again, and I darted back. I slipped on the gravel in the road, and he was on me before I could recover.

The weight of him crushed me down onto the ground and I couldn't breathe, couldn't think beyond the terror of knowing this might be the moment I die.

I heard a crack and pain flared through me. He'd just damaged a couple of my ribs.

Then he raised his head, staring into my eyes, and the swirling red shifted, as if he wasn't quite sure what to do next. It was only for a second or two. But the pause was long enough for me to snatch at hope. I craned my neck, reaching up and ignoring the pain of my broken ribs, and snapped my jaws shut on his throat.

He yelped and jumped off me. I hung on tight, coming with him and hanging off his neck as he stood and tried to shake me off.

His hot blood filled my mouth, trickling down my throat and

threatening to choke me, but still I refused to let go.

I had to hold on, or he'd kill me.

An almighty shake from his broad frame dislodged me, and I flew through the air to land on a patch of grass.

The breath was completely knocked out of me, and so much pain rushed in that I thought I might lose consciousness.

His throat was ripped badly, and he gave me a shocked look, before turning and loping away into the shadows, leaving a trail of blood in his wake.

I lay on my side and struggled to draw in shallow breaths, unable to believe that I somehow had just bested my ex, the Alpha's son of the Northwood pack.

And with a demon host on board, as well.

The urge to find Galen and make sure he was safe almost overwhelmed me.

I let the shift fade, rippling away until I lay in my human form, shivering on the ground and trying not to pass out.

Somehow, I struggled to my feet, my arms wrapped around my aching middle, and began to stagger back toward the Alpha's house.

I needed clothes, and then I needed to go find Galen.

Abigail, the shifter whose baby I'd carried earlier, rushed out into the street to meet me. She was carrying a set of clothes, which she helped me into because I was beyond trying to dress myself.

"Oh my God, Talia," she said. "I thought you were going to die. Come back to the house and let us help you."

"Thank you," I whispered. "But I have to find Galen, wherever he is."

Was he even still alive?

What the heck was going on lately?

Had everyone and everything in this world been driven mad by an influx of demons?

# CHAPTER 13
# TALIA

I staggered around a bend in the road and found Sarah tending to one of Galen's Betas, Tommy. He was sitting on the street, and by the look of the blood pooled around him, had been injured quite badly.

"What can I do to help?" I asked Sarah as I wobbled up to them.

My legs felt like Jell-O, but at least they still worked. Sort of.

"You can help me lift... oh my God, Talia!" Sarah stared at me. "What happened to you?"

I shrugged off her concern. "I'm okay. Just got into a fight with an ex."

"Maddox?" Tommy's voice was a croak as he piped up from his position on the ground. "I hope you killed the bastard."

Worry coursed through me as I saw how much blood soaked Tommy's chest and abdomen. I met Sarah's gaze, and wordlessly she nodded. Tommy's injury was bad.

I looked back down at him. "The gutless wonder ran off when I started kicking his ass," I joked.

Tommy chuckled, then groaned.

I stood straighter, my ribs still painful, but they would heal in time. Tommy needed help now.

"What can I do, Sarah?"

She looked me up and down. "Internal injuries for you, too?"

I nodded. "A couple of broken ribs, I think. Nothing punctured. I'm good."

Sarah pulled a vial out of her purse. "Drink this. It tastes disgusting but will help."

I didn't even question her. I just unstoppered the vial and tossed it back.

She was right about the taste—like dirt and bile and all gross things. But within seconds of the liquid going down my throat, the intense pain in my side began to subside.

"Wow. Thank you. Now. How can I help?"

"I need to move him inside. Can we get him to the nearest house?" She pointed to Tommy, who tried to get up and then sank back, half-lying on the ground.

I nodded and looked around. Abigail's place was just across the street. "We can go there," I said. "Can you give him something for the pain? Or do I need to sew something together before we move him?"

Sarah assessed him. "No sewing here, but you're right. He's gonna need pain killers." She searched in her bag, then pulled out a red vial. "This might help."

She handed the little bottle to Tommy, who followed my lead and swallowed it down without question. He groaned and sagged. The small amount of color that had remained in his face drained out, and fast.

"He looks worse!"

"We need to move him quickly," Sarah said.

"Come on, Tommy."

I bent down and put my arms around his body. He was big, but I was a shifter, and Sarah did some kind of incantation that seemed to give both of us a surge of energy. She stepped into his other side.

"Can you get your legs under you?" I asked him.

He nodded, and then groaned as we hauled him to his feet.

Blood gushed down his thigh from a laceration in his groin. "We've gotta move quick."

We staggered across into Abigail's house and managed to get him on the kitchen table. There, the two of us worked on him with haste. I stitched and held flesh together while Sarah cast spells and poured stinky solutions over his body.

"What the hell happened here?" I asked Tommy, as I moved up to his shoulder where there was a huge chunk of flesh missing from his deltoid.

"Vampire," Tommy whispered, turning paper white.

"I think we're losing him," I said in a panicked voice.

Sarah studied his face.

"No. It's just the pain. You can pass out, Tommy. We've got you," she said, before continuing to work on him.

I glanced down his body. Sarah was right. His wounds were beginning to heal already, the stitches I'd just given him holding. His bleeding was slowing down.

"You're going to be okay," I told him. "Pass out if you can. Let your body rest. You'll heal faster."

He nodded, then touched my hand.

"Yes, Tommy?"

He was moving his lips as though whispering, but I couldn't hear him. I moved closer and put my ear next to his lips.

"I was wrong about you," he said. "This isn't your fault."

I stood up straighter and smiled down at him. "Thanks."

His eyes closed and his head fell to the side.

I put my fingers to the pulse in his neck, finding it weak, but still beating.

"What did he say?" Sarah asked, as she waved her hands one more time over his chest.

"That this wasn't my fault," I said, staring down at the vampire bite. I had no idea how to heal it. "But part of me thinks it is."

Sarah gaped at me. "Seriously?"

"Well, the pack that attacked us was my old pack," I admitted, not looking at her.

There was silence, then she said, "Yeah, but did you see the demon influence? Red eyes all over the place. And those vampires that fought with them? That's not a natural pairing, Talia. Shifters and vamps don't play nice together, usually."

She frowned. "None of this was your fault, and it's not like they came for you."

"It's definitely not your fault." Galen's voice came from behind us.

I swiveled around to find him standing in the doorway.

Tears pricked my eyes. He was alive. I fought the urge to run at him and jump into his arms.

"If I hadn't..."

"No, Talia," he said, stepping into the house just as the sun rose and light filtered in around him. "Your old pack attacked us first, days before I found you, and that event started all of this."

I nodded, tears gathering momentum and threatening to fall.

I sniffed loudly, calling them back in. "Why do I always end up crying around you? It's not fair. I'm pretty tough until I see you walk in the door."

He smiled.

"I'll take it as a compliment." He stepped up and pressed a kiss to my hair. "I'm so glad you're okay. I've heard from several people already how brave you were in fighting off that asshole, Maddox. I'm proud of you, Talia."

He was proud of me? My heart swelled in my chest and a silly grin creased my face. "I'm glad you're okay, too, Galen, and we're all proud of you."

Sarah's gaze slid between us, but she didn't say anything.

"How's the pack?" I asked him.

Galen sighed and his brows came together. "We've lost quite a few people. And there's a lot who need healing." He nodded at Tommy. "How's my Beta doing?"

Sarah wiped her hands clean on a towel nearby and handed it to me to do the same.

I didn't know what to tell him about Tommy. "Well..."

"He'll be okay," Sarah said. "Thanks to some luck, a bit of magic, his own healing ability, and Talia's sewing skills, he'll be fine."

Galen's lips kicked up a little at the sides when he looked at me. "Yeah, I know, she's good at sewing flesh together. There are a lot of people who could use your help. Are either of you up to more healing?"

"Yes! Of course," I said, the pain in my ribs only slightly twitching inside my chest. "I want to help."

My run-in with Maddox had solidified how separate I was from my old pack now. It was almost a waste to even call them my old pack.

The Northwood pack was nothing to me. Not anymore.

Galen's pack was my pack now, and standing with them today, fighting against Maddox, had really reminded me how loyal I now was to Galen and his people.

Sarah followed us, and together we went out into the street, daylight upon us. We traveled from house to house, helping the injured how and where we could. The other witches helped with the healing, too, and went in and out of various houses along the streets. When we reached the end of the stretch of houses on the main street, Galen put out his hand to stop me.

"I think it's time you went back to Dad's."

I rubbed my hands together, feeling itchy, sweaty, and in need of a shower after having so much blood on me today. "All right. What are you going to do?"

"I'm going to help with the burials." His tone was grave, and my heart went out to him.

What a horrible thing to have to do for members of his pack. His people.

"I'm so sorry."

He nodded. "It's the last thing I can do for them."

I had to touch him, to reassure myself that he truly was okay. I stepped closer and went up on my toes so that I could press my lips to his.

I stood there, feeling his heat against mine as we kissed, then I stepped back. "I'll go and check on your dad. We hid all the women and children in his house, to give them the best chance with the protective wards in place."

Galen's face lit up. "That was really smart."

I reached for his hand and squeezed his fingers. "I'll see you later. Okay?"

He nodded. "See you then."

I turned and walked home, my heart going out to him, for what he now had to do. Bury some of his family.

When I got back, Norah was the only one still sitting in the living room. All the others had gone.

"Talia! Are you okay?"

"Yeah, I'm fine, why... oh." I glanced down at the clothes Abigail had given me after my fight with Maddox. The long yellow summer dress was now covered in blood. "It's not my blood. I've been helping to heal some of the other pack members."

Norah nodded, looking wan and exhausted. "Since you're back, I might leave. The Alpha has been quiet."

"How did it go here?"

She walked to the door. "We watched your fight with that large male wolf. You've got some go in you."

"Thanks, Norah. And thanks for staying with the Alpha."

She nodded and left.

I shut the door and exhaled slowly. Fuck. What a night!

"Talia. Is that you?" the Alpha called from upstairs.

"Yes, Alpha!" I headed into his bedroom, where he was sitting up in his bed. "Can I get you something to eat? Or drink?"

He shook his head. "No. Not at all. I've had a dozen women here for five hours. I'm full."

I chuckled. "I imagine you would be. Do you mind if I go have a quick shower? I definitely need it."

I indicated the mess I wore and backed toward the door.

"Talia."

"Yes, Alpha?"

"You should call me Max."

I blinked at him. "Alpha Max?"

He chuckled. "No. You can call me just Max, if you want. Or Dad, if that suits you better."

My nose tingled with impending tears. "But... I..."

"I'm not pushing, at all, but I know you and Galen are... close. It doesn't seem right that you wait on me day and night, and still call me Alpha."

I put my hand to my chest, over my heart which was fluttering fast. I'd never had such acceptance before. "Oh, Alpha, I..."

"Max," he corrected. "Or Dad."

I swallowed hard. I didn't want to insult him, but Galen and I weren't mated, and I'd only lost my father a few weeks ago. "Could we start with Max? And depending on what happens in the future..."

He inclined his head. "That sounds like a good compromise."

I laughed, feeling slightly hysterical, probably due to exhaustion. "Thank you, Max. Well, I'm going to have a shower and rest a little, maybe. But if you need me, call out, okay?"

My body was truly aching now that I'd slowed down. My ribs were making themselves felt once again.

"Go shower and rest. I'll still be here."

I smiled, as I ducked out and headed toward my bedroom.

The shower was pure bliss, hot water to wash away the stench of battle and the blood of my injured pack.

Once I was clean, my body ached so much I ended up crawling into bed and sleeping for a few hours. When I woke, a lot of my surface injuries were healed, and my ribs were barely an ache around my middle. I wanted to see what had happened to the rest of the pack, so I jumped out of bed and dressed.

By the time I'd made Max some lunch, Galen staggered back home.

"Come in, come in." I opened the front door and encouraged him inside. "Food or shower first?"

"Definitely a shower." He stumbled inside and hit the wall.

"Galen! That you, son?" Max called out.

"Yeah, Dad. Give me a minute. I've really gotta shower." Galen pushed himself forward, and into the main bathroom off the end of the hall. He could barely stand up and I couldn't bring myself to just watch him.

I raced down the hall and stepped into the bathroom with him. "Let me help you."

I twisted the taps, the shower head blasting out cold water, then warming up while I adjusted the temperature.

He wasn't wearing a shirt, but he pushed his jeans down his thighs and stepped out of them before moving into the cubicle. He was bruised and battered, dirty and bloody.

"Can I…" I didn't finish my sentence, because I shouldn't be asking.

Galen could barely move, and I needed to confirm that he was not about to keel over.

I tugged off the tank and denim shorts I'd only put on an hour ago and got rid of my underwear.

Then I stepped into the shower behind Galen's massive body and picked up the soap. "Do you mind if I help you?"

I set the soap in the center of Galen's back and began to run it in massive circles, helping the dirt and grime to dislodge.

"You know this isn't fair." He groaned, reaching out and pushing his palm into the tile and hanging his head beneath the water spray.

"What isn't?"

"I finally get you naked, and within reach, and my body couldn't be any more tired if I was dead."

I chuckled and stepped forward, wrapping my arms around his waist and pressing my naked body to his back. "I just want you to know I'm here for you."

And reassure myself that he was alive and well.

He'd buried a lot of pack members today, and I was so grateful that he hadn't been one of them.

# CHAPTER 14

# GALEN

**M**y cock wanted to stir, but my body was so hurt, and my heart so broken after the burial task today, that there was nothing left in me to respond to Talia the way she deserved.

"I'm so sorry." She pressed her lips against my back, her breasts caressing me from behind.

I sighed and closed my eyes, enjoying the feeling of her there. Her presence was comforting in a way I hadn't realized I needed.

Today had been so much harder than I'd ever thought a day could be. Watching the pack and the witches come together last night to fight as one had been inspiring, but seeing the grief-stricken souls today as we buried our dead and fought to keep the injured alive... It had taken every bit of my strength not to cry in front of everyone.

I was the Alpha in the absence of my father, and they were all looking to me to provide a strong lead.

"Thank you," I said, my voice husky from holding everything in. "For looking after my dad. For keeping the children and the women safe."

It had been a brilliant move to bring all those who couldn't fight into my dad's protected house. There was strength in numbers, and the wards over the property made it the safest place in the whole pack territory.

"I was just glad I could help," she whispered, her words tickling the skin of my back.

I lifted my head and moved beneath the spray, rallying enough energy to scrub my face and hair. I was covered in filth. Dirt from the graves I'd dug, blood from those I'd carried.

I wouldn't go to bed tonight with the reminder still engrained on my body, but I would carry the memories forever in my heart.

Talia soaped my shoulders and the backs of my arms.

"Could I have that?" I asked.

She smiled; I practically felt her lips lift upward. "Turn around and I'll do your front."

I was almost afraid to do as she asked. I didn't want to disappoint her.

"I..."

"Galen, just turn around. I'm only here to comfort you, not to put any pressure on you. Don't worry."

I forced back the fear and did as she asked, relief filling me when I saw no censure or disappointment in her expression. Instead, she simply grinned at me and began to wash my chest and belly in slow circles. I smiled down at her, enjoying the experience as calm washed over me.

"You know you have an Alpha edge to your voice sometimes," I told her. I hadn't heard it in many females. "My mom had it."

She'd been born an Alpha mate. But then, so had Talia.

She shrugged. "I just want what's best for you, and sometimes you're stubborn, so I need to be firm."

Spoken like a true leader.

When her hands headed below my waist, I reached for the soap. "I can do the rest."

Her gaze flicked up at me through her long eyelashes. "Could I?"

*Oh, God.* Was this the right moment for that? But I wanted her. Badly.

"If you'd like to."

I thought she'd hurry through it embarrassed, or shy. But she didn't. She lathered up her hands with lots of soap, then ran her fingers up and down my cock, before exploring my balls, one at a time.

I SHOULDN'T HAVE FOUND her ministrations so arousing. They should have felt clinical, her explorations tentative.

But the more she cleaned me, the more the distress of the day fell away and the pleasure of her touch shone through.

My cock stirred and began to harden, finally waking from its temporary stasis. "I think it's time we took this to the bedroom."

Her gaze shot up, her eyes wide and a little hesitant—a look I was getting used to from her.

"Oh... ah..."

I grinned as I turned off the taps. "I have an idea. Do you trust me?"

She nodded, something that made every Alpha inch of me crow with pride. "Then let's go, beautiful one."

I reached around her hip and playfully tapped her on her deliciously curvaceous ass. She squeaked a little, then jumped out of the shower cubicle and grabbed a towel for each of us.

I dried myself and waited as she did the same more slowly, then took her hand and led her to the bed. "I know you're a virgin and would prefer to be mated before you do anything too serious."

"Oh, um..."

"But there's lots of things we can do to pleasure each other that don't include taking your virginity."

I had a million little things I wanted to do with her.

She halted, and her face betrayed all sorts of emotions. Most of them not happy.

"But if you don't want to, I'll just go set up for a nap on the couch," I told her.

After all, it was still daytime, and she wasn't my mate.

"I'd, um... yes."

I frowned at her in confusion. "Yes, what? You want me to go set up on the couch for a nap?"

I hoped she didn't mean that, but I would definitely do it if she wanted me to. The last thing I would ever do was force any woman, let alone a virgin, into anything, even a kiss. Everything with Talia was forbidden, and sacred at the same time.

"Yes. I'd like to try some things. If that's okay?"

*Okay? Hell yes it was okay!*

I swung her up into my arms, loving the feel of her clean, naked body against my chest. She stared up at me with adoration and trust.

Now I had to find the strength not to make love to her the way I wanted to.

I placed her down on the bed and pulled out a bottle of the lube I kept in the top drawer.

"I want to touch you, is that okay?" I set the lube on the nightstand.

She lay on her back, shivering a little, and nodded.

I climbed onto the bed with her and slid under the covers, where she joined me in the warmth.

Today had been terrible, and a part of me really needed this affirmation of life. Another part just wanted Talia, plain and simple.

I turned toward her and gripped her waist. She wasn't moving, and her naiveté stalled me. I took a breath.

"Kiss me," I said, needing her to give me that last inch of permission before I showed her what pleasure could be found in a bed.

Her beautiful little nipples caught my attention as she turned to face me. She lifted her chin for my kiss.

It was all I needed. I grabbed her face and kissed her, feeling her warmth, her breath. I wanted to breathe life into the fire of the passion that was building slowly between us.

She moaned and kissed me back, grabbing my arms, clinging to me so tight I felt the twinge of her nails in my flesh.

I slid closer and began an exploration of her body with my hands and fingers. Her breasts were full and soft, filling my palm and making my cock swell further.

She moaned and moved forward, pressing her thighs into me.

I slid my palm into the indent of her waist and over her hip. She shifted, opening her legs a little.

I pushed her back so I could kiss her more easily. Then I grabbed the lube and squeezed some on my fingers. I wanted to make sure I didn't hurt her.

"Can I have some too?" she asked.

I didn't ask why. I was already too horny to speak at the thought of touching her virginal body. I just did what she asked, squirting liquid into her palm before sliding my hand between her thighs.

She moaned and gasped at the first contact of my fingers against her already swollen clit, bucking a little as if she wanted more.

The groan that ripped from my throat was feral, but she answered with another moan that shivered all the way down to my wolf.

I circled her clit with my fingertips, then slid a single finger down between her lips to feel the entrance to her body.

She was wet and open, and as I slowly slid my finger into her tight, warm body, she wrapped her hand around my cock.

Pleasure burst through me and we groaned in unison, the air around us filling with the sounds of our mutual desire.

I kissed her deeper, harder, and moved my hand on her, alternating between pressing on her clit and exploring the depths of her perfect pussy.

She slid her hand up and down me, squeezing occasionally, then holding onto the head as she bucked and gasped on my fingers.

When she arched her back and her pussy tightened around my finger, I knew she was going to cum. My own orgasm had been teasing me, but I'd managed to keep it under control. *Just.*

But as she cried out and rippled around my fingers, my control slipped and the heat of my desire for her was torn from my body.

I came between her fingers while she came on my hand, and I claimed her mouth with the longest, hottest kiss of my life.

When the heat between us eventually died down, and the ripples of pleasure subsided, I slid my hand out from between her legs and stared down at her awestruck eyes.

"You okay?"

She nodded, swallowing hard. "That was amazing."

I agreed, but there was a strange fullness in my heart—in that place where the heat of my passion for Talia had chased away the shadows. Then reality intruded and the shadows began to return.

"Shall we shower quickly?" I asked her, wanting to get up and reaching for the best excuse. "I've made a bit of a mess."

She reached for one of our discarded shower towels, wiped her hands, and then folded it over the wet spot.

"Let's have a sleep. I feel so... relaxed." She rolled onto her side and closed her eyes, the bliss of post-orgasm pleasure stealing over her.

"Let me just go to the bathroom. I'll be back." I kissed her lips, rolled out of bed, then stopped to tuck her in before I went to clean up.

When I looked in the mirror, the churning emotions inside me were obvious in my expression. Had Talia seen that, before she fell asleep? I hoped not. She didn't deserve that. But the darkness was back, along with the doubts, even though I didn't want to acknowledge them. Being with Talia had been too good. I'd felt things I'd never felt, and other things I hadn't experienced for far too long.

Jessie.

What had happened to her had followed me through the years. I couldn't go through that again. Losing the girl I loved had almost killed me.

Which meant getting close to a woman like Talia was dangerous, and that meant I needed to be more careful about guarding my heart.

And other parts of my body that seemed too eager to love her.

I crept back into my old bedroom and stared down at her. She was fast asleep. A huge part of me ached to climb back beneath the blankets and curl into her, reveling in her warmth and light.

But I couldn't.

I grabbed some clean clothes, dressed quickly, and went to see my dad. After all, I had a lot to report.

# CHAPTER 15

# TALIA

Waking up in the middle of the day was such a strange experience. I was disorientated for a minute, then I realized where I was. And why I was naked.

The memories of what Galen and I had done came flooding back, as did the feelings of complete exhilaration.

I rolled onto my back, tugged the blankets up to my face, and bit down on the sheets to stop the squeal from emerging.

Galen had been so incredibly thoughtful. And talented. And hot!

Hearing him groan as he came had made my own orgasm so much more intense.

Speaking of Galen... where was he?

I sat up in bed and glanced around the room, listening for anyone in the bathroom or the hallway outside the bedroom. Silence. How long had I been asleep?

I stretched out my hand to stroke the indented spot next to me on the bed. The space that Galen had occupied for a short, hot time this afternoon.

It was cold.

I must have been asleep far longer than expected, for him to have left me alone so long.

I slid out of bed and hurried to the bathroom for a shower. I dressed quickly, wanting to go and find Galen. The sun was low in the sky which meant it must be close to dinner time by now.

I rushed out of my room and found Max asleep in his room, and no sign of Galen anywhere.

Where was he?

I went into the kitchen and began the preparations for dinner. There was a basket of homemade bread sitting on the counter, delivered yesterday by one of the other pack women prior to the battle, and I figured the bread would go nicely with steak and a salad. I grabbed a knife and salad ingredients from the fridge and began to chop.

Was the battle really only last night? It felt like so much had happened since then—my sexy afternoon sojourn with Galen chief among them.

I was lucky my shifter genes had enabled my injuries to heal so quickly. I still had twinges in my chest from my ribs, but the pain was reduced to a dull ache that I could tolerate, and I hadn't even thought about them while in bed with Galen.

I still couldn't believe I had fought off Maddox. A frown marred my face. Nor that so many of Galen's pack had been injured or killed.

I felt a little out of whack due to being up most of the night, then sleeping twice during the day.

My emotions seemed a little bit all over the place, though I supposed there was a good enough reason to feel as if I were on a rollercoaster. The truth was, I felt a little dizzy. I drank a large glass of water and took a deep breath, raising my gaze to look out the kitchen window and try to center myself.

Outside in the street, pack members trudged up and down in front of the house.

An older man limped down the road, children surrounding him in support. A woman carried a basket of food, but her eye was cut and her face badly bruised. Another woman walked by, her left arm bent strangely as she hugged it into her chest. The signs of damage that my old pack had done to these beautiful people were all around me.

I dropped the knife to the countertop, my fingers tightening into fists. Fucking Maddox and his fucking Alpha father. All this hatred and death. And for what?

Pack lands?

More of what they already had?

They didn't even need more land.

"Fucking... Maddox!"

I picked up the knife, then slammed it down again on the countertop, unable to contain my anger. If they hadn't attacked Galen's pack in the first place, they wouldn't have lost.

My father wouldn't have made some 'mistake'.

He wouldn't have been murdered by the Alpha he loved, and to whom he had always remained loyal, no matter what.

And I wouldn't have been rejected by my mate and tossed away like trash.

No.

It was far worse than that. I'd been thrown away, then hunted down to be killed.

And all these lovely people from Galen's pack, who had been so welcoming to me, wouldn't now be dead, injured, or suffering.

No matter what happened, they didn't seem able to leave me alone. Even after they'd failed. Even after Galen beat their Alpha and made a deal with them to lay the hell off and stay clear of our pack and lands. Galen's people didn't deserve what had happened to them, and neither did I.

I pushed off from the kitchen counter and marched along the hallway, then turned and paced back just as forcefully. I didn't know what to do with all these feelings. I wanted to yell, and scream, and fight that bastard Maddox all over again.

This time, I wouldn't stop until I'd torn out his throat.

I wanted vengeance for my father.

For all the victims of Maddox and his asshole father.

And I wanted vengeance for myself. For the old life I'd lost. For the burgeoning new life here in Galen's pack that they'd tried to take, and failed.

I was so angry, my wolf began to howl, deep down inside me. She wanted to shift and tear things apart with her teeth.

"Talia!" Max called out, pulling me back to the here and now. "You okay?"

I strode to his room, still breathing hard, trying and only just managing to contain my rage. I kept my wolf tucked away.

"Yeah." My tone was gruff. It didn't sound like me. "I was just making dinner. Shouldn't take too long, if you're hungry."

He stared at me, blinking a few times as he took in my new sense of purpose. "You don't look like yourself, Talia. Are you sure you're all right?"

I crossed my arms over my chest and stood in the doorway, staring at the Alpha who'd given me leave to call him by his first name.

"No, Max, I'm not all right. I—"

"You're angry."

I nodded at him. "Hell yes, I am. My old pack... what they've done to yours and Galen's people. I'm so angry at them. I'm enraged."

My whole body was shaking.

He grinned at me with a flash of teeth and a gleam of the old wolf in his dark eyes. "Good. Hold onto that rage, my dear. Tamp it down but keep it ready. That's what you'll need to beat them."

A strange type of happiness filled me up seeing Max display

the strength that I knew was there beneath the surface of his illness.

I opened my mouth to say something positive along those lines.

A massive crash erupted at the other end of the hallway.

I turned toward the sound and called out, "Who's there?"

There was a whisper of heat on the breeze, but no one answered.

Hairs rose up on the back of my neck and dread trickled all the way down my spine.

I knew, deep down in my gut, that this intruder was no ordinary wolf shifter.

I exchanged a quick look with Max, and then ran out into the hallway, holding my anger ready to fuel a burst of energy, just as he had advised.

*You'll need your rage to beat them.*

There was no one in sight, but another thump in one of the rooms down the hall signaled the truth. Someone had broken into our house, knocking through our wards.

And I had the strangest sense that, whoever it was, they had come here just for me.

# WOLF OF SHADOWS

USA TODAY BESTSELLING AUTHOR

## AMELIA SHAW

# CHAPTER 1

# TALIA

I tugged my wolf shifter to the surface, ready for the fight I knew was coming. The ruckus I'd just heard could be something harmless, one of the witches' cats knocking stuff off my shelves maybe? Or a local kid playing a prank.

But according to all my instincts, that was doubtful. Very doubtful.

As I took another step down the hallway, my heart pounded inside my chest and my father's voice sounded in my head.

"Talia, when you grow up, you're going to have to fight 'em off with a stick."

Not a day had gone by without him uttering those words to me. He'd been right, but somehow, I doubted he'd meant 'fight' in the literal sense. Yet here I was in my kitchen armed with a broken broom handle, prepared to battle it out with whomever had broken into the Alpha's house.

Fight them off with a stick.

Yeah, thanks for that, Dad.

I could take care of myself in a fight. A fair fight. I had a sneaking suspicion that it was more than a rogue wolf shifter who was guilty of breaking and entering in this instance.

"Show yourself." With my makeshift spear at the ready, I crept along the corridor toward my bedroom. "I know you're here. What are you waiting for? Come out."

Under normal circumstances, taunting a person who had no qualms about breaking into someone's home wouldn't be a good idea. But my circumstances were far from normal. I'd been rejected by my mate, kicked out of my pack, and abducted by an alpha who had given me a home–and fueled more than a few heated dreams, I had to admit.

And that was just in the past week.

The hits kept on coming, and I was sick of taking them lying down. I was finally ready to hit back. Maddox had learned that the hard way when he followed his father's orders and attacked Galen's pack the night before. I wasn't the same wolf that had been used, abused, and tossed away like yesterday's garbage by my former pack. They couldn't hurt me anymore.

My old alpha, the pack members who wanted me dead, and even Maddox had lost their hold over me when I'd realized how little they cared for me. They'd had no use for me once my father was dead and buried.

And to think I'd almost married Maddox.

In stark contrast, Galen's pack had taken me in and protected me when they should have cut me loose the minute they realized I wasn't the bargaining chip they thought I was.

I'd fought Maddox the night before and claimed a narrow victory. Still, a narrow win was still a win and I'd take it. Besting a wolf like Maddox had gone a long way in proving myself to Galen and his pack. I'd surprised them.

Hell, I'd even surprised myself.

I expected my ex to go home and lick his wounds. Not the

physical ones he'd suffered during our fight—shifters healed too fast for that—but the psychological ones. He'd lost a fight with the girl he'd rejected and cast away. A burn like that needed more than aloe to heal.

My own injuries were all but gone. Just a few muscle kinks that could as easily be attributed to my afternoon make out session with Galen as they could an altercation with Maddox.

Still, if he wanted to square up for round two, I was ready.

"Maddox, I know it's you," I called out, assuming it had to be him, or one of his lackeys. Tired of the hide-and-seek nonsense, I tightened my grip on the wooden handle and stepped up to my bedroom door.

Max was bed-bound and resting in his room at the front of the house, still stricken with whatever illness plagued him. His spirit was strong, but his body—both man and wolf—had been weakened. He was vulnerable, unable to protect himself.

It fell to me to keep us both safe. But safe from what? I'd yet to see anyone. I'd heard the crashing noises of someone breaking in, but where were they?

I began to doubt the presumption that Maddox was behind the break in. If he, or one of his lackeys, was in my house, they would have made their presence known. Max and I were alone. The intruder had plenty of opportunities to attack, but they hadn't.

If it wasn't someone from my old pack, then who?

Or better yet, what?

I'd sensed a demon during the pack battle, felt its control over the wolves. It spurred on their thirst for blood and vengeance until the dirt was soaked in it. The dead and dying had littered the ground.

I was beginning to suspect a demon was behind this break-in attempt as well.

Maybe it wanted to test for weaknesses in our defense system and gauge how many wolves left in Galen's pack were willing and able to come to my aid.

Or maybe I'd already scared it off? That seemed unlikely though.

Back pressed against the wall, broom stick in hand, I took a deep breath and pushed open the door to my room. I thrust the jagged, broken end of the handle up and out.

I'd hoped to go on the offensive, turning the tables on the home invader, and catch them off guard but when I pushed open the door fully, no one was there.

Inside the room, the bed had been pulled from the wall and stripped of its sheets. The closet had been emptied; the contents scattered around the room. I assumed the upended bookcase had been the source of the crashing noise I'd heard.

Perhaps I was wrong in believing they were after me.

Were they looking for something in particular? I couldn't think of anything that would be of value to anyone. I'd been forced to leave a lot of my life behind when I was kicked out of my former pack and that included many of my material possessions.

If the intruder was a demon, they wouldn't be looking for money or jewelry. They were here for evil intent, and I intended to find out what that was.

Just as soon as I located the demon.

I hopscotched my way around the books scattered across the floor to the other side of my bedroom.

A creak came from the direction of the front door.

Fuck! Max was up at that end of the house. Get away from him.

Broom handle tucked under my arm like a javelin, I rushed to the front of the house.

A demon waited for me in the kitchen. The yellow slit eyes

that blinked at me matched the gnarled and stained teeth in his crooked grin.

This one looked different to the other demons I'd met. More human-shaped, less flame. But even creepier somehow.

"Hello, Talia," the demon said, stretching out each syllable and wringing every ounce of sound possible from those two words.

Adrenaline zipped along my veins. My legs trembled with the need to run away.

But I couldn't run. Not with Max here, vulnerable. This pack took care of its own and if I wanted to be a part of the pack community, I needed to do everything in my power to protect Galen's father.

Just like Galen would do if he was here. And what I wished someone had done for my father.

"Where's your Alpha?" The demon wrapped his meaty fingers around the kitchen counter edge, splintering the marble beneath the force of his grip. "He went and left you all alone?"

"Who says I'm alone?" I snapped the broomstick in half over my knee and twirled the two pieces in my hand, mimicking a move I'd seen in one of those blockbuster action movies.

"The sick old man doesn't count." The demon ran his hand along the counter as he stepped closer toward the front door, then he turned around and came back again. The treads groaned under his weight, threatening to give way. "You're wasting your time playing nursemaid. I can smell the death on him from here. Let me save you the trouble."

"I'm surprised you can smell anything over your own stench and if you even think about touching him, I will kill you where you stand." I steeled my spine, held my ground, and prepared to make good on my threat.

"Oh, I'll do more than think about it, little wolf." The demon closed the distance between us. His hot breath was as rank as his body odor. "But I think I'll play with you first."

Anger, unlike anything I'd ever felt before, raised its ugly head inside me. This was not the day I would die. Nor would Max. Not on my watch.

"Oh, you want to play?" I swung the stick and landed the first blow with a crack to the side of his face, splitting his almost-human cheek wide open. "Let's play."

He pressed his hand against his cheek, eyes widening at sight of his own blood staining his fingertips. The demon shoved all four fingers in his mouth at once and suckled them clean.

"I like your spirit, little wolf." He slid his tongue under his lip and sucked his teeth. "I'm going to enjoy feasting upon it."

The demon reached for my arm. I whacked him as hard as I could with the piece of broom handle in my left hand.

"Foreplay." His grin sent chills down my spine. "A wolf after my own heart."

"Demons don't have hearts." I dodged right, out of the way of his left hook, and swung the stick to hit him again. And again.

My muscles, still a little sore from the night before, ached in protest at another round of abuse, but I refused to quit swinging the stick. I didn't care how big or bad this demon was. I would fight to the last breath.

Just like I had with Maddox.

"Talia," Max shouted from the bedroom. "Are you all right? Tal—"

He erupted into a fit of coughing. The illness wreaked havoc on his respiratory system, reducing his lung capacity and making it difficult for him to raise his voice.

"Talia?" he called again.

"I'm fine, Max," I yelled, sweat breaking out on my upper lip.

That was a lie. I knew it, and he knew it.

It didn't stop me from telling another one.

"I've got it all under control."

Things were far from under control. A demon was in the house uninvited.

This didn't feel like the work of my old pack. Maddox and his father had never outsourced their dirty work in the past. They preferred to handle their own business.

"What do you want? Who sent you?" I doubted the demon would answer my questions, but I had to ask.

These demons had been following me for weeks now. I needed to know who they were, in order to find out why.

The demon lunged forward, arms outstretched, ready to grab ahold of me and presumably drag me off to Hell—or the person who controlled him. I leaned back, just out of reach. The tips of his blackened fingertips grazed my forearm.

He muttered something that sounded like Latin. I didn't know enough Latin—or any, for that matter—to be sure, but I had a terrible feeling whatever he said wasn't good.

He narrowed his slit eyes and crooked his finger, motioning for me to make another move. A request I was all too happy to oblige. I let loose a flurry of blows, hitting any vulnerable or exposed part of his body.

A viscous black substance oozed from his wounds and splattered the walls and floor. The demon spat out more of the thick darkened blood and left an inky splotch by my foot. He wiped his mouth from corner to corner on the back of his hand, revealing a vicious smile.

"My turn." The demon grabbed the floor lamp in the corner, swung for the stars, and connected with my right side.

Searing pain exploded in my shoulder socket and raced down my arm. Electric pain all the way to my fingertips was followed by a horrible pins-and-needles sensation, then nothing.

My fingers unfurled their grip from around my makeshift

weapon of their own accord. The half-broom handle fell from my hand and clattered against the floor.

The demon aimed for my left side and swung again, no doubt hoping to incapacitate me. I moved out of the way, and he missed.

Even though he had rendered my right arm useless, he could have done much worse given his strength and speed. He was a demon after all. Strange. He was holding back, wounding me but never issuing a killing blow. Why?

I wasn't going to be so generous.

With my left arm, I swung the stick at him. Each whack of my stick was harder than the last. I put everything I had into every hit, hoping to knock him out. With a quick twist of the wrist, I adjusted my grip on the one broom stick I had left, jagged side out, and lunged.

The makeshift dagger drove straight into his chest. Ugly black blood spewed out around the wound.

"I'm a demon, not a vampire." He locked his gaze with mine.

I staggered back, pressing my back against the wall. I panted hard.

The demon eased the broken handle out of his chest. If it was painful, his stone-cold expression gave nothing away.

Black blood waterfalled down his leathery chest, pooling at his feet before it soaked into the gray shag rug.

"Talia," the alpha called from his bedroom down the hallway, followed by more coughing.

"Not now, Max," I shouted behind clenched teeth.

The demon lunged at me. I dipped down into a squat to avoid taking another hit to my shoulder.

Laughter rumbled through the demon's chest like crackling thunder.

It was clear the demon was toying with me, and I wanted to know why. I also wanted to stay alive, and I wasn't sure those two things went hand in hand.

Death made interrogation difficult—for both of us—but not impossible thanks to the witches now living on the pack's land.

I called on my wolf and the inherent earth magic, fused into the genetic code of every shifter, that controlled our change.

It was past time for me to stop fucking around and take the demon down.

# CHAPTER 2
# TALIA

My wolf answered the call to arms in record time. The change came easier and faster than ever before. My muscles and bones shifted, and my skin and hair morphed into a thick, coarse coat with little pain.

Where I'd once stood as a woman, I was now a large gray wolf.

My lips curled back on a snarling growl, exposing sharp canine teeth designed for tearing into meat. A shiver ran down my spine, but I shook it out like I would water beaded on my coat.

My wolf loved to hunt, but even she was apprehensive about the taste of demon.

Hackles raised, I reared back on my haunches and lunged for his throat. The demon knocked me away with the ease of swatting a fly.

I hit the floor and slid toward the living room. I dug my claws into the hardwood floor, leaving four deep tracks and curls of the raw pine beneath the veneer in my wake as I grappled for purchase. I went after him again.

My teeth sank into his arm and the acrid, viscous blood coated my mouth, triggering my gag reflex. As expected, the demon tasted like shit. Wolves were carnivorous of course, but I found out the hard way there was at least one meat we wouldn't eat.

I heard Galen's heartbeat, recognizing its strong and steady rhythm, before I caught his scent. The demon's stench wreaked havoc on my sense of smell.

"Hell no. Talia!" Galen's voice was shocked. A quick glance showed him standing in the entrance of the opened front door.

As I released the demon's arm and staggered back, shaking the disgusting blood from my mouth, Galen pressed his index and middle finger beneath my jaw and raised my head until I met his gaze. He nodded and ran his fingers through my coat—as if to reassure me that he was there, that he was real—before he shifted.

Galen's wolf was the most beautiful beast I'd ever seen and every inch of him was Alpha. He attacked the demon with fang and claw, shredding flesh from bone.

I jumped into the fray after him.

With Galen on the attack as well as me, the demon seemed to sense his demise. He backed into the dark corner and attempted to make an escape into the shadows. Galen gave no quarter and charged after him. His jaw snapped shut like a trap on the demon's throat and with a single, vicious shake of his head, Galen ripped it out.

I shifted back to human form first, relief winging through my heart. He had appeared like a guardian angel and saved my life, and likely Max's, too.

Galen dropped the demon body to the ground, gagging and retching over the taste. I empathized with his position. Demon tasted worse than I'd ever thought possible. Like poisoned, charred flesh.

I waited for him to shift back to human. When he did, the

thank you I was planning stuck in my throat. Instead, shyness took me. I couldn't take my eyes off his beauty. He grinned as he surveyed my own nakedness, his gaze raking me from head to toe.

The heat of embarrassment filled me. I turned and raced down the hallway naked to grab a change of clothes. Bloody man. Even after saving my life, he could still make me blush as hot as Hades.

When I was finally covered up again, I popped into Max's room. He was still coughing, struggling to stay sitting up, his back against the headboard.

I hurried over to him.

"Everyone's safe," I said, helping him lower back down onto his pillows. "Just a little run in with a demon, but he's gone now."

"I know you said everything was fine, but I thought I should message Galen." Max tapped his cell phone nestled next to the TV remote beside him on the bed. "Just in case."

"Smart man. I can see why you've been Alpha for so long." I tucked the old pair of sweatpants for Galen I was carrying under my arm, bent down, and pecked a kiss on his cheek. "I'm sure Galen will come see you in a minute to fill you in on all the gory details."

"I love story time." The warmth of Max's smile wasn't enough to chase away the sadness in his eyes. His mysterious illness ravaged his body like galloping consumption, yet his mind and spirit were still that of a strong alpha wolf.

He didn't need to say how much he wanted to be out of his bed and back in the action. It was written all over his face, in the crease between his brows, the lines around his eyes, and the determined set of his jaw.

"Go on, give Galen something to put on. The sooner he gets dressed, the sooner I get to hear the details." Max patted my hand and sent me on my way.

Halfway down the hallway, the pungent smell of sulfur hit me like a sucker punch to the sinuses. My eyes watered and my throat tightened, but it didn't account for the vertigo and dizziness.

I set my hand to the wall for stability and paused to regain my balance.

"Talia? What is it?" Galen's bare feet padded across the hardwood floor.

He was close, but I couldn't open my eyes to look at him out of fear I'd fall.

"What's wrong?"

"Nothing. I'm okay. Fighting the demon took more out of me than I thought." I took a deep breath, forced my eyes open, and plastered a reassuring smile on my face, but there was no hiding my white-knuckled death grip on the wall. "I grabbed you a pair of sweats."

I knew exactly where all his clothes were since I was still sleeping in his room, and he was crashing on the couch. I hadn't moved any of his things and was still living out of a suitcase.

"Thanks." Galen caught the sweats I chucked at him. "Are you sure you're okay?"

He mistook my still-frozen position in the hallway for being injured when in fact, the sight of his naked body had rendered me immobile.

"Yeah, I'm good." I licked my bottom lip and let the truth fall from my lips. "I'd be better if you left those off though."

Max's raspy laugh from his room behind me was the douse of cold water I needed.

"I think we should talk about what happened first." Galen's devilish smile was a promise of things to come and caused a ripple of desire to run along my veins.

At least I have something to look forward to.

He eased the loose cotton pants up and over muscular thighs and chiseled hips, covering the well-endowed part of his body that had snagged my attention. Then he pulled the drawstring waist band tight below his navel. It was almost like he was teasing me, the way he did it so slowly, and it was with difficulty that I lifted my gaze up to his face.

"Okay." My tongue felt thick in my mouth, making coherent speech difficult.

Galen stirred feelings within me that I'd never experienced before. Being with him, the way he looked at me, the way he touched me, left me questioning the years I'd invested in Maddox.

"Come here." Galen offered his hand for me to hold as I walked back down the hall. "We're going to sit on the couch and talk this out until we figure out what—"

He stopped short when we reached the living room. The place was a mess. Scorch marks on the sofa. Books thrown across the carpet. The coffee table lay on its side.

"How about the kitchen? I'll make some coffee." I led him down the short hallway that connected the foyer to the kitchen.

"I think I'm going to need something stronger than coffee." Galen brought my hand to his mouth and brushed his lips against my knuckles. Instant reaction between my thighs. One I tried hard to ignore. In the circumstances, it seemed inappropriate to lust after Galen when the house was trashed, and demons were on the hunt.

He sucked in a breath as if he felt something too, and turned our entwined hands, exposing my wrist. "How did this happen?"

"How did what happen?" I rotated my arm for a better look at my wrist.

"That's a pretty nasty burn." Galen untangled our fingers and held my forearm with both hands. His brow furrowed and the corners of his mouth curved down while he examined the wound. "Does it hurt? We should see if one of the witches has a salve to put on that."

"I can't even feel it. Weird. I don't remember burning myself on anything." I stared at the blistered skin, watching it turn an angrier shade of red before my eyes.

The larger blisters engulfed the smaller ones, merging until a bizarre symbol that resembled a hieroglyph took shape on my arm.

"Um, this is..." Fear held me in its icy grip as I remembered the demon touching me and quoting Latin, raising goosebumps over my skin. A chill raced down my spine. "This isn't good, is it?"

"We need to talk to Marguerite and the coven. Now." Galen spun me around, flattened his palm against the middle of my back, and nudged me toward the front door.

The walk outside and along the road was like an out of body experience. I knew my legs were moving. I could see the bend of my knees as I took a step, one foot shuffling in front of the other, but I couldn't feel the ground beneath me.

The coven to which Galen had granted sanctuary had set up an encampment on pack lands. He had allowed them to use some of the cabins, but they'd also built their own private tents. Unlike the witches who still lived outside the property lines, the few who sought shelter from the wolves were symptom free of the curse that drove everyone mad and these coven members on pack territory remained untouched by the demons.

Which was more than I could say for myself.

It was obvious the wound on my arm was not an ordinary burn. I hadn't done anything to cause the injury and my wrist had been blemish-free prior to the fight with the demon. I'd been so preoccupied with not dying at the time, but there was no denying it.

I'd been marked by a demon.

Galen called Marguerite on his cell as we marched toward the cabins. He instructed her to lower the wards around their homes, giving us safe passage through to meet her.

It was the first time he'd spoken since we left my house. He explained the new lockdown procedures and intensified wards that had been put in place whenever there was an immediate threat to pack or property.

I wasn't an initiated member of his pack, and there were a handful of vocal wolves that made their opinions on the matter of my presence well known. But over the course of the short time I'd been here, Galen had treated me better than my own pack.

It was the most I'd belonged in my life.

Even when I'd been betrothed to Maddox, there had always been something missing, like I was the last piece of the wrong puzzle. All that had changed after Galen, which seemed crazy when I considered the circumstance of how we'd met.

Or maybe I was just crazy.

My life had been in a free fall with no end in sight for weeks now. A nervous breakdown seemed totally within the realm of possibilities after what I'd been through. How else could I explain my feelings for Galen and his father, or the rest of the pack, for that matter?

"Sarah is around. She's going to try and help us," Galen explained.

"Oh, great." I liked Sarah. She was younger than most of the other witches and had a nice nature.

Galen and I continued down the main road of the pack lands toward the south end where the witches were housed. Sarah waited outside one of the bachelor cabins that had been sectioned off for the coven.

Her long red hair was twisted up into a bun on the top of her head. She wore a black silk robe over matching pajamas, the fabric a stark contrast to her pale skin.

Sarah hurried down the steps of the cabin and stepped in front of one of the pop-up tents some of the witches had set up in the front yard. They'd complained about the size of the housing and worked some of their magic to add to their accommodations.

The tent looked far too small for one grown person, let alone the three of us, but on the inside, it was glamping to the max and large enough for a party of twelve. I'd experienced their expanding magic several times and it never ceased to amaze me.

Sarah unzipped the opening and pulled back the flap, holding it open while Galen and I crawled through.

"This never gets old." I spun a slow circle in the entranceway, marveling at the details within the spell she'd crafted. She had everything a witch could want, from couch to cauldron to kitchen sink. "Can you spell the Alpha's house? I'd love a bedroom, so I don't need to steal Galen's anymore."

"Of course, I can." Sarah grinned. "But I'm not sure how the Alpha will feel about that. Or Galen."

I slanted a look at Galen, who simply raised a brow at me.

"You're right." I focused on the idea of the Alpha, not the sexy man standing in front of me. "I'd better ask Max first."

It wasn't my house, so I really shouldn't have said anything.

She locked her fingers together, turned her palms out, and raised her arms above her head, sighing as she stretched. "So, Galen didn't rush you over here to discuss renovations. What's the emergency?"

Fear and shame drove me to clamp my hand over my wrist, hiding the mark seared into my flesh.

"It's not going to go away on its own, Talia. She needs to see it." Galen pried my fingers from around my wrist and lifted my arm up for examination.

"Holy shit." Sarah's wide-eyed expression did nothing to quell my fears. "That's a demon mark."

"Yeah, we kind of figured that part out on our own," Galen grumbled.

I had no idea what it meant for the future. Was it, like... a homing beacon? A tracker? Just a weird burn I'd have to deal with forever?

No-one seemed to know, or they weren't telling me. Either way, I wanted it gone.

"Can you…" I stumbled over my words, afraid to ask the question or hear the answer. "Can you remove it?"

"Of course, I can." With her finger, she traced the outline of the demon mark burned into my skin. "But it'll cost you."

I tugged my arm free of her grip and considered how much money I had left in my cash stash. Enough… maybe.

"I'll pay for it." Galen draped his arm over my shoulder and tucked me against his side, holding me tight. "Whatever it costs."

"You sure, sugar daddy? This one's expensive." I felt Galen stiffen at the same time as me at the offensive term. She raised her hands, palms out, in a placating gesture and backed up a step. "Sorry, I didn't mean sugar daddy. I meant pack daddy… Alpha, that's what I meant. Sorry, this is what happens when I have too many energy elixirs."

"How much is it going to cost, really?" I was more than a little concerned at the idea of being indebted to Galen, for what I feared would be a substantial amount of money, and how I would pay him back.

"It doesn't matter how much," Sarah said. She seemed to sense my apprehension over the looming debt. "He can't pay it."

"What do you mean, I can't pay it?" Galen scoffed, reaching for his wallet. "I said, whatever the cost, and I meant it."

"Trust me, if I could take your money, I would." She turned her attention back to me, an unspoken apology in her eyes. "But the cost is Talia's. She has to pay it, or the spell won't work."

In other words, I was screwed and on a fast track to Hell.

# CHAPTER 3

# GALEN

Things went from bad to worse in a hurry. Talia hadn't shared the details of her financial situation, but I knew it wasn't good. She'd barely had time to establish a new life outside of her pack before I snatched her away from it.

And I'd ruined her life for nothing.

It was becoming a pattern. First with my girlfriend Jessie, and now with Talia. It looked like I wouldn't be able to save her either.

Fuck.

I should have done my homework. If I had, I would have known she wasn't engaged to the Alpha's son, that she'd been tossed out of her pack, and taking her would be a waste of time.

Except, that wasn't true.

Nothing about Talia was a waste of time. I couldn't imagine a better way to spend my time than getting to know the strong, resourceful woman who'd chipped away at my armor and somehow managed to expose my heart.

"Well, I guess I belong to a demon." Talia slipped out from under my arm and flopped on the couch with an exasperated sigh.

"What do you suppose slaves wear in Hell? Uniforms? Jumpsuits? Or those coverall-looking things?"

"Oh, don't be so dramatic." Sarah waved off Talia's very valid fears and strolled over to a bookshelf on the far side of the tent. Her fingers danced along the book spines until she found the tome she was after. She plucked it off the shelf with a flourish.

"Easy for you to say. You're not the one shackled for all eternity to a demon." Talia hid her face behind a throw pillow, and I suspected she was trying not to cry.

Her pain hit me like an arrow to my heart. I would have given anything to make it my own, but according to the witch, there was nothing I could do to save Talia. I was helpless, hopeless.

Again.

"First, we don't even know if that's what the mark means." Sarah opened the book, licked her index finger, and flipped through the pages until she found the right spell. "And second, the spell doesn't require money. It requires a sacrifice."

"A sacrifice?" My experience with witches was limited, but from what I'd gleaned of their craft in the time they'd been on pack lands, the word sacrifice could mean anything from blood to sweat, to tears.

Or all the above.

"A few drops of blood." She leaned into the book, squinting as she read the words scrawled across the rag paper page of the old tome. She glanced up from the spell book, her eyes wide. "Or a pint."

"A pint?" Talia shot upright and dropped the decorative pillow in her lap. "A pint of my blood?"

"It could be a cup." Sarah's gaze flitted from the spell, to Talia, then me. "I think it's a cup. The ink is smudged and faded. It's a little hard to make out, but if Talia makes a blood sacrifice, the spell should work."

"Should?" Talia said, sounding as frazzled as she looked.

I didn't blame her. The demons were responsible for the curse that drove the witches mad and led to hundreds of casualties. Every death, including those of innocent civilians caught in the crossfire, could be laid at their feet.

And now Talia was connected to one of them through the mark on her wrist.

"They call it practicing witchcraft for a reason." The witch shrugged, as she bustled around to gather the other ingredients for the spell.

Despite her casual attitude, the slight tremor in her hands when she pinched leaves from a dried bundle of herbs and tossed them into a pot gave her away. Talia was her friend, and I had no doubt Sarah cared about her.

So did I. Which was why the spell had to work.

I sat down on the empty couch cushion beside Talia. I cupped her face in my hands and brushed my thumbs across her cheeks, erasing the tracks of the tears she'd shed behind the pillow.

"Talia, look at me." I waited until she fixed her soul-piercing violet-blue eyes on me, before continuing what I hoped would be a motivational speech. For both of us. "She's just messing around, all right? She can do this. You can do this. Hell, you lost more blood kicking Maddox's ass. You held your own in a fight with a demon. This is nothing."

That earned me the first genuine smile I'd seen on her face since the demon attack at my dad's house.

"You're right. I'm sorry. I don't know what's gotten into me. I just feel off my game." She tilted her head and pressed a kiss against my palm. "I guess the demon mark has me a little freaked out."

"Oh, my goddess." Sarah pressed her hand against her chest and expelled a deep breath of air. "Me too."

"Not helping." I closed my eyes and pinched the bridge of my nose, shaking my head.

Talia laughed and the sound was music to my ears. She deserved to be happy after all the shit she'd been through; was still going through. I found myself wanting more and more to be the person that made her feel that way.

"Okay, I'm ready. Let's do this before I chicken out." She leaned in close, her voice barely above a whisper when she spoke. "This may come as a shock to you, but I'm not big on the sight of blood. Especially my own."

"A lover not a fighter, huh?" I teased, taking her hand in mine. I couldn't get enough of Talia and seized every opportunity to touch her.

I knew better than to get involved. I knew how it would end—with a broken heart. Mine. I'd cobbled it back together after my last doomed relationship. I didn't think I had it in me to go through that again.

But the way she looked at me, like I'd hung the moon, made me want to try.

"Truth be told, I hadn't had a lot of experience in either area until recently. I mean, besides Maddox." One corner of her mouth curved up in a lopsided grin. "Who, coincidentally, fell into both categories."

The thought of her with someone else—with Maddox—ignited a jealous streak in me that I never knew existed. Not even with my ex, and I had been head-over-heels for that woman.

Or at least I'd thought I was.

The way I felt about Talia had me questioning every relationship I'd ever had and whether I knew what love truly was before I met her. It pained me to admit it, but I wasn't sure that I did. The one thing I knew for sure was that Maddox didn't deserve her or the years she'd given him.

What I wouldn't give for a fraction of that time with her, moments curled up beside her in bed.

This woman would be my undoing.

Sarah finished her preparations and handed Talia an athame. The short Damascus steel blade, used for rituals and ceremonies, was etched with runes down the center and razor sharp.

"Will you do it?" Talia set the dagger in my lap. "I don't think I can do it myself. Look at my hands. They're shaking."

Her nerves were getting the better of her. Talia had a lot riding on her friend's spell. So did I. If something happened to her, if she was hurt or the demon claimed her, I'd never forgive myself. I couldn't lose her.

Especially to a demon.

We didn't know what the symbol meant, but it was pretty obvious it wasn't anything good.

Demon marks weren't just handed out by hell-spawn. They were a form of currency among demons and a barter system with humans—and werewolves, apparently. Demons used them to seal a deal, a piece of your soul traded for a wish from the destitute and desperate. The mark was physical proof of a contract made, carried through life and claimed upon death.

But Talia had made no such deal.

The demon had branded her with its mark on her wrist, claiming a piece of her soul without Talia getting anything in return. That shouldn't have been possible.

I picked up the blade and turned it over in my hand, taking care not to nick myself with the sharp edge, contaminating the blood sacrifice with my DNA. The ornate handle, encrusted with opal and other semi-precious stones, felt lighter than I expected. In fact, the weapon was perfectly balanced.

Talia held my gaze and with a nod of assurance that she was ready, held out her hand. I supported her hand with my left and traced the line running across her palm with the blade of the athame.

Bright crimson blood welled to the surface and puddled in the center of her cupped hand. Sarah rushed over with a silver chalice to collect the sacrifice. Talia lifted her hand from mine and squeezed it into a fist over the goblet, pumping her fingers to increase the flow.

"Is that enough?" Talia looked a little green and I worried she might pass out.

"Let me see." Sarah peered around Talia's bloody hand into the cup. "That's plenty. Here, this will help stem the flow of blood and speed up the healing process."

She removed the cup from under Talia's hand, exchanging it for a bandage she grabbed from the side table, a wound dressing slathered with a sweet-smelling poultice. She wrapped the bandage tight, tucking the loose end into one of the folds and turned Talia's hand over to examine her work.

Satisfied with the dressing, she gave Talia her hand back and took the silver chalice filled with her blood to a small countertop cauldron with a firebox underneath. She blew on the smoldering embers, bringing them back to life as she stoked the fire. The sap in the pine crackled and popped, fueling the fire as it oozed out of the wood pulp.

Sarah checked the spell book, muttering to herself as she grabbed various jars and added a pinch of this and a dash of that. She finished the concoction with the dried herbs she'd already prepared and spoke the words needed to invoke the spell.

"Drink this. All of it." She thrust the goblet into Talia's hand. "Bottoms up."

"Why does it smell like landfill baked under the midday sun on the hottest day of summer?" Talia gagged when she brought the steaming brown potion to her mouth but tipped the cup back and choked down the liquid. "Blech, that was so gross. Now what?"

"Now we wait." Sarah reached over and rotated Talia's arm until the demon mark was visible. "The mark should disappear any moment now."

I ticked off the seconds in my mind, knots forming in my stomach with each one that passed. Nothing happened. The mark on Talia's arm looked as sore and irritated as it had before she drank the potion.

"What does this mean? Why isn't it working?" Talia cradled her marked arm to her chest and tucked it into her chin, her shoulders bobbing as she fought back tears.

The spell was an utter failure. That was what it meant. It didn't take witchcraft to figure that out.

"I... I don't know." Sarah sat on the edge of the couch cushion, pulled Talia into her arms, and rocked her back and forth. "I'm so sorry, Talia. I followed the spell's instructions to the letter. I don't understand what went wrong."

"What am I supposed to do now? Fight off every demon that tries to take me?" Talia shifted in her friend's arms and looked to me for answers.

I gave her the only one I had: "Yes. But you won't do it alone. I'll be with you, as will the pack."

My wolf paced behind my rib cage, ready to burst free at any moment. He wanted to hunt down whoever summoned the demon and deliver his own special brand of justice. Pack justice. As Alpha, it was my responsibility to enforce the rule of law. I was the judge, jury, and executioner.

I couldn't have agreed more. When we found them, and I had no doubt that we would, they would pay in spades for what they did to Talia.

"I can ask the other members of my coven. If there's another spell that will work, the high priestess will know it." Sarah used the cuff of her sleeve to wipe Talia's tears and brushed the stray hairs out of her eyes.

"I'm calling a pack meeting." I stood up, pulled my phone out of my jeans pocket, and paced the floor while dialing David's number. He answered on the first ring. "Hey, get everyone together to the meeting hall. We need to talk, all of us, including the witches. I'm at Sarah's place. We'll bring the coven and meet you there."

The demons had invaded the wrong town and fucked with the wrong pack.

It was high time somebody taught them a lesson. It was up to my pack and me to do it. School was in session, and I was the teacher.

# CHAPTER 4

# TALIA

The meeting hall wasn't large enough for all the pack members plus a full coven of witches, forcing Galen to hold the meeting outdoors. I shivered as a cold wind wrapped around my bare arms.

Galen offered me a sweatshirt he'd stowed in the back of his Jeep, and I nestled into the added warmth of another layer—and Galen's comforting scent permeating the heavy cotton fabric.

The sweatshirt hung down at my knees like a sack dress, drowning my small frame. I rolled the sleeves at the cuffs, leaving enough material to cover the demon mark on the inside of my wrist. Then I wedged my way to the front of the crowd that had gathered around Galen who was busy thanking everyone for coming on such short notice.

"I've asked you all here tonight to discuss the problems with the demons in our town. They're testing us, coming onto pack land, and tonight they attacked someone under my protection." Galen left out my name—and the demonic brand seared into my flesh—but everyone seemed to know who he was talking about.

I felt the weighted gaze of his pack members bearing down on me and was grateful he decided not to make the demon mark public knowledge until we knew what it meant or what it would do.

While most of the pack had accepted me, there were still outliers wary of a castaway from a rival pack.

Not that I blamed them.

After my former pack attacked them and the casualties suffered under the orders of Maddox and his father, I wouldn't trust anyone from my pack either.

In fact, I didn't.

Galen's pack was the polar opposite of the one I'd been raised in. This was a community where people supported each other and worked together. I wanted more than anything to be a permanent part of it. I had hoped to prove myself and earn a place among them.

That was before I was demon marked.

My world had been turned upside down. Again. I had no clue if the demon would kill me or claim me. Both of those scenarios were horrible but being claimed by a demon scared me more than anything. There had to be a way to remove the mark. I just needed more time to figure it out.

But time wasn't on my side.

It seemed determined to work against me. The demons in town grew bolder. Maddox and his father were hell bent on seizing control of the whole territory and usurping Galen. I wanted justice for my father's murder.

And the town residents were caught in the crossfire.

The universe threw everything it had at me all at once and I struggled to keep up. I thought the public humiliation of a broken engagement and being kicked out of my pack was the worst thing that could happen to me.

How naïve could one person be?

I saw things clearly for the first time in my life. Maddox had done me a huge favor without even realizing it when he'd ended our relationship. I'd thought we loved each other, but I couldn't have been more wrong. Being alone was better than being trapped in an unhappy relationship.

The Alpha of my pack had murdered my father. If he hadn't cast me out, justice would never be served. Not without a challenge. But outside of the pack, vengeance was mine.

And then there was Galen.

If I'd been engaged to Maddox and an active member in my old pack, there wouldn't have been a place for him in my heart.

And he'd taken up residence there in such a huge way. I now couldn't imagine my life without him in it.

Galen wrapped up the why of the meeting and moved on to the what—as in what he planned to do about the current demon situation.

"That's Marguerite, the high priestess, over there." Sarah had to elbow her way through the crowd to join me in the front row. She pointed to an older woman with silver hair and piercing blue eyes. "When the meeting's over, we'll ask her about... you know, your little problem."

Wolf shifters had excellent hearing, so I appreciated her discretion, but my problem was far from little.

It was a huge problem that left me feeling anxious and overwhelmed. Still, I was grateful to have a friend who stuck by my side and wanted to help.

We listened to Galen talk about the enhanced perimeter wards the witches agreed to install, along with their offer to upgrade the ones already in place. His decision to give them pack protection and allow them into pack lands had forged a powerful alliance with the coven.

It was an equal partnership and that meant the wolves wouldn't be able to rely solely on the coven's magic for protection. They needed to bring something to the table as well.

Which brought Galen to his second point in the meeting, one that grabbed my attention and refused to let go.

Watches were to be added to the regular security protocols in place. His Beta would assign each wolf a partner. The pair would then be given a four-hour shift patrolling the borders of the pack land and alert Galen or his Beta of any demon sightings.

Under no circumstances were they to risk the wards and engage with the demons unless the latter crossed the property line and entered pack lands.

I wanted to help protect the pack and planned to volunteer for a watch as soon as the meeting was over, and we'd spoken to the high priestess about my mark.

It was a chance for me to return the favor to Galen's pack for taking me in and to prove to the few skeptics that remained that they were wrong about me.

Two wolves, one stone. So to speak.

"I'm going to see if I can get Marguerite's attention, let her know we need her help, before she takes off to work on the wards." Sarah pulled me into a hug, squeezed tighter than normal, and whispered in my ear. "You'll be okay by yourself, right?"

"Of course. I'm a wolf shifter, remember? I'm never really alone." I swept away her worries with a much-needed laugh and squeezed her back.

The oversized sleeve of Galen's hoodie slid up my arm, exposing my wrist. I yanked the sleeve back down, clutching the cuff in my hand to ensure the mark stayed out of sight. To my relief, no one seemed to notice.

That was a close call. If someone saw the demon's mark, they might have reason to question Galen's leadership and loyalty to the pack for withholding information that could affect everyone.

That was something the members of my old pack would have done. Not out of concern for the pack, but as a power play.

Anything to gain the advantage and jockey for a better position in the pack.

Galen's wolves seemed different, less interested in individual power and more concerned with what was best for the pack as a whole—the way it was supposed to be.

Still, I didn't want to do anything to jeopardize Galen's position or cause more friction within the pack than I already had. It was a close call, and I needed something better than a baggy sweatshirt to hide the mark.

Before someone noticed and figured out what it was.

"Hey, Talia," a familiar voice said from behind me.

I glanced over my shoulder, surprised to find the newest member of Galen's pack looming there.

"Darius. Hi." I tilted my head back to meet his gaze and offered a meager smile. "I'm sorry, I didn't realize you were standing right behind me this whole time."

The odd thing was, he hadn't been there the whole time. Darius stood out in a crowd. I would have remembered nudging past him to get to the front and there was no way I overlooked him when scanning the crowd after exposing the mark on my wrist.

He must have seen me and made the effort to work his way through the crowd to reach me. But for what purpose?

Darius's sudden appearance was unnerving, but more than likely I was being paranoid. I'd felt off kilter ever since the demon attack and that, combined with everything that happened in the last week, made me suspicious.

I'd been through two break-ups, one with a fiancé and one with a pack, an abduction, a whirlwind whiplash rebound, and a demon mark.

On second thought, maybe a little caution was warranted.

"Listen, I wanted to talk to you about... you know..." His gaze flicked down to my wrist before he stepped to the side, invading my personal space. He draped his arm around my shoulders. "In private."

Goosebumps prickled my skin and red flags popped up, waving erratically, in my mind.

Danger. Danger. Danger.

How had he seen me, and the mark on my arm, when I hadn't seen him anywhere among the people gathered for the pack meeting?

I needed that question answered. Against my better judgment, I let him steer me to a secluded spot near a thicket of trees about a football field's length away from the safety and security of the crowded meeting area.

So much for caution.

"Galen left that out of the announcements." He hooked his finger on the cuff of my sleeve and hiked it up my arm, studying the mark. "You should be more careful. Someone other than me might have seen it and that could cause problems for the Alpha."

The way he emphasized the latter made me wonder if he wasn't the one who would eventually cause problems for Galen.

"We weren't planning to keep it secret forever." I shifted on my feet. The impulse to bolt in the direction of the crowd increased the longer his finger lingered on my wrist. "It happened a couple of hours ago and we were hoping to find out what the symbol means before we said anything."

"You don't strike me as someone who'd make a deal with a demon." Darius encircled my wrist with his hand and brushed his thumb back and forth over the burn which was still sensitive to the touch. "How'd you get it?"

I wasn't used to having a wound that didn't heal and winced when he traced the blistered skin. A smile appeared, then immediately disappeared from his face before it had the chance to fully form, as if he found pleasure in my pain but didn't want me to know about that particular kink.

"There wasn't a deal, because I didn't make one." I bit down on the inside of my cheek hard enough to draw blood and tugged my arm free of his grip.

The metallic taste coated my tongue and provided a much-needed distraction from the sting of the burn.

"Demon marks don't just appear out of thin air." Darius narrowed his eyes, a deep line forming between his pinched brows, and crossed his arms over his chest. "Something must have happened."

"A demon showed up in my house and attacked me." I shook my arm, encouraging the sleeve to slide back down, and bunched the rolled cuff in my fist. "I'm not sure when or how, but it marked me while I was fighting it off."

"You fought off a demon?" Darius looked me up and down. His gaze lingered on my breasts, giving me an unexpected reason to be grateful for the baggy sweatshirt.

"I held my own." I sidestepped to my right for a better view and looked past him to Galen and the small crowd of pack members surrounding him. "And then Galen showed up and finished him off."

"Galen." Darius said his Alpha's name through gritted teeth, muscles twitching as he clenched his jaw. "I'm glad he was there to save the day."

The flat tone of his voice and flicker of anger in his eyes said otherwise.

But it wasn't violence toward Galen that I sensed from Darius. His anger seemed to be projected inward, not out. As if he was upset that he wasn't the one who had shown up at my house when the demon attacked.

I neither expected nor wanted jealousy from Darius, but it was better than greed. I'd half expected blackmail to be the reason he asked to speak to me alone.

The need to get back to Galen and Sarah outweighed the need to know how Darius had seen my mark.

I should have waited for Galen to finish the meeting and sought his advice on how to handle the situation with Darius instead of running off with him.

In the short time I'd known Galen, I'd leaned on him quite a bit. Probably more than I should have. He had enough on his plate as it was. I'd hoped to handle Darius myself and not add to it.

As usual, things didn't go according to plan.

It was time I made my exit.

"Listen, I appreciate the advice about the mark. I'll be more careful and keep it covered. I'm supposed to grab a bite with Sarah. So, I should really get back." I stepped out of Darius's reach, relieved he didn't get physical when I walked away.

"I can help you." Darius jogged a few steps to close the distance I'd put between us. "With your mark, I mean. That's what I wanted to tell you. I think I can heal it."

How would an average wolf shifter know how to heal a demon mark? I recalled the adage about curiosity and the cat and decided not to stick around to find out.

"Sarah is already working on something for me. She's gone to a lot of trouble to help me, so... But hey, if that doesn't work, we could try your way."

"She's a talented witch but a demon mark is beyond her abilities." Darius matched my pace stride for stride. "I just want to help you."

Something about his eagerness raised my hackles. My wolf stirred from her restorative nap after the fight with the demon and stalked forward until I felt the weight of her presence in my chest.

She was done talking and ready to fight our way out of the conversation.

# CHAPTER 5
# GALEN

The meeting with the witches went off without a hitch. The coven wasted no time reinforcing the existing perimeter wards and Marguerite assured me that she would see to the new wards herself.

A few members of the pack were still leery of the witches living on pack lands, but the demons had grown bolder, and I was grateful for new allies.

Markus and I reviewed the security protocol one last time before we paired people up and assigned them a shift to be on watch.

It was all hands on deck until we stopped whoever was behind the demon attacks.

I checked two out of three items off the emergency to-do list. The last item on my list was for Talia to show Marguerite the demon mark and get the high priestess's opinion on how to remove it.

It looked like Sarah had things well in hand as far as the magical wards were concerned. She and Marguerite had their heads together and were deep in conversation.

Except, as I looked around, I didn't see Talia anywhere.

I thought she would have stayed with the coven while I wrapped up pack business but when I asked the witches, none of them had seen her. Marguerite agreed to examine the demon mark to see if anything could be done.

But that required Talia and she was M.I.A.

A few witches offered divination services to help me locate her, but I didn't need incense and a crystal ball to find Talia.

Not when my wolf could pick up her scent and follow her trail.

I backtracked to the last place I'd seen her and sniffed out the different scents in the air until I found the one unique to Talia— orange blossoms and sunshine. The strength of her scent trail ebbed and flowed, almost disappearing when I reached the spot where she had stood during the meeting.

There were too many witches and wolves in one place, muddying the trail. I closed my eyes, inhaling a deep breath through my nose, and let my wolf go to work.

There.

It was faint, but it was enough. I followed her scent away from where the crowd was gathered to a more isolated area of the property. The smell of orange blossoms intensified, but there was something else too.

Something not Talia.

Something male that put my wolf on edge. Neither of us were thrilled with Talia being alone with another guy. Jealousy reared its ugly head, making my fists tighten.

I recognized the other scent. Darius.

What's she doing with him?

There was something off about the newest member of our pack. I couldn't put my finger on what it was, but the more time I spent around him the more worried I became.

The decision to bring him into the pack was on me and I hoped I hadn't made a mistake.

With demon attacks and a curse on the witches, we needed as many wolves as we could get. I hadn't vetted him the way I normally would a new member. It was a rash decision made from necessity.

One I hoped didn't come back to bite me in the ass.

I caught a glimpse of Talia near a small grove of evergreen trees, a secluded spot perfect for an intimate conversation.

Or something more.

Wolves were skilled hunters, stalking their prey before they attacked. My wolf and I were no exception. I treaded lightly, each step precise and without a sound.

Darius came into view, his fingers curled around her wrist and a possessive streak in his eyes. It seemed he'd taken an interest in Talia as well. My wolf never doubted our prowess and welcomed the competition.

I wished I shared my wolf's confidence and had to stifle a growl at the sight of another man touching her—regardless of whether or not the touch turned out to be innocent.

When it came to pack business, I had the courage and determination needed to lead. The same could not be said for relationships.

Not after Jessie.

Her death broke me. I'd pieced myself back together for the sake of the pack and focused all my energy on our community, but the personal scars were still there.

I was damaged goods.

Talia was a salve to my tattered soul. I caught glimpses of a future I thought I'd lost whenever we were together, but if I examined it too hard or looked too long, it disappeared. As much as I wanted to, I couldn't open my heart enough to commit.

Her wolf called to mine in a way I'd never felt before, and it scared the hell out of me.

Talia seemed to have all the confidence I lacked and knew what she wanted. Or at least, she knew what she didn't want.

And judging by her body language, the only kiss lover-boy was going to get from her was a fist across his lips.

I shouldn't have doubted her.

"There you are." I kept my pace and my tone casual, closing the distance between us as if I were out for a moonlight stroll. "I was looking for you. Figured you'd need a ride home."

It wasn't the night for a challenge. Not after a demon had attacked Talia. There wasn't any room left on my plate for more problems. When this was all over, if Darius wanted to throw down a challenge over Talia, I would be more than happy to accept.

In the meantime, her safety, and the safety of everyone under my protection, was my number one priority.

"Well, considering you drove me." Talia unfurled her closed fist and stepped away from Darius, joining me at my side. "Darius kept me company while you were finishing up."

I'd spent enough time with her to pick up on subtle nuances when she talked. There was more to the story—no surprise there —and I'd hear the rest of it as soon as we were alone.

"Galen." From Darius's curt nod and clipped one word greeting, I assumed he wasn't all that pleased to see his Alpha.

I filed that away for later. One problem at a time.

"So, you're ready? Everything's all wrapped up?" Talia seemed eager to get away from Darius and hurried toward me.

"Think about what I said, Talia," Darius called after her, but he made the right choice and let her walk away. "I'm here to help."

"I appreciate it. If things don't work out, you'll be the first to know." Talia barreled past me in the direction of my truck and never looked back.

Darius took off in the opposite direction without as much as a goodbye. It was a blatant show of disrespect to his Alpha, but under the circumstances I was forced to pick my battles.

And I was all too familiar with needing space to lick love's wounds. I'd won this battle. Talia was heading home with me, so I decided to cut him some slack.

I waited until we reached my truck and the privacy of its extended cab before I asked, "What the hell was that all about? Spill."

"Somehow, he saw the burn on my arm." Talia rubbed the spot on her wrist where the demon had left his mark. "The crazy thing is I don't even know how. He wasn't there when I jockeyed my way to the front of the crowd. Or when I accidentally flashed the mark when I hugged Sarah. I know, because I checked straight after to make sure no one saw anything."

"Okay, he saw the mark on your wrist and wants to help you with the demons." I pulled my seatbelt across my chest, clicked it in place, and started the truck. "We can work with that. I mean, if he—"

"Wait, it gets weirder." Talia tugged at her seatbelt's shoulder strap and adjusted her position in the passenger seat, putting her back to the door. "He said he knows how to remove it."

"What?" I jammed on the brakes and threw the gear shift into park. This conversation required my full attention. "How in the hell would he know how to do that?"

"That's what I was hoping to find out, but then he started giving off a creeper vibe and my wolf was having none of it." The corner of her mouth curved upward in a lopsided grin. "Your timing was impeccable."

"I try." I met her smile with one of my own and unfastened my seatbelt, turning in my seat to mirror her position. "Did he give you any clues about the mark or how to remove it?"

"No, and I didn't get the impression that he would just hand over the information. It was like he wanted to be the hero or something." She twisted her long golden hair into a loose bun at the base of her neck and tucked a stray strand behind her ears. "I told him about the coven, that they were going to help us. He doesn't think they can. The whole thing was just so odd."

"Speaking of the coven, Marguerite has agreed to help, but she needs to examine the mark first." I tugged at the sleeve of the sweatshirt I'd let her borrow, struggling to ignore the way our scents mingled together, and inched up the sleeve to expose the demon mark.

It wasn't healing, which for a wolf shifter with accelerated healing ability, was odd. The blisters that made up the demonic symbol were still raised and red.

"The sooner you see Marguerite, the better." I put the truck in gear and headed for the coven's encampment on the other side of the property. "Removing the mark is top priority and the coven seems like our best bet. We'll keep an eye on Darius, but I don't think he really knows how to remove the mark."

"It was a bold statement to make if he couldn't follow through. Why would he even say that?"

Bewilderment clouded Talia's beautiful eyes.

"I can think of a reason." I couldn't help myself. I lifted my hand and ran my thumb over her cheek, down and around her jawline.

She shivered beneath my touch, but the warmth in her eyes showed me she wasn't repulsed. Her mouth parted slightly, and her teeth gently nibbled on her bottom lip, igniting instant heat in my groin.

I shifted in my seat. Now was not the time for desire to rear up, but when it came to Talia, everything about her made my senses switch into overdrive.

She dropped her gaze, breathing slightly faster than she had moments earlier, and I chuckled wryly. "We should get back," I said, reluctance obvious in my voice.

She nodded without looking up. "Uh huh. Yes. Good idea."

I turned my attention to the road. Talia didn't see the qualities I did when I looked at her. Qualities that went beyond physical beauty, though she was stunning. It was her quiet strength, the kindness in her eyes, and heart, that drew me to her.

After what she'd been through with her ex and her old pack, it was no wonder she undervalued her worth.

She needed a reminder of how beautiful she was, inside and out. I wanted to be the man to do that for her, make her see how perfect she was, but my heart had been closed off for so long, I wasn't sure if I could open up again. Not to the extent she deserved.

But she made me want to try.

"I want to help the pack." Talia pulled me from my thoughts, saving me from dwelling too long on the past and on things I couldn't change. "I'd like to be put on rotation for a watch. It doesn't matter which one or who you pair me with. Put me where you need me."

"You don't have to. The pack—"

"No. After everything the pack has done for me, it's the least I can do." She reached over and rested her hand on my forearm, giving it a gentle squeeze. "I want to do this. I need to do this. So, please, Galen, put me where you need me most."

What if where I need you most is by my side?

"Okay, I'll talk to David and see what we can come up with. I'm sure there's a few spots that still need to be filled."

"Thank you so much." She beamed at me. Happiness radiated from the passenger seat, filling the cab, and permeating my senses.

It was infectious. She was infectious.

I parked the truck outside Marguerite's tent, but I didn't open my door. Instead, I reached over the console, cupped the left side of Talia's face in my hand, and leaned over to her. It seemed that I just couldn't stop touching her. She rubbed her face against my palm and this time, closed the remaining distance between us.

Her lips found mine, parting when I groaned and deepened the kiss. She crawled over the console onto my lap and straddled my hips. My cock hardened and it was all I could do to control myself as she pressed against my flesh.

I trailed my hands over her ribs and around to her back, sliding lower until I cupped her gorgeous, rounded ass and urged her even closer.

The tiny mewling sound that escaped her drove me wild, spurring me on.

Then her hands were somehow beneath my shirt, warm fingers curling against my naked chest. I groaned as all my blood headed south. She drove me fucking crazy—in the best possible way.

Someone rapped on the window, the face and figure distorted through the condensation we'd managed to build up on the glass.

When I focused properly, it was Sarah. "Uh, sorry to interrupt." The witch feigned a cough to hide her amusement. "Marguerite is needed at the main gate to help with the reinforcement of the wards. So, if you want her to look at Talia's mark, you better come inside now."

"I guess we better go in." Talia rested her head on my shoulder and nuzzled into the crook of my neck. The warmth of her breath against the sensitive spot raised goosebumps on my skin.

"Yeah. I guess so."

Talia climbed back to the passenger side and got out of the truck.

"You coming?" She laughed, catching the double entendre after the words left her mouth. "Don't answer—"

"I was hoping to." I flashed her a mischievous smile and winked before flicking my gaze down to my lap and adjusting myself. These jeans were damn tight. "You go ahead. I need a minute."

She raked her gaze downward and pulled her bottom lip between her teeth.

"Not helping, Talia."

"Sorry." Her laughter as she shut the passenger door said she was anything but.

The sway of her hips as she followed Sarah inside Marguerite's tent didn't help my situation either.

The witches needed to come up with a way to remove Talia's mark, and fast. If something happened to her, I'd never forgive myself.

Talia deserved a happily ever after, and I was going to do everything in my power to see that she got it.

# CHAPTER 6

# TALIA

Marguerite examined the mark and sketched a copy of the symbol in a leather-bound journal. She questioned me about the attack and took particular interest in the physical characteristics of the demon.

I wished I'd paid better attention. My description lacked detail and left her with more questions than answers.

At the time, I'd been more concerned with staying alive than the color of the demon's eyes or scars marking his body.

She believed the solution to my problem, removing the demon mark and any claim he may have had on me, lay in uncovering his identity. According to Marguerite, we needed to summon the demon and force him to remove the mark while he was bound inside a summoning circle.

But to do that we needed his name.

Easier said than done. It wasn't like there was a demon directory where we could just look him up. She assured me that once she finished with the wards, translating the symbol, and locating the demon would become her top priorities.

It was hard to say who was more disappointed, me or Galen.

He stormed out of Marguerite's tent and waited in his truck while I said my goodbyes and apologized for his misdirected anger.

"No need to apologize, dear. I didn't take it personally." Marguerite took me by the hand and ushered me out of her tent. "Galen is a friend and ally. His feelings for you run deep and that scares him. So does the prospect of losing you before he has the chance to make you his."

Make me his?

The idea sent an immediate frisson of desire down my spine.

When I returned to the truck, I sat in the passenger seat with my hands folded in my lap and stared out the side window as we drove back toward Galen's house. I watched the coven's encampment get smaller while I considered what Marguerite had said about Galen's feelings for me.

He was physically attracted to me. That much was clear, but the rest of his feelings were muddied and left me confused. Whenever we got close to intimacy on an emotional level, I felt him pull away.

Something was holding him back.

Marguerite said he was scared, and I assumed that had something to do with his ex. I'd yet to hear the whole story, but I knew all too well about bad breakups and had my own scars to prove it.

Clearly, we both needed to work on resolving our past if we wanted to have a future.

Galen drove me home, escorted me inside, and checked the house for any sign of demons. After a thorough search of every room, he seemed satisfied I was safe—at least for now—and went for a quick visit with his father before heading out for his turn on watch.

That became our routine for seven uneventful days.

He split his time between his duties protecting the pack lands and checking in on me and Max. The bond he had with his father was a painful reminder that my father had been taken from me too soon. I missed my dad, and the need for vengeance grew stronger with each passing day.

The demons continued their attacks on the town but kept their distance from the pack lands—and our house. The witches had obviously done a great job with their warding.

Last night, before he'd headed out on his watch, Galen expressed concern for the coven. One of the witches who refused to relocate, choosing to stand her ground with the townspeople instead, had been afflicted by the effects of a demon, driving her insane. He worried about the witches under his protection, and whether he could keep them safe from the demons' effects.

I killed time waiting for my first watch by taking care of Max and tackling a few overdue chores. The Alpha said his house had never been so clean, but I could only rearrange the furniture so many times.

When the day for my shift on watch arrived, I was bouncing off the walls and driving Max crazy. The poor man needed his rest and that was hard to come by while I was dragging a love seat from one side of the living room to the other.

"Talia!" He called out from his bedroom.

I cringed at the slight annoyance in his tone and went straight to his room. "Yes, Alpha?"

"You need to calm down a little. I know you're going stir crazy in here, but don't you have a watch shift tonight?"

I nodded. "Yeah... I do."

"Great," he said with a grin. "How about you go for a walk? Or... something?"

He was as ready for me to get out of the house as I was.

I chuckled. "Yes, Max."

I was tying my sneakers when Galen walked in through the back door and set his keys on the kitchen counter. "Hey, there. I thought you would have headed out already."

"I'm leaving in a few minutes. Erica offered to walk with me."

I tossed my phone and keys into my bag and hitched it over my shoulder. "Your dad's awake. I just checked in on him and let him know I was leaving."

A knock on the front door had me smiling.

"That must be Erica." I made my way through the kitchen and living room, heading for the front door.

Galen cut me off midstride.

"Let me check." He strode to the window, pulled back the curtain, and peered outside. His posture softened and he offered a quick wave before closing the curtain. "It's Erica."

He was more protective than usual. Marguerite hadn't made any progress on deciphering the symbol which meant we still hadn't learned the demon's name. Galen was worried something would happen to me before she figured it out.

I was worried he had too much on his plate and was spreading himself too thin.

It was a vicious cycle.

"I'll see you tomorrow." He looked so worried, I stepped up to him and cupped my hands around his face, before pulling him in for a quick kiss. "Make sure your dad finishes his protein shake, please."

"It tastes like chalk," Max called out from his bedroom.

"You're going to drink it anyway and quit eavesdropping," I called back.

Galen chuckled and shook his head. He trailed his hand down my arm, taking my hand in his, and tugged me back for one more kiss. "Be careful, okay?"

Erica knocked again. "You coming?"

"I'm always careful." I smiled and bounded for the door. "I'll be fine. Stop worrying."

"I don't think I can. Not where you're concerned."

He was making it almost impossible to leave, but I managed to blow him a kiss and close the door behind me.

"Come on, let's go. We're going to be late, and Markus is going to be pissed."

"Sorry," I said as I jumped off the patio and walked alongside her at a hurried pace. "Galen came by to check in on his dad and we got to talking."

"You mean, Galen came by to check up on you." Erica jabbed me with her elbow and laughed as we marched toward the meeting hall.

"That too." I sighed.

"Hey, I was just kidding around. It's pretty obvious Galen's got it bad for you, but no one holds that against you. Well, there's probably some single ladies in the pack who might." Erica snorted when she saw my scowl and tried in vain to rein in her laughter.

"Great," I grumbled. I didn't like the sound of any other woman being interested in Galen. It raised my wolf's hackles and made her distinctly uneasy.

Markus was waiting for us when we reached the town hall. He glanced at his watch. "You're late."

"Blame Galen." Erica winked and jerked her head in my direction.

I groaned and glanced away into the forest. The two of them shared another laugh at my expense.

The ribbing didn't bother me. I'd experienced worse from my old Alpha, the man who would have been my father-in-law if I'd married Maddox. Besides, I knew that it was all in good fun. Erica and Markus were just joking around.

"I need you on the south side." He indicated a box next to the front door of the town hall where we could leave our clothes if and when we shifted. "Go on, get out of here."

"So, how do you want to do this?" I spoke with Erica, not rushing to undress since we hadn't yet decided on our plan of action.

"If we split up, we'll cover more ground. I'll head west, and you can run the line east." Erica bent her knee and raised her leg back, hooking her hand on her foot, and stretched out her hamstrings.

We both opted for two legs and not four, making communication easier if we came across something suspicious. I slid my cell in the phone slot of my leggings and tucked my purse into the clothes box with my sweater.

"Check-in in fifteen?" Erica set a timer on her phone, stowed it away inside her sports bra, and took off in a westerly direction.

I pulled my phone back out and set the timer before I headed east.

The pack's property was beautiful, having just the right amount of pasture and wooded areas to create the perfect habitat for wolves—and small prey.

No wonder my old Alpha had been so desperate to steal the land from Galen and his father. He'd been a terrible steward to the lands owned by his pack during his tenure as Alpha and needed better hunting grounds.

What my former pack needs is a better Alpha.

Leaves crunched on the forest floor just outside the property line to my left, followed by the snap of a branch.

I smelled her before I saw her. Natasha. She was my best friend Celia's older sister. We'd kinda grown up together, but Natasha didn't love me the way Celia did.

Natasha's wolf breached the boundary. She bared her fangs, snarling as she squatted back on her haunches. Then she launched, going straight for my throat.

She'd wasted the element of surprise with all the noise she'd made tromping through the woods. I was ready for her attack.

I clocked her with a roundhouse kick to her ribs, knocking her out of the air and onto the ground with a meaty thump. She pushed herself onto all fours, but she favored her right front paw when she circled around me, testing for weakness in my defenses.

She should have been thinking about her own.

I kicked her injured paw hard enough to elicit a yelp and punched her upside the ear. She dropped to her belly, lowered her head, and whimpered her submission.

"What are you doing here, Natasha?" I rested my hands on my hips. "We clearly can't have a conversation like this, so go ahead and shift back."

Natasha shifted from the sleek white wolf to a five-foot-seven platinum blonde. I envied her curves. I did not, however, envy her predicament.

"Well?" I tapped my foot, but the grass tamped the sound and dulled the effect. "How many more are there?"

"It's just me." She raised her hands in a placating gesture. "I swear it. He sent me here to scout the boundary and if I saw you, I was supposed to take you out."

"Well, Maddox and the Alpha are going to be really disappointed because you're a terrible scout and a worse assassin." I pulled out my phone and texted Erica.

"I think we both know that I wasn't really trying, Talia." Natasha scoffed and crossed her arms over her midsection.

As much as it pained me to admit it, she was right. I'd seen Natasha in action, and she was a gifted hunter and fighter. She held her own against the larger wolves in my old pack and earned her place as scout and once upon a time, my friend.

But that felt like a lifetime ago.

"Fine. You were holding back." I spared a glance over my shoulder in search of Erica.

The pent-up tension eased from my neck and shoulders when her gray coat broke through the shadows of the trees. She must have shifted to get to me faster.

"So, why even show yourself if you weren't going to follow through with the attack?" I slid my phone back in my pocket to keep my hands free in case she decided to get squirrely on me.

"You caught my scent." She shrugged as if that explained everything.

In a way, I supposed it did.

Erica burst onto the scene, tongue out one side of her mouth and panting. She padded up beside me and sat back on her haunches next to my leg. Her presence added to my strength and made it easier to confront Natasha—and my past.

"So, why did you pull your punches? What could you possibly have to gain by failing your mission?" I couldn't wrap my head around why she would choose to do such a thing.

"Not everyone in the pack wants you dead, Talia." She raised her head, jutted her chin, and met my glacial gaze.

"Why, because they miss me? Like they wanted me to be a member of the pack? Yeah okay, Natasha. Go peddle that bullshit somewhere else. I'm not buying it." I refused to believe anyone in my old pack could have a change of heart.

Even Natasha, who I thought was my friend, didn't stick up for me in the end. She'd stood by and watched as the Alpha threw me away. She didn't even say goodbye when I left.

"I didn't say they wanted you back. Just that they don't want you dead." Natasha jerked her thumb toward the tree line. "Can I get my clothes? It's a little chilly out here."

Erica took off in the direction Natasha pointed, tracked her scent to where she'd stashed her clothes, and trotted back with a bundle in her mouth.

"The Alpha and maybe half a dozen loyalists are the only ones pushing for your death. The rest of the pack was satisfied with your banishment. But there were a few who opposed that as well, like my sister. And Nyssa, of course." Natasha stepped into her jeans, hiked the denim over her long legs, and buttoned them at the waist.

That sounded more like the pack I knew. They had no use for me and didn't want me around. At least the majority of them didn't want me dead. The fact that Natasha disobeyed an order meant my old Alpha was losing his hold over the pack.

"I should have stood up or spoken up or… I don't know, done something." Natasha slid her arms through the sleeves of a navy-blue cotton shirt and tugged it over her head. "I'm really sorry, Talia."

"You didn't even come see me before I left. Not standing up to the Alpha I understood, but the cold shoulder? You totally blew me off like we were never friends, Natasha." I tried to hide my pain, but the wound was still too fresh, too raw, for me to cover it up.

"The Alpha threatened banishment on anyone who tried to help you or showed you any kindness."

I glared at her. "That didn't stop Celia or Nyssa from helping me."

Natasha shoved her hands in the front pockets of her jeans and rocked back on her heels. "I don't have anything outside of the pack."

"Neither did I."

If I sounded bitter, it was because I was.

"I know it doesn't make it better, any of it, but I am sorry for what happened to you and that I didn't step up in any way to support you."

Natasha's apology was my first step toward closure.

"I'm sorry, too." I raised my hand in response to the confused look on her face and to stave off any questions she wanted to ask. "Because this attack can't go unanswered. I have to call it in with Galen's Beta."

Erica huffed her approval.

I pulled out my phone and dialed Markus's number.

"We have a situation on the southern boundary," I said when he answered.

Natasha's fate was out of my hands. She'd crossed pack lines and invaded Galen's territory. She would have to answer for that.

And so would her Alpha. He wanted me dead and refused to stop trying. I wanted justice for my father's murder. Only one of us would get what we wanted.

I just hoped it was going to be me.

# CHAPTER 7

# GALEN

"What's on your mind, son?" My father dug his elbows into the mattress and inched himself up into a sitting position.

He was as pale as the sheets around him and the dark smudges beneath his eyes spoke of a desperate need for sleep.

"Why does there have to be something on my mind? I wanted to spend some time with you." I handed him the remote from the nightstand beside the bed.

"I'm your father. You think I can't tell when something is bothering you? I can read you like a book." His raspy laugh turned into a cough.

"Okay, okay, don't get yourself riled up." I picked up the pitcher and refilled his glass of water. "I'll talk."

His eyes softened and the corners of his mouth upturned in a gentle smile. He sucked down half the glass of water through the bendy straw as I held it in front of him.

"It's about Talia." I set the glass back on the table and plopped down onto the wooden chair beside his bed.

"Of course, it is." He leaned back on the pillows and closed his eyes. "You've never needed my advice for pack business."

"I ask for it anyway. Just because I don't need it, doesn't mean I don't want to hear it."

"Good, because I have plenty left to give. Now, tell me about Talia. What's bothering you?" His eyes were still closed, but I knew I had his full attention.

"Where do I even start?" I raked my fingers through my hair, tugging at the roots. "She's driving me crazy, and I mean that in a good way. I just never expected to—"

"Have feelings for her? Especially after you kidnapped her with the half-cocked plan to sell her back to her old pack?" He wrapped his arms around his midsection and stifled a laugh. "What's really unexpected is that she has feelings for you."

"Wow. Thanks, Dad." I knew he was just kidding around, but his words stung a little—probably because they held a ring of truth.

"The biggest thing standing in the way of your happiness is you, Galen." He clutched one of the extra pillows to his chest, rolled to his side, and coughed until he was gasping for air.

I hated seeing my father that way. He shouldn't have gotten sick. Wolf shifters didn't get sick and yet there he was, lying in a makeshift hospital bed in his bedroom. It didn't make any sense.

Nothing made sense. Not his illness, the pack territory war, the demons, or Talia's mark. "I'll take your silence as confirmation that I'm right." He turned back over to face me, his eyes wet with tears from his coughing fit, and reached for my hand. "You need to let go of the past, Galen. You would risk life and limb for our pack. You're going to have to risk your heart for love. Trust me, it'll be worth it, if you can bring yourself to let down that wall you've built around your emotions."

"Thanks, Dad." I squeezed his hand and held on a little longer than usual. I wasn't ready to let him go. "You always know what to say."

His grip had weakened along with his pulse. The illness had been killing him slowly, eating away at his strength, and it seemed that its appetite had grown. Whatever virus had him in its grip had doubled its efforts to devour him, body and soul.

I made sure he was comfortable, had plenty more water, and had his cell phone within arm's reach before I headed back outside.

My phone blew up with text messages before I made it out to my truck. They were all from David. Which meant we had trouble.

"We've got a problem," he said, in lieu of a greeting when I called him.

"What kind of a problem?" I began jogging up the main road toward the center of town.

"A five-foot-seven, one-hundred-and twenty-pound, bleached blonde kind of problem."

David's response caught me off guard. I'd expected him to mention another demon attack or a cursed witch who'd gone insane.

"Trouble on the first date?" I joked, turning left at the fork and heading up the hill.

I didn't normally make light of any situation where David called me, but with one emergency after another, I had to find the humor where I could.

"You're hilarious, and no. It was trouble on someone's first watch." David called out orders to run the perimeter again to a wolf in the background.

Talia. My heart lurched. "Son of a bitch. I knew it was a bad idea to put her on watch. I might as well have strung a slab of meat from her neck and rung the dinner bell." I began to run. "Is she hurt?"

"Talia's fine. The blonde, on the other hand is a bit worse for wear. She's got a few cuts and bruises. Nothing that won't heal with a shift. Listen, before you go off the handle, try to remember that Talia's a grown woman and just wants to help the pack."

David was more than just another of my Betas, he was my confidant and friend.

I trusted his advice almost as much as my father's.

"Yeah, I know, but I don't want her to get hurt. If something happens to her..." I didn't even want to think about it and tried to push the thought from my mind.

"Now who's the one having dating problems?" David said with a chuckle. "I'll meet you out the front."

The blonde must have been from Talia's old pack. It was pretty brazen of her to actually come onto our lands to attack her.

It was an act of war, and I would respond accordingly.

As promised, David was at the front door of the meeting hall to greet me as I ran up to the porch.

"Where's Talia?"

"Still at the southern boundary with Markus and Erica, keeping an eye on the prisoner."

"Son of a bitch sends an assassin into our land to kill someone under our protection." I flicked my gaze to David then back to the gravel-covered road. "This attack can't go unanswered."

"I don't think he expected this so-called assassin to succeed. According to Talia, she didn't put up much of a fight." David scratched the stubble along his jaw. "Honestly, I think he expected her to get captured or killed."

"He's challenging me." My wolf stalked to the surface, his growl rattling my ribcage. He was ready for a fight. That made the two of us. "I'm sure he'll be pleased to hear that I accept."

"You need to up the stakes. Put an end to this shit once and for all. We've got enough trouble with the demons."

"I know. We're spreading ourselves too thin, protecting the witches, fighting off a rival pack, and dealing with demons." I tilted my head to indicate I wanted to get walking, and David stepped into place beside me. "We can't keep this up forever."

"You already know the solution to one of our problems." David gave voice to my thoughts.

"A challenge to the death."

Like my father had said—life or limb.

I was ready to do whatever it took to keep my pack safe. Except tell Talia my plan. She had enough to worry about with the demon mark. She needed to focus on working with the witches to get it removed.

David's torch illuminated three people and one wolf near the pack's side of the property markers: Talia, Markus, a woman I assumed was the assassin, and Erica still in her wolf form.

I jogged over to them, and Talia rushed into my open arms. I wrapped myself around her, holding her close, and breathed her in.

This situation could have turned out differently. I could have lost her.

"I'm fine, Galen. There's not a scratch on me." Talia returned my embrace and squeezed her arms around my midsection. It was tough to actually let her go, but in the end, I had to.

"Want to introduce me to your friend?" I brushed a light kiss across her forehead and untangled myself from her arms.

"It's funny you say that. Once upon a time, Natasha was my friend." Talia's voice held a bitter edge.

I hated that she'd gone through something that made her feel that her friends had turned on her. I couldn't change her past, but maybe, just maybe, I could protect her from that in the future.

"What are we going to do with her, Galen?" Markus held Natasha's hands behind her back while Erica sat at attention by his feet.

"Well, after sending her on this little suicide mission, I'd say it's pretty clear her Alpha doesn't want her back." As I started walking over to the rival wolf, Talia slipped her tiny hand in mine. I gripped her tight, enjoying the connection. "Do you have anything to say for yourself?"

"I took the assignment but never planned on going through with it. I needed to get a message to Talia. She needed to know that the whole pack isn't out for her blood." Natasha lowered her head and averted her gaze in a show of submission.

"So, you're just a messenger?" I stepped forward, closing the distance between us, and exerted my dominance as Alpha. "I'm supposed to believe that bullshit?"

"Believe what you want. Dying by your hand is better than living under his thumb." Natasha bucked the natural instinct to submit to an Alpha, raised her head, and met my gaze.

The defiance only lasted a moment before she dropped her head again, but the steely determination I saw in her eyes gave me pause. If she had disobeyed the orders of her Alpha to reach out to Talia, then killing her would be an unnecessary and unjustified death.

"Take her to the meeting house," I said to Markus. "Erica can babysit her until I decide what to do with her." I wanted to speak to Talia in private, hear her side of the story and gauge what she thought about Natasha's intentions. "David, get a hold of Theo. Take Markus with you once everything is squared up at the meeting house and fill them in on what we discussed in the truck. I need to talk to Talia."

I waited for everyone to leave before following behind with Talia. She seemed distant, all of a sudden, as if she expected to be reprimanded for what had happened on her watch.

"I'm not upset with you, Talia." I draped my arm around her shoulder, tucking her against my side, and felt the tension in her body relax slightly. "Quite the opposite. I've been worried sick that something will happen to you, and I won't be able to stop it."

"I know that's why you don't want me to take my turn at watch, but I can handle it, Galen." She held the hand I had draped over her shoulder and cuddled closer. "I can't just sit around and pace the floors waiting to hear something from Marguerite. I need to do something."

"I know you do." I kissed her forehead and focused on walking in the dark. "You have David to thank for being added to the watch, by the way. He talked some sense into me. Given the fact that your old Alpha is actively sending people to kill you, would it be too much to ask that you stick with your partner and not split up?"

"I can do that." Talia beamed a thousand-watt smile at the news that she would still be on the watch rotation. "So, what's going to happen to Natasha?"

"That's what I wanted to talk to you about."

"Me?" Her smile faded and her eyes widened. "You want my opinion on how to handle the situation?"

"Of course, I do." I steered her around a tree and kept our walk at a strolling pace so no one could overhear us. "You have a history with Natasha. One that's different from the history I have with her pack."

"Well, the rose-colored glasses are off and have been sincethe day I left—when I saw the blood and rust on the relationships that had previously mattered to me." Her cheeks flushed and her pulse quickened with an obviously rising temper. "But for what it's worth, I don't think Natasha was lying."

"I don't either. I can usually sniff out a lie, and her words rang true to me." I shook my head and let out a frustrated sigh. "And therein lies the problem."

"I don't think she deserves a death sentence, Galen." Talia slid her hand from mine and rubbed her palms against her thighs. "There are plenty of people in that pack who deserve to die, but Natasha isn't one of them."

"Well, that's what will happen to her if I send her back." I closed my eyes and pinched the bridge of my nose. "I guess I better find a more suitable place to hold a prisoner than the meeting house."

"Galen." Talia twisted the hem of her shirt around her fingers. "I want to be the one to kill him."

It looked like I would be having a conversation with Talia about the challenge sooner than I'd planned. Which, prior to this moment, had been never.

"Listen, I know better than most how much you want justice—"

"He used my father as a scapegoat for his mistakes and then killed him in cold blood. I don't want justice. I want revenge." Her tone was fierce. She sucked in a breath between her teeth and grabbed her marked wrist, then winced. "Ouch."

"What is it? What's wrong?" I reached for her arm, but she jerked back.

"Don't touch it. It burns." She cradled her arm to her chest and rocked where she stood, groaning. "Why is it burning? Oh God, make it stop."

Her arm went limp suddenly, and she stopped rocking. Her eyelids fluttered shut and her head lolled forward, pulling her body with it. I jumped for her, and even with my shifter speed I only just managed to catch her before she hit the dirt.

What the fuck?

"Talia?" I turned her over and cradled her in my arms. "Talia, can you hear me?"

I braced her head in the crook of my arm and checked her pulse. It was strong and steady. I watched the rise and fall of her chest for any signs of difficulty breathing but she seemed fine—apart from being suddenly unconscious.

I had no idea what had happened to her.

"Talia, wake up, baby."

My sleeping beauty didn't stir. Was this related to the demon mark? Would she ever wake up again?

## CHAPTER 8

# GALEN

It had been several minutes, and Talia was still unconscious no matter how hard I tried to wake her. I held her against my body and reached for my cell phone.

I dialed David's number, hoping that he and Markus had already connected with Theo. It was easier to update them all at once. David answered on the first ring, put me on speaker, and I briefed my Betas on the situation.

"The witches better have a solution," I said. "It's been well over a week since Marguerite has given any updates and Talia is running out of time."

"Keep us posted, Galen," David said.

I ended the call and hauled ass across the property to the coven's encampment.

I ran in the direction of Marguerite's tent, skidding on the gravel and almost falling with my precious cargo.

Marguerite peeked out the flap to her tent and her eyes widened when she saw me carrying Talia. "Galen, while I always enjoy your visits, this clearly isn't a social call." She held the tent flap open. "Why don't you come inside?"

"Something is wrong with her." I rushed forward, hoisting Talia's limp body over my shoulder in a fireman's carry before bringing her inside Marguerite's tent.

"Oh, my goddess, you should have called me immediately. What happened?" Marguerite rushed around her tent, gathering herbs and dried flowers.

"We were just walking in the forest, talking. Someone from her old pack attacked tonight and she was upset." I adjusted my hold on Talia and cradled her in my arms.

Her breathing was normal, but she still showed no signs of waking.

"The mark on her arm started burning. She was in a lot of pain, Marguerite, and then she just passed out." I brushed a few strands of Talia's golden and red hair from her face and pressed a kiss to her temple.

Marguerite walked over to a bookshelf and blew on the wicks of three large white candles that sat on one of the shelves. The flames flickered to life. She piled chunks of charred wood beneath a small cauldron on a massive wood-planked kitchen table and lit the fire with a snap of her fingers.

"How long has she been this way?" She rifled through various jars next to the cauldron, knocking some of them over in her haste to find whatever stray ingredient she was looking for.

"Not long. Maybe ten minutes. We were at the opposite end of the property. I came straight here as fast as I could."

Shit. This was like Jessie all over again. Hurt and in trouble, and I couldn't do a thing to save her. Was I cursed to lose the women I loved in a violent or traumatic way? Was it some cruel twist of fate? Or karma?

"Set her down over there." Marguerite pointed to a cot in the corner. She grabbed a wooden spoon from a jar stuffed with utensils in the middle of the table.

I did as I was told without argument or question—something

I wasn't used to doing as my father's son, the next Alpha of our pack. But I would have done anything she said, even bartered my soul, if it meant saving Talia.

"Tilt her head back and open her mouth." Marguerite ladled her concoction into a small silver pitcher, grabbed the folds of her dress to raise the hem off the floor, and hurried to Talia's side.

She poured the thick liquid from the pitcher straight down Talia's throat.

"What if she chokes?" I asked.

It had been years since I'd felt this helpless. Not since Jessie, and the weight of the guilt I carried in my heart ever since she'd died, seemed quadrupled when it came to Talia. The emotions came rushing back, amplified, and threatening to pull me down through the ground to the depths of despair.

I wondered if Marguerite had a potion that could make me forget certain parts of my past—or at least one part in particular.

"Have a little faith, Galen. I'm high priestess for a reason."

Marguerite slowed the flow of the potion, letting gravity and nature take their course, then emptied the remaining contents of the pitcher into Talia's mouth. She pressed her palm against Talia's forehead and chanted something in a language that sounded like Latin.

Why are these spells always Latin? Spanish I could follow.

Talia shot upright on the cot; her eyes wide. She sucked in a deep, gasping breath.

I rushed forward to grab her, but Marguerite thrust out her arm, blocking me from picking Talia up and crushing her to my chest. "Let the girl breathe."

"Right, sorry." I gave Talia the space she needed to come to her senses fully.

Seconds later her eyes focused properly on me, and she smiled. "Galen." She took my hand, tugging me close. I sat beside her on the cot as she scrunched up her face and took in her surroundings. "Marguerite?"

"What do you remember, dear?" The high priestess pulled a ladder-backed wooden chair out from a small dining table and dragged it over so she could sit by the side of the cot.

"Galen and I were talking." Talia turned round, her sapphire-violet eyes on me. A frown marred her brow. "And then... how did we end up here?"

"It's okay. I'll explain everything in a minute. Just tell Marguerite what you do remember, all right? Then I'll fill in the gaps." I squeezed her hand to reassure her that I wasn't going anywhere, and that she had my support.

"I don't remember anything after that." Talia shook her head, her strawberry-blonde locks swishing on her shoulders. "There was just burning. Intense burning, like my skin was on fire, and then it was all black."

"You were upset, talking about your father and wanting vengeance. You said you wanted to kill your old Alpha." I directed my question at Marguerite. "Is it... reacting to her emotions?"

"Let's hope not." She pressed her lips into a pencil-thin line, and her brows pinched together.

"Why, what does that mean?" Talia swung her legs over the side of the cot and got to her feet despite my protests. "What aren't you telling me, Marguerite?"

"You're familiar with a rancher's brand on a herd of cattle?" Marguerite's question was rhetorical, so she plunged ahead without a pause. "A demon's brand is nothing like that. The rancher marks the cattle and that's the end of it. But a demon... when one of them marks you..."

"I'm connected to it?" Talia turned her arm and stared down at the mark on her wrist. "Right then. Cut it out, like a cancer. Once you get it all, I'll shift and heal."

"If I thought that would work, I would have operated when

Galen first brought you to me." Marguerite rested her hands on Talia's shoulders, as if to calm her growing agitation. "The mark is part of the demon and now part of you. It's an open connection between the two of you, and it grows stronger with every passing day."

"So, remove the fucking thing," I snapped, my temper getting the better of me. "You were supposed to have figured out a way to do that already."

I was furious that this was the first we'd heard about the open connection between Talia and the demon.

"Galen, I understand that you're—"

"No, Marguerite, I don't think you do understand." I felt my hold on my wolf slip. He was close to the surface and ready to break free.

"We still don't know the name of the demon that Talia is connected to. We need that name. There is one thing I can try but I can't make any promises that it will remove the mark." Marguerite retrieved an old leather tome from a bookshelf on the far side of the room.

"I really don't understand witches. If there's something you can try, then why haven't you tried it already?" I growled; my hands curled into fists at my side.

"You're under a great deal of stress, wolf. So, I'll give you a pass this time, but let me remind you that I am the Alpha equivalent among witches and deserve the same level of respect and decorum as your wolves grant you. Do you understand?"

The air crackled with electricity and the lights inside her tent flickered. I recognized the flash of power in her eyes. It was similar to the change in my eyes when I shifted.

Marguerite was not a witch to trifle with and I had overstepped my bounds with someone I considered a friend and ally.

Talia's gaze ping-ponged between us, worry fluttering across her face.

"You're right. Please accept my apologies." I dipped my head and bent at the waist into a slight bow. "This isn't your fault, and I shouldn't be directing my frustrations at you."

Talia released a small sigh of relief and gave me an appreciative smile.

"The reason I'm not throwing spells or potions at the mark with the hopes that one of them will work, is because I don't want to make Talia's situation worse—which is a very real possibility." Marguerite flipped through the pages of her grimoire.

"But you're willing to try it now?" Talia's voice cracked as she spoke. Her bottom lip quivered and her eyes watered.

I wanted to scoop her up and surround her with my essence, until no one could hurt her anymore.

"I am, yes." Marguerite set the open tome on a bookstand and went about collecting more ingredients from her stores. "But you need to be willing to accept the risk."

"The risk?" My query was sharp, despite my previous apology.

Marguerite stared at me calmly. "The risk that we might make it worse."

I opened my mouth to speak, then realized it was up to Talia to make the call. It was her body, and it had to be her choice. But she didn't need to do this alone. "I'm here with you, Talia." I pulled her into a side hug. "Whatever you decide."

Talia closed her eyes and relaxed into me. "Thank you, Galen. That means more than you realize." She took a deep breath, opened her eyes and looked at Marguerite. "Okay. Let's do it."

We waited for what felt like an eternity for Marguerite to finish preparing and cooking her spell.

Talia cringed as Marguerite slathered the gelatinous substance over her wrist. The witch hovered her hand over the demon's mark and made counterclockwise circles while she spoke and then repeated an incantation. Over and over.

Nothing bad happened. Nothing good happened, either.

Marguerite released her hold on Talia's arm and took a step back. "I'm sorry. I hoped this would work."

"You tried," I said, and I meant it. "We're all in unchartered territory. We'll figure this out."

I hope.

This was another failed experiment and another setback. At the rate things were going, Talia would be claimed by the demon, and I would lose her forever.

Or maybe not.

"What about Darius?" I turned to face Talia and rested my hands on her shoulders. "He told you he knew how to remove the demon's mark, didn't he?"

"Yes, but—"

"Then we should call him. See what he has to say." I pulled my phone out of my jeans pocket and scrolled through my contacts list in search of Darius.

"Galen, I don't want to call Darius." Talia grabbed my hand and pulled it away from my phone, stopping me from swiping the touch screen.

"Who is this Darius person?" Marguerite returned the grimoire to its place on her bookshelf and set about cleaning her cauldron and spelling equipment.

"A new member of my pack who appears to have a thing for Talia. It's probably bullshit, but he claims to know how to get rid of the mark. If he does have information, we need to find out what it is."

I expected Marguerite to agree that it was a lead worth pursuing.

"I think we need to ask ourselves where Darius would have gained this information." Marguerite poured herself a glass of wine and sat down in her wooden chair.

"Who cares where he heard it from?" I didn't understand the reluctance. "As long as we can get the mark off Talia's wrist, that's what matters, right?"

"That's a double-edged question, Galen." Marguerite took a long draw of wine from her cup and set it down on a small table that floated over to her from the front corner of her tent. "Knowledge is power. Especially this kind of knowledge."

"It's not like he could just stroll into the local library and find it in the reference section." Talia looked to Marguerite for confirmation. "Right? He couldn't do that, could he?"

"No, it's most certainly not in any library this side of Hell." Marguerite polished off the wine in her glass and dabbed the corners of her mouth with a cloth napkin. I noted that she hadn't offered any to Talia or me. Not that we'd likely feel like drinking it right now, but still, it would have been nice oh her to offer! "So again, where would he get the information?"

"You think he's just posturing, trying to get closer to Talia? Make himself seem important?" I scowled and shoved my phone back in my pocket.

"It doesn't matter why," Talia said. "I don't trust him, Galen. I get a bad feeling whenever I'm around him. Like, stalker vibes." She shivered.

Stalker vibes? What the hell? Had I let the wrong shifter into my own pack?

"Okay, I admit defeat." I raised my hands in surrender. "It's pretty obvious I'm outnumbered on this one."

I had to trust them. Talia had great instincts and they'd kept her alive so far. I made a mental note to keep a much closer eye on Darius from this point forward.

"Thank you for not forcing the issue." Talia reached for me, grabbed me by the shirt and tugged me closer. Then she pressed a kiss against my lips.

It was sweet, simple, and perfect.

We lingered over the kiss, which felt so gentle, and yet incited so much emotion in my chest. Eventually we pulled apart, and her gaze connected with mine, promising so much. If we could only get past our current crises.

"So, now what?" I felt like we were back to square one.

"I think we need to convene with an expert in demon matters." Marguerite looked like she'd sucked on a lemon. "A dark arts practitioner or a dark witch."

A dark witch? They summoned demons. The odds of a black witch being responsible for raising the demon that marked Talia were high.

And now we needed their help?

In other words, we were screwed.

# CHAPTER 9

# TALIA

Despite everything going on, Galen kept his word and left me on the rotation for watch duty. I looked forward to my shift each time. Not that I didn't enjoy my time with Max and looking after him, but I needed to get out of the house, to stretch my legs, and let my wolf run.

I'd handled myself when Natasha showed up, kept my cool, and called for backup. I had even impressed David, Markus, and Theo—or the Beta Boys, as I liked to call them. Not to their face. I wasn't trying to get myself killed.

There were enough people trying to do that already.

David scheduled me for an additional watch, upping me to two per week. Which still left plenty of time for Max. And Galen.

Which would have been great, if he had been around to spend time with. Unfortunately, that wasn't the case.

At first, I tried not to take Galen's absence personally. After all, he was the Alpha and Alphas were busy. He was no exception, but I could tell it was more than that. Ever since Marguerite suggested contacting dark witches to remove the mark, he had pulled back emotionally and physically, and I saw him less and less.

He even started sleeping at his apartment in town above the bar, even though he'd closed his business weeks ago due to all the pack drama. But at least he couldn't avoid me when he came to see his father.

A few of the women in the pack stopped by the house to introduce themselves formally and invite me to be a member of the events committee. I was pretty sure that Julia, Samantha, and Michele were the events committee.

I was a little concerned that there were only three members but welcomed the distraction from the backslide in my relationship with Galen.

And the demon mark. Though that was a little harder to forget about since I had a physical reminder on my wrist of the demon's claim on my soul.

Today, I'd been nominated to make several batches of brownies for a pack picnic the committee had planned for the weekend. The idea was to boost pack morale with something pleasant to take everyone's mind off the lurking danger.

The event trio deserved some credit for how hard they worked to maintain a semblance of normal. With everything going on, a picnic was the furthest thing from my mind.

The oven announced it was ready for baking with three loud beeps that pulled me out of my thoughts and back into the kitchen.

I slipped on my apron and set out the ingredients for the recipe. With everything premeasured and set aside, I set about mixing everything together. The baking dish went in the oven, and I repeated the process, measuring, mixing and baking until I was down to my last batch.

Galen strolled through the back door at that point and snatched one of the individually wrapped brownies. "It smells delicious in here. You made all these?"

"I did." I yanked the bag from his hands and set it back on the counter. "They're for the picnic this weekend."

"Julia, Samantha, and Michele got their claws into you, I see." Galen chuckled, snatched up another brownie I'd yet to wrap, and shoved half of it in his mouth before I could take it back.

His eyes widened with each chew until his eyebrows all but merged with his hairline.

When he could finally speak, he said, "This is the best brownie I've ever eaten. Are there mini chocolate chips in there?" He examined the inside of the remaining bit of brownie before he polished off the rest in one bite. "So good."

My heart swelled with pride at his pleasure in my baking skills, but I cleared my throat, trying not to care too much. The guy had been absent more than present recently, and I shouldn't have been getting so hung up on his approval. "I think I heard your dad." I dismissed him with a wave of my spatula.

I'd promised myself that I wouldn't hang around the house waiting for his visits with Max, just to be around him. If he wanted to pull back or slow down, then I needed to do the same.

My heart had suffered enough at Maddox's hands.

If I could spare myself any more heartache, I would.

"Thanks." Galen's shoulders slumped as he jogged across the kitchen. He stopped at the entrance to the living room and gripped the trim molding that ran along the opening. "I'm sorry."

"You don't have to apologi—"

"No, I do." He turned around and leaned against the jamb like he was shoring up the wall with his body. "I've had my hands full, and admittedly, I'm stretched a little thin, but I pulled back without any explanation to you."

"You don't owe me one. We aren't mated or anything." I set the spatula in the mixing bowl and wiped my hands on the front of my apron. "But I could do without the whiplash."

"You're right." He lowered his gaze and stared at the floor. "After Marguerite tried and failed to remove the mark—"

"Listen, if this is about working with dark witches, I'll understand if you don't want to. I can meet with them myself. It's fine."

"You say fine, which means it's definitely not fine." Galen met my gaze, a hint of humor in his eyes. "But that's not what freaked me out. It was the possibility of failing again, of not being able to fix this at all."

"Nobody is more scared of that than I am, but I don't have the option of hiding from it." I held up my arm and bared my mark. "I am constantly reminded about it."

"I know." He raked his fingers through his hair, tugging through a few tangles at the ends. "It's just, I've been through this type of thing before, and I couldn't save her. I backed off from you in an effort to save myself from more pain, but not being with you hurts."

"Galen, I don't need a hero. I need a friend. Someone I can count on, who isn't going to disappear on me when things don't go the way they planned. Life can be messy and painful, but I need someone who can be there for all of it. If you can't do that, I'll understand, but I need to know now."

I wasn't sure who was more surprised by my ultimatum—Galen or me. But it needed to be said. I was acutely aware of the fact that the demon mark might kill me. I didn't want to waste precious time on an emotional rollercoaster.

I wanted Galen to be my rock, but I wouldn't beg or force him.

"I can do that." He pushed off the wall and stalked toward me. "I am your friend, Talia. I won't bail on you again. I promise."

"Don't make a promise you don't intend to keep, Galen. I'm giving you an out. This is your chance to cut your losses and run." I leaned against the counter and crossed my arms over my chest.

Deep down inside, my wolf snarled. She didn't want Galen to

run. She wanted him to stay close, and she was mad at me for giving him the chance to get away from us.

"I never make a promise I don't intend to keep." He pinched my chin between his thumb and forefinger and raised my head until I met his gaze. "And I am not going to run. I will stay right here, by your side, no matter what happens."

"It's about damn time you came to your senses," Max shouted from his bedroom. "Stubborn ass."

"Dad, stop eavesdropping," Galen fired back. "This was obviously a private conversation."

"There is no such thing as privacy with my shifter hearing and these paper-thin walls. Besides, I'm bed ridden. I need entertainment and you two are better than daytime TV."

"Keep it up, Max, and I won't bring you any of these brownies." I was not above threatening him with baked goods.

"Shutting up now." The old wolf didn't make a peep after that.

"Take him a brownie when you go see him, please." I reached for one of the brownies already packaged in a bag.

"I was thinking I could stay down here with you for a while." Galen sounded unsure of himself, as if he expected me to say no.

"I'm just going to be baking. It's fine. Go visit with your dad."

"You said fine again." One corner of his mouth curved up into a lopsided grin.

"This is one of those instances where fine actually does mean fine," I said, mirroring his smile.

"And how exactly does one know the difference?" he asked with a laugh, but I suspected he was only half-joking.

"These are girl club trade secrets, Galen. I'd be breaking several club rules if I told you." I twirled a lock of his luscious hair around my finger. "But if you promise not to share the secret with anyone else, including the Beta Boys, I'll tell you."

"The Beta Boys?" Galen busted out laughing. "Do they know you call them that?"

"Of course not." I gasped at my slip. I hadn't meant to say that out loud. "Despite what the universe seems to think, I don't have a death wish."

That made him laugh harder and I was glad his sense of humor had returned, at least around me. Everything had been life or death and there hadn't been much to laugh about.

But you had to find your joy where you could.

I was tired of crying.

"Man, I needed that." Galen coughed and wiped his eyes, pulling himself together. "How about I give you a hand with the rest of the brownies?"

"Do you even know how to bake?" I asked, unable to hide the skepticism in my voice.

Maddox had been useless in the kitchen and had zero inclination to improve. He'd been more into traditional roles when it came to tasks around the house.

"Of course." Galen slid the cookbook in front of him and sorted the ingredients. He mixed and measured with the ease of someone proficient in the kitchen.

"I'm impressed." I pulled out a chair from the kitchen table and sat back to watch him work.

There was something incredibly sexy about a man who knew his way around a kitchen.

I swooped in when he removed the bowl from the electric stand mixer and dragged my finger through the batter for a taste test. Galen grabbed my hand and wrapped his mouth around my finger down the knuckle, sucking it clean.

"Mm, delicious." He ran his tongue around the tip of my finger once more for good measure. "You'll just have to wait until they're ready."

"Okay." I wobbled back to my seat on suddenly jelly-like legs.

He poured the batter into a glass baking dish, slid it in the oven, and set a timer.

"Twenty minutes. How on earth will I pass the time?" He padded across the vinyl floor toward me with a look in his eye like a predator stalking its prey.

My senses immediately heightened, heat pooling between my legs, as it always did when Galen showed his desire for me.

He bent down and brought his lips close to mine but waited for me to close the distance and initiate the kiss. I ran my tongue along his lips, deepening the kiss when he opened his mouth to me.

The passion between us flared and for long minutes I lost myself in his delicious kiss, until Galen eventually pulled away. I almost whimpered in denial—until he grabbed me and hauled me close against his obviously aroused body.

I needed him, and soon. But now was not the time. Especially with his father only a room away. I allowed a moment longer to enjoy the hard heat of his flesh against my belly, then shot him a wry grin and shook my head.

"How about a movie?" I wanted to make love to Galen, but my first time was not going to be on a kitchen table, with an audience listening in from the next room.

He sighed as if hard done by and leaned forward to kiss my lips softly. His expression said he knew why I'd stopped, and reluctantly agreed. "Sounds like a plan."

The brownies were done, and we were curled up on the couch with a bowl of popcorn and an old monster movie marathon playing on the TV when Galen got a call.

"It's one of the Beta Boys," he said as he picked up his cell.

His snicker at the nickname I'd come up with was cut short when David shouted on the other end of the phone about a full-fledged attack from the Northwood pack. We could hear growling and snarling in the background.

Both Galen and I jumped to our feet.

Fucking assholes never quit.

The wards near the main entrance to the pack lands were down, and several wolves had been injured.

I shoved the bowl of popcorn onto the coffee table and turned off the TV.

Galen was already in the kitchen searching for his keys. We could run of course, but we'd get to the pack's border a lot faster in Galen's truck. And that way, we could conserve our shifter energy for fighting if we needed to.

"Let's go." Galen said brusquely.

Galen pulled the truck forward, cut the wheel hard to the left, and hit the gas. We tore through the grass, over the sidewalk, and bounced off the curb into the street.

We pulled up near the perimeter of the pack's land in record time. There, the fight was still in full swing. Teeth were bared, and a blur of fur and teeth were everywhere as growling, snarling wolves of all colors and sizes ripped into each other.

Galen's wolf burst free of his skin the moment he was out of the car. He disappeared into the fray. I was right behind him, my wolf almost jumping out of my skin in her eagerness to be free. The Northwood pack had Galen's pack outnumbered, but not over-powered.

Maddox and his father generally filled their ranks with weaker wolves to ensure they weren't challenged and held on to the seat of power.

Galen's strategy was the opposite. He was confident in his own ability to hold leadership, and therefore welcomed strong wolves and independent thinkers. His pack was better for it. Especially in a situation like this.

Galen's wolves rallied when they saw him and fell into formation. They attacked as a group and tore through wolf after wolf from the Northwood pack.

Maddox howled, calling for his men to retreat. He left the wounded for Galen to deal with. It looked like the meeting house would serve yet another function besides a prison—emergency room.

A lesser Alpha would have left the enemy wolves in the field to fend for themselves. Or killed them once and for all.

But not Galen.

His good nature and leadership based on morality were just a couple of the things I loved about him.

Even in the midst of the fight, the word love gave me pause.

After years of associating the word with Maddox, it felt strange to think it in the same sentence as another wolf. But there wasn't another word in the English language to describe the feelings I had for Galen. I was falling in love with him.

I made a promise to myself to tell him how I felt if the demon mark was able to be removed.

But that was a really big if.

# CHAPTER 10

# GALEN

The Northwood pack had obviously figured out a way to break the wards, which had rattled me more than I wwanted to admit.

Marguerite and her coven had their work cut out to repair the damage Maddox had done to the magical protections placed around the property. The witch wasn't sure how he'd done it, but she suspected dark witches and equally dark magic were involved.

Dark magic was to blame for a lot of our problems, it seemed. And yet, we needed the help of the dark witches to have any chance of removing Talia's demon mark. It seemed the universe was not without a sense of irony.

Talia and I brought food and magical supplies to the witches who were working around the clock to rebuild the barriers. David, Markus, and Theo volunteered to help with the wounded. By the end of the battle, the Northwood injured members had outnumbered our own.

We'd patched them up and our prisoners were now resting in

the warded cabin in which I'd once kept Talia. Theo was on watch, but they couldn't escape. Not even if they were physically able to.

To my relief, the rest of the day had been uneventful. Once Maddox and his followers had retreated there had been no further signs of the Northwood pack, or their dark witch friends.

The next day was the day of the picnic and despite everything going on, I decided to allow it to go ahead. The pack needed something positive to enjoy at the present time.

I'd considered canceling the event, but in fact it was Talia who convinced me it would be good for the pack to come together. Even something as simple as a pack picnic might lift morale.

She was right, of course.

Julia, Samantha, and Michele had roped Talia into helping and she'd baked enough brownies to feed an army. We swung by Dad's house, loaded the trays of brownies into the back seat and tray of the truck, then headed over to the pasture.

I assumed that most of the pack members wouldn't attend; that they would prefer to tend to their wounds. Or just stay home for peace and quiet. But when we parked under a tree and I looked out the window, every wolf who was able to attend was there with blankets and casserole dishes in hand.

"What a turnout," Talia said with a grin.

I nodded, grinning back at her. "Better than expected. Let's go." We jumped out of the truck and started unloading. The picnic became a potluck. Talia and I dropped the brownies off at the dessert table and found an empty patch of grass in the middle of the field. She spread a blanket out for us to share and then dragged me into the line for food. We piled fried chicken and spoonfuls of every kind of salad known to man—or wolf—onto our plates.

The food was delicious and for the first time in too long, I felt like I could take a breath.

With so many attacks and the demons destroying the town, it amazed me that I hadn't been challenged for Alpha yet.

Emphasis on yet. It felt inevitable somehow. But for the time being, it seemed I had the support of my pack. And that was enough.

Despite the way Talia had found her way into our pack, she now fitted in just as well as anyone else.

When we'd finished eating, I lay back on the blanket. Talia groaned and rubbed her stomach. "Now I know what a Thanksgiving turkey feels like."

"A Thanksgiving turkey?" I stopped cloud-watching and rolled my head to look at her.

"Yeah, you know—stuffed." She giggled. "Oh, I shouldn't laugh. My stomach hurts when I laugh."

"Do you want me to rustle up some antacids?" I propped myself up on my elbows. "Michele probably has some in that Mary Poppins bag of hers. She's got everything else in there."

"She's kind of a den mother, huh?" Talia watched a group of kids running around the field playing a game of tag.

"Yeah, I think it just happens naturally after you've raised six kids." I lay back down, tucking my hands under my head. "With her kids grown, she's pretty much just adopted everyone in the pack."

"She's sweet." Talia laid down and curled up beside me, resting her head in the crook of my shoulder. One of her hands curved possessively on my chest, and I found that I liked it. I placed my hand over hers, keeping it there.

"That she is."

The sun on my face and the warmth from Talia's body pressed against mine lulled me into a much-needed nap.

We'd invited Marguerite and her witches to join us if and when they could. She agreed to send them in shifts so that they could rest and recharge.

When I woke, Talia sat up and rubbed her eyes. She'd obviously been sleeping too.

"Oh, there's Sarah." she said, pointing to the young witch she'd made friends with.

"Oh hi, you two." A weary smile fleetingly appeared on Sarah's abnormally pale face.

"You okay?" I asked her.

She put her hand up to her forehead as if she had a headache and swayed where she stood. "Yeah, I'm okay. I just... I'm a bit tired. That's all."

Talia met my gaze and suddenly seemed as worried as I was.

She jumped to her feet and took Sarah over to the table to get some food. But there was something off about the witch, and whatever it was couldn't be fixed with anything we were serving at the buffet.

She barely touched the food. Talia set Sarah up on a chair a few feet away from our blanket, and then hurried over to whisper to me. "I think we need to call Marguerite."

"We need to do more than that." I got up and dusted off my hands, concern churning in my gut. "We need to search for the goddamn demon. She's cursed, isn't she?"

"I think so." Talia frowned and nibbled at her lip. "I'll call Marguerite. You find David." She already had her phone wedged between her ear and shoulder.

I spotted David walking away from the dessert table with a plate piled high with baked goods and called out to him. He turned, half a brownie protruding from his mouth, and waved. I pointed to Sarah, who'd gotten out of her chair and was now staggering through the field in a haphazard manner.

"What in the actual..." He dropped his plate and rushed over to me.

"I guess one day of solace was too much to ask." I slipped an elastic tie off my wrist and secured my hair back out of the way. "She's cursed."

"I'm starting to think we all are."

Neither of us laughed. There was some truth to David's joke.

All things considered, the idea that the pack had been cursed wasn't an unreasonable conclusion. It made more sense than anything I could come up with for all the crap we'd dealt with lately.

"You keep an eye on her. I'll get Marguerite."

David nodded and followed Sarah around the pasture. She wasn't really doing anything wrong, but she looked unwell.

Talia rushed up to me. "Marguerite's on her way."

Some of my pack members were staring at me now, concern written in the lines of their faces. I smiled and waved, wanting them to continue to enjoy the day while they could.

It wasn't their fault that I couldn't go an hour without thinking of the demons that plagued us, or the wolves that wanted us dead so they could take our land.

We waited for Marguerite to arrive and, when she did, she came with three other witches.

"Where is she?" Marguerite asked.

I pointed toward the food tables where Sarah was now pushing David away from her. "Over there. She is not herself."

Marguerite sighed. "Half my coven is under the influence. That's the real reason I couldn't send most of them here for the picnic. They're under house arrest."

I groaned and ran my hand through my hair. "It's the demons, isn't it?"

She nodded. "I don't know how my witches became infected, but I'm doing my best to keep them safe until the effects wear off."

I crossed my arms over my chest. "I appreciate that, thanks."

The witches who'd gone insane in town due to demon influence had turned the whole place upside down.

"I'll take Sarah back and lock her in her tent."

I watched Marguerite gather Sarah up, and the coven members left.

The rest of my pack at the picnic seemed to immediately relax, which made guilt settle even heavier in my chest. I'd been the one to say the witches could stay. I'd offered sanctuary, hoping the demons wouldn't be able to find them here.

"What do you wanna do now?" Talia asked, the pleasure of the picnic forgotten.

David strolled over to join the conversation.

"I want to find the demon that has influenced the witches," I said, stripping off my shirt. "It has to be nearby to be affecting the coven like that."

David nodded. "I'll join you."

"I'll stay and keep an eye on everyone here," Talia said. "Unless you'd prefer that I join you?"

I shook my head. "No. Stay, please. I'll meet you back home in a few hours."

I caught her beautiful smile before I let go of my humanity and shifted. David joined me in wolf form, and we went in search of the demon.

David and I ran the property line together, taking extra care to check out the areas that had known weaknesses remaining in the wards. There were a lot.

Less than half of the wards had been rebuilt and it was unlikely any more repairs would be made if the witches were being influenced by a demon running loose on pack land. They needed every ounce of their magic to protect themselves until we found the creature.

And that wasn't looking good.

We ran the length of the property again with Markus and

Theo, then Markus split his group of twelve wolves into four smaller groups and marked off quadrants for each group to search more thoroughly.

There was no sign of the demon anywhere.

If I hadn't seen the cursed witch for myself, I wouldn't have believed a demon had made it onto the property.

I found it hard to believe the demon had cursed a few of them and left. The demons in town cursed as many witches as they could find. He wouldn't have had to look very hard.

There were plenty of witches on the property.

Hours went by and we came up empty-handed. There was no scent trail to follow or physical sign of a demon's presence anywhere. It was as if the demon had done his dirty work on the witches, then vanished into thin air.

We couldn't go on like this, especially without the safety of the wards. The pack and the coven were vulnerable.

I had to do something.

I shifted not far from the coven's area and spoke to my protective detail of wolves. "Go home those of you who aren't on night duty and get some rest. I'm going to speak to Marguerite."

They headed off and I ducked into one of the bachelor cabins and grabbed a pair of jeans. Most of the pack wouldn't care if I turned up for a meeting naked.

The witches would.

When I knocked on Marguerite's small cabin, she opened the door immediately. "Did you find anything?"

I shook my head. "Nothing."

"Shit." She groaned, putting both hands on her hips as though she were pissed off at my incompetence.

"I agree." I took a deep breath. "So, despite the fact that this goes against everything I believe, would you please set up a meeting with a dark witch?"

Marguerite's eyes widened. "Are you sure? I know it's not what you want to do."

I nodded. "Yes, I'm sure. Desperate times call for desperate measures. And this is becoming desperate times."

And if Marguerite was right, the dark witch may be able to help Talia as well as the pack.

# CHAPTER 11
# GALEN

Contrary to popular belief, wolf shifters are not immortal, just hard to kill—unless you're a crazed witch armed with tainted and powerful magic.

That seemed to be enough to level the playing field.

The demon's curse spread through the coven like wildfire. More and more witches became infected, and two had been crazed enough to attack members of our pack. They used magic to snap bones and cause massive internal injuries.

Luckily, the wolves who'd been attacked survived.

Unluckily for the witches, those attacks didn't end well for them. My wolves retaliated and killed them both.

It was horrible, and the unease that had existed between the wolves and witches grew into outright hatred.

My pack had been under attack from the Northwood pack for weeks before the demons began to intensify everything. When the witches I'd let into our pack began to attack us as well—from the inside—it felt like that was the last straw.

My alliance with Marguerite and her coven hung by a thread after the two witches were slain. It hadn't mattered to most of the coven that the deaths were the result of self-defense and an unprovoked attack by insane, demon-cursed witches.

A dead witch was a dead witch in their view, and that fueled anger on both sides.

I couldn't help but wonder if their reaction had something to do with their affliction. If they hadn't all been affected by a demon curse to some degree, would they have been more understanding?

I liked to think so.

At least where Marguerite was concerned. She was a level-headed and practical witch. I liked her. Surely, she couldn't expect my wolves not to defend themselves when attacked. Even if the attacker was under the influence of a demon curse.

I spent the morning as I had done for days now, running the perimeter, grateful the witches still unaffected by the curse had agreed to continue their work on repairing the wards after the pack retaliated against their sisters. There was still no proof that the demons had breached the property line. So how did they get in?

Something told me that when I found my answer, I'd find one for Talia, too. All our problems were connected, and I had a terrible feeling her mark was at the center of everything.

Running in wolf form was the only thing that took my mind off Talia's demon mark, so I picked up extra shifts on watch throughout the week.

Tonight, the full moon was covered by clouds, but I felt her silvery pull just the same. My wolf shifter ran faster, around a tree and into the field where the picnic had been held. It hadn't been that long ago, but it felt like a lifetime.

And yet, tonight, in the light of the moon, my heart lifted. What a magnificent evening!

I raised my snout and sniffed the fresh breeze as I trotted forward across the grass, then quickly lowered it again when I caught the scent of something not of nature.

Out of the corner of my eye, I saw something move. I turned to see a witch charging across the open field, her long blonde hair flying behind her like a long ribbon in the wind.

My instincts sent a growl of unease through my chest, and I skidded to a halt, hoping to stay out of her way. But she wasn't trying to avoid me. Quite the opposite.

She blasted me with a bolt of magic that sent me tumbling ass over tail. She raised her hand and fired again. Fuck! I rolled to the right and narrowly missed getting shot in my hind quarters.

When I had all four paws back on the ground I ran for it, cutting across the field in a zigzag pattern. As I hoped, it proved harder for her to hit a moving target. Somehow, I needed to circle back and subdue the witch without killing her.

Easier said than done when my best defenses were sharp teeth and claws.

Still, Marguerite and her coven would not forgive any more casualties and we needed their help as much as they needed ours.

Even with the witch affliction reaching the pack's lands, less witches had been infected here than in town. We hadn't seen signs of another demon. The same couldn't be said for anyone living in town.

I couldn't afford to make a mistake and hurt the witch hurling magical balls of death at me from behind.

Shit. Shit. Think. Think. What do I do?

I had to wear her down and lure her back to the coven encampment and Marguerite. It was a good plan, but it had one tiny flaw.

She needed to follow me.

The witch didn't seem to be all that interested in chasing me any longer. She wasn't running after me, and she was staring off into the distance in the direction of the town.

Fuck. Why would she chase me when there were wolves all

over the property that she could attack—probably more easily than me? Unfortunately for her, they would attack back.

I tapped into the pack bond and sent word for any wolf on pack lands to take shelter, and to hold off entering the picnic field unless they were scheduled for a security detail. I was setting a trap and didn't need one of my wolves inadvertently becoming the bait.

When there were no other wolves within sight for her to attack, she turned and glared at me, then began to follow me again. I didn't hit my full stride, wanting to ensure she kept up. But that proved to be a mistake. It turned out witches were faster than I expected. Or at least, this one was.

She ran up beside me, leapt onto my back, and grabbed fistfuls of fur. Pain ripped into my flesh and I tried to shake her off, but she dug her heels into my side and held on.

She twisted her fingers deeper into my fur until she touched skin and lit me up with a lightning spell. Every cell in my body was in pain.

I collapsed to the ground, writhing in pain with her still on top of me.

Oh my God...

I'd underestimated my opponent. That could be the last mistake I ever made.

The witch leapt to her feet, brushing the dirt and grass from her clothes. She lifted her arms and wriggled her fingers, clearly readying herself for another spell. I tried to get up, but my legs shook, and I couldn't get my paws under me.

The lightning bolts she conjured sizzled in her hands, but instead of shooting them out and killing me straight away, she held them for a moment at her fingertips.

I'd made an error earlier. Now, so had she.

I wasn't going to lie here and let her kill me. I seized the opportunity and launched at her, clamping down on her forearm and sinking my teeth into her flesh. I didn't want to kill her, but she'd survive one bite.

The lightning fizzled out and she screeched in pain. At the first tang of coppery blood on my tongue, I released her arm.

I gathered enough strength to make a final run for the coven, got to my still-shaking legs, and took off. She howled and raced after me, but I wasn't going to let her grab me this time. I put everything I had into th run. My heart pounded and pain screamed in every part of my body, begging me to stop.

You stop and you'll die. Just keep moving.

As we reached the encampment, the witch fired multiple shots in my direction. I kept running, weaving through the tents scattered about the grounds.

When I finally reached the cabin where Marguerite lived, her door opened, and she rushed out just as I collapsed on the porch steps.

The woman ran toward us. Marguerite stood in front of me, putting herself between me and the crazed witch.

Lighting magic shot our way, but Marguerite put up her hands, creating some sort of magical shield. The rest of the coven who'd appeared from various tents grabbed the blonde witch and held her down.

She screamed like a banshee, writhing and fighting against their braced arms. Sarah raced out of her house and joined them, holding a large potion bottle.

Marguerite took the potion bottle and chanted in a language I didn't recognize while she poured the purple potion over the blonde witch's face. The woman, who'd moments ago been dead set on killing me, stopped screaming, then passed out, collapsing in the arms of one of her coven members.

Marguerite ran her hand through the blonde witch's hair, spoke to the others, and they carried her away.

I gaped at the high priestess. What was she doing? Sedating her witch? Or curing her? That was beyond her abilities, surely?

I shifted back, wanting out of my pain-wracked body, and needing my vocal cords back.

My human body came back to me, but the pain was still there. Not as bad, but damn...

I shuddered as I got to my feet and stretched out my back, hoping to be able to soothe some of the quivering muscles.

Sarah came over to me, a pair of jeans in her hand. She glanced away. "I, ah... conjured these for you."

"Thanks," I said, grabbing the jeans and managing to slide my aching legs into the pants, before collapsing to sit on the steps once more. "Fuck... that hurt."

Sarah twisted around to stare at me. "She got you?"

I nodded. "Oh yeah."

"I'll be right back." She raced off into her cabin, then came back a few moments later with a small vial of red liquid.

"This is for the pain," she said. "It should help."

I didn't even ask what was in it. I just tossed it back, wincing at the strange, grass-like flavor.

Immediately, the pain of the lightning attack began to subside. I groaned with relief and sunk deeper down on the stairs. "Thank you. That's heaps better."

Marguerite had gone with the witches to put the blonde somewhere, so I took a minute to get my breath back. I'd made it without killing the witch, and everyone had seen me show restraint. Hopefully that would help to repair some of the rift between the pack and the coven.

"So, you're feeling better then?" Last time I'd seen Sarah, she'd been under the effects of the curse, too.

"Marguerite managed to stave it off before it fully took hold," she said. Then she shuddered. "Thank the goddess."

I opened my mouth to ask more when I heard a shout.

"Galen!"

It was Talia. I sat up to look for her. She ran over to me and I got to my feet. She wrapped her arms around me, enveloping me in a hug. "You're okay. I was so worried."

I hugged her back, tightly, enjoying the connection. There had been several moments when I'd worried I'd never be able to hold her again, so the relief pulsing through me now was a palpable thing. "How did you even know what happened?"

Sarah inched her hand up in the air, a sheepish smile on her face. I should have known.

It suddenly occurred me that Talia wasn't pack. She wouldn't have gotten the message to steer clear of the field. She'd integrated so seamlessly into my life and the daily life of the pack, I'd forgotten nothing had been made official.

And that oversight could have cost Talia her life. We needed to rectify that, and soon.

I pulled back from her hug and grinned down on her. "You didn't have to rush out here. I'm fine. Not a scratch on me."

It was a slight exaggeration, but she didn't need to know that. I hugged her again, harder than usual, until she oomphed and said I was squeezing the air out of her lungs.

"But I'm happy to see you." I released my hold slightly.

She tapped my shoulder blade and sucked in a deep breath. "I can see that."

Marguerite exited the tent where they'd taken the crazed witch, then walked over to us. "I want to thank you, Galen."

"There's nothing to thank me for, Marguerite." I let go of Talia and shook the witch's proffered hand. "I don't want any more harm to come to your witches or my wolves."

The coven hadn't needed an infirmary until the Northwood pack brought the wards down and let a demon in. Maddox would pay for what happened to the coven—and to my pack. I planned to see to it personally.

"Galen." Marguerite rested her left hand on my shoulder and squeezed, pulling me from my thoughts. "We've tried everything at our disposal and can't stop this curse from spreading. Like with Sarah, if we get to the witch early enough, we can help stop it. But mostly it's too late by the time we realize someone has been affected. Perhaps if we had access to more of our gardens and root cellars we left behind, but even then, I'm not sure."

"I'm sorry so many of your sisters have been afflicted." I covered her hand with mine. "I'm not sure what, if anything, we can do, but you know I'm here for you and yours."

"You may very well regret that offer, Galen, because there is something you can do for us." The fine lines at the corners of her eyes and around her mouth deepened.

The stress had taken a physical toll on the high priestess.

I knew how she felt. It had worn me down as well. We all needed a break but there was no relief in sight that I could see.

"Let's hope I don't regret it." I released her hand and crossed my arms over my chest. "What do you need?"

"As I said, we can't conjure a cure for the curse once it takes hold, but I know of a coven that might. In Jarrettsville." Marguerite tucked an errant strand of her silver hair behind her ear.

"Another coven?" I shook my head. "No offense, but that sounds like a witch thing to me. Wouldn't it be better if someone from your coven reached out to the other coven?"

"We would, Galen." Marguerite steepled her hands in front of her mouth and inhaled a deep breath. "But we're forbidden from dealing with them."

"Now I'm really confused. So, you can't make deals with this other coven, whoever they are, but you want me to ask them to help you?"

"Precisely. I need you to buy a potion from them. I'll give you all the details." She spoke as if that cleared up everything.

It didn't.

"It might help if we knew why you can't work with these witches," Talia said, prodding for more information.

At least I wasn't the only one who struggled to follow Marguerite's logic.

"Isn't it obvious?" Marguerite let out an exasperated sigh when she took in our baffled expressions. "They dabble in the dark arts."

"So, they're dark witches." Talia perked up at that bit of knowledge. "That's a good thing! They might know how to get rid of my mark."

"They're more in the gray area. I wouldn't expect them to know anything about summoning demons, but the magic they do practice crosses a line my coven will not." Marguerite turned her nose up over the other witches' preferred method of magic.

It seemed pretentious of her, considering her magic had failed to save her coven or Talia. She was too good to wield the magic, but she wasn't above using a potion that was a result of that magic.

A bit of a contradiction.

Not that I was in a position to judge. Talia and I needed help from even darker witches than the ones Marguerite wanted us to buy a cure from.

"I guess we're going on a road trip," I said to Talia, whose eyes lit up at the request.

Talia needed a cure, and so did Marguerite.

# CHAPTER 12
# TALIA

Dark magic had gone from being our last resort to our next best hope. I wasn't sure what that said about our chances, but it couldn't have been anything good.

Marguerite sent us on a mission behind enemy lines to make a deal with a coven that didn't just walk the line between good and evil; they danced right over it according to Sarah.

Magic was still a bit of a mystery to me, but I'd learned more about its mechanics thanks to Sarah and Marguerite. Prior to Galen taking in the coven, I hadn't had the opportunity to meet many witches, never mind learn about their magic.

I supposed that was something positive to come from being demon marked. The witches were inadvertently teaching me their craft as they researched ways to remove the mark. I wouldn't be able to wield magic because I wasn't born with that spark that made a person a witch, but it gave me a greater appreciation for who they were and a deeper connection to nature.

When we left pack grounds and drove through the nearby town where Galen's bar was situated, I hardly recognized the historic district. Stores had been looted and burned, windows were boarded, and trash littered the ground and blew across the street like tumbleweeds.

The only people on the streets seemed to be afflicted witches who stumbled along the sidewalks, bumping into lampposts and benches, like a horde of zombies.

There wasn't a mortal person in sight.

"Oh my God, Galen. It's so much worse than I realized."

He sighed. "Yeah. There's a reason I closed the bar, and it wasn't just the pack wars."

Galen slowed the truck to a crawl and took care not to rev the engine or hit any debris in the road. We didn't want to draw the attention of the cursed witches. They seemed to be a in a stupor, as if they were sleepwalking without anything left to attack.

We preferred not to make a target of ourselves.

The truck offered some protection, but Galen and I had seen cursed witches in action. The demons seemed to be able to make the witches' innate magic darker and more powerful. It was as if the curse enhanced and tainted their magic at the same time.

After seeing what was left of the town, I felt better about the choices we'd been forced to make in relation to taking in the witches and protecting ourselves with wards.

"Do you see any demons?" I looked away from the devastation outside my window and turned my attention to Galen.

"Just the aftermath." He gripped the steering wheel with his left hand and curled his right into a fist in his lap.

I put my hand to the window, wanting to heal the pain of the town and its people. "The witches have their work cut out for them when this is all over."

The shops on the opposite side of the street hadn't fared any better. It was a disaster area.

"We all have our work cut out for us." Galen spoke in clipped tones, but I knew his anger wasn't directed at me. "This is the pack's town as much as it is anyone else's. We've been supporting this whole area for years and we have a responsibility to the humans who live here to help fix it."

My heart went out to Galen. He was an Alpha to his very core, wanting to help anyone weaker than himself. Which, given his strength, was pretty much everyone.

He also owned a business and home in this town. Surely it upset him to see that go to ruin as well? I wasn't sure he was up to me asking questions about it though, so I kept my comments vague. "I think it's admirable that you and your pack have devoted so much of yourselves to supporting the community. The Northwood pack only cared about themselves. It was never about doing good, only what they could get."

"Maddox and his father give wolves everywhere a bad name. They'll get what's coming to them, Talia. I promise." Galen eased the truck into a lefthand turn and slowly accelerated when we reached the edge of town.

"Hey, can we chat about something else for a sec?" His tone indicated that this was going to be a serious conversation.

I twisted in my seat to look at him. "Of course. What's up?" It had to be about the pack, or us, or his dad, or the witches. Or even the demons, or my mark. Shit, we had a lot going on.

"David and I are in the process of drafting a challenge request to the Northwood Alpha. We wanted to take our time, make sure we cover every scenario and leave no room for error—no loopholes they can wrigglc out of."

I swallowed hard against the sudden lump in my throat. "Ah... okay." I didn't know what else to say. That hadn't been on my list of things to worry about at the moment.

Galen glanced my way. "I vow to end Maddox' and his father's reign over the Northwood pack, Talia. And, given your past with them, I want your blessing to do so."

I relaxed back into my seat and stared out the windscreen for a minute, needing to think. "You know I want to take them down myself, Galen. I want vengeance for my father. For me. For the life they stole. For everything bad they've done."

Even though I now knew that I would have been miserable married to Maddox, the damage that they'd done to me needed to be answered for.

"I know. But the last time you spoke of your need for vengeance, you passed out."

I sighed. "That's true." I hadn't forgotten I'd been so angry that my mark had burned and sent me into a temporary coma.

"So, would you leave the challenge to me? At least... to begin with?"

I bit my lip, thinking quickly. "I love that you want to do this, for me, and for the pack. But..." I trailed off.

Galen was an Alpha. If anyone could beat my old fiancé and his father, it was him.

"Look, I understand your need for vengeance, I have it too," he said. "You're one of the smartest, strongest, and most capable wolves I've met, Talia,but the Northwoods never fight fair—and I can't lose you."

His words made my heart sing and squeeze tight all at once.

"I can't lose you either," I choked out.

He reached out and squeezed my thigh. The touch sent heat right through me. "But you'll let me send the challenge?"

I nodded and gulped out, "Okay. Yes."

"Thank you." His tone wasn't triumphant, or gloating. It was respectful. Suddenly, I knew it was the right decision to let Galen do this. I didn't want to be hurt, or upset about this. If anything, I was proud of the fact Galen was willing and able to fight on our behalf.

But I also knew that I wanted to be there, fighting alongside him. This challenge wouldn't be one-on-one if I could help it.

We were silent for a while and I went back to staring out the window once the scenery changed to trees with canopies of gold and burnt orange leaves. "How far is it to the town where the dark coven is?"

"About an hour. Why, you have somewhere to be after this?" Galen chuckled and spared a glance in my direction.

"Yeah, I am super busy. I mean, my calendar is so full." I smiled alongside him.

We passed the time with a you-laugh-you-lose challenge, telling each other bad dad jokes to see who would laugh first. Losing had never been so much fun. My stomach and sides hurt by the time we cruised into the dark coven's town.

It looked a lot like ours.

I don't know what I'd expected. Some sort of Halloween town or Goth revival, maybe, but nothing was painted black or decorated with bats and spiders.

Nothing screamed 'Welcome to Jarrettsville, home to dark witches, circa eighteen-seventy-three.'

"Did Marguerite say how we were supposed to find the coven once we got here?" I marveled at the similarities of this little town to ours, but the major difference was glaring.

These shops and residences remained untouched by crazy cursed witches.

"We don't find them. They find us." Galen pulled the truck into a parking space and turned the key, powering down the engine.

"That sounds ominous." I was only half kidding.

"Looks like the coffee shop is open. I could use a cup right about now. You want anything?" Galen reached into the console and retrieved his wallet. He slid it into his back pocket as he stepped out of the truck.

"A latte would be amazing. I'll come in with you." I hopped out of the truck and followed him into the café.

On the surface, it appeared to be a normal coffee house with espresso machines brewing and frothing in the background.

Bakery cases filled with muffins and cakes led the flow of traffic toward the cashier waiting behind the counter.

But when I looked a little harder, I started to notice things.

Things like the drink selection: poisoned apple cider or the jack-o-latte. The day's special was soup bubbling away in a cauldron.

"Did we just get played by a bunch of witches?" Galen turned and looked at the décor. It had shifted from a retro diner with checkered floors and red booths, to haunted mansion with black walls and purple chairs.

"Maybe. This is weird, Galen. I was wondering what a town that dark witches lived in would look like and pictured sort of a Halloween vibe, you know?"

"A bit stereotypical, don't you think?" Galen bent down and examined the desserts in the glass cases.

"Yes, but I don't think that's really important right now." I crossed my arms over my chest and tapped my foot on the now black-tiled floor. "Do you?"

"Not at all." Galen straightened, turning toward me with a smile on his face. "Okay, so what do you think is going on right now? The coven is messing with you?"

"Yeah, I think so."

"But they'd need to have a mind reader to do that, right? You didn't say anything about it out loud until just now. So, the coven would have to have a powerful psychic to know what you were thinking." Galen took my hands in his and laced our fingers together. "I don't think—"

"It's not psychic ability," a young female voice said from the back of the coffee shop. "Just a little spell we crafted to read the intentions of people coming into our town here."

I squinted toward the back of the shop where the voice had come from, but couldn't see anyone.

Galen appeared to ignore the weirdness of the situation and

said, "Please tell me there's still coffee here." Galen looked over at the espresso machine like it was a long-lost lover.

"Galen," I chastised. "Now probably isn't the time."

"I know, I know. It's just been a really long month and I could use the caffeine."

It was hard to argue with that.

A woman emerged from the shadows and walked toward us. "So, the old crone sent you?"

The witch looked to be in her late teens with short platinum blonde hair tipped with indigo blue ends. So far, nothing about the town or its inhabitants was what I expected.

"You mean, Marguerite?" Galen leaned against the bakery case with his arms crossed over his chest.

He'd given up on his quest for caffeine and was back in business mode.

Marguerite had long silver hair and a few fine lines around her eyes, but she hardly qualified as an old crone in my opinion.

"That would be the old lady I was referring to, yes." The young witch slipped a black knit hat on her head, leaving just the blue bits of her hair exposed.

"What do you know about the demon curse that's afflicting the witches in town?" I asked, hoping to get the ball rolling.

"You're going to have to talk to Angelique." The young witch motioned for us to follow her. "I'm just the welcoming committee."

"I feel really welcomed, don't you?" Galen muttered.

"I lifted the glamour and let you inside, didn't I?" The witch led us down a narrow hall and out the back door. "We may not be shifters, but our hearing is pretty good."

I gave Galen a side-eyed glance and silent warning to curb his attitude. He raised his hands in a placating gesture.

"I'm sorry," he said to the witch. "I get abrasive when I'm exhausted. But that's no excuse for being rude."

"It doesn't bother me, but I would be on your best behavior with Angelique. She's not as warm and fuzzy as I am."

I'd met old wool blankets warmer and fuzzier than our escort, but I kept that comment to myself. No need to offend her again.

We followed her down an alleyway that ran parallel to the stores that lined the main street through town. There were metal doors on the left side, each stamped in white paint with the store name. Matching aluminum trashcans were set on the left side of each door and a large dumpster sat on the far end of the back alley.

The witch turned right out of the alley and onto a residential street dotted with brick, ranch-style homes and a couple of small two-story homes with dormer windows and screened-in front porches. It reminded me of my old neighborhood.

I looked at Galen, arching a brow. He seemed to pick up on my train of thought because he nodded and mouthed the word, 'weird'.

It was like a carbon copy of our town.

Except for the old Victorian house that sat on the corner lot.

We didn't have one of those and I assumed that it was the home of their high priestess.

"Is that Angelique's house?" I pointed to the massive black and white three-story with scalloped wooden siding and a clay-tiled roof.

"What gave it away?" The young witch had the angsty teenager routine down pat, but I suspected she was older than she looked and acted.

"Just a good guess." I barely contained my eye roll.

We weren't off to a great start, and I hoped things would improve when we met Angelique. The witches back home were running out of time.

The young witch opened the gate in the hip-high white picket fence that surrounded the property. The front yard had herb gardens on either side of a concrete walkway that led up to an expansive front porch.

She pressed the doorbell and the front door creaked open, revealing a grand foyer with a Tiffany chandelier swaying from the ceiling.

I felt like I'd stepped back in time. Everything was matched to the period the house would have been built.

"Bring them in, Aubrey." A woman's gentle-toned voice carried out into the foyer from a parlor off to the left.

"Well, don't keep her waiting." Aubrey ushered us into the living room with a flap of her hands.

My wolf growled inside of me as my heart began to pound. We had little defenses against witches and here we were, just walking into the lion's den.

Galen slipped his hand into mine and interlinked our fingers. We shared a single, worried look for a moment, before following Aubrey's request, and walked into the large sitting room.

I wasn't sure what I was expecting, but a beautiful woman in a flowing white dress was not it. She was sitting on an elegant lounge, glasses perched on the edge of her nose as she stared at us.

There wasn't a witchy thing in sight. Just a huge book case and luxurious rugs and cushions.

Now that she'd dropped us off in front of the high priestess, Aubrey made her exit through a doorway on the opposite side of the room.

"I have to say, I'm disappointed my sister didn't come and speak with me herself," the high priestess said, her tone all honey and sugar.

I gaped at her. Oh my God. Angelique was just a younger version of Marguerite. Gorgeous long hair, and the same blue eyes.

Our visit to dark coven territory just got weirder and weirder.

"I'm sorry, did you say your sister?" Galen sounded as mystified by her statement as I was.

"She didn't tell you?" Angelique steepled her fingers in front of her face, the gesture oddly familiar. "I'm not surprised. She wrote me off years ago. I told her not to be so judgmental, and that she might need my help one day. And here we are."

"So, you know about the curse, then?" I felt a glimmer of hope rise within me. "Can you help us?"

If she knew about the demons plaguing our town, and had a cure for their influence, maybe she could remove my demon mark too.

"Of course, I know about the curse. Unlike my sister, I make it my business to know what is happening in the towns around my own. Things like this have a tendency to spread, and I don't want my coven members affected by any demons."

Marguerite had told us at least one truth about the coven before she sent us out here. If Angelique didn't want her witches tainted with the demon affliction, she wouldn't have condoned calling them. Angelique's coven wasn't as dark as I'd hoped.

It was a strange sort of disappointment. As much as I didn't want to be in the same room as a full-fledged dark witch, according to Marguerite, I might need one to remove the mark.

Angelique was the coven's best chance at a cure, but she probably wasn't the witch I was looking for.

The mark on my wrist itched in response to my thoughts about having it removed. It was becoming more sentient and in tune with my emotions. And that meant the demon who marked me was, too.

Marguerite and her coven weren't the only ones on a clock. I was, as well, and it was ticking down.

I lifted my chin, determined to get things moving. "Marguerite hasn't been able to conjure a potion strong enough to lift the curse once it takes hold. She can contain it to an extent, but not cure it."

I wasn't sure if Marguerite wanted me to share that little piece of information with her estranged sister, but honesty seemed like the best policy if we had any chance of leaving here with a cure in hand.

"Well, that much is obvious, or you wouldn't be here. It should have been obvious to my sister too. She's limited herself, relying solely on herbs. It has made her weak and now her coven is paying the price." Angelique rose from her perch with the grace of a panther.

The witch's graceful stride and long, full skirted dress gave the appearance that she floated across the room. She stood in front of the fireplace and warmed her hands over the crackling fire.

"She can't expect to fight something otherworldly with earth magic." Angelique tsked. "My sister should know better."

"But you can, right? You have the magic to fight the curse and make a cure for Marguerite's coven?" I hoped the subtle appeal to the strength of her powers would be enough to sway her to help us.

"Of course, I can." Angelique turned her back on the fire and faced me, meeting my gaze. "But it will cost you."

Galen and I had expected as much. Witches loved to barter. Magic wasn't free. With Marguerite, it had been an even exchange: shelter on pack lands for wards surrounding the property.

But I had a sinking suspicion, nestled in the pit of my stomach, that neither Galen nor I would be able to afford what Angelique was selling.

# CHAPTER 13

# GALEN

ngelique was Marguerite's sister. I hadn't seen that one coming. The fact that Marguerite hadn't shared that piece of information with me before sending Talia and I out for a cure shouldn't have surprised me. That woman played things close to her chest.

Something I related to as Alpha. I didn't share any more than I had to with pack outsiders. Still, a heads up about what Talia and I were walking into—on her behalf—would have been nice.

The witches in my town preferred to blend in with the community. Here, the witches were the community and the town operated as a front for their coven. They used glamours to conceal their presence and limited their contact with the outside world.

The less people knew about their dark magic practices, the better. They were less likely to be arrested that way. Humans were fine with the supernatural until things got messy—and dark magic was definitely messy.

"Tell me, Alpha, are you willing to pay the price for the cure to save my sister and her coven?" Angelique opened an ornate metal box on the mantel, retrieved a cigarillo, and proceeded to smoke it, flicking her ashes into the fire.

"It depends on how much you're asking." I was pretty sure she wasn't going to ask for cash, but I could hope. I did have some money stashed away for emergencies. I figured a demon curse qualified as an emergency.

"No, that's not how this works. It's a yes or no question." Angelique took a long drag from the small cigar and blew a smoke ring in my face.

"I like to know what I'm buying." I folded my arms over my chest and held my ground. I wasn't agreeing to anything without the details first.

"You know what you're buying. You're buying a cure for the demon afflict—"

"And how much I'm paying for it," I interjected, since she seemed hell bent on splitting hairs.

"You're either willing to pay it or you're not." Angelique turned her attention from me to Talia and my stomach clenched up in knots.

Talia had already sacrificed enough. She had a demon mark. I wouldn't let her take on a debt for Marguerite when the witch couldn't offer anything in repayment. She'd already said removing the mark was beyond her.

Talia didn't need to owe anyone anything.

"What about you, little wolf? I see you're willing to make deals with demons." Angelique pointed her cigarillo stub at Talia's wrist. "What about with a dark witch?"

"I didn't make a deal with a demon." Talia jutted her chin and squared her shoulders. "The demon marked me, but I never asked for or received anything in exchange."

"You're telling the truth." Angelique's eyes widened as she flicked the rest of her tiny cigar into the fire. "That is very unusual. A demon doesn't mark a wolf for no reason."

"I'll pay it," I growled, drawing the witch's attention away from Talia.

"Excellent." The witch clasped her hands together and stepped away from the fireplace, the flames flaring behind her. "Your firstborn for the cure to the demon curse."

"What?" Talia's hands curled into fists at her side.

I hadn't given children much thought since Jessie died. I hadn't seen a future with anyone else.

Until I met Talia. She made me want things I hadn't in a very long time—including a family. Love. Commitment. Children.

"Oh, your faces." Angelique swept her long blonde hair to one side and draped it over her shoulder. "I'm just kidding."

Talia didn't relax her hands. If anything, she looked even more upset than I was.

"No one's laughing." I moved to put myself between Talia and the witch.

As much as Angelique needed to be knocked down a peg, we needed the cure she had to offer.

"So serious." Angelique rolled her eyes and sighed. "Fine, fine. We'll just get down to business then. The terms of this agreement are final and binding."

She ran through the legalese of a contract that bound us to the terms of the exchange. Terms we hadn't negotiated because all sales were final and sealed in blood.

Sacrifices had to be made.

Angelique revealed a small athame hidden in the folds of her skirt. She ran the blade over the pad of her thumb and sliced it open. Blood welled to the surface and ran down the back of her thumb, across her palm, and down onto the carpet.

"I, Angelique Lilith Marchand, high priestess of the Noctum coven, offer this potion and the knowledge of my foremothers needed to imbue it, to Galen, Alpha of the Long Claw pack." She slid the blade back into the folds of her skirt and clicked her fingers, a scroll appearing out of nowhere. Then she swiped her thumb across a leathery scroll and marked it with her blood.

I wasn't sure what the parchment was made out of, but it wasn't rags or wood pulp. I decided it was best not to think too hard on it. Otherwise, I might lose the nerve to touch it.

"You haven't said what you're asking in exchange for the cure," I said.

"Well, since you so rudely refused my first offer..." Angelique's mouth curved into a devilish grin. "I'll take a marker to be called in at a later date of my choosing."

"A marker?" Talia seemed confused by the witch's request. "Is that like a favor?"

"Yes, that's exactly what it is." I pinched the bridge of my nose and closed my eyes. "A favor for her to call in whenever she wants."

"At my beck and call." Angelique dangled the scroll in front of her. "Your name in blood is all that's required to seal the deal, Alpha."

"What kind of favor?" Talia leaned forward. She narrowed her eyes into slits as she examined the document's fine print.

"Anything, really." Angelique yanked the document back, rolled it up, and held it behind her back. "But if those terms aren't satisfactory to you and your... friend, another offer has just come to mind."

"I think you should hear what the other offer is before you decide, Galen." Talia wrung her hands together. "A favor to her could literally be anything. It's better to know ahead of time what you'll be giving up."

I wasn't thrilled at the idea of owing Angelique a favor either, but I had a gnawing suspicion that whatever her payment up front was, it would be worse than the lay-away.

"What's the other option?"

"I'm glad you asked, Alpha." Angelique's ruby lips peeled back in a wide smile that revealed sharp incisors, no doubt filed to a point on purpose, and a small black crystal embedded on each side along the gumline. "Your seed."

Man, I hate being right.

"Think about it." The witch sighed like a well-satiated lover. "A half-witch, half-wolf child. The blood of a high priestess and Alpha running through her veins. She would be magnificent—a force of nature."

"No!" Talia's answer on my behalf was like a gunshot going off in the room.

She wasn't my mate, but she'd just laid a claim in front of Angelique.

"Does she do all the talking for you?" Angelique pulled the scroll out from behind her back and ran it down my chest. "According to the lunar cycle, it is the ideal time for creation and conception. One night of your life, Galen Long Claw, for the lives of many."

"You're asking for more than one night. That's a lifetime commitment." I ignored the pointed stare Talia gave me for putting that much consideration into the offer.

Angelique hadn't been kidding about the firstborn. We'd just assumed the worst and she had some sadistic ritual in mind. But what she really wanted was a child.

She'd been steering me toward a coupling from the moment I'd asked for the cure.

Her eyes turned sultry as she said, "I'm in need of a donor, not a co-parent."

Father a child, then abandon it? I don't think so.

Talia was growling, low in her chest, as if her wolf was about to rise up and break free.

"I'll take my chances with the marker." I snatched the scroll out of her hand, bit down on the tip on my index finger hard enough to draw blood, and scrawled my name across the bottom of the contract.

Talia's sigh of relief pierced the awkward tension building between me and Angelique.

The witch pouted. "More's the pity."

The scroll retracted with a snap of Angelique's fingers and disappeared into thin air. "Aubrey, bring the potion."

Aubrey waltzed into the room balancing a silver tray on the flat of her hand. She rotated her arm and extended the serving tray to Angelique. In the center of the tray was a liter-sized clay jar with a cork stopper. A paper tag dangled from twine cording wrapped around the neck of the bottle.

"As we agreed." Angelique removed the potion from the tray, checked the tag, and handed the bottle to me. "One cure for the demon curse. My sister will know what to do with it, but I've included detailed instructions in case she has any questions."

"Thank you, Angelique." I passed the jar off to Talia and extended a hand to the high priestess.

"Don't thank me yet, wolf. Save your gratitude for when I call in my marker."

Angelique's laughter followed us out of the parlor, into the foyer, and onto the front porch.

"Galen." Talia stopped midstride and clutched my arm. "What's to stop Angelique from using her marker for... for her hybrid child?"

"Nothing, I'm afraid." I turned and cupped her worried face in my hands. "I'm not the only Alpha around. She has her fair share to choose from. We just have to hope that when the time comes for her to call it in, there's something she needs even more."

It wasn't much, but it was the only consolation I had to offer her.

The marker was a blank check for Angelique to cash whenever she wanted. It was possible all I'd done was delay the inevitable.

Still, I had the cure, and the witch was without child. And Talia's wolf had settled back down behind her beautiful eyes. I had to take that as a win.

"Let's get going while the going is good." Talia cradled the jar to her chest, leapt off the front porch, and rushed down the side-walk and out onto the street. It was like she couldn't wait to put distance between us and Angelique.

I was hot on her heels.

Aubrey didn't see fit to grace us with her presence to escort us back to the coffee shop where we'd left my truck. Talia and I retraced our steps through the alleyway. Instead of cutting through the coffee shop, we followed the alley out to the end, banked a right at the corner building, and hauled ass down the sidewalk back to the coffee shop.

"If I never come back to this place, it will be too soon." Talia was buckled up in the passenger seat the second I unlocked the door.

At least one of us had the option never to return.

I climbed behind the wheel, threw the truck into reverse, and tore out of town.

We reached the main gate on the pack's property an hour and a half later. Marguerite and Sarah were waiting for us on the edge of the coven's encampment. Both were eager to have the cure in their hands so they could replicate and administer the potion to their witches.

"You might have warned us about Angelique." Talia thrust the clay jar into Marguerite's hands.

"It was imperative you went in with a clear mind, free of influ-ence from me. Had she sensed my influence in relation to your opinion, she may not have helped us." Marguerite checked the tag hanging from the neck of the bottle.

"I don't think she was helping us at all," Talia grumbled. "She helped herself."

"My sister only ever does anything if she stands to gain from it." Marguerite handed the cure over to Sarah with instructions to place it by her cauldron and wait for her before she began the replication process. "What was the price?"

"A baby." I pinned her to the spot with a stern gaze.

It was a good thing she had given the clay jar to Sarah, otherwise she might have dropped it on the ground and lost her one chance at saving her coven.

Her hands clutched at her throat. "You didn't promise her one?" Marguerite's concern over her sister's desperation for motherhood confirmed my choice to roll the dice with a marker instead.

"Not quite. My options were to impregnate her tonight or agree to an undisclosed favor to be called in at a date of her choosing."

"We can only hope and pray to the goddess that she finds herself in need of something else from you in the future." Marguerite lowered her hands in front of her and bowed. "My coven and I are in your debt, Galen. The price for our salvation was higher than I anticipated and for that I am truly sorry."

Her contrition did a lot to soothe the jagged worries in my soul. "Just take care of your coven, Marguerite, and finish the wards surrounding the property as soon as you're able."

My phone buzzed in my back pocket. I recognized the pattern of the vibration for the silent ringtone. It was the one I'd assigned to my father's number.

"I need to take this call." Phone to my ear, I excused myself and stepped outside. "Hey, Dad. How are you feeling?"

"I've felt better, son." His voice was thready and weak.

The illness had ravaged his body, but up until then, his spirit had remained strong. He didn't sound like himself, and I feared I was losing him. "I'm coming, Dad."

I hung up and popped my head back into the tent. "Talia, I have to go."

She'd grown fond of the old man in the time she had been staying with him, and she took as good, if not better, care of him than I did. She prepared his meals, kept his room clean, but more importantly she kept him company.

"I'll come with you." She started for the entrance to the tent.

"It's been a long, strange day and there isn't an end in sight, so why don't you stay here?" I went back into the tent and pulled her into my arms, resting my chin on the top of her head and breathing her in. "We're both on the schedule for watch tonight, so I'll go check on my dad and be back here in an hour or so."

"We could really use another set of hands here, if you don't mind helping out, Talia?" Sarah zoomed by with an armful of ingredients, busy as she and her comrades were trying to replicate the cure.

"Okay, let him know I'll be in to check on him in the morning and give him a hug for me." Talia held on a little longer before letting me go.

I jumped in the truck and zoomed home. There, I slipped inside and sat next to my father's bed.

He'd deteriorated since I'd seen him last. The illness was working harder to take him away from me, and my father—our Alpha, the strongest man I knew—was too tired and weak to fight it off any longer.

I was losing him.

This man was more than my father; he was my best friend and confidant. A sounding board when I needed advice, a shoulder to cry on. He'd raised me to be the man I was today. I owed him everything.

I sat in the chair beside his bed and filled him in on everything that had happened with the witches, the demons, and the pack. I spared him the detail that he'd almost been a grandfather. I wasn't sure his heart could take that little snippet.

I listened while he doled out more sage advice about my life. More specifically, my love life and Talia.

"She's the one, Galen." He gripped a pillow against his torso and coughed. "Marry her or I will. She won't refuse a dying man his last request. I'll steal her right out from under you."

"You think so, huh?"

"She lets me win at checkers. I'm telling you, she's as good as mine if you don't make a move." He rolled to his side and settled deeper under the covers. "Now, get out of here. I need my beauty sleep. I've got a hot date in the morning."

Our roles had reversed. It wasn't something I'd expected or prepared myself for. He had taken care of me all my life. It was my turn to do the same for him in his final days.

My heart hurt as I tucked him in the same way he used to tuck me in at night when I was a little boy, pulling the covers up over his shoulder, kissing his temple, and wishing him sweet dreams.

I wasn't ready to let him go. I doubted if I ever would be.

· CHAPTER 14

# TALIA

I was worried about Max. Galen had left earlier to check in on his father and spend some quality time with him before he was due back for security detail. I'd hoped to get an update on how Max was doing but didn't want to intrude on their time together.

Galen would let me know how Max was, whenever he got back.

Until then, I had my hands full helping Sarah and Marguerite administer the cure to the afflicted witches.

They'd followed the instructions Angelique provided and brewed enough of the potion for each member of the coven to receive a dose. Some of the witches, most likely the first affected by the curse, needed a double dose.

Even Sarah took some, just to be on the safe side, even though her affliction seemed to have passed.

Marguerite started another batch while Sarah and I measured out the doses.

The two worst affected witches were still sedated and strapped down on cots in the makeshift infirmary. Sarah and I worked in tandem. She held their mouth open, and I poured the potion down their throat.

The second batch of the cure cooled in a cast iron cauldron on the table. Marguerite planned to administer any second doses needed herself once the potion was ready.

Sarah and I completed our rounds of the more stable, but still affected, witches. By the time we reached the last witch, our first patients were waking up. It was a huge relief to see them all coming back to good health.

Like shifter healing ability, there was something to be said for the healing properties of magic.

And for Angelique's recipe—though I'd never admit that to the dark witch. "This is amazing." Sarah took my tray of empty paper cups and set it on the long wooden table. "They're already so much better. Look at them."

"Do you think they remember what happened? What it felt like to be cursed?" The demon mark on my wrist itched again.

"I'm not sure, but Marguerite will no doubt have a lot of questions for them when she feels they're ready to answer them." Sarah's gaze traveled to my wrist, her mouth forming a little 'o' when she put two and two together on why I'd asked. "So the curse and your mark aren't the same type of demon magic."

"Demons have their own magic?"

That was news to me.

"It's not like ours." Sarah shrugged. "It means a lot to me that you're here, Talia. With everything you have going on, you took the time to help us. I won't forget that. Marguerite won't either."

"That's sweet, Sarah, but you're my friend. You don't owe me anything for helping people who need it."

Besides, the only thing I wanted, they couldn't give me.

I checked my phone for an update from Galen. Nothing. I supposed no news was good news.

It was almost time for my watch. I said my goodbyes to Sarah and Marguerite and headed over to the meeting house to check in with Markus. I was grateful for the time alone. The walk afforded me a much-needed opportunity to clear my head. So much had happened recently, all of it strange.

Especially our trip to Jarrettsville.

Angelique had freaked me out, mostly because of her request for a hybrid baby with Galen. My wolf had almost jumped out and forced me to shift right there and then on the spot.

No way was that woman—or any woman—getting her hands on my man.

My man? I couldn't help but feel proprietary over Galen. My feelings for him were growing stronger by the day and the thought of him spending intimate time with someone else had instantly gutted me.

I had hoped to get information about my mark during the visit, but hadn't gotten anywhere. It was obvious she knew something about it, but uncovering what she knew would likely come at too high a price.

They weren't the only dark coven out there. I would find my cure and get the demon mark removed one way or another.

The moon hung low and heavy in the sky. There weren't too many shadows thanks to the moonbeams illuminating the path, but I couldn't shake the feeling that something was lurking in the darkness beyond the tree line.

I decided to investigate, following my intuition to the spot where I'd sensed someone watching me, but there wasn't anyone there.

Damn, Talia. You're really freaking yourself out. Knock it off.

I started back for the path.

A crunch came from farther back in the woods. It was like Natasha all over again. Someone was out there, most likely waiting to attack. Which meant, it was likely one of the Northwood pack members.

"There you are." My old Alpha leaped out from under the cover of the trees. "I was beginning to think you weren't going to show up tonight."

My blood boiled at the sight of the man who'd murdered my father. "What are you doing here?" I spat the question at him.

"Looking for you, obviously." He leered, exposing his canine teeth. "It's no surprise I would find you prowling around. Just like your mother used to."

"My mother?" It was the first time I'd heard anyone say anything about my mother in years.

My father had always hated talking about her. It hurt him too much.

"Like mother, like daughter. She was a whore too. Ask your father. Oh wait, you can't. I killed him. You'll just have to take my word for it." His vitriolic words and acidic laughter shattered the peace of the night.

I glared at him, feeling my wolf rise up ready for the call to shift. "My mother wasn't a whore, and neither am I."

I was still a virgin. Not that I was about to tell him that, but calling me a whore was the last insult I'd take personally.

"Maybe not. But she was just as dark, just as tainted as you. That mark on your wrist is proof enough. She wasn't sure if your father was really your father. Did you know that? He was too stupid to care and married her anyway." He stalked forward, closing the distance between us.

I inhaled sharply, clenching my hands into fists. "You're baiting me into a fight and I'm not going to fall for it."

As much as I wanted to beat his ass into next month, Galen had drafted papers to formally challenge him and I'd promised to respect the process.

Of course, that had been before the Northwood pack Alpha showed up on pack land, looking for me and spewing all kinds of hateful bullshit.

Galen couldn't blame me for defending myself if this asshole attacked me first.

I couldn't hide the smile that crept across my face. I hoped he would attack. Then I could beat the system and have vengeance without going back on my word to Galen.

I just needed to play this stupid wolf's game and get him to hit me.

Piece of cake.

"You didn't waste any time moving on to the next wolf. How long did you wait after your breakup with my son to jump into bed with Galen?" The Alpha spat at the ground beside my foot. "Power hungry bitch. Your mother was the same way. Fucking every wolf she could just to get ahead in the pack. You don't believe me? I'm speaking from experience, sweetheart."

Vomit. Gross. No way.

"You're talking a whole bunch of bullshit is what you're doing." I kept him talking, trying to make him mad enough to take a swing. "No one cares about what you have to say, especially not me. It's why you're hemorrhaging wolves. You can't keep your own pack together."

His lip lifted in a snarl. "Ha, the wolves who left are useless creatures anyway. My pack is better off without people like you or that worthless girl Natasha." He circled around me, stalking his 'prey'.

Only, I wasn't his prey. He just didn't know it yet. My plan was working and it wouldn't be long before he struck.

Like a villain in a movie, he kept monologuing. "I suppose you think you're clever. Trading up from my son to Galen. After all, Maddox won't become Alpha for decades, but Max will be dead in days."

I bit down hard on my lip to stop myself from screaming out at him. Bastard.

The Alpha kept going. "But it won't last. He'll see you for what you are soon enough and when he does, you'll be tossed out of another pack. Assuming you live beyond tonight."

He lunged without warning, fist raised, in a superman punch maneuver. His fist slammed into my chin. My lower jawbone cracked and shifted out of alignment.

I staggered sideways, groaning at the pain splintering through my head. But I used it to focus. He'd drawn first blood, which meant it was game on.

I'd watched him fight off challengers enough times to know all of his moves. When he came at me with a left hook, I was ready, blocking it with my right and landing a looping left to his temple.

I caught him off guard and made the most of the opportunity by throwing another punch. And another.

He shifted his hands and swiped at my midsection with razor sharp claws, shredding my shirt. I ran my hand over my stomach, expecting to feel gashes and come away with blood on my fingers, but the only thing he'd slashed was cotton fabric.

The demon mark on my wrist pulsed. I felt a rush of energy unlike anything I'd ever experienced before. Was it giving me extra power?

"You made the biggest mistake of your life coming here, old man," I said through my clenched teeth and fractured jaw. The bones had begun to set crooked. I would have to have it rebroken for it to heal properly.

"A mistake? Hardly. I tried to rid my pack of the darkness. It started festering inside your mother when she was pregnant with you. And then you were born, and I knew it was inside you too. I could see it, smell it on you." He let his hands go in a flurry of punches.

I dodged most of his strikes, copping one solid punch to my ribs that knocked the wind out of me.

When I got my footing, I wheezed in a breath. "If you hated me so much, why did you let Maddox and I get engaged?"

I didn't understand why he felt the way he did about me. I wasn't a dark or evil person. I'd been an upstanding and loyal wolf in the Northwood pack.

None of this situation made any sense.

"My stupid son gets an itch he can't scratch, and you think that meant I endorsed your engagement? Please. Whatever evil you got in you, girl, is what lured him in. Poisoned my son until you had your way with him."

He swung again, but I dipped left and dodged the blow.

I tapped into the burst of energy from my demon mark and threw a series of devastating blows to his face, each one hitting their mark. My knuckles screamed with pain, but the effect was satisfying. His nose broke, his eyebrow split open, and blood poured down his face.

Galen's wolves howled in the distance. The cavalry was coming.

But for once, I didn't want back up.

I wanted to take out this bastard myself, and make him pay for what he did to my father.

To me.

To my mother's memory.

I hit him again. And again.

Markus was behind me, shouting something, but the words were a garbled blur. I was lost to my rage and the pulse of power from the demon's mark on my wrist.

By the time Theo and Markus reached me, my former Alpha was a beaten, bloody mess. He was curled up in the fetal position, begging for me to stop hitting him.

The only thing that stopped me from killing him was the knowledge that I would have then been in the running to fill the Alpha position for the Northwood pack. I had zero interest in ever being a part of that pack again. I kicked him once more in the ribs for good measure.

Galen wanted to challenge him, and he was welcome to officially unseat the Alpha. I didn't see any reason to merge the two packs.

Except maybe Nyssa and Celia.

The memories of my old friends softened my heart, pushing the red haze further into the back of my mind.

"Talia, are you oaky?" Theo grabbed me by the shoulders and spun me around.

Markus checked the defeated Alpha. Satisfied that he wasn't dying from his injuries and would live to attack another day, Markus ordered him off the property.

The Northwood Alpha turned and hobbled back through the woods.

Asshole.

"Why does this stuff always happen when you're on watch?" Theo joked and poked me in the ribs.

"Ow." I gripped my jaw. "Don't make me laugh—it hurts. Don't make me talk either. That hurts really bad too."

"Let me take a look at you." Markus came over and examined my jaw. "It needs to be realigned. If we don't set it tonight, your bite will be off."

Theo offered me his hand to squeeze while Markus reset my jaw. White hot pain spiderwebbed across my face and settled behind my eyes. My knees threatened to give out, but the two of them kept me on my feet.

"Galen needs to know what happened. Do you want me to call him for you?" Markus rubbed soothing circles in the center of my back.

I nodded. As much as I wanted to talk to him, the pain and swelling in my mouth limited my ability to talk. I needed a few minutes to recover and then shift to finish the healing process.

"Hey, are you okay? I just heard what happened." Darius jogged up the path, ignoring the others as he rushed to my side.

"I'm fine." I pressed my hands on either side of my face, supporting my jaw so I could respond.

The sooner I answered, the sooner Darius would leave.

Or at least that was what I hoped.

I wasn't sure how he'd heard about the attack so soon. The only other wolves on watch were Markus and Theo, and I hadn't seen anyone else when I left the witches.

So, who told him?

"Why don't I take you up to the meeting house? There are still a few cots left in there from the craziness with the witches." Darius gently squeezed my shoulder before trailing his fingers down my arm and reaching for my hand.

I shook my head and pulled away from his grip. I didn't want to go anywhere with Darius. He totally creeped me out. Big time. I needed to go with my gut and trust my instincts.

If I had done that earlier, I probably wouldn't have gotten kidnapped.

Oddly, that scenario worked out for the best. Still, that was a fluke situation and Darius was nothing like Galen. That nagging voice in the back of my head assured me that if I went anywhere with Darius, the situation would not have a happy ending.

Markus and Theo had Galen on a speaker call. They were both preoccupied with answering the multitude of questions he fired at them in rapid succession and hadn't seen my signal for one of them to intervene.

"Are you sure?" Darius asked in soft dulcet tones, the way one might speak to a child. "You need to rest, Talia. Just relax and let me take care of you."

He reached for me again, but I stepped back out of his reach. This time Theo caught the uncomfortable interaction.

"Talia, Galen wants to hear your voice. Even if it's a little garbled right now." Theo waved me over, inviting me to join in on their call and providing me with an escape route.

I'd bested my old Alpha in a fight, and I was shaking from relief. I felt confident I could take Darius if I had to, but so far, he hadn't done anything that warranted it.

He was weird and set off all sorts of internal alarms for me, but that was about it. I couldn't justify punching him in the face when all he'd done was offer assistance.

Darius had ingratiated himself into the pack. He'd spent time making friends and alliances, while I'd been busy running from one disaster to the next and leaving a trail of damage in my wake. The best thing I could do for the time being was to politely turn him down and avoid him whenever possible.

But if Darius started something, I wouldn't be afraid to finish it.

# CHAPTER 15

# TALIA

Galen was on his way. Markus, Theo, and I all tried to convince him to stay with his father. The threat was over and there was no need for him to rush to me and miss out on time with Max.

He didn't listen.

He wanted to check the boundaries himself, meet with Marguerite for an update on the witches' recovery and work out a timeframe for the completion of the new wards.

And check up on me.

He was not convinced when I told him on the phone that I was fine. May have had something to do with my broken jaw that hadn't healed at the time of our conversation.

In this particular case, he was probably correct, and Galen may have had cause to worry. I was an effed-up, insecure, neurotic, and emotional mess.

My altercation with my old Alpha had made me feel strong. But five minutes after he'd left, and my jaw was hurting like the blazes, the tears began to run. I shifted into my wolf form to help with healing, but also so I could hide from the pain inside of me.

The tipping point for my breakdown had begun.

I didn't want to be coddled and told everything was going to be all right. Because the mark on my wrist said otherwise. I wanted to be alone. There was so much rattling around inside my head I needed to process it all, and I couldn't do that with Galen or one of his Betas hovering over me.

The pain in my jaw subsided as soon as the shift happened and would be one hundred percent better when I shifted back from four legs to two. Our ability to heal serious injuries was just one of the perks of being a shifter.

Speed was another.

I cut across the property, zigzagging through the trees, kicking up clumps of dirt and grass whenever I took a hard turn.

The crisp, clean air, along with the smell of fresh pine and even the decomposition of foliage on the forest floor, soothed the voices in my head.

But it didn't shut them up entirely.

The Alpha of the Northwood pack's voice remained loud and clear inside my mind. He'd used a two-pronged attack—mental and physical. I'd heal the physical injuries easily, but the mental? Well, that would take more than a shift to fix the damage.

He'd accused my mother of being a power-hungry gold digger and alluded to having an affair with her at some point. The thought of his hands on my mom disgusted me.

Worse than that, he accused her of being tainted by darkness. Of being evil. As if she were to blame for whatever plagued the pack.

He was a revolting man and unworthy of the title Alpha. It was time for him to be dethroned.

He'd accused me of being just like my mother, not wasting any time moving up the ranks after my break-up with Maddox.

My relationship with Galen was still complicated, but I was in love with him, that was for sure. Our connection wasn't because I pushed him or manipulated our feelings. My new life was none of the Alpha's concern—or anyone else's for that matter.

After all, he'd kicked me out of the Northwood pack and forced his son to end our engagement. He even made Maddox attack the Long Claw pack and me.

Just like he sent Natasha after me.

I'd earned my happiness and I was going to enjoy every second of it. Just as soon as I got rid of the demon mark on my arm.

All of my dark thoughts were like a storm cloud that hovered over my head and blocked out the sun.

I should be happy. The Northwood Alpha had attacked, and I had defeated him. I'd beaten him. Not Markus or Theo. Not Galen. I did it on my own.

After years of living under his thumb, after the death of my father, and my life being destroyed, I'd stood my ground. And I'd won!

It wasn't quite the vengeance I'd wanted, but it was a victory, nonetheless.

So why did his words hold such power over me? Why was every single negative thing he said still ringing in my ears?

Running wasn't having the usual restorative effects on my mood, but I pushed harder, and ran faster, in the hopes that I would feel better. I wondered if Sarah or Marguerite had a potion that could cure the melancholy that had settled into my heart and mind.

Something, anything, to wash away the hurt and anger.

I ran the length of the boundary and cut across open ground at top speed through the field. The smell of my former Alpha's blood lingered in the air.

His words continued to haunt me.

What had my father or I ever done to become the focus of his ire? He'd killed my dad because of a mistake, then tossed me aside like I was nothing.

The Alpha had said he wanted to cleanse the darkness from his pack. He'd tried it with my mother and then again with me.

I didn't understand what he meant.

Had my mother passed something down to me? Why hadn't my father ever said anything about it?

I always thought I was a good person. Had I been fooling myself? Did he know something about me, and my family, that I didn't? I found it hard to believe that he would be privy to the Linetti family secrets while I'd been left in the dark.

That mark is proof enough.

The Alpha knew I'd been marked. What else did he know?

The demon's symbol on my limb flared to life. It throbbed in time with the beat of my heart and seemed to grow stronger whenever I was angry or upset.

As if it fed off those darker thoughts and feelings.

The demon was feeding off me, eating my emotions.

The connection with the demon terrified me and I was frustrated that we hadn't made any further progress in getting the mark removed.

The longer it stayed on my arm, the deeper the demon's claws sank into my skin. The demon had a hold on me—had laid claim to my soul. It was just a matter of time before it came to collect.

Part of me wished it would.

At least then the waiting would be over. All the uncertainty was wearing me down. I was always putting on a brave face while everyone else's emergencies took precedent, and the most pressing matter in my life was put on the back burner once again.

If the demon would only come for me, then I could at least fight him and try to win my freedom. To prove that the darkness wasn't really a part of me. At the very least, I could attempt to find out his name.

But the demon never made a move.

Its pieces were all on the checkerboard, safely in the back row, while I was forced to wait for it to make a play and advance across the board.

Galen called my name, but I couldn't face him. I'd gone to the dark corners of my mind, and I wasn't ready to come back to the light.

Not yet anyway.

I continued to run. Dirt packed in between the pads of my paws and in the grooves of my claws. Bits of grass and leaves clung to my coarse coat. I must have looked like a wild and feral beast.

In some ways, I was.

In the Northwood pack, I'd followed the rules, did what was expected of me, and never spoke up. I'd played the part assigned to me by Maddox and his father.

But I wasn't that wolf anymore. In truth, I never had been. I'd made myself smaller to fit inside the box they'd put me in.

A box that turned out to be a cage.

I'd thought I loved Maddox and worse, I'd thought he loved me. But Maddox didn't know what love was any more than I did.

We were both wrong. It wasn't love at all.

But maybe he and his father were right about one thing. I was moving on too fast, clinging to Galen and the safety net he provided. Not because of a desire for power but for security.

But is it really too fast when the whole world is crashing down and coming to an end?

Demons were running lose, cursing witches, killing humans, and attacking wolves. The town was destroyed, and the people looked to the pack to fix it. But the packs were at war with each other, and dark witches might have been the reason behind all of it.

When I thought about everything that had happened since Galen made the fateful mistake of kidnapping me with the hopes of gaining an advantage over the Northwood pack, my feelings didn't seem rushed at all.

It felt like I knew exactly what I was doing. At least where Galen was concerned.

The rest of it, well, I was making it up as I went along. There wasn't really a precedent for demon marks outside of a deal struck.

Galen was intentionally loud, lumbering around in the woods, stepping on branches or piles of dead leaves to make his presence known. He stayed close, following my every move, but never invaded my space.

He respected my need to be alone and at least tried to give me some semblance of that. It went against his better judgment as an Alpha, and as my kind-of-sort-of-maybe boyfriend. I knew that he just wanted to keep me safe.

But I wasn't sure that he could.

Not if what the Northwood Alpha had said was true.

How could Galen keep me safe from myself?

We continued like that, with me running and Galen following. He never pushed. He just waited, giving me the space I needed to work out everything on my own.

He was a patient wolf.

The story of how we met was an unorthodox one, but it was ours and I was grateful he had crashed into my life.

Galen filled the cracks of my broken heart and mended it back together. He showed me that a true partner didn't expect you to lessen yourself, but instead built you up and helped you shine.

He showed me what real love was.

And now I was running from him.

I reached the lake and padded out to the end of the dock. The placid black water looked like glass in the moonlight. I smacked my paw against the surface and watched the ripples spread out, distorting my reflection.

The tiny wave I'd created dispersed, and the mirror finish of the lake's surface returned.

I hardly recognized the wolf staring back at me when I peered down over the edge of the dock. The pointed ears, long snout and black nose, and the thick, dark gray fur coat were all mine and familiar.

But the eyes belonged to someone else.

The intense sapphire-violet eyes I normally boasted in my wolf form were gone. They'd been replaced with fiery red orbs. An unnatural, unholy color that belonged to a demon and not a wolf.

Terror gripped my heart.

What is happening to me?

I smacked the water again with my paw, destroying the reflection, and waited for the surface to calm once more, willing the image to be different.

The same wolf stared back at me—red eyes and all.

I gave voice to my fears and howled at the moon.

Was I all those things that the Northwood Alpha said I was? A vessel for the darkness. Wicked. Evil. Damned.

The proof seemed to be staring me right in the face.

Was this how a demon was able to mark me without being summoned or a deal being struck? It sensed some sort of evil inside me and claimed it for itself?

Like recognized like.

Galen answered my call with a howl of his own. He must have sensed my distress and decided enough was enough.

He prowled out of the tree line and approached the dock.

Panic set in. He couldn't see me like this. If he sees my red eyes, he'll freak out.

I couldn't bear to see the fear or disgust in his eyes when he saw me like this. It would shatter my already fragile heart.

"Talia?" Galen shifted back to human form and charged down the dock. "What's wrong?"

I prayed to all the gods in the universe that my eyes would return to normal when I shifted.

Please, please let them be normal.

When I was human again, I gripped the edge of the dock and peered over into the water. The red glow was gone, and I was back to myself.

Whatever it was that had caused my eyes to turn a hellish shade of red seemed to only affect my wolf. At least that bought me some precious time. It was still a problem, but one I could work with short term.

As long as I didn't shift around any of the other wolves, and that included Galen, the problem could be contained. I could search for an answer. It had to be connected to the demon mark.

My best chance at finding a solution to the mark and glowing red eyes lay with a dark witch.

One darker than Angelique.

Still, she was a starting point. I'd sworn I would never go back to Jarrettsville, but I needed help. Help I couldn't get anywhere else.

Angelique's knowledge and power came at a price. One I hoped I could afford. And yet, what choice did I have? I would have to pay whatever it cost.

"Are you okay?" Galen knelt beside me, the flat of his hand caressing the small of my back. "Talia, talk to me. Tell me what happened, please."

I did the only thing I could.

I lied.

~

THE END
The story continues in **Wolf of Thorns.**
Click here for the next boxset for books 4 – 6:
https://books2read.com/u/mZqp5e